In Safe Hands

JANE SANDFORD was born in Oxfordshire. Her work has been appearing in major magazines since she was sixteen. Now married to an American she lives in America. *In Safe Hands* is her first novel.

JANE SANDFORD

In Safe Hands

FONTANA PAPERBACKS

First published in America by Fawcett Gold Medal Books 1984
First published in Great Britain by Fontana Paperbacks 1984

Copyright © Jane Sandford 1984

Made and printed in Great Britain by
William Collins Sons & Co. Ltd, Glasgow

'We can't just go to sleep and leave that girl lying in there terrified,' Claire told her husband firmly. 'When I gave her a hug good night, I could feel the fright coming off her like heat off a stove lid.'

Chuck had already pulled off his boots and shirt, but he undressed no further. Clearly he would not be getting to bed until this was straightened out.

'Isn't there anything you can do to make her feel better?' he asked, without much hope. If there had been, Claire would be doing it, instead of sitting stiffly against the headboard with her handsome, worried face brooding above the fleecy wool shawl like a mountain peak collared in cloud.

'I could if it was me she was afraid of,' his wife said, 'but it's him. The Lord knows what's gone on between the two of them. Kate didn't say and I wasn't about to ask, but there's one thing certain – he scared her half to death. Now she's alone she'll go to pieces, I know it.'

'You want me to talk to her?'

'No, dear heart, talk to him. He's the one got her into this condition, maybe he can get her out.'

Barefoot, his bare chest copper brown above his jeans, Chuck went downstairs, candlestick in hand, and dropped into a seat at the kitchen table. The man across from him had his chair tipped back; his head drooped forward as he looked up at Chuck from under his eyelashes.

'Things not too good?' The voice was attractive, basically upper-class British but with the trace of an Irish lilt.

'Our hostage is in bad shape. She needs help.'

'How do you know? I'm not saying you're wrong, mind you, I'm just curious.'

'Indian draw on deep source of ancient wisdom, get sitrep from spirits of wise ancestors. Also plenty smart squaw. Claire says the girl is scared sick – breakdown level sick.'

'Yes, well, I wondered about that. She did look a little shocky after supper.' He sighed. 'What, specifically, is she afraid of, does Claire know? I mean, is it the whole situation, or is it me?'

'All of us, maybe,' Chuck said with tact.

'Rubbish. Just because she's frightened doesn't mean she's totally lost her marbles. I hate to be the one to tell you this, *kemosabe*, but you're about as intimidating as Winnie the Pooh, and as for Claire, don't be ridiculous. Afeni? Nothing to spook her there, I wouldn't have thought. There is Sam, of course. If Kate knew about Sam, she'd go off into strong hysterics and with reason, but she doesn't – and I thought he was pretty good this evening. Hardly the life of the party, but at least he didn't regress. No, my faithful Indian companion, there's only one Idi Amin in this woodpile, and I'm it.'

'This is an impertinent question, but you didn't, er, do anything to her?'

'Gentle Jesus meek and mild. I merely kidnapped her, doped her, handcuffed her, and inadvertently managed to give her the impression that I was about to cut her throat. Apart from that, Mrs Lincoln, she's had a perfectly splendid time. And now I suppose she thinks I'm going to rape her,' he added gloomily.

'Why would she think that?'

'Oh wake up, will you? God, you're thick this evening. For one thing, it's the basic abduction victim scenario: once aboard the lugger and the girl is mine, right? The other little difficulty is that I find her rather appealing.' He laughed and rubbed his face hard with his knuckles. 'National Euphemism Week. She's a complete and utter darling and I'd like to fuck her brains out. Stop looking like a dowager at a dogfight. I shan't lay a glove on her. We've enough complications already, and besides it wouldn't be fair. She's as safe with me as she would be in a convent – safer, probably. But young as she is, this can scarcely be her first encounter with some poor sod afflicted with impure thoughts. Presumably she can recognize the symptoms. Only this time she can't call a taxi and go home.'

'Yes, but if you've given her no reason –'

'Logic will be your downfall, cocker. Look, if I'm any judge, Kate's a late bloomer. Even the sexual revolution has its dropouts. I don't say she's a virgin, though it wouldn't surprise me, but she's not a part of the dance, she hasn't learned the steps yet. She just doesn't *know*: therefore, anything is possible. Reminds me of the adorable ninnies of my youth who equated a discreet smooch in the shrubbery with a proposal of marriage. All I have to do is look at her sideways and she expects me to hurl myself upon her like some randy great cossack. Which is a remarkably

6

tempting thought, but don't tell Claire I said so. Or anyone else, as if you would. Concealment, like a worm i' the bud, shall feed on my damask cheek. Snivel. It's a terrible waste, but things being how they are, I am not, repeat *not*, in the market.'

'I believe you,' Chuck said. 'Now you have to convince her.'

'And how do you suggest I go about it? Short of having myself gelded before her very eyes, which would be quite horrid for both of us, I really don't know what the hell to do.'

Chuck smiled, stood up, and relit his candle, curving his palm protectively about the flame – a needless gesture, since over the last two hundred years the farmhouse had settled into itself until it was as free from draughts as a bank vault.

'Talk to her,' he said as he headed for bed. 'Tell her what a nice guy you really are underneath. She might even believe you. God knows it's the truth.'

Left alone again, the man looked at his watch. This was a time wasting tic, a couple of seconds gained before the confrontation he dreaded, but the position of the hands caught his attention. Twenty-four hours, to the minute, since the girl and her boy-friend had come out through the swinging doors of that restaurant in New Lymington and roared away in a red Porsche, happily oblivious to the hunters behind. Twenty-four hours: it seemed inconceivable that so much had happened in so short a time.

Phase One of the operation had been an astonishing success, and now Kate Harper, the one indispensable factor in their desperate endeavour, was safely at the farm as they had planned. What had not been planned, had not crossed anyone's mind even in the most far-fetched and freewheeling of those endless preliminary discussions, was that he would fall haplessly, embarrassingly in love with the bloody woman. The crippling disadvantage of having been brought up to behave like a gentleman, allied to the kind of conscience that would have cramped the style of an elderly nun, meant that any blithe surrender to instinct was out of the question. Besides, the girl was petrified of him.

At least he could do something about that, or try to. All very well Chuck saying, 'Talk to her,' he'd talked to her already, for hours, and deep down where it really counted she still saw him as a monster. He lit a candle, extinguished the lamp, and made for the stairs. Halfway up he checked, struck by an idea of dazzling simplicity: he would tell her the absolute truth. What she

7

made of it was up to her. He reached the door of her bedroom and knocked.

'Who is it?' Her voice was shaky.

'It's me,' he said. 'Can I come in?' Damned silly question, what was she going to say, No? There was a moment's pause.

'I guess so.'

He went inside, closing the door behind him, knowing that Claire was awake in the next room. Sturdily hoping for the best no doubt, while wondering whether she wouldn't have been wiser to let bad enough alone. He set down the candle and inspected his prize. Even in the narrow bed she looked tiny, a scared bundle of bones under the faded quilt. Standing, he towered over her: better put that right, but if he sat down on the bed she'd probably pass out. He pulled up a straight chair, turned it so that the high back was towards the bed, forming a slatted barrier between them, and straddled it. Then he fell silent and waited for her to speak, partly because he wanted Kate to feel she had some control over the conversation, but also because he was fascinated to find out what she would say.

'What is it?' she asked him at last, her grey eyes immense and dark with fear. 'What do you want?'

Unbidden and untimely, the classic answer to her second question popped into his head out of the swamps of memory: that immortally corny riposte, '*Bon dieu*, are you not woman enough to know?' *The Sheikh*, it came from, a mildewed copy discovered in his father's library and blissfully devoured the summer he was thirteen. He managed not to say the words aloud, he even contrived not to laugh, but he could feel the irrepressible grin spreading across his face.

'Guess,' he said cheerfully.

Twenty-nine hours earlier, hundreds of miles away, and in an entirely different world, Kate had been on the telephone.

'Well of course I'm having dinner with you tonight.' She shifted her weight from one foot to the other, wishing the college would go mad with generosity and provide a chair under the pay phone in the hall. 'I mean, it's Saturday, isn't it?'

Even as she said the words she thought how awful they sounded, as if a date with Charlie was some kind of recurring chore, like laundry. She pushed the pale hair out of her eyes, registering the slightly slick feel that meant it was about to go lank on her. Whenever she could, she slipped over to wash it at her mother's house, in her own pale blue bathroom with the shower, the stack of fluffy clean towels, the wall-to-wall carpet, the blessed privacy. Ought one to forgo all those comforts for a quick, sordid sluicing in the communal bathroom, where other people's hair always seemed to be inexplicably braided through the holes in the drain, just to look nice for Charlie, who was more like a brother than a boyfriend? She supposed one ought.

'I have to wash my hair,' she told him. 'And Howard and Mary Beth are having this party and I promised to show up, but I could meet you after. I don't plan to stay long – like Howard's *parents* are going to be there and that sister of Mary Beth's, the one that's a model in New York, you know? Being sweet and dear and unspoiled and calling me honey-lamb because she can't remember my name. Yuck.'

'Yeah, I met her,' Charlie said. 'Thirty-one, twenty-one, thirty-one. A man could cut himself. I'll be there too. Howard wants me to keep his mother happy. He says she calls me that nice polite boy who doesn't have a beard. What an image.'

'You could go in black silk socks and a necktie with nothing in between. Kind of Dow-Jones streaker.'

'No way. My glorious body is for you alone.'

'I'll be bringing my own, thank you,' Kate said. 'Why would I want yours?'

'You will, baby, you will. This ancient Turkish aphrodisiac –'

9

'Sure, I know. Six parts gin to one part dry vermouth. Gotta run. See you later.'

'Want to meet me before the party? Rocco's at seven? We could have a beer there and then go together.' Kind Charlie, he knew how she hated to walk into a room full of people by herself, even people she knew.

'That'd be great. Rocco's at seven, right? And thanks, Charlie.'

Later, sitting on the bed in the room she shared with Mary Beth, she watched her roommate applying eyeliner. Whenever Mary Beth made up her eyes, which was often, she always parted her lips and put out the tip of her tongue, lightly pinched between the two halves of the perfect bite that had cost her long-suffering father four thousand dollars. Kate turned off her blow-dryer.

'What do you do that for?'

'Do what?'

'Stick your tongue out that way.'

'So I won't blink.'

'Uh-huh. And crusts make your hair curl.'

'It's *true*. If you took the trouble to do anything about yourself, you'd know.'

'Doing something about yourself' was Mary Bethese for painting your face as if it were a wall. Kate, who simply kept hers clean and put on lipstick when she wanted to look old enough to drink, was her roommate's current reclamation project. In an exasperated moment of utter despair, Mary Beth had called her the representative slum of Beresford College, although she apologized afterwards. But Mary Beth came from Atlanta, where going around in public with your naked face hanging out made you a traitor to your sex, unless you were postmenopausal, in which case the hell with it. Howard's mother had earned Mary Beth's disdain for the opposite reason: at fifty-six she raced around in her designer jeans, took karate three times a week, was thrilled with the results of her first face lift, and was currently rumoured to be weighing the advantages of a tummy tuck. Mary Beth had told Howard that having your face lifted was trashy, and Howard had refused to speak to her for two weeks. But now it was all forgiven – more's the pity, Kate thought selfishly, since their reconciliation had spawned this terrible party and now she had to go to it. Still, at least Charlie would be around, sweet faithful Charlie who bought her a steak every Saturday night and never abandoned her at parties and didn't try to bully her into bed.

10

'Kate Harper!' Mary Beth yodelled, 'you are *not* coming to our party dressed like *that*! Levis and a sweater, whatever next.'

'Tell Howard's mother it's cashmere. Hand knit in the lamaseries of Tibet. Tell her my father brought it on yak-back all the way from the Forbidden City. No, just tell her Jackie Onassis has one exactly like it, that'll turn her on. See you.'

As Kate flew breathlessly into Rocco's, late as usual for the patient Charles, a graduate student named Sean Devlin sat in a top-floor apartment in a rundown building two miles across town, trying, with only limited success, to stave off total panic. This is like one of those puzzles in the newspaper, he wrote on the yellow legal pad in front of him. *Two people asleep, one worried to death, one dangerous, one can't talk. How many people are in the apartment? What's the name of the engineer? Who's on first? I saw Esau sitting on a seesaw. How many S's in that?* 'Jesus God,' Sean said aloud, tearing off the sheet and crumpling it before he tossed it into the wastebasket. 'I'm losing my immortal mind, and no wonder.'

The baby, her fists curled like damp petals, lay quiet in her crib. Above her head a mobile of tiny glittering fish bobbed in the breeze from the open window. Sean, who was the baby's father, sat at the kitchen table, numbly maintaining the appearance of working on his dissertation. Most, if not all, of what he had written tonight would have to be scrapped when he came to reread it calmly – if, that is, he ever had the chance – but the act of writing made this seem a little more like a normal evening. At least, he supposed, he was better off than if he had paced the floor howling, or yielded to the ignoble, but profoundly attractive, impulse to welch on his obligation by getting pig-drunk.

He wrote in longhand, which was irksome, but the typewriter would have disturbed the visitor sleeping on the double bed in the next room. At least, he had been asleep last time Sean had checked him, sprawled in his shirt-sleeves on top of the covers, limbs splayed as if an explosion, or the rough hand of God, had tossed him there. The sound of typing would not have bothered the baby, who was as inured to it as country children are to crickets; but although the man on the bed could have slept on peacefully through bombing raids, mortar fire, and all the impersonal racket of war, small intimate noises woke him at once. It was simply a matter, he explained deprecatingly, of what you were used to.

At eight o'clock Sean stood up, stretched, and went over to close the window. Then he shuffled his papers into a tidy stack, dumped the reeking contents of the ashtray, and methodically crushed two empty beer cans before putting them in the garbage bin under the sink. His wife was a sweet-tempered woman, but one of the few things that made her furious was if he forgot to flatten the cans. Uncrushed, they filled the bin in no time, and it was five long flights down to the basement of the old brownstone where the communal dustbins stood in a verminous row. Marietta would be back from her mother's before ten, and there was a lot to do first. Right now he had to go out. If little Julia should wake up and cry while he was gone, the man on the bed would hear it and see to her. He knew a great deal more about babies than Sean did.

Sean splashed his face with cold water, checked his pockets for money and keys, made sure he carried no identification, and took from the kitchen drawer, where it lay innocently among vegetable peelers and egg whisks, a shining length of heavy-gauge wire. Tradition recommended a bent wire coat hanger, which was why anyone found with a wire coat hanger concealed about his person was automatically booked for stealing cars, which was why Sean wasn't taking one. He put the wire in his pocket, along with the rubber gloves Marietta used for housework. Softly he closed the apartment door behind him, hurried down the stairs, and emerged into the quiet street on the first of his errands, which was to steal a car. Not just any car, either, but one that would not be reported missing for several hours. Infinitely tedious research over the last three weeks had turned up half a dozen possibilities. Surely to God one of them would work out. If he came back without a car, the operation would have to be cancelled. Shutting his mind to this seductive thought, Sean Devlin went on his way, scared stiff.

At eleven o'clock Sean's dangerous visitor was sitting in the front seat of a shabby Plymouth, halfway down the block from Larry's Weigh Inn Steak House. Sean himself was crouched over beneath the bonnet, pretending to tinker with the filthy engine. He and the other man had been taking turns at this bleak charade for the last half hour, and his back was killing him. At last the couple they were waiting for came out into the fading warmth of the spring evening. The small girl with the straight blonde hair was laughing. She was not really so very small – five-five or thereabouts, Sean

12

figured – but her body in the shrunk jeans and clinging ribbed sweater was fine-boned and narrow, with an adolescent fragility. Next to her escort, an enormous youth with the shoulders of a footballer, she looked a child. As the young man steered her possessively towards his red Porsche, Sean's companion stared at her with the concentration of a naturalist observing one of the last examples of an endangered species. This was only the second time he had seen her, except of course in photographs, and the resemblance to Alice Mary was even more marked than he had at first supposed, but at the moment he could see no way to turn this unexpected element to advantage. File, under 'C' for 'Coincidence', and forget. One must not let oneself be distracted by peripheral details, no matter how striking. It didn't matter what she looked like, only who she was. Catherine Danbury Harper, daughter of Charlotte Danbury Harper and of her former husband Pendleton Reville Harper, secretary of state. Pen Harper's only child and only weak spot, laughing and careless in the mild spring air.

The young man handed her in, scrunched laboriously into the driver's seat, and drove off with considerable racing of engine and squealing of tyres. Sean jumped the wires, slammed down the bonnet, dived into the Plymouth, dragged the door shut with the help of the loop of string thoughtfully provided instead of a door handle, and they were off. For several blocks they followed the red car at a discreet half-block distance, and then Sean sucked in his breath and said, 'Shit!'

'Now what?'

'He's not taking her back to the dorm. That's the turning, right there. Fucking weeks I've followed them, dinner at Larry's every Saturday and then she goes back to the dorm as regular as the church clock, and tonight of all times they have to go joy riding!'

'How like the young.' The other man spoke mildly. 'No consideration for others. Cheer up, we'll see if we can wing it. Only whatever you do don't lose them.'

Sean had been twitchy before, and the sudden collapse of so much careful planning produced in him a dismaying tendency to babble. The other man saw no point in stopping him. His own nerves were comfortably in hand, and if it eased Sean to keep up a profane running commentary, let him get on with it.

'Where are they going, where the fuck are they going? He wouldn't take her to a motel – well he'd like to, I bet, but she'd never go; she's not the type. Looks like they're heading for the turnpike, but what for?'

'What else is out in this direction?'

'Couple of suburban developments, ticky-tacky boxes, not their territory at all, and anyhow they wouldn't be going visiting at this – preserve us, what are they up to now?'

The car they were following had swung off to the right.

'Well?'

'God knows. Only thing up that road is Adams Park. There's an amusement park, rides and so on, and a lake with paddle boats, but it doesn't open till Memorial Day weekend. Hey, maybe he's taking her up Winter Hill.'

'What's that?'

'Place kids go to make out in cars. Or used to. That boy must be sexually retarded.'

'The world's full of them. Will there be orgasmic teenagers under every bush, would you think?'

'Don't imagine so. These days, they mostly do it at home.'

'Better with your boots off. With any luck, then, our pair may have the shrubbery pretty much to themselves, which'll be a lot easier than picking her up after he drops her at the college. Is there any way you can tell ahead of time whether they're actually making for this what's-its-name, Winter Hill, or not?'

'There's a turning to the left in about a quarter of a mile. It's a narrow cut that goes up through the trees, and there's a clearing at the top, with a view over the river. Moonlight on the pollution.' Sean knew he was blithering, but he couldn't seem to stop. 'Look at the lovely scum on the water, lamby-pie, while I just get your panties off your cute little – there they go now.'

The taillights veered away to the left and vanished almost at once.

'Okay. Pull off the road and park on the verge. I don't want to drive up. How much of a walk is it?'

'Ten or twelve minutes, not more.'

'Good. Now belt up, cocker, and pay attention: here's what you're going to do.'

Sly and wary as a pair of poacher's dogs, they moved up through the dark trees.

'No, Charlie, don't. I don't like it. Oh, quit that, damn you!'

She pushed away the demanding hand and pulled her sweater

down. At once his hand was back, creeping under the hem, sliding over her skin, kneading and squeezing. She dug him in the ribs, hard, with her elbow.

'I mean it, Charlie.'

'Oh, man. Listen, I don't want to upset you or anything, but you really have a problem, you know? Maybe you ought to see a shrink. I mean this just is not normal behaviour.'

'No kidding. If I don't enjoy being prodded around like a lump of dough, I'm frigid. You cheated, too; you said you only wanted to talk. Otherwise I wouldn't have come up here. I like you a lot, Charlie. I just don't want to wrestle with you. It makes me feel foolish.'

'Jesus, Katie, you are eighteen – years – old! What are you waiting for, the Second Coming? What's so terrible about me?'

'There's nothing terrible about you, dummy. I'm truly fond of you, I always have been, even when I was a kid and you were so rotten and wouldn't let me play on your softball team because I was a girl. But I'm not in love with you, that's all.'

'If you'd only let me be nice to you.' He was sulky and insistent, his usual good humour gone. 'I could teach you things. You don't know how great it can be. Oh Kate, honey, I want you so much, please let me.'

'Hey, I'm sorry. I don't want to hurt your feelings, but this is *me* – I can't hand myself over like a – a sandwich or something. Come on now, take me back to the dorm, will you? I was working on a paper till three o'clock this morning, and I'm so tired I can hardly – Charlie look, look over there!'

A dozen yards from the car where they sat arguing, a man had stumbled out of the trees. He swayed a few steps towards them and then collapsed face down on the turf. They heard him moan and then start to cough, rackingly; he sounded as if he were choking to death.

'My God,' she said, opening the door, 'he's sick, or he's been hurt. We've got to do something.'

'Hold on a minute, Katie.' He was gripping her arm.

'Hold *on*? What for?'

'If he's been mugged, the guys who did it may be still –'

'Well if you won't help him, I will!' She pulled away and was scrambling out of the car.

'No, wait. I'll go. You stay right here while I take a look.'

'But, Charlie –'

'Don't argue. And don't leave the car. If you see anything that doesn't look right, don't wait for me – get the hell out of here and find help.'

She stood by the open car door, gripping the door frame, as Charlie crossed to kneel down by the huddled shape retching on the road. As she watched him begin to turn the man over, a gloved hand clamped painfully over her nose and mouth and an arm whipped around her, immobilizing her arms and thumping her back against an unyielding body, with an impact that left her half winded.

'Keep quiet and keep still,' a voice said close to her ear. 'I don't want to hurt you, but I will if I have to. Do you understand?'

Against the pressure of the hand Kate managed to nod her head. *Never try to fight.* She had had that drummed into her since junior school, when she was first promoted to walking home alone. *If you're near people, scream; if you see a chance to get away, run. But never, never try to fight.* She nodded again, more strenuously, and the harsh, smothering grip relaxed a little.

'Stand quite still,' the voice said quietly. It was a soft voice, educated, but not American. English or Irish, she wasn't sure which. 'Don't turn around,' it said. Quick fingers were tugging at her belt, reaching for the zipper, yanking her jeans roughly down around her knees. Oh Christ, it was going to be that, then. She stared wildly out across the moonlit clearing, looking for Charlie, and hope died. The two figures there had exchanged roles, and now it was Charlie who lay unmoving on the grass, with the former casualty bending over him. There would be no rescue. Whoever these people were, whatever they were going to do to her, there was nothing to stop them.

'Quite still, please,' the voice said again. 'This'll sting, I'm afraid, but you really mustn't wriggle.' Something jabbed into the large muscle at the front of her left thigh. Fiery pain spread from the site of the injection, and she gave a yelp.

'Shhh, it's all right.' Hands were holding her up now, which was just as well, because her legs were no use at all. She was losing herself fast. *There's been a mistake,* was her last conscious thought.

'But I already had my tonsils out,' she complained, blurred but reasonable, as the man lowered her onto the ground. He stopped to check her pulse, let her wrist fall back, and went over to Sean.

'Everything okay?'

'I think so. He wouldn't hold still, though, and I had to hit him. I was scared I'd break the needle or stick it in the wrong place or

16

something. You better check him out.'

A swift but thorough examination ended in a grunt of relief.

'He'll do. Good job you didn't hit him any harder.'

'I hit him as hard as I fucking well could; I thought he was going to kill me.'

'Never mind. Give me a hand and we'll tuck him up for the night.'

Between them they lugged Charlie back to his own car and wedged him, foetally curled, inside.

'Out like a light, bless his heart. I wouldn't be him in the morning, when he has to try and talk his way out of this lot.' By the flame of his cigarette lighter, he read the name on the car registration. 'Charles B. Eisinger. What a thing to do to you, Charlie boy; it's enough to turn a man off sex for life.' He moved away. 'Sleep tight, cocker, and may God go with you.'

'I'll bring the car up,' Sean offered. His nerves were recovering, but he had no wish to be left alone with the two unconscious victims. What if the stuff didn't work, and they woke up? He was a philosopher and a scholar, he told himself defensively; he belonged in a library. He was no damn good at this kind of thing.

'You're doing beautifully,' the other man said, as though Sean had spoken his doubts aloud. 'That deathbed scene was a zinger – next week, *East Lynne*. Take it slowly now, there's no rush, and if you sprain an ankle on the way down we're in trouble. I'll look after these two.'

When, a few minutes later, the man heard a car coming and saw the glow of its lights, he knew it wasn't Sean. It was too soon. That was the risk, of course, when you were obliged to operate in the local lovers' lane. He'd have to scare them off. He lifted the girl, carried her a short way from the car, and lay down on top of her, his face prudently hidden in the sweet-smelling tumble of her hair. Her jeans were still at half-mast, which was all to the good. Slipping his own pants down, he began to move against her as the headlights found them.

The two high school kids in the car reacted predictably. The boy gave an embarrassed laugh, and the girl was affronted.

'Yeccch, how gross,' she said. 'Some *people*. Let's get out of here, Petey, it's disgusting.'

The car swung around in a wide circle, Petey trying to sneak another look without the girl catching him at it, and then they were gone. The man pulled up his trousers and wiped his wet face on his sleeve. Close, very close. He didn't need any more like

17

that, thank you. The next car to climb the hill was the terrible Plymouth. Sean spilled out of it, shaking.

'That car – I saw the lights –'

'It's all right. I got rid of them. No harm done, but I'd just as soon not hang about.'

He straightened the girl's clothes, and they arranged her in the front passenger seat of the Plymouth, with a blanket tucked around her and a rolled-up jacket as a pillow for her lolling head.

'All set?' Sean asked, getting into the back.

'Almost.' The other man returned to the red car, leaned in the window, snapped Charlie's keys out of the ignition, and tossed them far into the trees.

'It's a long walk to the beach,' he said, sliding behind the wheel next to the unconscious girl. 'Tolerance for that muck varies a good deal, and he's a substantial item; we can't afford to screw up the timing. Oh sod it, I forgot. Sean, be a good chap and jump the bloody ignition again, and let's see if this pile of junk'll hold together a little longer.'

Just before dropping Sean on the outskirts of New Lymington, the other man ran through the instructions for the last time.

'And Sean –'

'Yes?'

'When you're talking to the mother, don't come on too strong. We don't want her to panic and blow the whole thing. Promise her the girl won't be hurt as long as they keep the lid on: no cops, no hue and cry. She's to call the college in the morning and say the girl's with her – she didn't feel well and a friend brought her home. Must be the virus that's going around.'

'What virus?'

'Any old virus. There's always a virus going around, that's how internists get Cadillacs. Tell her she just has to be cool and nobody'll come to any harm. Harper's a different matter. You can lay it on as thick as you like, I want that bastard softened up. Curdle his blood for him, if he has any, but keep it short, we don't want them getting a fix on the call.'

'Will do.'

'Sure you've got enough change? Those damn pay phones fairly gobble it up.'

'Yes, I'm sure. Put me down here, at the next corner. It's not that far to McBurney's, and there's plenty of time. Good luck.'

'You too. You're a hell of a fellow, Sean. The children shall rise up and call you blessed.'

'That was the Good Woman, you ape. And I've never been above rubies, myself.' They grinned at each other, and then Sean was out on the sidewalk, watching the car draw away and thankful that no bits of it were actually dropping off yet. He fell into an easy stride, heading for the saloon that was to provide his makeshift alibi. He'd have to stay away from the apartment at least another three hours, in any case; there were those calls to make, when the time came, and he couldn't do that from his own phone.

Suddenly he realized he was still wearing Marietta's gloves; that'd be clever, by God, to have a police car come by and spot him with those on. He worked them off with some difficulty – they were clammy inside and stuck to him – and carried them squeezed up in his palm until he could find a trash can and get rid of them. He couldn't risk being picked up, as any random pedestrian at this hour might easily be, and having the damn things found on him, they'd be worse than a coat hanger. Marietta would hunt for them for days, poor soul; he'd better buy a new pair tomorrow and plant them somewhere just unlikely enough for her not to have looked there. Would she be able to tell that they were new, though?

Jesus, Mary, and Joseph, it was all a nightmare. He hated to think of his wife weeping at home with the baby, desolate after the quarrel he had deliberately provoked so as to have an excuse to slam out of the house and stay away half the night. He hated deceiving Marietta; he had hated knocking out that harmless young man; in fact he hated just about everything to do with this whole business. The only thing he hated more was the thing they were trying, he and the rest of them, to stop. He supposed it was worth it. It had better be.

An hour later the wheezing Plymouth pulled up in front of an immaculately kept Jeep that was parked just outside a prosperous village, fifty miles north of the college town of New Lymington. A young black man sat in the driver's seat of the Jeep.

'No sweat,' he responded to the other man's enquiry. 'Man, this place is so peaceful they should check its vital signs; I think it died in its sleep.'

He swung himself out onto the pavement. He wore a long-sleeved turtleneck shirt. His left arm ended not in a hand but in a metal and rubber prosthesis; the right hand was gloved. He helped transfer the girl to the Jeep and then got into the Plymouth himself and found his way around the controls, while the other man shifted a picnic basket and various odds and ends from the trunk. The motor was still running, and the car shuddered in a loud, metallic ague.

'Don't let it stall, whatever you do; it may never start again. Just keep heading north, okay, Tom? Ditch the poor old wreck in a couple of hours, or sooner if you can't stand it another minute. Don't get picked up.'

'Your mamma,' Tom said pleasantly. 'My family been heading north for years. You ever lose your compass, just look around for the Tullivers. Whichever way they going, that's north. And we don't *never* get picked up.'

He drove off. The other man climbed into the Jeep and peeled off his gloves, scuffed and stained now and no longer needed. He took a moment to settle the girl more comfortably and, again, to take her pulse. He thumbed open an eyelid, examined the pupil, and laid his ear against her chest for a moment to listen to her breathing. Her small breasts were distractingly soft and round, intruding on his professional appraisal. He lifted his head again quickly and started the Jeep. Some fifty yards further on he reversed into a side road and set off again going south, back the way they had come.

At three o'clock that Sunday morning Pendleton Reville Harper, secretary of state, was drifting into sleep in his charming, hideously expensive house in Georgetown. It had been a most satisfactory day: he had gone around the golf course in one under par, the president had called in person to congratulate him on having extracted a further increase in military aid to South Vietnam from those venal nonentities on the Hill, and his current mistress had been gratifyingly inventive after dinner. Best of all, she had slipped tactfully away and left him to sleep alone, as he preferred. He was a tall, bulky man, and he liked to have his queen-size bed to himself.

Harper's likes and dislikes had been anxiously studied and meticulously met for three years now, ever since his predecessor, Fritz Kraemer's star pupil, known to his detractors as the Flying Hun, had emplaned once too often and vanished into the ocean somewhere off the Azores. As the president's speech writers had so pithily put it, Harper had grasped the precious baton of freedom passed on by the great runner who would run no more – a curious description of a determinedly sedentary man, but

20

speech writers must be allowed their little fancies. Poor old Hank: the most powerful man in the world one minute, and fish food the next. Of course, he'd never really been *accepted*; that impossible accent, the tantrums, and that appalling lone-cowboy gaffe. Without the office he would have been nobody, whereas his successor was a Harper, Endicott Harper's son, Samuel Alden Harper's great-grandson, last of a long line of public servants in the finest New England tradition. Not 'latest', unfortunately, but last. What a pity Charlotte had never given him a son; not that he would have traded Kate for a boy, or for the moon and stars if it came to that, but a boy as well would have been pleasant. Even now it was not too late. Some suitable young woman – not too young, he didn't want people snickering behind his back, but say thirty-two or so; a widow, or else divorced, though a widow would be tidier, but with at least one child to prove she was capable. No sense going through the exhausting farce of courtship only to find himself saddled with some useless female as barren as a mule. It was time he started looking around. Pendleton Harper nuzzled deeper into the down pillows, and smiled in his sleep. He was still smiling when the telephone rang.

Ten minutes later Mr Secretary Harper, his large face pale and sweaty above the red brocaded silk of his robe and his heart thudding in a most unstatesmanlike manner, was on the phone to his former wife in New Lymington.

'Yes, Pen,' she was saying, 'they called me too, a few minutes ago. The man said he expected I'd be hearing from you. We have to keep the whole thing absolutely quiet, they insist on that. Is that what they told you?'

'Pretty much. It shouldn't be difficult, but it's awkward about the Eisinger boy. The New Lymington people will just have to find him and keep him under wraps until I can get someone sent up there to take over. One way or another, that kid's mouth has to be kept shut.'

Though Charlotte Harper was sick with fear for her daughter, she was not so far gone in shock that she missed the callous purpose in her former husband's tone.

'Stop it!' she said strongly. 'All you have to do is ask him, you know that. Don't be ridiculous. Charlie's a good, responsible boy, and he's devoted to Kate. We can depend on him.'

'Couldn't depend on him to keep her safe from any thug that happened to be passing, that's obvious. But I won't quarrel with you. Now then, Charlotte, did they give you any idea what their

21

demands are likely to be? Is it money? They wouldn't tell me – just said I'd be "informed in due course", of all the gall.'

'They wouldn't tell me either. I hope to God it is money. We can raise that somehow if we have to, but I don't think it is. I think it may be political, but I've no real evidence – it's just a feeling. All the man said to me was that they had her, that I'm to square things with the college, and as long as there's no publicity and no police she won't be harmed. He said her – her future well-being would be up to you, Pen, and that he knew you would want to cooperate. He was very – polite. Oh dear God, I'm so frightened.'

'Now, now, Charlotte, everything will be all right.'

'You'll do what they say, won't you? No matter what it is?'

'If I can, my dear. If I possibly can. Look, I have to make some calls now. There'll be people coming up to go over all this with you, and I'll be in touch myself as soon as I have anything. Now you're not to worry. We'll soon have her back, safe and sound. And meanwhile, I intend to devote every ounce of energy and every resource I possess to making these gentlemen wish their parents had died childless.'

Irrepressibly, Harper was ballooning into his podium manner. Charlotte dug her nails into her palm and prayed for patience.

'Never mind all that now,' she said, as levelly as she could manage. 'For heaven's sake, Pen, never mind about that now. Just don't put the child in any worse danger than she's in already. This is not the time to send in the Marines; we want her *alive*. You can worry about punishing people afterwards.'

'Trust me. Everything that's humanly possible will be done. Now I have to get moving. Try to keep calm. Goodbye, Charlotte.'

Kate's mother put down the phone and rubbed her fists, hard, against her cheeks.

'Calm!' she said aloud. 'Calm! Dear sweet Jesus.' She stood up and began to pace the pretty bedroom. She felt a fierce hunger for action, but there was absolutely nothing she could do except wait. She was even tempted to call the Dean of Kate's college right away, to fulfil the only instruction she had been given, but she knew it must wait until morning. One must above all try to behave as normally as possible, and panic calls in the middle of the night were not in character for her.

She went down to the kitchen, made tea, and sat drinking it at the sky blue kitchen table Kate had made her buy. She tuned her transistor radio to the local news station. The announcer was chatting on soporifically about a fire in an abandoned building on Pine Street, word of a possible strike of apartment house maintenance workers, the latest incomprehensible release from the governor's office, and all the other minutiae that speckle the airwaves in the bad hours when happy people are asleep.

At least there were no dramatic bulletins about the abduction of Catherine Danbury Harper, eighteen-year-old daughter of the secretary of state. Nor was there any word of a college senior named Charles Eisinger being picked up dazed and wandering near New Lymington. Charlotte rinsed her cup and saucer, turned out the light, and went back to bed, taking the radio with her. She did not even try to go to sleep, but sat hunched against the pillows, half-listening to weather reports, 'Word from Washington', the latest increase in the price of canned tuna, waiting until it was time to call the Dean and tell the first of the many lies ahead of her.

SUNDAY, 29 APRIL 1973. 3.30 A.M.

At about the time one of Pendleton Harper's top aides was rousing the New Lymington chief of police out of a sound sleep, the man in the Jeep was driving along a narrow country road that ran through woods. When a track opened up to one side he turned off and followed it far enough to be hidden from the road; then he steered in among the trees themselves, the four-wheel drive carrying him safely over the spongy, rutted surface. After the Jeep rolled to a stop the first thing he did was fill up the petrol tank from one of the spare cans. Then he pulled on a sweater against the delicate bite of the night air and checked his passenger again. She was snoring gently, like a baby with a head cold. He took off his belt, used it to buckle the girl's wrist to his own, and settled himself for a nap.

The first wash of dawn was showing between the branches when he woke. It was a dead light, cold as the moon, bleaching everything it touched to wintry monotones. He looked down at the girl beside him. She might have been newly drowned; her face was marble pale and her hair, flopping disorderly around it, seemed by contrast the sad colour of wet sand. It was the first time he had really looked at her closely and the first time he had thought about her at all except as an abstraction: a pivotal element in his plans, but, as a person, inconsiderable. She was prettier than he had realized, even in this unhelpful light. The likeness to Alice Mary remained, though at such close quarters it was less striking: a matter of colouring mainly and the set of the eye sockets, the straight line of the brows. It occurred to him, troublingly, that she looked like what his father would call a 'thoroughly nice girl'. He caught himself feeling sorry for her and stamped down hard on the weakness. As he watched, the eyelashes that brushed the upper curve of her rounded, still childish cheeks fluttered a little, and she turned her head away and moaned deep in her throat. He unfastened the belt and threaded it back through the loops in his corduroys; then he straightened up, combed his hair with his fingers, worked his shoulders briefly to loosen them, and climbed down from the Jeep. As soon as she recovered consciousness she would almost

24

certainly throw up, and he wanted her outside before that happened.

Through the lingering fog of the drug that had kept her under, Kate was aware of being lifted, moved, and put down somewhere, lying flat. She was in the hospital, that was it. The bed was not only hard but extremely lumpy. She opened her eyes, expecting a white ceiling, white walls, white coats, and perhaps her mother leaning over her. Someone was certainly leaning over her, but it was nobody's mother. A man's face, unfamiliar and severe. A hard mouth, a narrow beak of a nose, hard eyes staring at her; lines like parentheses harshly scored into the flesh below the cheekbones; thick, straight hair, longish, but not fashionably long, more as if he hadn't bothered to get it cut. He was wearing a dark sweater over an open-necked shirt, with a scarf knotted at his throat, and behind his head were the tops of trees and, beyond them, an oddly luminous sky the colour of watered ink. Man and background alike appeared to her with such hallucinatory sharpness that she thought she was dreaming. She shut her eyes, squeezed hard, and opened them again. The man was still there. He had no business to be there or she had no business to be here. Or both. Something was horribly wrong.

'You're not a doctor,' she croaked accusingly. The hard mouth tipped up suddenly at the corners.

'As a matter of fact,' the man said, 'that's exactly what I am.' She had heard the voice before, but could not for the moment remember where.

'You may not know it,' he continued, 'but any minute now you're going to be sick. Sit up a bit, can you? There's a good girl.'

He was none too soon. It was as squalid as it always is, but he did not seem to mind. He supported her, one arm around her heaving shoulders and a firm hand on her forehead, until the humiliating performance was over. Then he picked her up and moved her away from the mess, wiped her face, and gave her water to rinse her mouth.

'That's better,' he said, after she had gargled and spat. 'Take it very gently.' He had brought the plaid wool blanket from the Jeep; he spread it on the grass, moved her onto one side of it, and drew the rest over to cover her against the cool air of morning. She tried to sit up, but he pressed her shoulders down and wiped her face again with the wet cloth.

'Easy, just lie still.'

'What happened?' she asked. 'Was there an accident?'

'In a way. Don't talk yet, rest a bit. I'll tell you all about it later.'

Her eyelids weighed a ton apiece. She let them fall and drifted off again. When she came around for the second time her mind was much clearer, and anxiety dropped over her like a net as soon as she opened her eyes. She struggled up onto one elbow.

'Charlie,' she said. 'What have you done with Charlie?'

'We left him having a nice zizz. I imagine by now he's blundering around looking for a policeman, if they haven't already picked him up.'

'You – you didn't kill him?'

'Of course not. He got a healthy wallop behind the ear, and he'll have a shocking headache, but not much worse than yours. We don't believe in killing people; in fact we're very much against it.'

'Well that's good to know.' She sat up, hugging the blanket around her. The birds were carrying on like lunatics, and the light was growing stronger every minute. There was nothing to see, though, but the man, the Jeep, and the trees. She had no idea where this place might be, but wherever it was she was alone in it with an unknown man who had brought her here without her leave, and the more she thought about her situation the more unpleasant it looked.

'What would happen,' she said carefully, 'if I stood up and started to walk away?'

'Right now this minute? You'd fall flat on your face.'

'No, but – if I could walk, I mean – what would you do?'

'Stop you.'

'That's what I thought. I am being kidnapped, then?'

'Oh dear. Well, yes, you are, but please try not to be frightened. Nothing awful's going to happen to you. Couple of weeks in the country, lots of lovely fresh air and so on, and then you can go home. You're not in nearly as much trouble as you think you are. Honestly.'

On the grass beside him was the canvas bag he had taken from the Jeep. He stowed away the water bottle and the wet cloth, and took out a Thermos flask and two mugs.

'Coffee,' he said, holding a mug out to her. 'And take these, they'll make your headache better.'

She swallowed the tablets meekly. The coffee was hot and strong and very heartening; she drank it down and gave back the empty mug.

'Is there more?'

'Later. If you have too much at one go you'll start being sick again. Want a cigarette?'

'Yes, please.'

He gave her one, lit it for her, and took one himself. He sat leaning against a tree trunk, serenely drinking his coffee. He was not looking in her direction, so she felt free to look at him. The sun had come up at last and brought the colours back. She could see now that his hair was a dark, dull gold, like expensive butterscotch. His eyes were slitted against the cigarette smoke, and she could not be sure of their colour. Grey seemed likely, cold, puddles-in-November grey. It was hard to tell how old he was. His hands and his body – what she could see of it – were those of a relatively young man, but his face was lined and worn under the tan. He could have been anywhere from a racked-up twenty-five to a man of forty-plus in hard physical condition. She searched his face anxiously for clues to the kind of personality she had to deal with. It told her very little. It was not an evil or a brutish face, which was something; in other circumstances she might have thought it pleasant, even attractive. But there was no hint of compromise there, no margin at all. He looked, primarily, intelligent, tired, and effective – as flatly functional as a bread knife. He glanced up then and caught her examining him. She blushed furiously, and he laughed and suddenly looked much younger.

'There's no charge,' he said. 'Although I can think of nicer things to look at.'

She asked the first question that floated into her head.

'Why did you say you were a doctor?'

'Because it's true. I'm not a professional criminal, you know; this is strictly a sideline.'

'You really are a doctor?'

'Paediatric surgeon. Three fucking years of it in Vietnam. Gunshot, grenade fragments, and napalm a speciality, amputations while you wait. You get sick of it after a while,' he went on conversationally. 'Patching up the poor little beasts so they can go out and barge into another daisy cutter. If you're not careful you start brooding about ways to reduce the supply of patients. And then you end up sitting in a very damp wood at a godless hour with Pendleton Harper's daughter. You can have some more coffee now, if you like.'

'Thank you. I guess it was what you saw in Vietnam, then, that made you join a terrorist group.'

27

'Good God.' He looked taken aback. 'I'd never thought of it quite like that, I must say. Any terrorizing that's gone on has been strictly by courtesy of your father's lot. I mean, have you ever seen what napalm does to the human body? Silly question, of course you haven't. It's remarkable stuff, though. There was one child, we never were sure if it was a boy or a girl, you couldn't tell any more. It hadn't any face left, either, just a big, lopsided hole to scream through. Everything else was sort of melted. It was dying, but not nearly fast enough. I killed it myself in the end, shot it full of enough morphine to knock over an elephant. Only time I've ever killed anyone – intentionally, that is.'

'But that's horrible!'

'Yes, ma'am, it was. Very horrible. Your father made a speech the next day, it was in all the papers. About how despite our continuing troop withdrawals, military aid to the democratic government of South Vietnam must be increased to protect the lives and liberties of the civilian population. Round about then it occurred to me that I was working at quite the wrong end of the production line.'

He had repacked the canvas bag while he talked. Now he got to his feet, stooped down, and pulled her up beside him, steadying her with one hand while with the other he whisked up the blanket and threw it across his shoulder. She tried a step forward. Her left leg seemed weak, the thigh muscles knotted and painful, and also the ground was much further away than she had expected.

'You'll be a bit groggy for a while,' he said. 'Hang onto me.'

She felt extraordinarily foolish leaning on his arm like a rheumatic dowager; besides, she did not like having to touch him. What was worse, she had the unpleasant impression that he knew what she was feeling and was sourly amused by it. When she was back in the Jeep, he opened the glove compartment and pulled out a long, thin length of chain and two metal bracelets, one much broader than the other. The heavier cuff he locked onto her left wrist. Then he doubled the chain through between metal and wincing skin, hitched the remainder of the chain through a heavy steel ring that was bolted to the Jeep's floor, and slipped the free end onto the other cuff before snapping that shut on her right wrist.

'Sorry about that,' he said, as she opened her mouth to protest, 'but people get such damn silly ideas. Comes of watching all that crap on television. I've a great deal to do, and I don't intend to wind up dead in a ditch because you had an attack of misplaced

28

initiative and took a grab at the wheel.'

Since this was exactly what she had been hoping to do, she swallowed her disappointment and did not answer. Then, to complete her helplessness, he brought out a pair of wraparound sunglasses and fitted them carefully on her face. The lenses had been coated so that they were completely opaque. Light leaked around the edges, but that was all; she could see nothing.

'If you don't see where you're going,' said the soft, hateful voice close to her ear, 'then you can't tell anyone where you've been.'

They drove in silence for a while. The chain had greatly reduced her options. It was long enough to allow her hands to rest in her lap, but only just. The controls were well out of her reach, even if she could have got rid of the glasses long enough to see which was which, and, tethered as she was, any chance of being able to jump out when the Jeep slowed for a curve was gone. Surreptitiously she tested the cuffs to find out if she could wriggle her hands free of them, but they fitted snugly around her narrow wrists. Probably custom-made, she thought bitterly.

There seemed to be very little traffic on the roads they were travelling. Her hopes rose involuntarily each time she heard another vehicle, but she could think of no way to attract attention that would not put both herself and her potential rescuers at too great hazard. She had not seen any gun, but almost certainly the man was armed, and she did not suppose he would hesitate to shoot. There was nothing more dangerous than a rebel with a cause. In the noble name of peace and justice, people like the man sitting next to her had done things that would make the average felon sick to his stomach. The Tupamaros, the IRA, the Black September, those terminally mixed-up creatures who believed that social justice, like power, came from the barrel of a gun. Their violence swathed in rhetoric, the flag that covers the corpse, they seemed to have no difficulty persuading themselves that a few innocent lives might legitimately be sacrificed for the higher good.

Her father's crew, of course, had a remarkably similar attitude, and she'd never liked them either. The only real difference lay in the degree of power and the view of what constituted a higher good. This man who had abducted her clearly believed that what he was doing was right, and that was what made him terrifying. Probably he would kill her, if he thought it necessary, with far less reluctance than he had expressed over easing a ruined child out of life. Kate was not a coward, but she had enough imagination to know when to be afraid, and now that the cushioning effect of the drug was wearing off she was beginning to be very scared.

'My mother will go out of her mind when she finds out about this,' she said at last, voicing the end of a train of thought. It was not that she expected sympathy or even attention; it was only that she had arrived at the point where she had to talk to someone, and he was all there was.

'She's already been told. Your father, too.'

'You do know we haven't much money? Mother and me, I mean. Father's quite well off, I suppose, but he's not rich – not *rich* rich. It hardly seems worth your while.' She was doing her best to sound nonchalant and worldly, and might have been more successful if her voice had been steadier. Fortunately, her peculiar captor was too annoyed by what she said to notice how shakily it came out.

'Whatever the hell gave you the idea we want money? Don't you listen to anything people say to you? Jesus Christ.'

'What *do* you want, then?'

'Pendleton Harper's resignation. Look, let me make it very simple for you. With your father out of the picture, Ted Faraday's pretty well certain to get the job. He's hardly my idea of a dove, but he doesn't have Harper's clout. Nobody does. Even the Congress could stand up to Faraday, and now that all the American troops have been evacuated, there's more than enough grass-roots pressure to make 'em do it. People are fed up, in case you hadn't noticed. Only Harper could have kept the miserable business going this long. So he's going to retire, is your dad, for reasons of health. Your health.'

Kate examined this bleak statement and drew a reasonable and beastly conclusion.

'You mean you'll kill me if he doesn't do what you want.'

She heard the man sigh. He sounded like her high school maths teacher when she had failed to grasp the principle of negative numbers.

'Try not to be silly,' he said. 'Nobody's going to kill you. Nobody's going to do anything to you at all. Why should they? All that matters is for your father to believe we're capable of it. And by the time we've done with him, he will.'

'It won't work.'

'I don't see why not. For a man with his racial views, the prospect of having his daughter ravished by platoons of hairy

30

black subversives ought to be tolerably effective. And if that doesn't do the trick, we can always offer to send him your head in a plastic bag by registered mail.'

She gave a little choked-off cry, and he turned to look at her, startled.

'Oh, for God's sake, girl. We're not going to do it: it's only a horror story to frighten your father. If he knew anything about us, it wouldn't work, but luckily he doesn't. For all he knows, we're the spiritual heirs of Genghis Khan. Besides, he'll be receptive – he knows about this sort of thing; it's his stock in trade. I don't mean personally, of course,' he went on, 'men like him don't get themselves all sweaty and worn out torturing people. They have it done at a nice safe distance, and call it pacification or winning hearts and minds or something equally hilarious. Might put them off their dinners otherwise. But he knows what goes on, so he'll be apt to take it seriously when it's aimed at one of his own.'

Her chained hands were clenched in her lap, the knuckles as white as bone. He took his right hand off the wheel and covered them. Kate flinched at the unexpected contact, but he kept his hand there. Hers were very cold. *Shock*, he thought, exasperated; *well damn it to hell, how many more times do I have to tell her?*

'I *told* you,' he said patiently. 'You won't be harmed. Quite apart from anything else, there's no reason for it – surely you can see that? I wish you didn't have to be mixed up in this at all. We did try to find an alternative, but in the end it always came back to you, because you seem to be the only human being on the face of this earth that your father cares tuppence about. Look, you're a lever, that's all. We need you to pry the s.o.b. out of the State Department, but once that's done we'll let you go.' His hand tightened over hers for a moment before he took it away. 'If it's any consolation, which it probably isn't,' he added, 'I'm not enjoying this either. It's no treat to me to have you sitting there shaking like a leaf. You couldn't possibly manage to stop being quite so scared, I suppose?'

'I don't see how,' she said carefully. 'Okay, you keep on saying you're not going to hurt me. What does that cost you? People can *say* anything. In Nazi concentration camps they used to tell the prisoners they were going to the showers, when really it was the gas chamber. They just didn't want them screaming and struggling and making things harder. If I'm going to die anyhow, I'd have nothing to lose by making as much trouble as I can. You could be telling me all this soothing stuff just to keep me from being a bother to you.'

'Yes, well, I'm not, as it happens. But if I were, obviously I wouldn't admit it, so that's not much help. What can we do to cheer you up? I could tell you the story of the Three Bears, but you've probably heard it before. Would you like me to recite? I used to be pretty hot stuff when I was about ten. "You know we French stormed Ratisbon; A mile or so away, On a little mound, Napoleon stood, Upon our storming day." No good? No, perhaps not. It goes better with gestures, anyway. I'll sing to you if you like, but you might not care for it. Desire has a tendency to outrun performance. When I tried serenading the cows Chuck made me stop; he said it was bad for the milk.'

'Cows?'

'Definitely cows. Not to mention calves, cats, pigs, a rather dim-witted pony, and an arthritic basset hound called Bagel. Then there's hens, of course, but they don't really count – one can't get emotionally attached to a hen, at least I can't. Those evil little faces, and besides their habits are not nice. Oh, I forgot about the geese.'

'It sounds like a children's zoo.'

'You're not far off. In theory it's an ordinary working farm, but the livestock end of things has been known to get out of hand. That's Claire, bless her. She goes on the principle that if it moves, you take it home and feed it. She'll probably start a campaign to fatten you up as soon as she sets eyes on you. I hope you like dumplings.'

'I don't think,' Kate said, 'I don't *think* I understand what you're talking about.'

'Of course you don't. How could you? I never was any good at explaining things, that's why I went in for surgery. At the critical moment the customers are decently unconscious. I'd never make a living in China, with everybody wide awake and all that merry chitchat among the scalpels. Anyway. I have this farm, and that's where we're going now. It's very isolated, which is why we're using it for this lark, but it's comfortable enough if you don't mind rather peculiar plumbing. Some friends of mine live there, and they work the place when I'm away, which is most of the time. You needn't start getting nervous about them, they're very much nicer than I am. In fact I'm the only real bastard in the whole set-up. Claire says I'm ruled by intemperate wrath, and she's not far wrong.'

'Is Claire your wife?'

'No. My wife died a year ago. Not quite a year.'

'I'm sorry,' she said quickly. 'I didn't mean –'

'It's all right; how were you to know? Claire's a very old friend. She's the daughter of the man who used to own the farm. I spent a couple of summers there, donkey's years ago, when my papa was attached to the Embassy in Washington, and I fell madly in love with her, as only a fifteen-year-old boy can fall in love with a woman who feeds him five magnificent meals a day. She was my first older woman. In later years I made the basic error of introducing her to my friend Chuck, who knew a good thing when he saw one and married her on the spot, the cad. They have two children, a boy of ten – he's my godson – and a girl of seven.' He was stacking up facts like a mason laying bricks, building a shelter against her vaporous fears. She realized what he was doing and yet was comforted by it; surely there could not be anything too villainous about people whose lives were defined by cows and basset hounds and children. Always supposing, of course, that any of it were true. One noticeable hole in the story presented itself.

'If it was her father's farm, how come it belongs to you now?'

'Remind me to give you a lecture on the economics of agricultural life in this country. Like most small farmers, the old man had hardly any actual cash, and when he died the place had to be sold to pay the taxes. I happened to hear about it, so I put up the money and then hired Chuck and Claire to run the farm for me, and we split the profits, or we would if there were any. Actually I own it in roughly the same way that a fisherman owns the bit of ocean he trawls. It's my name on the papers, and that's my lot. For all practical purposes it's their farm. Which is as it should be. You'll like them,' he went on. 'Of course the children won't be there, they've been packed off to Chuck's old mum for the duration. Claire's not too charmed with me about that, but they'll be safer out of the way.'

'What do you think I am, a child beater?'

'It's not you I'm worried about. Face it, your father's not the most sensible man in the world. He's been strictly enjoined to keep the goons out of this, but who knows? And some of those lads with the Bureau are a bit weird. It's the boredom that does it, I imagine. Think of having to spend months on end taping the grocery orders of some unfortunate housewife who once sent five bucks to Another Mother for Peace. Then one day somebody sticks a gun in your hand and tells you there's a bunch of godless, pot-smoking Communists miscegenating away like mad in that house across the street, and you're apt to get overexcited. Mind you, I'm hoping your papa will have enough elementary grasp of reality to do as he's told and keep the lid on, but you never know, and I can't risk having the children caught in a firefight.'

'I'd rather not be caught in one myself, if that's all right,' Kate said wearily.

'Poor kid, you've about had it, haven't you?'

He reached an arm into the back and fished up the old tweed jacket. One-handed, he rolled it into a makeshift bolster shape and tucked it behind her neck.

'We've a fair way to go yet,' he said. 'See if you can get a nap.'

She closed her eyes and leaned back. There was no way she was going to sleep, she was far too jumpy; but at least it would be a respite, a chance to think. The steady growl of the engine was soothing, and the man beside her had begun to hum softly to himself; a Shaker hymn, of all things.

> '*Tis the gift to be simple,*
> *'Tis the gift to be free,*
> *'Tis the gift to come down*
> *Where we ought to be . . .*'

Automatically, her memory fitted words to the plain, familiar tune.

> '*And when we find ourselves in the place just right*
> *We shall live in the valley of love and delight.*'

Presently, she slept.

Kate woke, much later, with a heart-stopping jolt, the initial panic of disorientation flowering like a slow explosion into real, reasoned fear. But at least the hateful goggles had been removed while she slept; it would have been worse to wake in that blank darkness. The Jeep was no longer moving; looking out, she saw that it was parked on the edge of a broad clearing surrounded by trees. The sun was high and it was very hot, more like summer than spring. A tickling rivulet of sweat ran down in front of her ear, and when she tried to lift a hand and brush it away she found she was still chained. The driver's door stood wide open. A small bug wavered in, lost its bearings, and began to bump doggedly against the windshield. That tiny, frantic buzz, and the twittering of invisible birds, were all she could hear.

There was no sign of the man, and she wondered, with a sudden internal lurch, whether he had simply gone off and left her. He had said she would not be harmed, but perhaps he was a literalist, like the good Buddhist who will not take life but sees no harm in fishing – he does not kill the fish, he only removes it from the water; and what happens to the fish after that is not his responsibility. As her father's daughter, Kate was well acquainted with letter-of-the-law lying, where the incomplete but literal truth is used to shore up whole structures of deception. The man could have meant it when he said he would not kill her, and still have felt no compunction about leaving her, like the landed fish, to do her own dying. It would be a very bad death.

When the door next to her swung back, she was so relieved to see him that she actually smiled. He smiled back, the fine wrinkles suddenly very noticeable around his eyes, which were not grey, as she had thought, but deep blue and surprisingly kind.

'First call for luncheon,' he said, leaning in and unfastening the chain, leaving only the wide cuff on her left wrist. He lifted her down, setting her on her feet and letting go of her at once. Thank God, she thought, he doesn't seem to want to paw me, anyhow. Her left leg still bothered her, as though she had a bad cramp, but she set her teeth and managed to walk without limping,

35

so that he would not offer to help her. The plaid blanket had been spread in the shade of a walnut tree. A basket stood open next to the blanket, and the paraphernalia of an almost Edwardian picnic – china plates, linen napkins, baskets and bowls and platters of food, everything but the footmen – were set out in all their unlikely opulence.

'Claire was afraid there mightn't be enough,' he said, answering her bewildered look. 'She's the only Quaker Jewish mother I know. Come and dig in.'

There was a cold roast chicken, moist and plump and perfumed with tarragon; there were thin shavings of brownish, strong-flavoured ham that contrived to be dry and melting at the same time; there was farm butter in pale, dewy curls, a fresh-baked loaf, potato salad with slivers of onion bathed in homemade mayonnaise, and crisp, dark green pickles only a couple of inches long. There was hard cider with a sour, fresh bite to it and a great wedge of golden, richly crumbling cheese. Kate, who would have sworn that her appetite had gone for ever, discovered a raging hunger and was embarrassed to find herself packing away more food than she normally ate in two days.

'It's a pleasure to watch you eat,' the man said finally, flicking away an overconfident ant and wrapping the cheese in its red-and-white check cloth. 'I can't stand women who pick at their food. Would you like to start again at the beginning or shall we have some coffee?'

'Coffee, please. I'm stuffed. Do you always live this way?'

'Dear me no, that was a mere snack, a little something to stave off the pangs until supper.' He poured the coffee and passed her a cup.

'This is crazy,' she complained. 'Sitting here making polite conversation, as if everything was normal. I ought to be – ' She paused uncertainly.

'Ought to be what? Weeping and wailing and guh-nashing your teeth? What good would that do? Of course, if you feel you owe it to yourself to have hysterics, by all means go ahead, but I can't see the point of it myself. Besides, it's bad for the digestion.' He was rewrapping the carcass of the chicken. 'I think you're behaving very sensibly. And look at it this way – at least you know now that we don't believe in starving our prisoners.'

'I wish I knew what you did believe in doing to them. Or am I better off not knowing?'

'We chain them in the root cellar and beat them savagely three times a day. Don't *worry* so.' He seemed to be in an annoyingly good mood.

'No, but what are you going to do, really?'

'Keep you safe. We'll take very good care of you, and send you home as soon as we possibly can. It'll be like summer camp, except you don't have to play volleyball. *Or* make an ashtray to take home to your mother.'

He finished packing the basket and buckled the straps around it.

'I'm afraid I can't offer you a bathroom,' he said, 'but if you could bear to improvise, there's some handy-looking bushes over there to your right.'

'Could I have – or maybe you didn't bring it – my bag? It was in Charlie's car when you, when –'

'Yes, of course. I'm sorry, I should have given it back to you before. It's in the Jeep. I'll get it.'

When he came back she took the bag and slipped the strap over her shoulder, blushing and irritated with herself for blushing (after all, kidnapped or not, people still had to go, and at least he hadn't made her ask), and walked in among the trees. Keeping his back politely turned, he busied himself about the Jeep, stowing the gear. Presently it occurred to him that she was taking a damned long time. He turned around, scanning, but there was no sign of her. Caught in this unusual social dilemma, he gave her another two minutes before chucking decorum to the winds and going to investigate. There was no answer to his calls, and Kate was nowhere to be found. Cursing himself and her, he ran for the Jeep, hauled a square black leather case out of the back and, still cursing, opened the lid.

Kate was sobbing as she ran. It was not much of a chance, she knew that – hardly a chance at all, really. But there might not be another. At the farm, if there was a farm, she would really be a prisoner, probably locked up, certainly watched every moment. If she were ever to get away it must be now. She had been so close to giving in, meekly letting herself be blandished into captivity like a sleepy child being carried up to bed. The hot day, the sheer, visceral comfort of that beautiful food, and, most of all, her abductor's elaborately ironic refusal to behave like a conventional villain, had combined to sap her will.

Now, with the adrenalin of flight racing in her blood, she could not believe how nearly she had let herself be lulled, or how hard

37

it had been to abandon the sham safety of inaction and make a run for freedom. She was not heading anywhere in particular, except away, but she soon found that the terrain was forcing her uphill, for she clung to the thickly wooded slopes. On the more open bottom land he would be able to spot her from a distance, and there was no way of knowing how much of a start she had. He looked very fit; almost certainly he could outrun her and outlast her too. Her only hope was, somehow, to lose him.

She came to a shallow stream, and unhesitatingly splashed through it to the far side, though she could not have said why: some vague memory, perhaps, of childhood stories about bloodhounds. At least there seemed to be plenty of water in this part of the country. You could survive for days in the wilderness, if you had water. Her strength was beginning to give out now. The wet jeans were clumsy and hampering, and her left leg was very painful, but she told herself she must not slow down, unaware that she had already dropped her pace to a leaden jog.

Her unprotected face and arms were whipped and stung by the crowding undergrowth, and her legs grew heavier with every stride. Twice she tripped and went to her knees, wrenching her ankle the second time. As she struggled to her feet the cuff on her wrist caught in a brier. She jerked it at frantically, and thorns ripped the flesh of her arm as she tore herself free and pounded on.

The ground rose more steeply here. Her feet were on a stony track, partly overgrown with spindling trees and bushes, that wound around the side of the hill. She drove herself on at a wounded, shambling trot, searching all the time for a place to hide and rest. It would have to be soon, for she was almost done; but there was only the hillside at her left, rocky and gaunt, and on the right the ground fell away sharply, with no more cover than would hide a cat.

'Oh – God,' she was gasping over and over, 'oh – God – oh – God – ' It was more of a protest than a prayer, but as she blundered around a great jagged boulder that blocked the path it seemed her appeal had been answered anyhow. There was a gap in the cliff face where the boulder had broken away. She could not see how deep it went, but it hardly mattered. She could not go any farther. Hands groping in front of her, she stumbled gratefully into the dark.

At first, the enormous solace of not having to go on running acted as an opiate and she simply crouched in the darkness, as far back as she could get, as numb to exterior signals as if she were asleep. But after a while the flood of relief subsided enough for her senses to begin, however hesitantly, to resume transmission. The cave smelled foul and was not altogether silent. Water dripped somewhere, and a muted scuffling and scrabbling betrayed the presence of sitting tenants whose peace she had disturbed, but the loudest sounds came from her own ragged breathing and the blood beating like surf in her ears. She took a deep breath, held it, and listened.

Now she could hear it: the swish of branches when there was no wind. Pebbles skidded, and a boot sole scraped on rock. Someone was coming up the hill. *This is the end of it, then,* she thought, curiously calm, almost relieved, now that the worst was on her and could not be escaped. *He will see the cave, as I did, and he will come in and find me. He will be the last thing I shall see. Please God, let it be over quickly, don't let it hurt too much. I don't even know if he has a gun. Perhaps he'll do it with his hands. Oh, please, please let it be quick.*

The entrance to the cave, the narrow oblong of light that gave onto green leaves and a glimpse of sky, was suddenly blocked by a dark shape. Trembling, she stood up.

He waited just inside the opening, letting his eyes adjust to the dark. She was there, all right, backed against the far wall. He could distinguish her face after a moment and the pale glimmer of her hair. He could not be sure, but it seemed to him that her eyes were shut.

'Oh, there you are,' he said in a matter-of-fact tone, as though they had arranged to meet and she had been waiting for him in the wrong place. 'I've been looking everywhere for you. I don't think much of the accommodation, I must say; it's as damp as a charnel in here. Stinks like one, too. Full of bats, I shouldn't wonder.'

He took a step towards her.

'Come on, let's get you out of here.'

He had taken two more steps when she screamed and went on screaming. The sound in that enclosed space was appalling, a wrenching, primitive horror that raised the hairs on the back of his neck. He backed up dismayed, his hands flying out sideways, palms forward, in a classic disavowal of harm.

'Hey. Hey, stop that! Easy now, girl, easy. Gently now. There's nothing to be afraid of, it's only me. I won't hurt you. Come along.'

She did not move, except to press herself even harder against the rock, as though another miracle might open it for her to pass through.

'Katie, don't be an idiot. You can't stay in a hole for the rest of your life, and anyway where's the sense in it? You're no safer here than you are outside. Look, you've got two choices: you can walk out under your own steam, or you can be dragged out by me. I'd advise you to walk – starting now.'

He sounded very much like a parent telling a child to get that damned bike out of the drive this minute. Kate was in no state to make a rational assessment of anything, but something in his tone of exasperated, adult authority got through to her. Painfully, she forced herself away from the illusory protection of the cave wall.

As she limped towards the mouth of the cave he could see her more clearly. Her clothes were filthy, and so was her face; under the dirt and the scratches it looked pinched and sick, as if she had been through a long illness. Simply putting one foot in front of the other was clearly almost more than she could manage. He stretched a hand out to help her, and she winced like a dog afraid of its master. *Now look what you've done, you bastard*, he told himself, queasy with guilt.

'Wait a minute,' he said aloud. 'I'm going to carry you. Don't scream.'

She stood passive, head drooping, the butter-coloured hair falling like a shredded banner over her face. He bent, slipped one arm behind her knees, and lifted her into his arms. As he started down the hill, leaning back to balance the extra weight, he glanced down and saw that she had closed her eyes again. Although she didn't weigh much, she was awkward to carry because she held herself rigid, the stiffness shaken only by fits of violent trembling. *Sweet Jesus*, he thought, *now she's going catatonic on me*. He took care to hold her quite impersonally, as if she were not a woman at all but a valuable piece of furniture. It seemed a long way down the hill.

As soon as he could, he set her down on the grass, with her shoulders against the trunk of a tree. It was important, when people were badly frightened, to give them what security you could, and the back was always vulnerable. It did seem to help a little; at least she relaxed enough to lean against the rough bark, and her face lost some of the clenched and desperate look that so disturbed him.

The sun was warm on her skin, beating against her closed lids. When at last she opened her eyes, the light blinded her for a moment, but then she saw him standing over her. His hands were at his throat, untying the knot of the silk handkerchief around his neck. She did not like to think what he might be going to do with it. Strangle her, perhaps. Or gag her. Or use it to tie her hands, so that he could rape her with less trouble. Whatever he did, there was nothing she could do except endure it.

Slung over his shoulder on a strap he carried a black leather box. She did not remember having seen it before. A camera, perhaps, to film her dying throes? A tape recorder to preserve her screams? She had read of murderers who indulged themselves in such baroque refinements, but she was too wretched to care. If only, whatever sick plans he had for her, he would just go ahead and be done with it.

He stood there still with the kerchief in his hands, looking down at her in an oddly abstracted way, as though he had been going to ask a question but couldn't remember what it was. Then he turned away, walked a few yards, and bent down. Soon he was back, with the rag of silk dripping water. He dropped neatly onto his heels in front of her and started to clean her face.

'That looks a bit more seemly,' he said when it was done. 'Recognizable, anyway. Hands, please.'

Like an obedient child she held them out. He went over them with the same grave thoroughness, frowning over a fingernail snapped off at the quick, frowning again at the crusted wound above her wrist. He cleaned around it carefully, went back to the stream to rinse the kerchief, came back with it wrung out, and used it to bandage the hurt place.

'It's the best I can do for the moment. There's a first aid kit in the Jeep; I'll dress it properly later.'

He took a flask from his hip pocket, pulled off the outer cap, and poured it nearly full. 'Here,' he said, offering it to her, but she made no move to take it.

'Lord God of Israel, *will* you do as you're told! It's damned good whisky, and you take it and drink it, or I'll pour it down your stubborn little throat.'

She put her hand out for it then, and sipped until the liquor was all gone. She was trembling still, though not as violently as before. When she gave back the dented silver cup he poured a measure for himself, knocked it back in two swallows, tucked the flask

41

away, and brought out a pack of cigarettes. He lit two, leaned across, and put one between her lips. Charlie did that sometimes, loading the gesture with innuendo. This man was as neutral about it as if she were an anonymous casualty in some field hospital. She drew in the smoke and relaxed very slightly, very warily. He hadn't hurt her yet. It was just conceivable, after all, that he might not intend to.

'Feeling better?'

She nodded.

'Splendid.' His voice had an edge of irony. 'Then perhaps you won't mind telling me what in God's good name all that was about. From the noise you were making, anyone would have thought I was going to murder you.'

'I thought you were.'

'You thought – you can't have!' He was gaping at her in disbelief. She just looked at him.

'You really did, though, didn't you? Well thanks a whole hell of a whole lot.' He raked a hand through his hair and sighed. 'Look, lady, I'm only a humble kidnapper. I don't go round doing people in. What on earth gave you a horrible idea like that?'

'I was afraid you'd be angry. Because I tried to get away.'

'It's not a capital offence,' he pointed out reasonably. 'The first duty of a prisoner is to escape, and if that isn't in the Geneva Convention then it ought to be. Anyway, it was my fault for being slack enough to give you the chance. But no matter how angry I was I wouldn't have hurt you. What sort of a monster d'you think I am?'

'I don't know,' she said in a small voice.

'That's right, you don't. I forgot. Well, you can't go on like this, thinking every moment's going to be your last. You'll make yourself ill. You do realize, I hope, that you're not being exactly logical?' He looked at his watch. 'Fifteen hours, I've had you in my hands, and I haven't done anything very awful to you yet. If I'm secretly burning to beat you up or rape you or murder you, what the hell am I waiting for? Of course,' he went on, 'that's assuming I'm more or less sane. I can see it's quite possible, theoretically, that I'm some sort of dreary nut case, saving you up for the next full moon. But it's not very likely, is it? After all, if I were *that* loopy, surely you'd have noticed.'

'I don't know what's likely and what isn't any more,' Kate said. 'I wouldn't have said it was likely I'd ever be kidnapped, and now I don't have anything to go on. I don't know what the rules are.

All I know is you've taken me away, and I don't know what's going to happen to me, but whatever it is I can't do anything to stop it. And I'm scared.'

He looked at her thoughtfully.

'Yes, I see that. That's understandable. A lot of people feel the same way in hospital – no control over events. You give 'em a bell, and then they push it and nobody comes, and they fall apart. I don't blame them.'

He bent down and pulled up his trouser leg. There was a leather strap around his calf, just above the top of his sock. Stiff with fright, she watched as he drew out a wicked, gleaming little knife. The handle was of some black wood, carved into an intricate design of braided knots. He held it out to her, hilt first.

'Here,' he said, 'you take this. Well go on, take it; it won't bite you. Now. The balance of power has shifted, d'you see? You thought you were going to be killed. Now, if you feel like it, you can kill me. Ever stabbed anyone before?'

'Of course not!'

'No need to be uppity; lots of people have, you know. In some parts of the world it's practically a way of life. Any special technique appeal to you? You could cut my throat, but I don't really recommend it. Awfully messy and very hard work. Windpipes are extraordinarily tough. You'd do better to go for the heart. Slide it in about here, at an angle because of the ribs. If you leave the knife in the wound there'll be hardly any blood, but I'll die quicker if you pull it out. That's a decision you'll have to make for yourself. There's always the gut, of course. Just shove it in any old where, you're bound to hit something fairly crucial. It probably won't finish me off right away, but I shan't be in any condition to run after you.'

She had gone an alarming shade of greenish white, and her eyes were round with shock. The knife tilted slackly in her hand.

'Or if you're squeamish,' he went on ruthlessly, 'you could do it in the back. High up, above the shoulder blades – go in fairly close to the spine, with the blade pointing downwards. You'll get a lung, and that should fix my wagon for me. And you won't even have to look at my face while you do it.'

'What's the matter with you? Are you crazy?' She shouted at him, goaded at last out of her deathly passivity. 'Why do you want me to kill you?'

'I don't in the least want you to kill me. All I'm doing is making

43

it physically possible, so if you really believe you have to, then you can.'

'But *why*?'

'Watch what you're doing with that thing – you'll cut yourself. Can you swim?'

He really is mad, she thought. What's the best way to deal with mad people? Humour them, I guess; act as if everything they said made sense.

'Yes,' she said quickly, trying to sound friendly and responsive, and achieving some sort of placatory grimace. 'Yes, I can swim. I love swimming.'

'Do you remember learning to float? Lie on the water, I expect they told you. Lie still and the water will hold you up. Well, it worked, didn't it? You've been thrashing around tiring yourself out, and it's time you stopped. Just lie on the water, Kate, just be still. You won't drown. But it's easier when you know you can put a foot on the bottom if you have to, and that's where the knife comes in. You have a choice, now. You can make up your mind to trust me, and I hope to God you do. But if that's too difficult – ' he spread his hands ' – use the knife. Use it now and go free. It's up to you.'

'It's a trick.' She had forgotten all about humouring him. 'You don't mean it at all. The minute I tried, you'd stop me –'

'Would I, though!' He wrestled angrily with the buttons of his shirt and yanked it open, baring his chest. The tanned skin was smooth, except where a fine red-gold fleece curled damply around the nipples.

'There! No, not like that, woman, use both hands. Get a proper grip on it, it's not a bloody paintbrush.'

He went down on his knees in front of her and grasped her hands, positioning them impatiently on the hilt of the knife, bringing them up until the point of the blade just pricked the skin close to the breastbone.

'That's about right.'

He let go her hands and dropped his own. She stared fascinated at the knife. There was a single bead of blood, bright scarlet, next to the shining tip where it had scratched him. She looked up at his face. He was watching her with an air of intensely private concentration, as if he were meditating. The space between them was charged with such tension it made her eardrums sing, and her skin prickled. Her hands were starting to shake. She threw the knife away from her into the grass with as much revulsion as if

44

it had suddenly turned into a snake, and covered her face with her hands. She began to sob, loudly and unrestrainedly, like a very young child.

After a while her hands were taken and drawn gently, but very firmly, down to her lap.

'It's not so easy to kill someone in cold blood, is it? I couldn't have done it either.' She could barely hear the words through the raucous din she was making. The sheer volume of noise had begun to frighten her, but she could not seem to stop. He brushed away the streaming tears with the back of his fingers.

'There now, sshh; it's all right. It's all over now. Don't cry, lovey, nobody's hurt.' The old-fashioned nursery endearment brought tears springing again. She was too weak, and too shocked, to tolerate kindness.

'But – but I might have killed you!' she blurted between sobs.

'For a moment or two there I thought you were going to.'

'Why – why weren't you scared?'

'I was. Petrified. Since you ask.'

'Then what did you d-do such a crazy thing for?'

'You tell me something. Do you still think I'd kill you?'

The question caught her off balance. She thought about it and, in thinking, discovered that she had stopped crying.

'No,' she said finally, sniffing. 'No, I don't believe you would.'

'That's why.'

He got up, bent to cup his palms under her elbows, and lifted her to her feet. He had the controlled, precisely applied strength of a dancer, or a first-class athlete – a kind of physical intelligence. It was impressive, and formidable. She could not imagine how she had ever thought she could get away from him.

'Got a handkerchief? Here, use mine. And now we'd better move, we've lost a lot of time. Do you think you can make it to the Jeep, or shall I give you a piggyback?'

'I'll make it.'

He looked down at her, consideringly.

'I shouldn't be at all surprised. You're quite a girl, Kate Harper. You must take after your mother.'

He retrieved the knife from the grass, thrust it back into its sheath, and picked up the black leather box.

'Okay? Let's go.'

Back at the Jeep, he swabbed the ragged tear on her arm with antiseptic and taped a square of gauze over it. Then he pulled out the chain and the second cuff, and stood jingling them in his palm.

'I don't want to put these back on,' he said, 'but I don't want any surprises either. How would it be if you gave me your word you won't do anything tiresome?'

'How d'you know I'd keep it?'

'Same way you know I'm not going to massacre you, I suppose. Besides, if you were going to try anything, you'd never have asked. I'm not proposing unconditional surrender, just a temporary cease-fire for mutual advantage: I let you off the shackles, and you keep your paws to yourself. Is that fair?'

'I guess so.'

'Thank God for that. You'll still have to wear the blinders, I'm afraid, for your own sake. It really won't do for you to know where you are.' He fitted the goggles in place, tossed chain and cuff back into the glove compartment, and shut her door.

For Kate the rest of that ride was a journey through limbo, unanchored to any kind of reality outside the vibrating steel body in which they were enclosed. The claustrophobia-inducing dark that began at the tips of her eyelashes completed her sense of displacement. Now that her hands were free, she could have snatched the goggles off; but then he would chain her again. There was nothing she could do that would not make things worse; safest, then, to do nothing, hide inside the dark. She was no longer thinking about trying to get away. She had done as much as she could; had endured a flight, a pursuit, and a recapture, far more terrifying than anything she could have imagined. She had survived, but it had taken every scrap of fight out of her. When the man spoke to her, she answered. The rest of the time she simply sat, lapped in a lethargy so profound that he grew professionally anxious.

He had told the truth when he said that he meant her no harm, but naturally he was not in the habit of seeing himself as he must appear to her: cruel, deadly, and probably mad, a figure of purest nightmare. The harm was real and inevitable, ingrained in the

46

situation, as he should have had the sense to realize from the start. The operation they had toiled over so high-mindedly for months had collided with a human being, and hurt it.

He supposed he ought to have kept her under drugs, but he didn't know her medical history and had balked at the risk. Now it seemed that concern for her physical health had blinded him to other, equally valid dangers. Like many surgeons, he was apt to concentrate on the narrow use of his particular skills, doing his best for the bodies and leaving the minds to heal, if they would, on their own. But he found he could not so easily shrug off Kate's terror; because he had caused it, it was up to him, if he could, to mend matters. The episode with the knife had been a clumsy form of shock treatment, primitive enough to give any responsible therapist fits, but at the time it was all he could think of. Certainly, since that storm of weeping, she had been calm. But that was the trouble, she was entirely too calm. The situation being too bad to be borne, she had simply withdrawn from it.

With a familiar pang, he remembered the children at the Refuge of Mary, Heart of Mercy, in Cam Loc. For the first two or three days after they were brought in, they would weep and rage, howling for the mother who had been fragmented, the worn-out grandmother who had died wordlessly on the sleeping mat, the harried older sister who could either care for a child or whore among the soldiers for the money to feed it, but not both.

Pretty soon, though, when they found out all the kicking and screaming in the world didn't change anything, most of the children became very quiet. Even the youngest, when they fell and hurt themselves, never cried. The more optimistic of the staff would refer to this as 'making a good adjustment'. His wife, Simone, had called it by its right name, which was despair, and she had fought it like a good Catholic warrior, right up until the moment some hash-happy South Vietnamese navigator, miles off course, had spotted the roofs of the orphanage and mistaken the untidy complex for an enemy headquarters.

They had found Simone under the rubble, Mother Mary Paul told him afterwards, crouched over two of the babies; apparently she had tried to shield them with her body. The children were dead too. Mother Mary Paul, red eyed, had assured him that Simone was with God. When he shouted at her that his wife's place was here with him, that he needed her a lot more than God did, the old nun was patient and polite and tactful enough to spare him further Christian comfort. She was a nice woman and had

47

loved Simone too in her way, but she was cut off from his world of blood and pain and shattered bones by her unquestioning conviction that God was in charge, and that He knew what He was doing.

The man had believed that himself, once; it seemed a long time ago now. You did the best you could. You amputated the little smashed hands, debrided the filthy wounds, picked splinters of bone out of the blessedly anaesthetized flesh, and sometimes you caught yourself muttering, 'Breathe, you little bugger *breathe*!' But you didn't go whining to God about it, except for an occasional exasperated request for Him to kindly keep His fingers out of the machinery.

With an effort, he dragged his mind back from the past, when at least he had known exactly what he was doing, to the far less manageable present. Up to this morning the girl beside him had figured in his calculations with no more emotional weight than a plastic counter on a board. It was monstrous of her to insist on turning into a real person, with needs and fears and all the rest of the distressing baggage real people lug around with them. She had no right to be real; it was going to screw everything up.

He did not want to feel pity for her or responsibility or guilt – let alone the sensation that, unforgivably, he was saddled with now. There was no time to spare for such irrelevant complications; it was so entirely unexpected and so unfair. He had not felt even the mildest interest in any woman since Simone's death. For a time this had worried him a good deal, but lately he had almost given up bothering about it. A switch, apparently, had been thrown, an intricate circuit of feelings, responses, and desires had quietly gone dead. And now of all times, for this of all people, the whole tyrannical apparatus had come to life again to plague him.

When, after throwing away the knife, she had huddled there with her face in her hands, bawling, while the tears ran down between her thin wrists, he had reached out his arms for her without even thinking. What had stopped him, as effectively as a pailful of ice water, was the discovery that he was not just going to comfort her, he was going to make love to her. For once that wasn't a euphemism, either. He was no stranger to the sexual imperative that rides the coat-tails of death, urging the birthrate up in heartless compensation, but it hadn't been like that at all. He hadn't just wanted to fuck her; he had wanted to melt in her, become a part of her, change her, by the addition of himself, as

48

irrevocably as she would change him.

Appallingly, he had been clobbered by a genuine *coup de foudre*, a phenomenon he had never quite believed in, and it left him feeling as if he'd been in a train crash. Just one of nature's rotten jokes, and in very bad taste as usual. What was worse, it was dangerous. He had work to do; he could not afford to be distracted. Other people depended on him: Chuck and Claire, Afeni and Sam, Tom Tulliver, Sean – the whole damn network. There was no way he was going to imperil his friends for the sake of some grotesquely mistimed biological spasm. This girl was nothing to him. And then he turned his head to look at her and was done for.

The oversized dark glasses gave her a wounded look, as if she were really blind. What could be seen of her face was still quite dirty in spite of his efforts, and her whole appearance was bedraggled and somehow apologetic. It was also familiar, and in a moment he realized why; she had the numb, tentative, almost embarrassed air of the refugee. All the gleam was gone, and it was his fault.

He knew, better than most, that the heart is nothing but a muscle, a reasonably efficient pumping mechanism, and in no way the seat of the emotions. Yet when he looked at her he was sharply aware that somewhere inside his ribcage something was causing him pain. Too much Elizabethan poetry in the mid-teens, that was his trouble. Obviously he was suffering from delayed adolescent nostalgia, which at his age was humiliating as well as absurd. 'Let me not to the marriage of true minds/Admit impediment . . .' Marriage of true minds my ass. I only want her because I can't have her.

A nice, specious explanation. What a pity it wasn't true. From a practical point of view, he could have her any time he liked. All he had to do was be a little rough, or threaten to be. Not even that: vulnerable as she was, it would be the easiest thing in the world to make her love him. Carefully regulated doses of kindness and reassurance, plus the occasional oblique reminder that, having total power over her, he chose not to abuse it, and she would drop compliant into his arms, dizzy with gratitude because he had not forced her. 'Those that have power to hurt and will do none' have got it made, he thought; there is no aphrodisiac more potent than mercy. Only I can't take advantage of it, precisely because she is so defenceless. God help us all, somebody's got to look after her, and I'm the one that landed her in this mess in the first place, so it had better be me. He had a swift vision of himself grimly standing guard outside her bedroom door, shielding her from his own unseemly appetites, and began to giggle. Light-headed with fatigue, he found laughter spilling and bubbling out of him as the stretched nerves involuntarily, gloriously relaxed.

Kate turned her sightless face towards him in alarm.

'What is it?'

'You may well ask.' He wiped his eyes and sobered up. 'It's all right, just something silly that would take too long to explain. You must be awfully bored. Have you ever played the Clergyman's Cat? My aunt used to fall back on it to keep me from grizzling on long car trips when I was small. I'll start: the Clergyman's cat is an affable cat who absolutely adores artichokes. Now it's your turn. You do B.'

The Clergyman's cat, that versatile beast, easily eluded eels, masterfully mesmerized Mongolians, and zealously zoomed around zenanas. After that they went a few rounds with Botticelli. 'Have you a pet named Captain Flint?' 'No, I am not Long John Silver.' 'Did you go over the sea to Skye?' 'No, I am not Charles Edward Stuart.' It was extraordinarily soothing. Next they inventoried, in French, the contents of *Le Manoir de Mon Oncle Georges de l'Indochine*. This led eventually to a mild squabble over whether or not that cluttered estate had included *un potager plein de parapluies*.

'A vegetable garden full of umbrellas? That's ridiculous, and you're cheating.'

'I am *not* cheating. I only cheat at cards. Anyway, you don't know my Uncle George. Grow anything, that man could. His coat hanger plantation was the envy of the neighbourhood. It's your turn.'

'You're a pretty weird sort of kidnapper,' Kate said, abandoning the game.

'I dare say. You'll simply have to make allowances for lack of practice. Don't forget I've never done this before.'

'Neither have I.'

'On-the-job training, they call it. I'd take it as a kindness, by the way, if you could suggest any improvements. "If a thing's worth doing at all, it's worth doing well," as my grandmother never tired of saying, poor tedious woman that she was. D'you think it might help if I grew a moustache?'

'What for?'

'Intimidation. You twirl it, in a sinister manner, and laugh gloatingly. Or is that just when you're foreclosing mortgages and booting widows into the snow? Oh, sod it all.'

'Huh?'

'Nothing. I was just thinking how nice it would be to scrub this caper and go to the movies instead. Or a baseball game or a concert in the park – something harmless and ordinary that you don't go to jail for. And afterwards I could deliver you to your mum's front door at a respectable hour, and you could ask me in for a cup of coffee. And then when I'd gone your mother would say: "Well, darling, he seems quite nice, but isn't he rather old for you?" And you'd say: "Oh, Mo-*therr*, he's just a friend." That's what I'd like, and I know it's out of the question, and it's making me bloody bad tempered. That's all.'

For a moment the glaze of civilized mockery had cracked, and he sounded sad and honest and desperately tired. Against her will, Kate was touched.

'You could be my friend, I guess. If you really wanted.'

'Not a chance. If I were, I'd turn the Jeep round right now and drive you home, which is the one thing I can't possibly do. I'm not your friend, I'm your perishing keeper.'

'Well, I'm sorry it bothers you, but I didn't ask to be kidnapped.'

'No. You just got yourself born into the wrong family. Sheer carelessness. If you'd had a particle of judgement this whole thing could have been avoided. Do you like him?'

'Who? My father? I don't like him or not like him, I don't know him. I was only eight when they split up, and even before that I scarcely ever saw him. He wasn't home much, and when he was he'd shut himself up in the study and nobody was allowed to make a sound. My best friend Alison, *her* father used to play checkers with her, and Go Fish, and he even taught her how to ride a bicycle himself. I couldn't stand it, I was so jealous.'

'Who taught you to ride a bike?'

'Nanny Bristow. She ran along behind, holding onto the seat, and then one time she let go and I found out I could do it myself. Father was home that day, for once, and I was so proud I went barrelling in to the study before they could stop me to tell him how smart I was. Boy, did I get it.'

'But he took you with him on that South American jaunt last year.'

'Oh, that. That was public relations. They'd told him his image

51

was too cold or something, so he thought he'd make like a parent for *Newsweek* and *Time*. And then *Newsweek* had a box about how he never once came to see me when I was at school, at Miss Hampshire's. I don't know how they found out; I guess it was one of the maids. Father was really mad. And the whole idea backfired anyhow, because having me along reminded people about the divorce, and they're all Catholics down there so it wasn't tactful.'

'Did you spend much time with him on the trip?'

'Not really; he was pretty tied up in meetings. We'd do the motorcade bit together, but that was about all. Mostly I got shuffled off onto the press secretary's secretary, which wasn't so bad. Marge Hollings, her name was. She could curse a blue streak, and she used to take me shopping and let me use her Arpège. In Montevideo she even fixed it so I could go out sailing with the naval attaché without father finding out. I mean, he does care about me, you're not wrong, but he's kind of strange. Mother says he'd like to keep me locked up in a tower, and visit me on alternate Tuesdays. He doesn't think mother raises me right. She's always getting these stuffy letters from him: Don't let Katie do this, don't let her do that. He thinks she's too casual. Would you believe he wanted me to have Secret Service protection, in case anyone tried . . . Well, maybe that wasn't so dumb after all.'

'It wouldn't have made any difference. A properly mounted operation takes all the factors into account,' he said pompously. 'If you'd had a watchdog puffing along after you, we'd have had to set things up a little differently, but the end result would have been exactly the same.'

'You're pretty sure of yourself, aren't you? You really think this nutty scheme of yours is going to work.'

As soon as the words were out of her mouth she regretted them. It was bad policy to annoy the enemy. She had done her best to appear cowed and submissive, which hadn't been difficult because, while not precisely cowed, she was certainly scared and deathly tired as well. After the cumulative shocks of the last few hours, she had regressed almost without thinking to the polite schoolgirl she had been at fourteen, civilly going along with the efforts of well-meaning adults to keep her entertained. And he had tried to be kind, she supposed; at least those silly games had helped to take her mind off the mess she was in. But she ought not to make him angry, she knew that much. Luckily, it seemed she had not.

'Of course I think it's going to work,' he said. 'Otherwise I wouldn't be here, and neither would you. I may be rash, but I'm not suicidal. And you have to admit it's going rather well so far.'

'How do you know the whole countryside isn't out looking for me? Why, there might be a roadblock right around this next corner.'

Oh, this is dumb. Why do I bait him? Why can't I keep my fat mouth shut? I'll only get in trouble.

'You mustn't underestimate us,' he said calmly. 'We have all the latest electronic gadgetry to keep us informed. There's the radio, for instance; we're very proud of that. If you turned it on now, you wouldn't get all that "Breaker, breaker" stuff and a lot of crap about smokies. What you'd get is my friend Sam, who is sitting with one ear glued to a very fancy ham wireless outfit and the other bloating under the impact of every news bulletin since midnight. We have an awful lot of other friends, too, some of them in the most peculiar places, and they're very good about keeping in touch. If anything was going on that I ought to know about, someone would get word through to me. As a matter of fact I'd better try and raise Sam now, let him know we're going to be late.'

'We must be almost there, then. CB radios have a pretty short range, don't they?'

'Ordinary ones do. This is what you call a custom job, though. Every stitch done by hand in our own workrooms, madam. It's faked up to look like a standard model because linear amplifiers are illegal, and so are some of the other little extras we built into this baby. Very handy toy to have around. Now let's see if it works.'

A whine of static was succeeded by a crackling noise, and then a man's voice, a soft Georgia drawl.

'Aurora Grain and Feed Store, hahdy,' said the voice, absurdly.

'Retriever to Aurora. Anything in on the drums?'

'Not a word. Where the hell are you at?'

'About two hours from home. We're running behind schedule.'

'No shit. Jesus, boy, we been worried half to death. I'd of called in, but I figured you weren't alone.'

'I'm not. Cargo on board as per bill of lading. Put a light in the window. Retriever going off the air.'

'Aurora to Retriever, Merr' Christmas, we gone.' The crackling cut out.

53

It had shaken her badly, he could tell that. Probably it had made the situation real to her again. The insulation had given way, the fragile intimacy that had begun to grow between them – for it had, surely it had – shattered by the voice from outside. It couldn't be helped. The adversary relationship, the only one they could ever really have, was back in operation. Recess was over. He didn't want to talk to her any more. He was afraid of what he might hear in her voice.

'You must be done up,' he said. 'Better get some sleep.'

She dozed for a time, miserably; jolting, confused awakenings alternated with periods of troubled sleep that were haunted by distorted faces and loud, angry voices gabbling words that made no sense. At last exhaustion came to her rescue with a long, healing stretch of deep unconsciousness. The light was beginning to go, and presently the man leaned over and took off her goggles. She stirred and whimpered, but did not wake.

In the dusk the strain of the day no longer showed so clearly on her face, and he was glad to be spared the sight. It was a relief, too, to have her asleep. There was no longer any need to talk, no need to school himself to reveal nothing more personal than good-humoured detachment. He would have traded almost anything, except the success of the operation, for the right to reach across and pull her close against him, to have her wake and know him, and be glad he was there. Fat chance; but the fantasy would not be banished. Her head would lie heavy on his shoulder, and from time to time he would rub his cheek against her hair. He'd drive with his left hand on the wheel and his right hand resting on her thigh, immobile, unthreatening, like the sleeping head of a large, friendly dog.

At this moment he wanted nothing more, and, as he drove on, scrupulously avoiding the smallest contact, he wanted it so much that his whole body hurt with the effort of not touching her. He had loved Simone, his exquisite friend – his lover, his wife, but his friend most of all – knowing the problems, cursing the bureaucrats, fighting alongside him to save the children. When she was killed, his grief had marked him, reduced him, like an amputation; he was not the same man he had been before, any more than if he had had his legs blown off by a mine. But what was happening to him now was like discovering that for thirty-six years he had been split in two: here was the other half of himself within arm's reach, alive, warmly familiar, *necessary*, and he wasn't allowed to fit it back on. To be so close, and yet separate, was continual pain.

He tormented himself further by brooding guiltily about what he was letting her in for, and the damage she was bound to suffer from this trap-door slide out of her soft, easy world. 'You won't be harmed,' he had told her, but how could he possibly prove it? Only by not harming her, and even so she would not be sure until the ordeal was safely over. Up to the last second of her captivity the threat would still be there, and with it the terror. They could hurt her if they chose to, and she could not prevent them. That was the reality, as she must see it, and it would take a personal note in God's own handwriting to convince her she was in no danger.

And this was only the first day, only the beginning. If he himself had frightened her so badly – and it was clear, though still surprising to him, that he had – then how would she react to the others? Sam Aitken, for instance. Sam, Sam, on the lam . . . On the lam now from his former masters in the CIA, from a dead man on the floor of a washroom in Pennsylvania, from an unkempt little crew of ideologues building bombs in a West Side loft. What in God's name would this sheltered child at his side make of Sam, with his Company manners and his nightmare past? Not that she would need to know any of that, and yet it showed, or something did. If you weren't used to Sam, as they were, would you be afraid? He thought it probable.

Afeni ought not to be very alarming; at least she was another woman, and close to her in age. But that was calendar age. Although Afeni was only twenty-two, she was decades – centuries – older in experience. Kate might well appear to her a pampered, overprotected brat whose hardship dues had gone too long unpaid. Afeni wouldn't be overtly cruel – she would never twist an arm or slap a face – but she could be as daunting as a duchess when she felt like it, with a tongue that could flay mules. Better not count on Afeni to act as prisoner's friend.

It was hardly likely Chuck could frighten anyone. In looks and temper he was closer to Cesar Chavez than to Sitting Bull, and though the smartass-Indian act he sometimes amused himself with could be disconcerting, the essential kindness of the man was as immediately obvious as the trunk on an elephant. But he was still one of the kidnappers, and that alone could be enough, he supposed, to make a snaggletoothed demon out of clever, gentle Chuck. That left Claire, who was loved by even the most

55

cantankerous of elderly neighbours, and whose apron pockets were always out of shape because she kept them stuffed with treats for any chance-met child or animal. She was his best bet. If anyone could make the next two weeks less dreadful for the captive, it would be Claire.

It was dark by the time they came to the farm. The last twenty miles of road were little better than a series of wagon tracks, and the Jeep lurched and rolled. Still she did not wake, and when he drew up in front of the sprawling old frame house she never stirred. As he switched off the engine, Chuck Lainez started down the porch steps holding a lantern. By its light the man took a last look at Kate's face while it was still open and soft with sleep. Then he allowed himself the piercing luxury of putting his palm against her cheek to rouse her.

'Wake up, Katie. We're home.'

Her eyes opened, empty at first and then widening in fright as she remembered who he was and what had happened. He stroked her hair back from her face because he could not help it.

'We're home,' he said again.

Entering the unfamiliar house, with the man beside her holding her elbow, steadying her, Kate felt she was being brought before a hostile tribunal: the trial would be the usual French Revolution burlesque – she was doomed to the guillotine whatever happened. (Sidney Carton, where are you now that I need you?) The dark, middle-aged man who had come out to meet them was still outside, unloading the Jeep. While not quite ignoring her, he had not once looked her in the face, and she remembered that a jury, when it brings in a verdict of guilty, is said never to look at the defendant. The destruction of hope was, for most people, an embarrassing act.

She had misread Chuck's feelings completely, as strangers usually did. It was a delicacy that kept his eyes from her face; after the first appalled glance at this weary, dishevelled scrap of a girl, he had not looked again because he was certain she wouldn't want to be stared at. He had been stared at too often himself. Before his father rode one wild horse too many and broke his neck, Chuck had hung around the dusty, small-town rodeos, and people had stared at him then because in looks he favoured his mother, a pure-blooded Sioux. All Indian kids were thieves, everyone knew that. The men would stare, and then someone would give him a shove and say, 'Get on out of here, kid, you know you got no business here.' Then he would have to explain again that his daddy, Charlie Lainez the rider, had told him to stay right there and not move. Usually, they let him alone after that, but they would stand a few feet away, talking low and laughing, and looking at him in a way he didn't like, until his daddy came, sweaty and smelling of bad whisky, to take him back to the trailer.

It wasn't much better after he grew up. When he was with the MASH unit in Korea, the wounded didn't care if he was a two-headed Bulgarian as long as he could put in an IV so it didn't infiltrate within a couple of hours, and he always could. But afterwards, in that fancy hospital in New York City, the sick, rich people would look at him mistrustfully when he came in to restart an IV or take a blood sample. They weren't paying all that money to have some drunken Indian fooling with their veins. Only on the paediatric floor did he feel at home. He was deft and never hurt the children, and some of the long-term ones would hold out for hours with a hot, swollen arm or a faulty heparin lock until they knew that he would be on duty to make them comfortable. The children were realists, and besides, they liked Indians. In western movies on television, it was always the cavalry they booed. 'Ugh!' they would greet Chuck when he came in with his needles; 'How! Me wait many moons for Big Chief Blood Bottle,' curling up in bed and hooting at their own wit. It always broke him up, and that made them laugh harder. Maybe, later on, he'd be able to make this frightened Harper child laugh too.

Kate passed through the screened porch and on into a hallway, lamp lit, plank floored, and shining, its smell of wax polish interlaced with great fragrant gusts of garlic. On the left a door stood open into a formal parlour, with a red chenille cloth on the round table, a piano, and stiff portraits of ancestors glowering with shyness on either side of the fireplace. The man steered her in the other direction, through a doorway on the right, and she found herself in a huge, warm room that seemed to combine the functions of kitchen, dining-room, library, living-room, and plant nursery. She saw a gigantic dinosaur of a range, a very modern refrigerator, a massive pine refectory table, a Welsh dresser, two oak settles flanking the broad brick hearth, a rocking chair, a braided rug covering the flagstones in front of an old leather chesterfield, and everywhere shelves: shelves upon shelves of pots and pewter and crocks and books and pitchers and seedlings and tools. Over everything shone the soft yellow light of the oil lamps. There were half a dozen cats in the room, one basset hound, and three people, all staring at her. The oldest of the three came surging up to them, hands held out; she must have been six feet tall, and was built in proportion. Without a word she drew Kate straight into her arms. It was like being hugged by a ship's figurehead, only softer, and after the first surprise Kate found it very consoling.

'Conor!' the immense woman said accusingly, over the top of Kate's head. 'What in the world has thee done to the child?'

'Cross-country run. My well-known charm let me down – she didn't really want to come.'

'And small wonder. Frightened the daylights out of her, I suppose. Men!' The arms around Kate tightened protectively. 'Not worth duck eggs, any of thee.'

'She'll be all right, Claire. She's just tired and scared and a bit

58

grubby. It looks worse than it is.' He sounded defensive. Claire Lainez paid no attention to him at all. Shifting her hands to the girl's shoulders, she held her a little away and looked her over, shaking her head.

'Hot water and clean clothes, for a start. And a comb. Thee come with me.'

Nobody had taken quite this line with Kate since she grew too old for Nanny Bristow. Torn between amusement, relief, and a recurring impulse to cast herself onto that splendid bosom and wail, she submitted to being partially undressed, clucked over, scrubbed with yellow soap and dried with a rough towel, buttoned into someone else's shirt and jeans (obviously not Claire's since, with the legs rolled up, they almost fitted), and finally having her tangled hair subdued to nursery smoothness with a vast whalebone comb that belonged in a museum. Clean and chastened, she allowed herself to be led back into the kitchen and installed in the rocker by the fireplace. The man called Conor put a glass in her hand.

'Knock this back; it'll do you good. After that you can have some of Claire's soup. It heals the sick, comforts the afflicted, and makes dead men walk. Now then; social amenities. Claire you've met. That's Sam over there, dancing the hornpipe sitting down without moving a muscle. Not everyone can do it. And this is Afeni.'

Sam, from his chair in the corner, nodded a dour acknowledgement. He was a big, broad-shouldered man of about thirty, red haired, with the white skin and the dusting of freckles to go with it. He would have been handsome but for the small lower jaw, too pinched and narrow for the face above it. He had a watchful, uncommitted air, not unlike the Secret Service operatives who guarded her father; here was the same feeling that you were being assessed, your potential for causing trouble automatically computed. He did not smile, but Afeni did, with a flash of perfect teeth.

'Hi,' she said. 'Glad you got here. Guess you can't exactly say the same though. Don't know what you could say, come to that, except maybe, "Get me the hell out of this." Ain't that just like Emily Post, never does tell you what you really need to know. Don't be scared now, girl, we don't none of us bite, not even old Bagel here.'

The dog lying by the hearth thumped his tail twice heavily, and looked hopeful.

'What you want from my life? Oh, come to mama, then, you old fool,' Afeni said, and he lumbered over and slumped, sighing, beside her chair, parking his dewlaps damply on her foot. She leaned down to scratch the back of his head with her long, finely shaped fingers. She was quite the blackest black woman Kate had ever seen, deep, shining blue-black, like a well-polished stove. Her hair was braided in cornrows, emphasizing the elegant shape of her skull, and her lovely neck was long enough to have accommodated a record number of brass collars. She had on Levis and a washed-out blue T-shirt, but if she had been robed in silk and furs she could not have been more exotic or more intimidating.

The brown-skinned man, the Indian, had come in so unobtrusively Kate did not see him until he stood in front of her chair. He was an inch or so shorter than Claire and about half her bulk. His mouth, when he smiled down at her, was humorous and mobile, but the black eyes remained serious. Punctiliously he held out his hand.

'My name is Carlos,' he said, 'but these white-supremacist Anglos here call me Chuck, so you may as well do the same.'

'And since when,' Afeni asked sweetly, 'have I been an Anglo?'

'You people are worse than anyone. Who helped the white-eyes steal our land? Who burned my people's lodges in the Indian Wars? Buffalo soldiers. Jackals of the imperialist aggressor. And such habits! While we were apologizing to the deer before we killed it –'

'You did not either; it was the Choctaws did that –'

'Whatever. While we were behaving in a decent and ecologically responsible manner, you poor ignorant savages were eating missionary stew.'

'You mind your mouth, redneck –'

'Red*skin*, woman, red*skin*!'

'That's your story. I don't see no feathers. And if you don't quit knocking us Americans of African descent I ain't going to wait for no stringy old missionary. I'll have *you* for supper. With fried grits and collard greens.'

'There, you see? What can you expect from people who eat such garbage? Now a fine roast dog . . .'

'Don't talk that way in front of Bagel; you know it upsets him.'

All this, Kate supposed, was a double act of long standing. They were putting on a show for her: see, we are human like you; we make silly jokes; you needn't be afraid of us. Clearly they meant it kindly, but she wished they would stop.

'Childish,' Claire said from the stove. 'Purely childish. I'm ashamed for the both of you. Now come to table and try to act like Christians.'

The soup was all that had been claimed for it and more. A deep, translucent red, ballasted with rice, it tasted of garlic, tomatoes, brandy, herbs, and chicken broth strong enough to skate on. Its restorative effect was immediate: Kate could feel it going straight into her bloodstream like a transfusion. The rest of the meal was also remarkable – a stew of leeks and tender young rabbit, with parsley-flecked dumplings that dissolved on the tongue like mist, followed by preserved pears and thick yellow cream. But it was the soup that made the deepest impression on Kate. She had never tasted anything remotely like it before. This huge, handsome woman, who sat at the head of the table regally dispensing wonders with a silver ladle that must have weighed a couple of pounds, was no ordinary farmer's wife. She was an alchemist, a brewer of potent magics in enormous pots. As a rural Ma Barker, the matriarch of a murderous clan, she was frankly impossible. Kate had begun to feel better.

After supper was over, Afeni and Chuck disappeared into the scullery to wash the dishes, and Sam wandered away to the parlour, from which there presently floated a succession of soulful Victorian ballads played on the piano. Claire brought out a baby bottle and filled it with warm milk. Kate was unsurprised; it stood to reason, with a fertility goddess like this in charge, that there must be a baby around somewhere.

'I'll take him now, Conor,' she said, sinking into the rocker and disposing her skirts about her. From a wooden box in the corner between hearth and settle, the man extracted a flannel-wrapped bundle and set it in the valley of Claire's apron. It was a tiny piglet, white eyelashed, pink bodied, with an anxious expression that went oddly with its meaningless piggy smile. It clamped onto the rubber nipple like a squid, making loud, blissful noises as the level of milk in the bottle began to fall.

'It's the dillun,' Conor told Kate, 'the runt of the litter. The others kept shoving it off the teat, so Claire's raising it by hand until it's big enough to stand up for its rights.'

'Poor little thing.' Claire patted it absently. 'Always hungry. I believe it's a waste of time – these little runty creatures hardly ever do thrive – but I couldn't sit with my hands in my lap and watch it dwindle.'

Out of sheer habit she rocked the piglet like a real baby while it fed. Looking up at Conor, she asked, 'Was that food all right?'

'Fantastic.'

'I wasn't hopeful it would keep fresh, fixed all that time ahead.'

'It spent most of yesterday in the refrigerator, and I refroze the cold packs and did absolutely everything else you told me to. It was fine.'

'Seemed like a shame not to stuff that good chicken, but a bread stuffing can turn sour and taint the whole bird when the weather's hot. I guess I did right. There's just something kind of sad though, about a chicken with nothing in it but air.'

'Stop fussing; everything was delicious. Kate loved it, didn't you?'

'It was the best picnic I ever had.'

Kate was taken aback to realize, after she'd said it, that this was literally true. Which was absurd. One was not supposed to enjoy the fringe benefits, if any, of being abducted. Here she was, spending incomparably the worst day of her entire life, scared green and in continual danger of God knew what, confined in the hands of criminals and no help anywhere, and yet somehow she had managed to tuck away two enormous meals and take pleasure in every bite. There must be something very wrong with her. Or maybe this was what life was really like; terror and tragedy mired in the mundane, robbed of their proper solemnity by cold roast chicken and bottle-fed piglets and – good God, was it possible? – 'The Lost Chord' on the parlour piano. One anguish to go, please, with a large order of fries. On the other hand, perhaps she was simply losing her mind.

Claire, cocking a knowledgeable eye at her, recognized the symptoms of emotional concussion.

'Bed for you, child,' she said, presenting Conor with the satiated piglet and heaving herself out of the rocker.

'Half a minute.' He tucked the creature back into its box and, straightening, addressed himself to Kate. 'One thing we'd better get clear. You won't be locked in. Please don't get the idea, though, that you can take off any time you feel like it. If you're silly enough to run away you'll be brought back, be very sure of that. And then you bloody well *will* be locked in, and you won't like it. This isn't Devil's Island, but it's not Sunnybrook Farm either, so don't play the fool. I'm not a particularly patient man. Do you understand?'

'Yes.'

'Right; that's all.'

He turned away, unsmiling, and made for the scullery, where Chuck and Afeni could be heard wrangling amicably above the chink of pots and silverware. Claire took Kate upstairs and carefully explained the intricacies of the plumbing. Hot water, which downstairs came from a propane heater in the scullery, helped out by the reservoir perpetually kept full in the old-fashioned stove, was supplied in the second-floor bathroom by an immense galvanized tank with a wood-burning stove in its base. After all that had happened in the last twenty-four hours it was not logical to be so much struck by the oddity of a bathroom with a half cord of logs stacked outside the door, but Kate was past logic by this time.

'And you see this little brass weight here, at the end of the string?' Claire was saying. 'Now when that weight reaches the red line *here* – You're not listening.'

'Sorry.'

'When the weight reaches the red line, don't run off any more hot water or this whole thing is liable to blow up. Just give a holler to one of the men, to pump more cold water up. That's important, so you remember. My father didn't believe in electricity, and this boiler was the apple of his eye, but it's like a cranky old mule. It takes knowing, and it takes humouring. Here's your towels now, and a new brush for your teeth, and this is your bedroom, right next to the bathroom. It's my Beccah's room ordinarily, and there's things of hers in the closet, but you won't mind that. I put you here to be next to Chuck and me. We'll be right in there, so if you need anything, just tap on the door. Or if you get scared in the night.'

'I *am* scared,' Kate pointed out. 'I'm scared right *now*.'

'Well of course thee is.' Claire's periodic lapses into the old plain speech were involuntary. Like all bilingual persons, she switched gears without even being aware of it, and strong feelings usually triggered a reversion to the language of her Quaker upbringing. 'Be a queer thing if thee wasn't scared,' she went on, patting the girl's shoulder. 'And easy to say "Don't be", and mighty hard advice to follow. Thee doesn't know us yet. But think on this: if the Lord had meant for thee to be harmed, He never would have let Conor bring thee here to me. It may be his name on the papers, but when it comes to what goes on, and doesn't go on, under this roof, this is still my house and well he knows

63

it. Thee get to bed now. I've put one of my nightgowns out; thee'll swim in it but it can't be helped. Afeni don't wear 'em. Say thy prayers like a good girl and wait on the Light; that's where the strength and the comfort come from. And be sure and blow the candle out before thee goes to sleep.'

Kate lay awake in the dark bedroom. In spite of the blanket, the quilt, and the engulfing folds of Claire's best drawn-thread-work nightgown, she was freezing. It was a mild night, but cold seemed to radiate outward from her bones in deadly waves, and her hands and feet were like ice. Alone, released from the obligation to keep up some sort of front in the face of the enemy, she could admit to herself how frightened she really was. Not of death, oddly enough. Like most people of her age who lived comfortable lives, she had always felt somehow immunized against death, as if she had had shots for it, like polio and whooping cough. But the sudden collapse of this pleasant illusion of immortality was something she found she could take pretty well in stride. Death, at least, was a natural matter. It was part of the package, something you let yourself in for by being born. Dying itself would probably be horrible, but once you were dead they couldn't get at you. You would be safe.

Trying to put her thoughts in order was like putting weight on a broken ankle, but she felt that it had to be done, some kind of coherence imposed on the chaos of the day. Since it was not the possibility of death that filled her with such dread, what was it? Being hurt, probably – the prospect of pain, inflicted casually or, even worse, with sick enjoyment; arbitrary pain, begun for no particular reason and therefore with no reason for it ever to stop. Being beaten up, abused, humiliated. Violation of civil rights, she thought wryly, and wondered if this was how black women had felt when they were dragged out of the line of march, tormented with dogs and cattle prods, and thrown into cells by men whose deepest fantasies were fed by the chance to brutalize what they so deeply feared. At least those women had a faith to hold onto; they were part of a movement, they stood for something. I don't stand for anything, she recognized drearily. I'm here because I am my father's only weakness. A lever, the man had called her. I'm not even a human being to him, only a tool, and if I break I'll be thrown away. Terminated, that was the word her father's people favoured. Terminated with extreme prejudice. If they had no further use for you, if you were inconvenient or potentially

64

embarrassing, they did not order you killed. Not being significantly alive in the first place, since you were not, by their reckoning, a real person, you could not be said to be killed. You were just terminated.

She wasn't afraid of the women – she was used to women. Claire, especially, looked more like an ally than a threat, as protective of her as if she were a small child in trouble through no fault of its own. Afeni was more detached, with a certain bracing cynicism that reminded Kate of Miss Clifton at school. It was easy to imagine Afeni cleaning a scraped knee with meticulous care and a stream of scalding comment on the idiocy of roller-skating downhill in the first place. Kate couldn't see her as a torturer, though – she would be far too fastidious for that. The men were another matter. She thought of them, simplistically, in terms of their women. Chuck would not harm her, she was sure, because Claire wouldn't allow it, and besides Claire would never have married the kind of man who was capable of hurting a helpless prisoner. But Sam scared her; he looked so cold. And Afeni would be no protection; she wasn't the type to interfere: 'Well, if you want to be disgusting that's your business. I have to feed the hens.' One danger, however, she did not anticipate from Sam. Those pale green eyes had rested on her as impersonally as if she were nothing more than an unusual slice of tissue under the microscope. He might hurt her, he might kill her, but her body, her femaleness, did not interest him.

The other man was different. It was no use shutting her eyes to what she really feared; it had to be faced. Sexual assault, molestation, rape; police report language, grist for the tabloids and the gossip columns, unthinkable things that might happen to other people but never to oneself. Pain of any kind was frightening enough, but such intimate pain, the sweet uses of love perverted to hurt and shame, must be unbearable.

She could understand now why so many cases of rape went unreported. It was too bad to talk about, too bad even to think about. She knew that some women were said to indulge in sexual fantasies in which they were raped, but she didn't believe a word of it. 'A fate worse than death' was just a gag line nowadays; people thought it amusing, but she realized that it might be literally true – the sort of emotional maiming that could wreck you for life.

And the other man, the man they called Conor, wanted her. Kate was not sure how she knew this. Since she had first woken in the woods at dawn, he had behaved towards her with friendly formality, as if some quasi-professional relationship existed between them: doctor and patient, or even teacher and pupil. Nobody could say he had taken advantage, as Nanny Bristow would have phrased it. There had been no gropings or encroachments, no covetous glances down the front of her sweater. Yet she knew he wanted her.

The girls at Beresford, like the ones at Miss Hampshire's, had grimly assured her that men, even the nicest of them, were only interested in one thing where girls were concerned. 'You want to be loved for your beautiful soul, honey, go find a faggot,' Mary Beth had told her trenchantly. 'Any normal guy takes you out, sooner or later he'll try to get into your pants.' Your safest bet, it seemed, was to follow the rules, avoid situations you might not be able to handle, and invoke the blessed shelter of the social conventions. Of course if you fell in love, it was understood that you would want to 'do it', probably would 'do it', and that meant a whole new set of rules, with different penalty clauses, and complications like the Pill.

Kate had not been in love since she was sixteen, when she had suffered delicious agonies over the art teacher at school. Entire screenplays, in which he kissed her wildly and touched her breasts (through her clothes, of course) with trembling hands, had whiled away a whole term of algebra periods. But since the art teacher, a saturnine but unsusceptible man with four children and a mortgage, was far more concerned with her colour values than her romantic potential, she had never had the chance to find out whether reality would have measured up to her tingling daydreams. Certainly she had never felt like that about anyone since.

There was Charlie, of course, but she'd known him since she was six. There was nothing mysterious left about Charlie, and anyhow it was hard to feel anything warmer than friendship for someone who had spent three years teasing her about her retainer. There was also Bill, who had composed a pavane for her and kissed her several times, but it had seemed to her a slobbery and unrewarding business, more embarrassing than pleasurable.

And there had been, and were, plenty of other young men who gazed hopefully at her across lecture halls and cafeteria tables, and made eager, clumsy overtures. Most of them seemed nice enough, awkward and friendly as half-grown puppies, but she didn't know how to respond to them, she didn't know what to say.

It seemed there was some special code to which she lacked the key, some prescribed set of moves that other people were born knowing, and that she would never learn. She wondered if Charlie's unkind gibe about being frigid was truer than he knew. Perhaps there was something missing in her nature. But none of that mattered now. What mattered was that she had been pitchforked without warning or ceremony into the grown-up world, and she hadn't the least idea how to cope with it.

Shivering with cold, she rummaged through the events of the day, looking for scraps of comfort. The man had pointed out himself that if he had wanted to do anything awful to her he would surely have done it before now, and that made sense. Besides, he hadn't acted like a sex maniac – not that she had any reliable data on how sex maniacs did act, but you ought to be able to tell if somebody was one after being alone with him for so long. And yet there was something: nothing overt, but certainly something, a prickling at the nape of the neck, a heightened consciousness of her own body, a sense of something extra in the air, like the brooding heaviness before a thunderstorm.

The situation itself was loaded, which was part of the trouble. Events had whisked her outside the haven of the rules, and there was no more security anywhere. Perhaps she was imagining things, creating a bogeyman out of her own fears. But anything could happen, anything at all.

There had been that terrifying byplay with the knife. It seemed to have broken something inside her, though she was not quite sure what: some unexamined assumption, perhaps, that the world was a predictable, orderly place. Curiously, the immediate aftereffects of that melodramatic confrontation had been benign. For one thing, she had been illogically pleased to discover that no hidden strain of violence festered within her. Whether her reaction had come from Christian forbearance or simple lack of guts was really not important, she was still relieved to know that nothing could make a killer of her. Abruptly forced to weigh her own freedom against someone else's death, she had opted for life, and felt the freer for it. She might have killed the man. Since she had chosen not to, it could be argued that it was by her own choice that she was here at all, and for a while that piece of sophistry had made her feel less helpless.

But now, alone in the dark, the gimcrack rationalizations broke down, and she was left with the memory of the knife in her hands and the bead of blood on his skin and the tension that had shimmered and pulsed between them – a tension for which the imminence of death was only partly responsible. Kate was inexperienced, but she was no fool. Unwillingly, she was beginning to understand what had happened to her. Her mind had already been raped, so expertly and with such confidence that she had accepted the assault without protest. It was obvious what had to come next. The only question left was whether it would happen now or later. When the knock came at the bedroom door, it was almost a relief.

'Who is it?' she called and got the answer she expected.

'It's me. Can I come in?'

'I guess so.'

It was no use saying 'Stay out', but it was as if she were being made a co-conspirator against herself. She hated it and did not know how to stop it. If she were going to lose everything else, she would have liked to keep a little pride.

He came in carrying a lighted candle and shut the door behind him. He put the candlestick on the night table, brought up a high-backed chair, set it down by the bed with its back to her, and straddled it. Then he folded his arms across the chair back, propped his chin on them, and sat and stared at her. She decided to wait him out and did for more than a minute. It felt like a week.

'What is it?' she asked, when she could not stand the silence any more. 'What do you want?'

He grinned, his teeth gleaming in the candlelight. One front tooth was slightly chipped. Viewed objectively, it was an attractive flaw, but to Kate it made him look predatory, a fanged beast ready to rend and tear.

'Guess,' he said.

'Oh.' She looked down at the quilt that covered her. It was an old one, with intricate ellipses of faded raspberry and brown and blue, made to warm bones that had long since gone to the graveyard. It had not been able to warm hers. Try as she might, she could not stop shivering, and that made her angry. He would think it was fear, but really it was the terrible chill that shook her so. It seemed suddenly very important that he should not think she was afraid. She'd made a complete fool of herself once already today and once was enough; this time let's try for a little dignity, with maybe a touch of well-bred disdain, if she could manage it. Think of Charles I on the scaffold: 'He nothing common did or mean upon that memorable scene' – and that was from one of his enemies, too. Think of Walter Raleigh or Mary

Queen of Scots. No whining. She took a deep breath.

'Well. No use saying I'd rather die, because I'm not sure I would. Anyhow, you're not giving me the choice. I can't run away, and I'm not strong enough to fight you. If I scream, there's no one to hear me but those friends of yours, and even if they wanted to they couldn't help me; you wouldn't let them. I could cry, I guess, and plead with you. Maybe I'll end up doing that, but I hope not – it wouldn't be any use, and you'd probably enjoy it. So you'd better go ahead and do what you want to do, and get it over.'

'My poor girl, you make it sound like a hanging. Do I really revolt you as much as that?'

Scraping up the last of her courage, she raised her head and looked at him.

'What difference does it make how I feel? I can't stop you.'

'You can't, no. There's only one person who can.'

'Claire?'

'No, not Claire. Me. Stop trembling, I'm not going to touch you. My God, I want to, though, and I imagine it shows,' he added ruefully. 'Thanks to my superb self-control, which won a gold medal at the Brussels Exposition in 1910, I can just about keep my hands off you. What I can't seem to do is switch off the current. You're very young, I know, but you're not half-witted. Eventually, you'd have noticed. In fact I shouldn't wonder if you had already. You certainly didn't seem very surprised when I walked in just now.'

'No. I was afraid you would.'

'I thought so; that's why I came up. Pretty grim, I should think, lying in the dark wondering when you're going to get pounced on. Well, you can stop worrying. You may have to put up with a good deal of heavy breathing and the occasional burning glance, but I promise not to jump you.'

'You're really not going –'

'I'm really not going to. Well, Christ, you have to draw the line somewhere. If I'd met you in a normal sort of a way, at a dinner party or something, I should be making the most strenuous efforts to seduce you. But going after someone who can't possibly get away . . . There's a word for that, and the word is not seduction. Naturally I wouldn't dream of forcing you, but then I wouldn't have to. In the end you'd do anything I wanted, partly to "get it over", as you so dauntingly put it, and partly because you'd be afraid of what might happen to you if you didn't. And that would

69

be rape, just as surely as if I'd held a knife to your neck.'

He stood up, replaced the chair, and stooped to straighten the quilt over her. She drew away, reflexively, and saw his mouth tighten.

'Calm down,' he said flatly. 'I've never yet inflicted myself on a woman who didn't want me, and I'm much too old to start now. You're perfectly safe from me for as long as you want to be – ' a ghost of the grin came back ' – and not one half-second longer, so watch it.'

He picked up his candle and walked to the door. Halfway through, he paused and looked back.

'Tomorrow, if you're a good girl and eat all your vegetables, I'll teach you how to milk a cow,' he said, and shut the door behind him.

It was not until she was almost asleep that Kate realized she was, finally, warm.

When Claire roused her out of bed early next morning –
'Breakfast be on the table in ten minutes, with you or without you'
– Kate threw on her clothes and shot into the bathroom. She felt
curiously cheerful, even excited, as though she really were on
vacation instead of a hostage in the keeping of polite but
potentially deadly guards. The weather might have had
something to do with it: a blameless spring morning, limpid and
cool, the dew on the pasture grass touched with a dazzle of
diamonds in the slanting sunlight. Looking out of the bathroom
window as she brushed her teeth, she could see Chuck, with Bagel
wallowing at his heels, turning a cluster of glossy caramel cows
out of the barn and through the gate into the meadow. Five geese
and a gander fussed officiously in their wake. It was the most
peaceful, reassuring sight imaginable.

Then Conor appeared, carrying two pails of milk across the
yard to the house, his scarlet shirt as arrogant as a flag, and
suddenly the pastoral scene lost its innocence. He was singing, the
son of a bitch, in a light, true baritone, as gaily as if there were
nothing on his conscience at all.

> *'Give your lover warning*
> *To be on his way by morning,*
> *I'm taking the night boat to Cork.'*

He glanced up and saw her at the window before she had time
to step back.

'Good morning! If you want breakfast you'd better get fell in
or there won't be any left.'

She was down in the kitchen in three minutes and sat in silent
amazement as fried eggs, country ham, sausage, fried potatoes,
and great mounds of cereal were methodically demolished by the
others, who seemed to have been up for hours. She settled for
coffee and a modest helping of cereal, drawing concerned
enquiries from Claire about her health.

'I feel fine, thank you. It's just I haven't been working.'

'We can soon put that right,' said Conor, helping himself to more ham. 'Always plenty of jobs going on a farm. Only if you want to, of course. You can sit on a cushion and sew a fine seam if you'd rather, but you might find it a bit dull.'

'I'd like to have something to do.'

'Sensible girl. Chuck, when d'you reckon Lady Godiva'll calve?'

'The spirits of my ancestors came to me in a dream. "Check the gestation table, dummy," they counselled me, "likewise the herd book." You want to go by that old stuff, it ought to be Monday. A week from today. But you know that cow. Twin crocodiles on Memorial Day wouldn't surprise me.'

'I hope she doesn't pop while I'm gone. Remember the time we had with her last year?'

The conversation became technical. Kate was not crazy about bovine obstetrics but at least, she reflected as she helped to clear the table, it was a relief to find her captors taken up with something else besides her own presence. The last thing she wanted was to be the centre of attention. Apparently the man would be going away, which was a plus of a sort for her – one less to worry about, especially if his vaunted self-control didn't hold up – but why was he going? To negotiate with her father, she supposed, about the terms for her release. She wondered how they would go about it. They couldn't make use of the media, as others had done, because publicity would wreck the whole deal. She hadn't understood about that at first, but she'd worked it out finally and it made sense. For her father's resignation to be managed convincingly, it was essential that as few people as possible should even suspect he was quitting under duress, with his retirement as the price of his daughter's life.

And how were these people going to prove they actually had her? Her bag, with all her identification inside it, had got lost at some point during her attempt at escape the previous day. Perhaps they would force her to make a tape, begging her father to do what they asked, spelling out what the consequences would be if he didn't cooperate. What if she refused? So far, except for that abortive dash for freedom, she had been a model prisoner, quiet and obedient, giving no trouble, and they had treated her well. If her behaviour altered, so, surely, would theirs.

Kate had never been confident of her ability to withstand pain. A grateful member of the Novocaine generation, she was both awed and puzzled by people who held up under torture, unable to imagine how anyone could do it. The man – in her own mind she resisted using his name – seemed civilized, even gentle, on the surface, but she was very conscious of the inflexible purpose beneath, and the prospect of defying him made her stomach knot like a fist. Since the knife episode she had been careful to avoid an open clash. When she had diffidently asked, the evening before, if the metal cuff could be taken off her left wrist, only to be refused on the gravely preposterous grounds that, without her ID bracelet, they wouldn't be able to tell her apart from the other babies in the nursery, she had dropped the subject at once, although the steel band chafed her spirit as well as her skin. And later, when he had come to her room and skewered her with that savage-seeming grin, she had simply waited, with queasy resignation, for him to begin to hurt her. But making a tape would be something else again. He could do things *to* her, because he was bigger and stronger than she was, but could he make her do things herself? Kate hoped very much that she would not have to find out.

Probably it was the fault of her years at Miss Hampshire's, where trivial issues had loomed so large that the wrong kind of knee socks could lead to months of misery. In any case, faced with a situation that might well end in her death, Kate found herself bothered by something no bigger than the single pea under the princess's twelve mattresses. It was ridiculous to feel shy about such an irrelevant matter. Nevertheless, she let several opportunities go by before nerving herself to ask. Finally, late in the morning, when he paused by the sink where she was peeling potatoes, hooked his finger around the strand of yellow hair that was hanging down annoyingly over one eye, and tucked it back behind her ear, she turned to face him.

'I've got a problem.'

'Yes, I know,' he said, looking amused. 'We've never been introduced, and you don't know what to call me.'

'How did you know it was that?' She was reluctantly impressed.

'Well for one thing, you've managed to avoid calling me anything up to now, and eventually it's bound to get awkward. Think if the house caught fire and I was the only person within earshot – the place could burn to the ground while you dithered about making your mind up whether to shout "Sir!" or "Hey, you!" In any clash of alien cultures,' he went on seriously, 'it's the silly little social nuances that cause the most trouble. Like foreigners in France, always giving dreadful offence by *tutoyer-*

ing people they shouldn't. Afeni's right about Emily Post; I don't suppose there's one word in there about formal modes of address to kidnappers. Now if only I were a bishop, we could look it up.'

'If you were a bishop I wouldn't have to; I know all that stuff by heart. Besides, if you were a bishop you wouldn't be doing this.'

'Oh I don't know; there are some very militant clergy about these days.'

'You're getting away from the point. And I know it sounds dumb, but it *is* awkward. I've heard what the others call you, but I don't know if it's your first name or your last, and it makes a difference. And I don't think it's fair of you to laugh at me that way.'

'I'm not laughing at you. I'm just happy – which must be very irritating for you, come to think of it. Sorry. Conor is my middle name, as it happens, and I'd like you to use it. Now I suppose you'll go right on not calling me anything at all, and serve me right for being familiar.'

'Conor. Conor, Conor, Conor.'

'Amazing grace, how sweet the sound. Don't scowl. Here, I'll finish the spuds, your fingers are getting all crinkled. There's a stool over there. Stay and keep me company, and I'll tell you the story of my early years as a barefoot bog-trotter in Holy Ireland.'

'*Were* you? A barefoot bog-trotter?'

'Only during the summer, alas. At the school I went to in England they made everybody wear shoes.'

'What school was that?'

'Place called Eton. It's near Slough, where Charles Dickens kept his mistress. A peculiar choice, I always felt, like setting up a love nest in Newark, New Jersey, but then he did have a sort of nervous fondness for squalor. Tell me, what are your views on *The Mystery of Edwin Drood*?'

'Miss Marple did it; I thought everybody knew that.'

'Box of Mars bars to the lady in the fourth row. Now for two thousand dollars, here is the next question: did Little Nell really die?'

'No. They had to fake her death because the truth about her bigamous marriage to Tiny Tim was about to come out. She emigrated to America under an assumed name, married Ralph Waldo Emerson –'

'More bigamy?'

'It had gotten to be a habit by then.'

'You left out the bit about her years in the brothel in Yonkers, but otherwise pretty good.'

Sam came into the scullery and, ignoring Kate, addressed himself to Conor.

'Ready when you are, C. B.'

'Oh. Oh all right. I suppose we'd better get it done.' All the laughter had vanished, and he looked as grim as when she first saw him. 'Kate, come with me.'

He took her hand and led her outdoors. Behind the barn Afeni was waiting. A bedsheet had been tacked up against the wooden siding. Without a word Sam and Afeni each caught hold of one of Kate's arms. They had the length of chain and the other cuff. In seconds she was pinioned in front of the sheet, arms outstretched, her wrists shackled to ringbolts set high in the wall, the slack of the chain looped around her bare throat. No one had spoken to her, and she was too astonished to cry out. Sam and Afeni moved aside, and she saw Conor facing her. There was a gun in his hand. She could not believe it was happening until she looked at his face. The misery she saw there convinced her as nothing else could have done.

'Don't look,' he said, and his voice was like silk tearing.

'Conor! *No!*'

'I'm sorry. I'm *sorry!*'

Time went slow. There were only the two of them, victim and executioner, grief with the gun and despair numbly waiting for the bullet, and they faced each other for ever.

'Perfect,' Sam said, and lowered his camera. Conor dropped the pistol and sat down abruptly beside it on the ground.

'Afeni,' he said, in a painful gasp that sounded as if the wind had been knocked out of him. 'Get Claire. Take that fucking chain off and get Claire.'

Afeni released her, the long fingers tremulous but quick, the fine face troubled.

'Baby, it's all right,' she murmured, putting an arm around Kate. 'It was just for the photographs, you dig? You had to look scared, like really scared. We couldn't tell you. Oh, Jesus, I'm sorry. That was a bad thing. Here, you come on in the house and we'll find Claire. Come on, now.'

Both of them were shaking as Afeni urged her across the yard. Conor waited, hunched over with his knees under his chin, until they had disappeared indoors. Then he rose stiffly, went over to the thick clump of honeysuckle at the corner of the barn, and threw up.

'What's wrong, boy? Something you ate?' Sam asked when he came back. 'Or you getting the hots for that cute l'il thing? Never did go for them eentsy l'il tits myself, but if that's –'

Conor hit him in the mouth. It was not a very heavy blow, but Sam wasn't expecting it. He sat down hard in the dust and came up spitting blood from a cut lip and looking like murder.

'Oh shit. I didn't mean to do that. But you've a way of putting things . . .' Conor sounded remote now, almost bored, as if they'd been through all this before. 'I'll do what I have to, you know that. Have done it, and will do it. But there are times when I find it bloody hard to take, and you're not helping. You've got your snaps; take 'em into the darkroom and get on with it. And take this with you.'

He kicked across the empty pistol and walked off around the barn. Minutes later Claire came storming onto the porch in time to see him ride out of the gateway on Barley, the bay gelding. She shouted after him, but he took no notice.

'Thee keep out of my way, then,' she hollered at his back. 'Thee just keep out of my way till I'm cooled down. For all of me, thee can keep right on going till thee gets to Jericho.'

She went back to the kitchen, fuming. There was no sense berating Afeni any more – the black girl was almost as upset as the white – and Sam had prudently gone to ground. The thing was done now, and nothing for it but to try and repair the damage. But she'd stand for no more. Keeping the child here was one thing; she'd agreed to that, full of misgivings but yielding to the urgency of Conor's arguments. Mistreatment was another matter entirely. She'd not have it, and if they didn't know that then they were about to be set straight.

'Afeni,' she said, 'thee's done enough harm for one day. Thee can go do something useful. I noticed a patch of weeds in the vegetable garden, right at the far end by the marrows. Thee get on out there and take a hoe to 'em. As for thee, child, thee's going to help me with the bread. I can use an extra pair of hands with the kneading.'

'I don't know how to do that,' Kate said shakily.

'Thee cannot learn sooner. Go wash your hands now, and we'll get to it.'

It was late afternoon, and Kate was in the barn. She had fed the

76

calves; Chuck and Claire seemed to have decided that what she needed at the moment was not mothering but something legitimate to do, and between them they had found a string of simple chores to keep her busy. She leaned on the edge of the pen, watching the animals as they bumped and bucketed around. They were attractive to look at, knock-kneed and leggy, with coats like crumpled velvet and huge, moon-blue eyes. Doomed to the butcher, she thought, but they're better off than I am; at least they don't know what's coming to them.

She heard someone approaching, assumed that it was Chuck, and stayed where she was. Then hooves clicked on stone, leather creaked, and there was the wiffling sound of a horse blowing out through its nose. It was too late to escape, but if she didn't turn around maybe he would go away.

Tack jingled, she heard the slithery, sucking sound of a saddle coming off, then more horse noises, and after a while footsteps, coming nearer. A pair of hands closed on the rail on each side of her elbows. Tanned, big-knuckled, capable-looking hands. Conor's hands. He was standing so close she could feel the warmth coming from him, but he did not touch her. She did not turn around, only stood waiting for those damnable hands to move, grabbing, hurting.

'If it would make you feel any better,' he said, 'I'd let you cut my heart out with a rusty trowel. Though if it comes to that, Claire will probably beat you to it. She's not very happy with me just now. That was a filthy thing to do to you, and it's no good saying I'm sorry because it doesn't help. You do know, don't you, that nothing like that will happen again?'

Slowly Kate shook her head.

'I've been thinking,' she said, staring straight ahead. 'Not because of what you did, though, just – just general thinking. As far as I can see there's no way out of it, sooner or later you'll do it for real. You're going to have to kill me.'

'Kate, that isn't true. A callous son of a bitch I may be and am, but I swear to you, on anything you like, I would never do that. Or allow it to be done.'

'Look, I don't believe you want to. Maybe you've really managed to kid yourself you won't have to. But you can't keep me here for ever, and you can't let me go, so what else is there?'

'Turn round.'

Reluctantly, she turned. Even with her back pressed hard against the rails, he was only inches away. He smelled of horse, tobacco, soap and, not unpleasantly, of sweat.

'Would you look at me, please? Come on, lovey. I can't talk to the top of your head, look at me.'

He took her chin between finger and thumb and tilted her face up. Mutinously, she glared at his shirt collar. Its shouting red framed a vee of golden throat. She could see a pulse beating there.

'My God, you're stubborn. Nanny Bristow must have had her hands full. I can stand here all day, you know; I'm not proud.'

When at last she capitulated and met his eyes, he wanted so badly to put his arms around her that he was afraid the pain must show in his face. He need not have worried. To Kate he only looked concerned and rather annoyed.

'That's better. Now then, tell me. Why can't I let you go?'

'Because I've seen your faces, of course. I know your names. I know what you look like, your voices. I can identify all of you. I can describe you down to the last detail. If you meant me to go free in the end, you'd wear masks or – or keep me blindfolded or locked up in the dark. If you don't care what I see, it's because I'll never have the chance to tell anyone. You won't face up to it, because you really don't like to hurt people, otherwise you'd have hurt me more than you have. But when push comes to shove you'll do it. You'll feel terrible about it, but you'll do it just the same.'

'Oh, Kate. Oh, my dear girl. Have you any idea what it does to people, being kept in the dark for days on end – or weeks? Or being surrounded by enemies with no faces? It's as good a way as any to lose your mind. Simple sensory deprivation. The guerrillas picked it up from the secret police, and it works – oh dear me yes – it works. If you'd ever seen anyone after they'd been put through that, you wouldn't ask why we didn't do it to you. Okay, you know our faces. But you don't know where you are, and it's a big country. If anyone's going to put us in clink, they'll have to find us first. We may seem a bit casual around here, but don't let the rustic ambience fool you. We're not a gaggle of village idiots. Anyway, think a minute. I dare say at the moment you find it immensely satisfying to visualize us all behind bars, but honestly what good would it do?'

'You mean you're counting on me not to turn you in?'

He laughed at her indignant face. 'Hardly that. There are – contingency plans. *Not* including murder. But I don't think they'll be necessary. When all this is over and you're safe at home, the

78

thought of locking up Claire and Chuck and Afeni and Sam and me won't seem nearly as enticing as it does now. Certainly not worth dragging through endless weeks in court. The moral ramifications can't have escaped you altogether. You've been horribly frightened, I know, but you haven't been hurt, and you won't be. I wish you could see some of my children; it might help you to see our side of things a little.'

He paused, and his face relaxed. 'I seem to be making a speech,' he said. 'How tedious of me. I didn't mean to go on and on at you as if you were a public meeting.'

'No, that's okay. If I've got to – to go through all of this, I'd at least like to understand why.'

'All right, then, look. The people of this country are being mulcted to pay for a peculiarly beastly little war that no longer has anything whatever to do with them – if it ever did – and would be over in months without the money that's being skimmed off their wages. There's no free neighbourhood clinic they can take their kids to, because the funds needed to build it and equip it and staff it are being spent to incinerate other people's kids ten thousand miles away. It's absurd, it's wicked, and it's gone on far too long already. All we're trying to do is make life a little less horrible for a lot of thoroughly bewildered Vietnamese and Cambodians who are much too young to understand that they're only being sacrificed to make the world safe for democracy. If we're successful, what's the worst that can happen? Your old man will be out of a job. I don't think he'll have much trouble finding another one, do you? Yale would take him back in a minute, more shame to them. I feel bad about scaring you, and I feel bad about worrying your mother. And I'm truly sorry about old Charlie's thick ear. But weigh all that in the balance against the poor fucked-up Southeast Asians and I can't see there's any contest. It's got to be stopped.'

'Yes, I see that. And you're right, I guess. But you're going about it all wrong. There are legal, constitutional ways.'

'They've been tried, and they haven't worked. This may. Now listen to me, young woman. After this morning, there's no very compelling reason for you to believe a word I say. My credit's gone, if I ever had any. But whether you trust me or not, you're stuck here for the next couple of weeks and you may as well make the best of it. If you hate the sight of us you're entirely within your rights, but at least get this straight: *we are not murderers*. That sort of lark may be all in a day's work for your

79

father's funny friends, but it's not our speed so you can put it smartly out of your mind.'

She had meant to say something acid, but it was so obvious that, of all incongruous things, his feelings were hurt, that she found herself rashly protesting, 'But I don't hate the sight of you – I don't hate the sight of you at all!'

His eyebrows shot up, and she felt herself beginning to blush. She hoped the dimness of the barn would hide it, but he touched his cool, hard palm to her heated cheek and smiled at her, making it worse.

'Well, you probably should,' he said. 'For your own good. We're not exactly the sort of people your mother would want you to know. It's very attractive, by the way – the blushing, I mean. I didn't think girls did that any more. What I meant to ask you, Kate, before we got sidetracked, is whether you want me to buy anything for you in what is grandly known as "town". I have to take a set of batteries in for charging and pick up a fresh propane tank, so if you need hairpins or horse liniment, or a couple of sacks of linseed, now is the time to ask.'

'Could you get me a comb? And a box of Kleenex and some cigarettes? I lost my bag yesterday. I must have dropped it in the woods.'

'Oh Christ, did you? No, that's right, you hadn't got it when I found you. Well that's handy. You've no idea where you might have left it?'

'Could have been anyplace between the Jeep and the cave. Does it matter?'

'It will if anyone finds it. Not that that's likely, but there's always Murphy's Law. I suppose it had your driving licence in it and your credit cards and stuff, with Catherine D. Harper stamped all over them? It would. Dear oh dear. As the burglar said when he saw the judges going into the Old Bailey, these things are sent to try us. You are a careless creature, aren't you?'

'God damn it, I was running for my life.'

'Not really. You only thought you were. Okay. Comb, Kleenex, cigarettes. What kind?'

'Kents. And if you should see a pie with a file in it . . .'

'Very funny. All the world hates a smartass. Now get out of here, will you please? Run along and polish the pigs or something. I've more than enough to worry about without you taking my mind off my work. Off you go.'

She collected the empty milk pail and marched out. She was

doing her best to be haughty, but the irrepressibly youthful switch of her small backside in the tight jeans ruined the effect. Simultaneously tormented and beguiled, Conor watched her out of sight.

By the afternoon of her second day at the farm, it was clear to Kate that her apparent freedom of movement, while it made life far pleasanter than if she were confined, was not going to be much help when it came to an escape. The keys to the Jeep and the pick-up were kept in a cupboard when not in use, and the cupboard was locked – not with a key, but with an elaborate battery-operated mechanism, a row of electronic push buttons. When they were pressed in a coded sequence, the cupboard door sprang open. A key she might have stolen, but there was no way to steal a string of numbers from someone else's brain. The telephone was kept in the same cupboard, and once when Claire was using it Kate had glimpsed a dull sheen of metal on the back wall that might have been a gun.

Exploring the house earlier that day, when she thought all the others were outside, she had gone up to the attic. There were three rooms up there: one obviously a young boy's room, with models and half-completed projects, and football posters on the plank walls; the second was a storeroom, piled with trunks and clutter, and the third she could not enter. Its stout door was equipped with another of the electronic locks, and beyond it she could hear, faintly, Sam's unmistakable drawl.

'Aurora to Sleeper One, Aurora to Sleeper One, do you read me?'

It was the radio installation Conor had spoken of, and she couldn't get at it. Cross that off, then, no way of establishing contact with the outside world. Kate had had hopes of that radio. She had had hopes of a number of things. In the country, neighbours would be dropping by unannounced; some visiting farmer would show up, and she could slip him a note asking him to get the police. But twice callers had arrived, and each time she had been hurriedly escorted to her bedroom several minutes in advance. Each time, too, Afeni or Sam had stayed with her until the visitor had left, making sure she kept quiet and stayed away from the window. The second time, she had asked Afeni how they knew when people were coming.

'You know the things the cops use to catch speeders? Kind of a cable thing that just lays across the road, and when a car runs over it a signal goes off? We got a trap set up just this side of the fork, 'cause like there ain't nobody else but us on this road since old man Sonnenfeld died. Any time we hear that bell sound off – that one makes a noise like a cowbell only a lot louder – we know somebody's on the way here, and we just tuck you under wraps till they're gone.' Kate's face, always transparent, showed her disappointment, and Afeni laughed.

'No sense getting restless, girl. You just take it easy – you going to be with us a while yet.'

That took care of callers, and now the radio was off limits too. They really had thought of everything, damn them. Kate crept back down the narrow, slippery stairs to the safety of the second-floor hallway, where her presence could easily be explained if she were seen. There was yet another lock on one of the bedroom doors, which she supposed must be Conor's, so she couldn't snoop around inside. (She doubted, anyhow, if she would have had the nerve.) All three locks were recessed into the wood, and thin matching panels could be slid over to hide them. They would not have fooled a professional searcher, but to a casual visitor nothing would show to raise questions or excite suspicion.

While she had never been naive enough to dismiss her keepers as – what was Conor's phrase? – 'a gaggle of idiots', she certainly hadn't realized how relentlessly thorough they were. Beneath the amiable charade of hospitable country folk entertaining a friend from the city, she was as much a prisoner as if she were in Sing Sing. It seemed extraordinary that they should have gone to all this trouble, when they could so easily have kept her locked in her room. It would have been unpleasant: lack of exercise, squalid sanitary arrangements, fear and loneliness and grinding boredom. It would, when she thought about it, have been horrible, but it wouldn't have killed her, and it would have been infinitely simpler for them. She supposed it was Conor's peculiar conscience she had to thank. He had taken her away because he needed her, but he would inflict nothing upon her that was not essential to the operation. There was another possibility she recognized, which was that she was being deliberately seduced – not sexually, but emotionally. It would be hard to feel vindictive towards people who had put themselves at risk just to make her comfortable.

None of this was bringing her any closer to the main objective, which was to get the hell away. It was all very well being told to relax, take it easy, make the best of it; she couldn't. She was as quietly frantic as a cat in a box. They'd buttered her paws all right. They had been kind; but she was dependent for her life upon that kindness, clinging to it and at the same time despising her dependence. She had to be her own person again: Kate Harper, not 'child' or 'my dear girl' but a young woman with a car and a bank account and credit cards, and the inalienable right to go where she pleased and do as she chose. If only she had been free to leave when she liked, she would have wanted to stay. The farm was less a jail than a huge, live plaything, and its orderly working made her preoccupations at Beresford seem, by contrast, both boring and unnecessary. She was beginning to learn a little about the ancient, complex skills of survival, the knowledge painstakingly amassed since the day the first hairy ancestor dragged a sharp stick across the first unpromising field, and it was a lot more absorbing than English Lit. But she hadn't been asked, that was what stung. She had been scooped up and dumped down here, was being held here, constrained (however considerately) to submit to an authority she did not acknowledge, and she couldn't stand it.

Objectively, Kate understood why these unlikely people had undertaken such a bizarre conspiracy. Although with the recent withdrawal of US troops from Vietnam the antiwar movement had lost much of its force, there were still plenty of people, friends of hers among them, who agonized over the continuing saturation raids on Cambodia and the huge sums funnelled into South Vietnam to prop up that crumbling regime. The people at the farm, instead of merely deploring the situation, had decided to do something about it, that was all. She wasn't even opposed to their aims. Her father droned on sanctimoniously about peace, but there was no peace, and wouldn't be while he stood at the president's elbow, prodding and manipulating that dim, beleaguered man. She was quite prepared to admit that it was grotesque for people to be dying in Vietnam while Pen Harper jetted impressively around the world, issuing statements, conducting negotiations, addressing assemblies, and feeding as implacably as a lamprey on the fat substance of his own mystique. She had no fondness for him. He had made her mother wretched, and his obsessive, cold devotion to herself had nothing human about it that she could respond to. It was the sort of attachment a man might feel for an immensely valuable jewel, locked away in a safety deposit box. She was dear to him because she was his;

84

and also, perhaps, because she was beautiful.

Kate knew she was beautiful. It struck her as a not very interesting physical fact, like her height and her blood group and her double-jointed elbows. Given a choice, it was probably better to be nice looking than ugly, but it wasn't an attribute for which she could take any credit. Her father, she knew, felt differently. Secretary of State Harper's lovely daughter. '*Linda, linda!*' the crowds in South America had shouted, and he had appropriated the praise even while he seethed at the liberty. If Conor and his friends wanted to force his resignation, good luck to them. She didn't care, but she wouldn't be *used*. She wouldn't stay obediently revolving around the farm like a plane in a holding pattern while they plotted their careful moves out in the world. She wanted to go home, and she didn't intend to be stopped.

By day she was watched. They tried to be tactful about it, but she was watched all the time. If she wandered as far as the end of the vegetable garden, one of them would discover an errand in the same direction. When she went to the creek for watercress, Claire came too, 'for a breath of air'. But her door was not locked at night. There might be an alarm system, but she had examined the windows and doors as minutely as she could without being conspicuous about it, and she could see no sign of one. Possibly they took turns standing guard, but she didn't think so. They were all up early, looking clear-eyed and rested, with no telltale yawns over the breakfast table. In any case, she had to try. It was her only chance, and the sooner she took it the better, because these people were getting to her. A few more days exposed to their peaceable ways and the insidious rhythm of their life, with its seamless meshing of logical tasks, where everyone did what he or she could do best, and no one ever seemed harried or put-upon – a few more days of this and she would be theirs. They would have brought about the greening of Kate Harper, drawing her in with bonds more powerful than any chain, and she couldn't risk that.

Her forehead pressed against Annabel's satin flank, she squeezed the rubbery udders until her fingers ached. The milk tanged musically into the pail, and Conor told her how clever she was to have got the knack of it so quickly and what a help she was turning out to be. She smiled, and squeezed, and made her plans.

Jobie Parrish was good and mad. Miss Melvin had picked on him all day, and he couldn't seem to get hold of long division worth shit, and his mother had put margarine on the bread for his cheese sandwich again even though she knew right down well he only liked plain bread with cheese because he'd told her and *told* her. And when he got home, after trudging all that way from the corner where the school bus let him off, she had been so taken up with that stupid new baby, who couldn't do anything interesting but only sleep and squawl and piss itself, that Jobie might just as well not have been there at all.

He had removed himself, therefore, in a monumental huff, and gone off with the old .22 to take out his annoyance on the squirrels and pigeons of the countryside. And even that trusted safety valve was letting him down; it was one of those days when he couldn't hit the side of a barn. Glowering hideously, he took a great kick at an unoffending tussock of grass, caught his toe in something, and went ass over elbow, which was about what he might have expected, considering the way his day had been going.

He sat up, using language that would have made his mother faint, and looked to see what had tripped him. It was a brown leather strap. He tugged on it, but the ends seemed to be caught. Investigating, he found the strap was attached to a leather satchel. The satchel part was snagged halfway under a bush, which was why he hadn't seen it right away. He freed it, and settled down cross-legged to examine his prize. It was good leather, he could tell that, thick and glossy, with a lovely rich smell. He unfastened the heavy brass catch and looked inside. It was even lined with leather (a different kind, all soft), but there was nothing much in it: a comb, a lipstick, a pocket-size pack of Kleenex, a beat-up Zippo lighter and half a pack of Kents, a felt pen, and a wallet.

Feeling guilty, he opened the wallet. A few coins and a house key were in one side of it, and there were some notes. He counted them: two tens, a five, and a couple of singles. There was nothing else in the wallet except a driver's licence and a bunch of credit cards. Jobie knew what the cards were because he'd seen pictures of them in the newspaper advertisements, but he'd never seen a real one before. His father didn't approve of them; he said they could get a man in debt and in trouble faster than a crooked poker game.

The name on the cards meant nothing to him, and the driver's licence was different from his pa's and bore the imprint of a state far away to the northeast. That decided him. It wasn't like taking something that belonged to a neighbour – the satchel must have been lost or abandoned by some careless traveller from out of state, and it didn't look as if the person who owned it was about to come back for it. The leather had been rained on, and there'd been no rain since the thunderstorm on Sunday night. The find was his, God had left it there for him to fall over, and there was no sense letting a thoughtful gesture like that go to waste. It was the satchel itself he really coveted; it would be just right for him to carry his lunch in, instead of a cruddy old paper sack that fell to pieces when it rained. Nobody else at school had anything half so fancy, and it sure would take the starch out of old Emily Cotton and her store-bought tin box with the pictures of Mickey Mouse and Goofy and the special place inside to write your name.

The money tempted him very much. It was more cash than he'd ever seen in one place at one time, and he hated to leave it behind. But taking money was stealing, real stealing, they could send you to reform school for that. Besides, how could he ever spend it without being found out? Everybody knew the Parrishes were as poor as Job's turkey, never mind how hard his pa worked. So were most of the folk around the Hollow, except for those uppity Cottons. Jobie got a quarter a week, provided he did his chores and finished his homework before supper, and if he started flashing ten-dollar bills around, Sheriff Black would get him for sure.

After long thought, he took two quarters from the change purse, closed it, then opened it again and took out a dime, and shoved the wallet back under the bush. He put the Kleenex, the lipstick, the lighter, and the cigarettes with it. He kept the comb – it was a nicer one than his – and the felt pen, which was something he'd wanted for a long time but never had the willpower to save up for. A lot of boys would have kept the cigarettes and the lighter, but Jobie didn't smoke. Miss Melvin said smoking cigarettes gave you cancer. Jobie's grandfather had died of cancer, year before last, and he didn't want to go that way; by the end the old man must have weighed less than he did.

He stood up, slung the satchel over his shoulder, and set off briskly for home. He hadn't done his homework yet, and it would take him at least an hour to get back to the house. He didn't usually come this far except on weekends or school vacations, but he'd been walking off his mad and hadn't paid attention. For his next birthday, when he was twelve, pa had promised him a watch, but he could tell time pretty good by the sun, and he reckoned he was running it close. Two rotten pages of long division to get through before supper, or pa would dock him a nickel off his allowance. Then he remembered the sixty cents in his jeans pocket and felt better, but he did not slacken his pace. Catching hell from pa and having his mother sigh and go on at him about how he had to do his schoolwork so he could go on and make something of himself was almost worse than losing a nickel.

He dropped off the satchel in a dark corner of the shed, walked into the house whistling, and spread out his homework on the kitchen table, dutiful as could be. It was just his bad luck that pa should decide, when supper was through, to fix that wobbly chair leg his mother had been complaining about for a month. Jacob Parrish came back from the shed with a hammer and nails in one hand and the satchel in the other.

'All right, boy,' he said, 'where'd you get this?'

'I found it, pa. I found it today when I was out huntin', over to Little Crick.'

'What you hide it for?'

'I – oh, gee, pa, please lemme keep it. I can put my lunch in it for school and my pencil box and ever'thing. It's just an old thing somebody throwed out. *Please* lemme keep it!'

'Jobie Parrish, do you think I am a fool? Bag like this must have cost twenty, thirty dollars, and it ain't hardly been used. You didn't take it from nobody, did you?'

'No, sir. I found it, like I said. It was lyin' under a bush, and the strap was stickin' out, and I caught my foot and tripped, and that's how I come to find it.'

'And when you found it, was it prett' near empty, the way it is now?'

Jobie had often wished he could lie to his father; it would make his life so much easier. He could lie to plenty of other people, and frequently did, because adults had such cockeyed ideas that often it was kinder to lie than go upsetting them with the truth. But when his father fixed him with those steady eyes that somehow managed to look hopeful in spite of everything, he just couldn't seem to get his tongue around the words. His shoulders drooped in defeat.

'No, sir, it wa'n't.'

'What all else was in there?'

Jobie told him.

'What you do with it, son?'

'I stuck it back under the bush. It's all there, just the way I found it, except –' he gulped '– except I took sixty cents.'

His father held out his hand, and Jobie dug down into his

pocket and handed over the money. It was kind of a relief, in a way, though he minded about the satchel. He didn't even mind about that quite so much when pa put his arm around him and gave him a very hard hug.

'You are a good, truth-tellin' boy, and I am proud of you. Now about how far is it to this bush, would you say?'

'It's a good hour, walkin' steady – hour to get to it, that is, and an hour to get back.'

'Too late to go now, then; it'd be dark before we was halfway there. You show me the place in the morning, and then I'll give you a ride to school in the pick-up so you won't be late, and I'll drop the whole caboodle off at the sheriff's office. Might even be a reward out on it, you never know. Meantime, Jobie, you get yourself off to bed, and don't forget to brush your teeth.'

After Jobie was in bed, his mother sat rocking the baby, who was fussing again. The doctor in town said it was just colic, but she didn't know; didn't seem like Jobie had been fretful this way when he was a baby, but that was years ago and maybe she'd forgotten. She sighed.

'Twenty-seven dollars and some-odd cents. That's an awful lot of money, Jacob, to be just givin' away like it was a piece of candy. Whoever left that bag layin' out there, don't seem like it was nothing to 'em. And so many things we need.'

'I know, honey. But it ain't ours. Don't you worry now, I saw Ben Cotton just this mornin', and he said he might be gettin' his house painted. He can't see to it himself on account of his arthritis, and he was figurin' he'd ask me to help him out. So don't you worry none.'

He rubbed her shoulder gently and went to work on the chair.

If you're silly enough to run away, you'll be brought back, Conor had warned her, but if she could only get clear her chances looked good. It hadn't been difficult to figure out the best time for the break. Like all farm households, this one rose with the sun, and she would need all the margin she could get. But she would not be able to move fast in the dark, and the risk of injury was greater. With luck, her absence would not be noticed until Claire came in to call her at a quarter to seven. If she could slip out just before dawn, that should give her a useful start.

It wasn't much, but it would have to do. After all, Conor wasn't psychic; he couldn't look into a crystal ball like the Wicked Witch of the West and track her down. Dogs would have posed a danger, but she couldn't see old Bagel making a very reliable bloodhound. It was as much as that animal could do to find his own feet. She didn't know which direction would lead her to the nearest town or how far away it was or even what it was called, but this wasn't the desert. It was farm country, and somewhere there must be other human beings.

What kind of a story she would tell when she encountered one, she hadn't quite decided. On the one hand, Conor and the rest of them were criminals; criminals of an unusual sort, certainly, but that didn't alter the fact that kidnapping was a very grave offence, and if they failed this time they might try again with someone else. The president himself had a young daughter; suppose they went after her? On the other hand, there were those other children to be considered, the ones she had never seen; the boy who had built the model planes in the attic, the little girl whose gingham dresses, pink and lilac and blue, hung in her bedroom closet. With their parents in prison, what would become of them?

Perhaps Kate could pretend she had lost her memory. After all, no one could prove she hadn't. Or she could say she'd been drugged and then dumped from a car. After all their kindness, she didn't want to be responsible for sending these people to jail. She just wanted to go home, and if that showed a lack of civic conscience then tough. The vast resources of the Secret Service were there to protect the president's family, and if they weren't up to it, we might as well give up and hand over the country to anyone who could be bothered to run it.

She tried not to think about the escape except when she was alone. It wouldn't be safe, with such eyes observing her. Conor often seemed able to pick her thoughts out of the air, and Chuck, too, was preternaturally acute. It was better to keep her mind empty, as if she were passing a savage dog that would fly at her if it sensed fear. After supper Sam brought out his guitar and sat on a stool by the fire, singing melancholy songs in a husky, pleasant half-voice.

> '*The water is wide, I cannot get over,*
> *And neither have I wings to fly . . .*'

The companionable peace that permeated the kitchen, as alluringly as the smell of vanilla in a pastry shop, rasped Kate's nerves almost to screaming point. If she was going she wanted to go now, this minute, away from the warmth and the people who were becoming so perilously attractive. The piglet snored contentedly at one corner of the hearth, and at the other Bagel twitched and hunted in his dreams. Claire sat in the rocker patching a pair of Chuck's jeans, the steel-rimmed spectacles she used for close work poised halfway down her nose. Afeni's long limbs were folded on the hearthrug, her head just touching Sam's thigh as he played. Kate and Chuck shared one settle, and Conor lay draped the length of the other, his heels higher than his head, a cat idly kneading at his stomach. Even sprawling, his body looked trim and serviceable, ready for emergencies, and it occurred to Kate that she had never seen him truly off guard. Like a mountain lion blinking in the sun, he was relaxed but totally aware, the muscles ready to bunch at an instant's notice.

She had dreamed about him the night before. In the dream, he came in to her out of the snow, with ice on his eyelashes and in his hair. He had on an immense orange-coloured cloak that fell to his feet. Smiling, he had wrapped its folds about her, and together they had swept through the door and high into the air, soaring safe and warm between the frozen stars. It was the most beautiful dream she had ever had; waking, the memory of it scared her sick.

After tonight, if she was lucky, she would never see him again. No more anxious hollowness under the ribs when she entered a room and found him in it, no more crawling of the scalp when they passed in the yard, no more the constant sense of something feral and dangerous, too lightly leashed. How soothing it would be to return to the familiar routines. A movie on Friday with Bill and Howard and Mary Beth; Saturday evening at Larry's with Charlie, poor Charlie; Sunday dinner at home, roast chicken with mashed potatoes and beans, while in the basement the washing machine thumped and gurgled over a week's accumulation of her dirty clothes. How safe and comfortable it would be.

Unexpectedly, a tiny treacherous voice somewhere inside her whispered, 'How *dull*.' She repressed it at once and willed herself to concentrate on Charlie Eisinger, poor Charlie who was so devoted to her, and whose devotion had been rewarded with a punch on the head and a hypodermic full of dope. She wondered what he was doing, and if he was all right.

Charles Belfort Eisinger sat on the edge of the cot and stared at the wall of the small, windowless room. He had finished his supper – or was it lunch? He was beginning to mix things up, particularly since they had taken away his watch. No, lunch had been a hamburger, cool and leathery, with some tired french fries and a carton of milk. Supper, the remains of which still sat on the metal table, had been ham and swiss on rye, with a salad of iceberg lettuce daubed with some anonymous dressing, a cardboard tub of wilting vanilla ice cream, and acrid coffee in a Styrofoam container. Two little paper bags of sugar, with blurred pictures of the birds of North America on one side and 'Enjoy Your Meal' on the other, and a wooden tongue depressor in place of a spoon. A minuscule plastic bucket declared itself as containing non-dairy creamer; the ingredients, printed in incredibly tiny type, sounded better suited for wall paint than human consumption. Charlie, who normally drank his coffee with cream, refused to touch it. It was one of the few choices he could still make.

Presently the man who never spoke would come for the tray (lightweight plastic, quite unsuitable for belting anyone). After that another man would come and sit down on one of the two chairs bolted to the floor on each side of the metal table, and Charlie would get up and go sit down on the other chair, and it would start all over again.

'But I've told you all this stuff already,' he complained, half an hour later. 'I told that guy in New Lymington, the one that brought me down here, wherever the hell this is, and I told the other guy yesterday, twice, and I told you this morning. This afternoon I told that shrink with the ink blots, and now you want me to tell you *again*?'

'That's right, Mr Eisinger. Just run through it again for me. Maybe you'll remember something more, something that just slipped your mind. These things can happen, you know. Now let me see, let's start when you left the restaurant.'

'Larry's. We always go there. I guess it was around ten after eleven when we left. We just came out and got in the car and drove off.'

'And you didn't notice anyone waiting there? You didn't see a car pull out and follow you?'

'No. I already told you, no. I don't say there wasn't – I guess there must have been – but I didn't notice anything. Why should I? I wasn't expecting a thing like that to happen.'

'You say, "There must have been"; why do you say that, Mr Eisinger?'

'Well, it's obvious. How would they know where we were going unless they followed us?'

'They couldn't have known in advance?'

'How? I'd never – Kate and I had never been up there before.'

'As I understand it, your normal pattern of behaviour on Saturday evenings was to take Miss Harper to dinner and then drive her back to her dormitory immediately afterwards; is that right?'

'Yes, but –'

'Then why, on this one occasion, did you vary that pattern? Why, instead of taking her back to the campus, did you take her to Adams Park?'

'Christ, man, I *told* you.'

'Tell me again.'

'I took her there because I was hoping to – to fool around a little, see if I could get some action. I've known Katie since we were kids, and she acts like we still were, and I wanted – I wanted – oh shit, this is embarrassing.'

'There's no need to be embarrassed, Mr Eisinger. I'm a married man, and nobody gets to be a married man without – ah – fooling around a little, as you put it. That's normal. In fact if you had felt no desire to fool around, given the opportunity, with an attractive young woman like Miss Harper, I might be inclined to worry about you. But you've never had any problems of that sort, have you?'

'No!'

'Never. Not even in prep school. You've never done anything, anything at all, that you might be ashamed of. Nothing someone might have found out about. Nothing that could be used, perhaps, to exert pressure on you.'

'No. I told you. I haven't done anything, nobody's ever tried to pressure me, and I wasn't blackmailed into taking Katie up to Winter Hill so somebody could kidnap her. You people are insane; you think everybody else plays the same kind of games you do. I took her up there because I've been buying her filet mignon every Saturday for months and I've never even got to first base and neither has anyone else. The older buys call her the Snow Queen. Guess I was hoping to warm her up a little. And that's all. Can't I have a cigarette?'

He looked longingly at the pack of Marlboros in the other man's shirt pocket.

'Fire Department regulations, Mr Eisinger. No smoking in the building. Now this man came out of the trees, you say, and he appeared to be injured or in some kind of extremity, and you went to his assistance. He was the only man you saw?'

'Yeah. He was lying face down, coughing his lungs up, and I was afraid he'd choke. I started to turn him over, and he wrapped his arms around my neck and heaved, and next thing I knew I was down and he was kneeling on my chest. I tried to buck him off, and he slugged me, and then while I was still groggy from the punch he stuck a needle in my leg and I went out, and that's all I remember till those cops showed up around daybreak.'

'And you can't give us a better description of the man?'

'It was the middle of the fucking *night*, for Christ's sake! Sure, there was a moon, but barely into the first quarter, and how much can you see by moonlight anyhow? He was sort of medium tall, and sort of skinny, and he had dark, wavy hair. I think it was dark; it's hard to tell in that kind of light. It *looked* dark. I never got a real look at his face. If you brought him in here right now, I might recognize him or I might not. He was just ordinary looking.'

The other man sighed.

'So you have no idea how many people were involved?'

'The only one I saw was the guy that slugged me. There might have been an army, out there in the trees, or he could have been on his own. I would think it's likely there was at least one other person, though, to grab Katie while my guy was taking care of me, otherwise she'd have taken the car and gotten out of there, like I told her to.'

'I notice you say "one other person", not "one other man". Does that mean you think it might have been a woman?'

'For all I know, it might have been the Easter Bunny.'

'You don't seem to be taking this very seriously, Mr Eisinger.'

'Oh, I'm serious. When the victim of a crime gets treated like a criminal himself, I think it's pretty *damn* serious. First I get beaten up and drugged, then I get arrested, then I get shoved into a limo with funny glass in the windows, shanghaied half across the country by a bunch of goons who won't answer questions, locked up in a fancy nuthouse, and harassed by relays of imbeciles asking impertinent questions and making some very unpleasant implications, I might add. You can bet your bureaucratic ass I think it's serious, and the first thing I'm going to do when I get my hands on a telephone is have the whole motherfucking bunch of you seriously fired. After that I'll find me a hotshot lawyer and sue the living shit out of whatever cockamamie government agency was dumb enough to hire you in the first place. Is that serious enough for you?'

'You have nothing to gain by being abusive. I've spoken to you before about these outbursts of hostility. They don't give at all a good impression. In fact Dr Lescher is extremely concerned about you. "An aggressive, immature personality, poorly integrated, with a tendency to indulge in fantasies of revenge, and consequent impaired perception of reality." That's what he put in his report after your interview this afternoon. You are not about to have anyone fired, sir, and it would be more appropriate if you began instead to consider the ambiguity of your own situation. Miss Harper has disappeared. Presumably she was abducted, and you were with her when it happened. You are the only witness, and a far from satisfactory one. We'll return to that a little later. Right now I'd like to go back to that trip you made to Canada last summer. You visited Toronto, did you not?'

'You know I did.'

'And while there, according to your statement, you made contact with a draft evader by the name of Kevin Clarke.'

'I met a guy in a bar.' Charlie was getting very tired. 'We got talking, and it came out he used to go to Beresford too. We had a couple of beers together. If you want to call that making contact, then I guess that's what I did.'

'And the man Clarke, on that occasion, introduced you to a woman named Anne Mallaby, whom you took to dinner the following evening and subsequently accompanied to her apartment, where you remained overnight.'

'Yeah.'

'Do you still maintain that you were at that time ignorant of Miss Mallaby's connection with the antiwar movement, and the part she had played during the Mayday riots in Washington, D.C.?'

'All I knew about Anne Mallaby – and all I know now, as far as that goes – is she was a friendly, sexy, good-looking broad, and I liked her a lot. We didn't get into politics. We got into bed.'

'Would you say you were in the habit of having sexual relations with women you have known only a few hours?'

On and on it went, over the same well-trampled ground. Charlie's head ached, and his back ached – the metal chair was designed for shorter legs than his, and a less massive body – and when he rubbed his eyes, or shifted in his seat, the man across the table commented on it smugly, as if he had somehow betrayed himself. At last the interrogator shut off the tape recorder and went away.

Charlie threw himself onto the cot, which was inches too short for him, and lay staring at the ceiling light behind the wire grille. The light was never turned off. He had been wearing the same clothes for three days now, and they felt as if they were growing to him. There was a dwarf-scale closet off his room with a seatless toilet and a sink, and they'd let him have a toothbrush and a free-sample-sized tube of toothpaste, but that was it. He could understand, just barely, their refusal to give him a razor, but surely an electric shaver wouldn't have hurt? He despised the sight of himself in the steel mirror over the sink, stubbled and scruffy, hopelessly one down compared to his pressed and barbered inquisitors. No one had said it in so many words, but he got the message anyhow: showers and shaves and clean underwear were not a right but a privilege, bestowed only upon those who cooperated. Apparently they didn't consider him cooperative enough.

The open-ended misery of his predicament had come to occupy his mind to the exclusion of everything else. Katie's plight, which normally would have driven him frantic with worry, had receded until it seemed little more than a mechanical failure, the front tyre blowout that had caused the accident in which he had broken his back. If it hadn't been for Katie, none of this would be happening. After a while he turned over, his feet hanging over the end of the bed, and laid his cheek on the thin, hard pillow and fell asleep.

The night alarm system had been there all along, practically under Kate's nose, and she'd never even recognized it. She had been looking out for something scientific and modern, like the special locks, not for a safeguard going back a couple of thousand years. She had been so careful, too. It took her what felt like an hour just getting down the stairs, hugging the wall where the treads were less apt to creak, shifting her weight an ounce at a time from toes to ball of foot to heel to toes; barefoot, her loafers clutched in one hand while the fingertips of the other skimmed lightly, desperately lightly over the varnished pine boards that lined the stairwell.

The hallway reached at last, she padded with infinite stealth to the porch door. If she went out through the kitchen, Bagel might bestir himself for once and bark. Besides, Chuck and Conor would find the back door unbolted when they turned out at first light to fetch the cows for milking, and they would be after her before she'd had a fair chance to get clear. Greased with the Chapstick she had stolen from the bathroom cabinet, the bolt on the door to the porch slid back without a sound. She eased the door shut behind her – the hinges squeaked a little, enough to make her throat close up but not, she realized thankfully, enough to wake even the lightest sleeper on the floor above – and crossed the porch. It was dark still, but not quite pitch dark. She could see where the screen door was, and she felt along the door frame for the hook and, holding her breath, slipped it free.

She flowed like a cat around the edge of the half-open door, pushed it to, and picked her way down the rough steps, feeling with her toes for the edge of each tread. Now there was hard-packed dirt under her feet, gritty and cool. She drifted silently across the yard, past the barn, hulking black against the sky that was scarcely a half tone less dark. She almost walked into the bumper of the Jeep, which had been left parked nearer the house than usual, and paused a moment to regain her balance and her breath. Dew-wet grass thrust softly between her bare toes as she approached the pen where the geese were shut up at night. And then all hell broke loose.

It was enough to wake the dead, let alone the household: a fearsome chorus of honking, guttural complaint, like a kennel of hounds with the croup. For perhaps three seconds she was numbed by it, immobilized with shock. Then she took off like a rocket, flying over ground she could not see, following the route she had planned the day before: head for the creek, left at the watercress beds, and then straight into the woodland that bordered the pasture. Once in the woods she could slow down – would have to slow down if she didn't want to trip and sprain something or break something – for by then she would be shielded from the house. The geese were still at it, trumpeting the news of her escape with spiteful persistence, but she could not give up now. She ran headlong into the first of the trees, bruising her cheek and shoulder, and halted momentarily, just long enough to pull on her loafers. She glanced back towards the house. There was a glow at one of the upstairs windows, and as she turned away she heard an engine start up, and then the stammering whine of the pick-up. *Keep clear of the road then, stick to the rough country, and you may make it yet.* Slowly, carefully, restraining the urge to run, she moved on through the woods.

It was the geese that woke Conor. The racket they made was so extravagant he almost missed the sudden electronic chatter from the black leather-covered box that stood, open-lidded, on the table next to his bed. He pulled on a pair of jeans, kicked his feet into shoes, grabbed a sweatshirt, a flashlight, and the black box. On the bed in the room next door Afeni and Sam lay intertwined, covers on the floor, black limbs and white in a particoloured tangle. Sam was not a man who could safely be startled while he was sleeping. Conor found a damp washcloth hanging on the old-fashioned wooden towel horse, balled it up, and pitched it at his target, hitting him squarely between the shoulder blades. Sam was off the bed and into a practised crouch, hands reaching, in one smooth movement.

'Cool it; it's me. The girl's gone. You take the pick-up and cover the left fork, I'll take the right. I've got the monitor. Stay in touch, but I don't want her picked up right away unless she heads for the Crossing. I'll let you know if she changes course. And watch what you say over the radio.'

Across the hall, Chuck was already half dressed, the flame of the bedside candle leaping in the draught as he flapped into a shirt.

'She fooled us,' he said equably when Conor came in. 'Miss Goody Two-Shoes is tougher than she looks. Shall I take Barley?'

'Yes, but there's no rush; it won't be light for another half-hour. I'm leaving now, and Sam's taking the pick-up. As soon as you and the pony can see where you're going, take the handset and move out and cover the woodland. As of now, she's going due east, but check in with me by radio before you leave. Keep in touch. You're the one that's most likely to spot her. I think she's smart enough to stay off the road. If you do, call in, okay Chuck? Don't pick her up until I say so.'

Claire was sitting up in bed, swathed in yards of calico, looking distressed.

'Oh mercy,' she said. 'Oh, that poor child.'

'Poor child my bloody foot. Stupid little pest. You and Afeni will have to see to the milking; God knows when we'll be back.'

He raced down the stairs, collected the keys from the cupboard, tossed one set up to Sam as he appeared on the landing, and ran to the Jeep. Even as he ran, he knew there was no real need for haste. On foot as she was, she'd have needed at least a half-hour's start to be beyond the range of the monitor, and it was in the highest degree unlikely that she would meet anyone at this hour in the barren tract of country she was making for.

Barring miracles, she couldn't get away. They had been careful to make that impossible. All the same, he felt a powerful pressure on him to stay close to her, not necessarily to recapture her at once – it might be better to let her run her string out, get the drive to escape out of her system once and for all, and collect her at leisure when she was tired of running – but because he was worried about her. She could break a leg or even her intractable damned neck. As far as he knew, Conor had fathered no children of his own, though he'd spent most of his adult years repairing other people's. Now he had a sudden, chilling glimpse of what it must be like to be a parent. Strings, attachments, haunting and unreasonable anxieties. Never a moment's peace.

He peered ahead at the dirt road, straining for a sight of her, knowing she would not be there.

'You do yourself a mischief, my girl,' he muttered, helplessly split between anger and love, 'and I'll wring your neck.'

Earlier, Kate's shirt had been soaked with sweat. The sun was high now – it must be close to noon – but the heavy cotton had dried on her. She was getting dehydrated, and the pitiless sunshine baked the moisture out of the fabric faster than her body could produce it. She had thought of herself as in good shape, but the years of winter skiing and summer tennis had done little to prepare her for a forced march under these conditions. She had brought no water with her and had found none fit to drink; only a muddy pool at the edge of a marsh, and that had tasted so vile she spat it out and settled for wetting her head and arms. She had longed to take off her loafers and soak her feet in the scummy puddle, but the risk that, once off, the shoes might never go on again had held her back. Her mouth was full of thick, gummy stuff that seemed to form again as fast as she got rid of it. She was near water now, though; she could almost smell it. Ahead the scrub was broken by an irregular line of trees, real trees with their roots in cool, damp earth. There must be water there.

There was. She lay down on the bank of the little stream and plunged her cupped hands into it. Too much cold water too fast could make you sick; she knew that and tried to be moderate. Indeed, it was such a difficult, clumsy way to drink that she gave up before her thirst was fully satisfied and began splashing water over her shoulders and head, shivering in the sudden, beautiful coolness. The dappled shade of the trees was seductive, the grass she lay on cool and silky-soft. *I ought not to be out here in the open; they might see me,* she fretted. *I ought to get back into that horrible scrub.* Intellectually she was positive she had shaken off any pursuit long ago, but her feelings were not amenable to reason, and she still felt hunted. *If I stay here, I'll fall asleep and they'll catch me. I have to find a house. There must be a house some place,* she thought, remembering the earlier disappointment of the cabin that had turned out to be empty, abandoned, with the morning-glory vines growing thick over the windows, and the half loaf of bread on the table mummified, hard as brick. *I have to find a house with people, get help, get home to mother. I have to get home.*

She forced herself up, wincing, and plodded on, bearing away from the cool, sweet water, moving awkwardly because her feet were painful. She wished she knew what time it was. Out of habit, she glanced again at her wrist, but there was only the blank steel cuff clasped around it. Her watch was lying on a shelf in the repair shop in New Lymington, with a ticket tied to the strap. Old Mr Leibowitz had promised it for Monday – 'I make it for you special quick, doll, only for you because you asked so nice' – and here it was Wednesday. He would think she was thoughtless and casual, wheedling him into fixing the watch over the weekend as a favour, and then not even bothering to come in and collect it. Ridiculous tears of frustration smarted in her eyes because Mr Leibowitz would be thinking badly of her when it wasn't her fault and she was in such trouble.

When she came on a narrow, dusty track that seemed to be going more or less the same way she was, she followed it gratefully. The surface was easier for her feet, and the trail, reassuringly, too narrow for vehicles – though really it was time she stopped brooding morbidly on possible pursuers and began thinking in terms of seeking out someone who would help her. Where there was a footpath there had been people, and would be again, but a road would be better.

She had followed the track no more than a mile when, somewhere ahead, she heard the bell. The noise was a flat, dry, irregular clank, but certainly it was a bell of sorts, and with it came a thin and dismal bleating. The track ran gently downhill, and she soon found herself in a small valley. At its farther end was a house, paintless and weathered grey, dwarfed by a sagging barn. Between Kate and the homestead grazed and wandered a scruffy herd of goats, one of them with a bell tied on a piece of string around its neck. A skinny little girl of seven or so, in torn jeans and a filthy T-shirt, seemed to be in charge of them.

'Hi,' the child said, revealing the lack of two upper front teeth. 'You want somebody?'

'Is anyone home at the house down there?'

'Sure. Daddy Samson and Daddy Paul're gone to market, but Mummy Charity's home. Mummy Grace and Mummy Consolation are there too, but they got their hands full with Daddy Brujo – he has been smack out of his fucking head since yesterday morning, like gone, you know? Mummy Consolation's madder'n hell. She can't figure out where he got the acid, and she says he knows damn well we don't allow none of that shit at Harmony. Not even pot, any more. She says soon as he gets back in his right mind she is going to toss that dumb fuck right out on his ass.'

She beamed gappily up at Kate. This vignette of home life in the valley was not encouraging, but it was the first inhabited place she'd found all day and might be the only one for miles, so she left the child cussing out an errant goat with sunny affability and a steel worker's choice of phrase, and made her way slowly towards the house.

This, at last, was the road home. There would be a telephone; she could call mother collect and mother would take care of everything. Someone would come fetch her and take her home. She supposed the police would want to question her, or the FBI or someone. She was certain, knowing her father, that he would have ignored the instructions to tell no one of her abduction. But she needn't say much, just that she had woken in the middle of the night, alone in the wilderness, and had started walking as soon as it grew light. She would say she remembered being with Charlie in Adams Park and being attacked there, but nothing more.

They might not believe her, but they couldn't prove she was lying. And the way she must look by now, it wouldn't take much to convince them she was in shock. For that matter, she supposed she really was in shock, at least to some degree. Probably that was why she felt so dreary, so emotionally dead, without any of the elation she had expected. She'd read somewhere that 'absence of affect' was one of the symptoms of shock.

On the porch a pretty, exhausted-looking woman was working at a wooden loom. She beckoned Kate up the steps, smiling.

'Hi, come and set awhile. You look real weary, honey. You come from far? Just let me get done with this little piece here, and I'll pour us some lemonade. It's real fine of the Lord to send the sunshine and I thank Him, but it sure does make for thirsty walking.'

There was something not quite right about the voice and the words as well. The country lilt was too studied, as if she were an actress in one of those TV series gluey with neighbourliness and the old simple values. Kate registered the anomaly without interest. This young woman with the tired eyes was a link with the real world, beyond the claustrophobic circle of Conor and his friends. To Kate she was not so much a human being as a facility, like a petrol station.

'Could I use your phone? I lost my way, and I've been walking for hours. I need to call my family and tell them where I am.'

It occurred to Kate as she spoke that she didn't in fact have any idea where she was, not even which state, and she'd better find out. But already the woman was shaking her head.

'Why honey, we don't have the telephone; we live close to the bone here, you know? No phone, no electricity, no trucks or cars. Paul and Samson took the buggy to market first thing with a load of goat cheese and eggs and lettuce, and when they get home maybe one of them could give you a ride into town, if the pony ain't too tired. But right now, best thing you can do is take a little rest. You sure look like you could use it.'

'You don't understand. I'm sorry, but I really do have to get word to my mother right away, it's an emergency.' Kate was beginning to panic. It was like one of those dreams where everything will be all right if you can only run, but your shoes are nailed to the floor. The woman rose from the loom and took her by the arm.

'Wish I could help you out, I truly do, but there is no way until the men come home. Now you step inside and have a nice glass of cold lemonade and lay down awhile, out of the sun.'

The terrible sound of sobbing had been faintly audible on the porch, but Kate had been so absorbed in her own concerns she had scarcely noticed it. Once indoors it was inescapable, filling the untidy room to suffocation. On a folded sleeping bag in one corner crouched a man. His legs were drawn up, his arms wrapped tightly around his shins, and his forehead drooped on his knees. Kate could not see his face at all, it was hidden by a mass of long, dark hair that swayed from side to side as he rocked and wailed in unimaginable sorrow. Beside him on the floor, hieratic and unmoving, like supporting figures on a tomb, sat two young women. Both were dressed, like the weaver, in long crumpled cotton dresses, one a baleful shade of plum and the other a stagnant green.

Looking at the girl in green, Kate found her so familiar, yet somehow so deeply disconcerting, that it was a moment or two before she realized she was staring at a distorted mirror image of herself. The pale oval face, the straight golden brows over grey eyes, might have belonged to a twin sister, if the sister had been simultaneously neglecting her health and cultivating an assortment of inner furies. Even the hair, if it had been washed and cut shorter, would have been the same. Only the mouth destroyed the illusion: ravenous, bitter, its downward line betrayed such grievous disappointment that Kate felt like a privileged infant by comparison.

The shock of this bizarre resemblance was succeeded by a second jolt, this time purely feminine. That green dress was a four-hundred-dollar Italian import Kate had noticed in Bendel's window on her last trip to New York.

'He looks awful bad, Consolation,' said the woman who had brought her inside. 'You think we should try to get the doctor?'

'Let him sweat, the son of a bitch,' the girl in green answered shortly. 'If he weren't so sick, I swear to God I'd strangle him myself. Where did he ever get the stuff?'

'Nowhere around here, that's for sure. All you can pick up in the Crossing is grass, and not much of that. He must have brought it back from Silver Spring after New Year's.'

'But Paul went over every inch of him when he came back,' the third girl objected.

'Stashed it some place nearby. Oh, Grace, you know how they get, my daddy was the same way with his old bourbon. For every secret hoard mama threw out there was always a couple more she missed; it was like he was playing a game with her. "It'll kill me in the end, honey-button," he used to say with that shit-eating grin on his face, and he was right about that if nothing else.'

Charity turned away and poured greenish liquid from a pitcher into two glasses, thoughtfully fishing out a drowned fly with her finger before handing one of the glasses to Kate.

'We always put ginseng in it,' she said. 'It's a natural, healthy stimulant. Just if you're not used to the taste, it's a little strange at first.'

It was tepid and sour, with a musty overtone that reminded Kate of cellars full of mice, but it was wet. Repressing thoughts of the fly, she drank it down.

'See if Brujo'll take some; the vitamin C might help him.'

Consolation took hold of one of the man's hands and unfastened it, finger by finger, from its rigid grip on his ankle. She put the glass in his hand and wrapped the stiff fingers around until he was holding it. Still weeping, he lifted his head, and Kate saw his face for the first time. The tormented eyes, red slits between bruised and puffy eyelids, looked straight at her.

'Hi, Princess,' he said between sobs. 'When did you get here? You want some lemonade? It's pretty terrible stuff, I'll say that for it.'

The tears continued to roll down his plump, baby cheeks, soaking the dark stubble of his beard. One lodged in the corner of his mouth and he licked it in slyly, with the tip of his tongue.

'I'll drink your lemonade, and *you* drink *mine*,' he went on. ''Cause why? 'Cause they *put* something in mine; yes they did so they did. Thor-a-*zine*, they put in mine, I bet you. Good old zombie juice, so I'll quit em*barr*assing all you kind people and zonk out, and then you can take me back to Doctor Shithead Schwabing's cute little dungeon where the crazy people are. Why do you betray me, Princess? Why do you do Big Daddy's dirty work for him? He wants me dead, you know that? He let them send me to fucking *Nam* 'cause he was hoping I'd buy the farm out there, you know? Buy the old rice paddy and not come home no more. But I fooled him, I did, I fooled Big Daddy, 'cause I did not die, no sir, my sergeant he took care of me, he did. My sergeant, he took better care of me than Big Daddy ever done, or sainted-Mummy-up-in-heaven-with-the-angels, or *you*, Princess, you fucking bitch!'

Like a spring released he suddenly catapulted to his feet and dived at Kate, but the two girls were too quick for him. They grabbed him and wrestled him back onto the sleeping bag, and Consolation lay across his chest while Grace sat on his legs, until he stopped struggling and went slack, and the anguished crying began again.

'He thinks you're his sister,' Charity told Kate, as if that explained everything.

'Listen, oh, will you please *listen* to me!' Kate had had all she could take of Harmony and its alternate lifestyle. 'I have to get to a telephone, I *have* to. I was kidnapped, do you understand? By some radicals. My father's Pendleton Harper, the secretary of state, and these people kidnapped me but I got away. But they're looking for me and I have to get to a telephone, don't you see? Before they catch me. If you'll just show me which way to go I'll start walking, but I have to get to a phone before they find me. Oh please, you must help me!'

'Why that's a terrible story,' Charity said. 'That's just awful, but don't you fret, honey. You are safe here. It's twelve, thirteen miles to town, you never could walk that far, the shape you're in. You stay right here with us till Paul and Samson come; we won't let no bad people take you away. You stay right here and rest.' She took Kate's hand in hers, and stroked it lightly.

'I'm all right. Just tell me the way to go.'

'No, honey. You are in no shape for walking. Lord knows how you made it this far. I could not take it on my conscience to let you leave.'

Kate took a deep, shuddering breath.

'If they find me here, those people who were keeping me prisoner, they'll do anything to stop the police from finding out where I am,' she pointed out, trying to sound calm and logical. 'They are dangerous people, truly they are, and now that you've talked to me and you know who I am, you're in danger too. For your own sake, you have to help me get away, can't you see?'

Instead of answering, Charity cocked her head to one side, listening. All Kate could hear were the dry, hiccupping sobs of the boy Brujo, but Charity ran to the warped screen door.

'There's someone coming,' she said over her shoulder. 'A man on a pony, riding the same way you came. I can't tell who it is; he's too far off still.'

'Will you hide me?'

'Go in the barn. You can hide there. Use the other door and keep low, the woodpile's between you and him. Run, now!'

Inside the barn it was almost dark. The place was an obstacle course of neglected tools and miscellaneous rubbish, but in a corner Kate found a heap of old burlap sacks. They stank of mildew, but she burrowed in under them and, wriggling around, pulled the disgusting things over her, trying not to gag. Straining her ears, she picked up the clop of hooves on hard-packed dirt, and then a murmur of voices. After a while the voices ceased, and there was the sound of hooves again, fading, and then silence. She huddled under the sacks, half suffocated, while she mentally counted One-Mississippi, Two-Mississippi all the way to three hundred, and then cautiously dislodged the nasty covering and peered out. Her face was almost at ground level, so the first thing she saw, inches from her nose, was the boot. The leg belonging to the boot was wearing Levis, and she knew those Levis. Even in the gloom of the barn, she could make out the fresh patch, darker than the faded cloth around it and edged with meticulous feather-stitching, that stood out just below the knee. The evening before, she had watched Claire as she sat in the rocker sewing it in place.

Chuck leaned down and pulled her out of hiding.

'Me heap smart Indian,' he said complacently. 'Follow sign heap good. White-eye maiden come on back to reservation now, or this Indian miss Happy Hour in tepee, be plenty damn mad.'

It was the same nightmare to be lived through again, but with one difference. When Conor had trapped her in the cave she had been like a rabbit caught in the beam of a car's headlights, paralysed with dread, unable to speak or move. This time, desperation brought with it a reckless courage. The moment he let go her wrists she feinted to one side, dodged as he grabbed for her, and slipped past under his arm, racing for the doorway. As she reached it, it was suddenly blocked. She was going too fast to stop, and the momentum carried her, with an audible thud, tight into Charity's braced young body. She struggled furiously as the woman's arms gripped her, not cruelly but with practised competence.

'Easy, honey, hold still. I don't want to hurt you. My, Chuck, it's good you warned us about this one ahead of time, she came on pretty strong to start off with. If she hadn't gone and blown it with that crazy story about you-all kidnapping her, I'd just as likely have loaned her Paul's old bike and sent her on into town. Funny how they all seem to have this hang-up about being prisoners and like that – Brujo's the same way.'

'Poor girl, she had a bad time. It's lucky Conor is visiting us, otherwise I think we would have to put her back in the hospital.'

'Oh, don't do that, they treat them so bad. That place Brujo was locked up, it's nothing but a thousand-dollar-a-week snake pit – they used to beat up on him and everything. Alice Mary – Consolation, I mean – she said he had bruises all over his body, poor dumb baby. You take good care of this kid, you hear? Nobody knows what's good for addicts except their friends; they're the only ones have the patience to take all that shit. Peace and love is what she needs, and you and Claire and the rest of you can give her that better'n any hospital.'

'Don't worry, she'll be safe with us.'

'He is *lying*, can't you tell he's lying?' Kate was breathless with

107

rage. 'They *did* kidnap me, and I'm not an addict. I'm Catherine Harper. If you don't believe me, you just call the FBI – they'll tell you who I am!'

'Sure the FBI knows who she is,' Chuck said sadly, 'and if they ever find her they will throw away the key. You know how we feel about the Weathermen, Charity, but she was only a camp follower – they let her make the coffee while they made the bombs. Bad enough that her comrades exploited her, without letting her be chopped up in little pieces for a grand jury to chew on.'

'He's lying, he's lying–'

It was too much. Between fury, humiliation, and defeat, Kate started to cry. Charity stroked her hair.

'Shh now, honey, don't you cry. You go along with Chuck like a good girl, and another time when you feel better maybe he'll bring you over to visit.' She turned to Chuck. 'I got to go help out with Brujo so Grace can get some rest; this pregnancy of hers is a bummer, she just can't seem to stay awake. If he gets worse, can I send Paul over for Conor? He was so terrific before, he just about saved Brujo's life.'

'Sure, just let us know. He'll come if you need him. But I wish you people would get yourselves a telephone; that pony of yours would thank you if no one else did.'

'Well, I'll speak to Paul again, but you know what he'll say. "Corruption creepeth in by little and little" – that's what he always says. That's what he said when Samson wanted the tractor so bad. Tell Claire I was asking after her.'

The bay gelding stood quietly by the porch rail where he had been tethered, switching at the flies with his tail.

'Conor will meet us at the bridge with the Jeep,' Chuck told Kate. 'They don't like anything with a petrol engine coming on their land. Last fall, when they first moved in here, I brought the pick-up down with a load of hay, and Paul let the air out of all four tyres. The hay was a present, too.' He sounded more amused than indignant. 'You're limping,' the observant red man remarked alertly. 'Never mind, let's put you up on Barley.'

He lifted her into the saddle and began to walk the pony along the track.

'That Brujo,' he said, in a tone between pity and contempt. 'Some wizard. You ever see that Disney movie *Fantasia*? Mickey Mouse as the Sorcerer's Apprentice? That's Brujito, messing with more magic than he can handle. His real name is Alexander

108

Blair. He's Cator Blair's son. Dropped out of school, dropped out of college, now he's trying to drop out of life, the hard way. Last time this happened he started convulsing. Conor had to come over and sedate him. He was here three days and never went to bed. You picked the wrong people to run to, Kate. Those girls think Conor is the PR man for God.'

'I suppose that's why she believed all your lies, and when I tried to tell her the truth she thought I was raving,' Kate said resentfully.

'She knows us; she doesn't know you. You show up here, an obvious runaway, with some crazy tale of kidnappers and persecution, what do you expect? She has heard it all before, from Brujo. Did he tell you his father had him sent to Nam?'

'Yes, he did, but he looks too young to have been drafted that far back.'

'Brujo was never closer to Vietnam than the Maui Hilton. It was his elder brother, Cator Junior. Little Cat. Cat was a patriot, he believed all that crap from his daddy's speeches, and he volunteered to help save Asia for democracy. They brought him home in a bag, what they could find of him. That was the first time Brujo flipped out. In a way it's true, you know? He is as much a casualty of that crummy war as his brother was.' Chuck sighed and patted the pony's neck. 'Poor Cat, he was such a nice kid. Straight, moral, the Ten Commandments, all that. One time in Saigon he stopped an infantry colonel from raping a girl. She was a bar girl, and there are people who will tell you a prostitute can't be raped, which is like saying it's okay to steal from a store because they were going to sell the things anyhow. The colonel wasn't happy, and Cat got to spend a lot of extra time in the field, and a grenade got him, and the colonel felt pretty good about that. Until Sam knocked three of the colonel's teeth out and broke his jaw.'

'You and Sam knew the man?'

'Everybody knew everybody. For the Americans, it was a small war. Small, but very shitty. Look at us – all of us. Cat should be living in the suburbs with a sexy little wife and a baby and a dog, and Brujo should be in college and so should you. Afeni's brother lost a hand in Vietnam, and Conor lost his wife, and Sam – God knows what Sam lost. His mind, maybe.'

'I didn't know Conor's wife was killed in the war – he just said she was dead.'

'Why should he tell you? So you can be sorry for him?' Chuck spat. 'He would never tell you, but I will. Simone was born in Saigon – her father was French and her mother was *tonkinoise* – but she trained here in the States, at Cornell. Child psychiatry. Afterwards she went back. She wanted to use what she'd learned to help her own people. She specialized in traumatized children – amputees, burn victims, the blind. She spent two days a week at our clinic, and the rest of the time she worked at the orphanage at Cam Loc. She was killed when the orphanage was bombed.'

'Was it the North Vietnamese?'

'No, that time it was the South. It was a mistake, of course. Everyone was very sorry. Either way, the people were just as dead. Seventeen children were killed and three of the nursing nuns and Simone.'

'So that's why Conor is doing this – because of her.'

'I said that once, and he blew his stack. Said I was arguing *ad hominem* and my head needed an oil change. He said he and Simone were in a war zone because they chose to be, but the children had no choice. They committed the sin of being born in the wrong place, at the wrong time. Then he quoted from some writer – I forget the name: "They are punished for having been punished." He called it Belial's Law. Conor wants life to be fair, and it will never be fair, so he will never be satisfied. Such a civilized guy, so pleasant and polite – is that what you thought? Conor is the most truly angry man you will ever meet.'

Kate shivered in the burning sun. She had been right, then, to be afraid. Conor was dangerous, even his friends thought so.

'What happens now? What – what will he do?'

'To you?' He glanced up at her, eyebrows raised. 'Nothing. What did you think he would do, whip you? All you did was run away; we were prepared for that. There was an emergency procedure set up; it worked; we found you; that's the end of it. No harm done.'

'How did you find me, anyhow?'

'We heard you calling us.'

'But I didn't –'

'But you did.'

He touched the metal band on her wrist.

'In here is a homing device, a transmitter. Sam made it; he's brilliant at that kind of thing. He used to do it for the CIA; now he does it for us. He invented our early warning system, too, and all the other gadgets. The homing device sends out a continuous signal to a portable receiver. When the person carrying it, which

110

is you, is separated from the monitor by more than two hundred yards, the alarm goes off. The system is directional, so whoever has the monitor, which is Conor, can tell which way you're going. Science is wonderful.'

'That's not fair,' she complained, and realized how ridiculous that sounded as Chuck laughed.

'It's not supposed to be fair. But isn't it better for you to wear a little bracelet than to be locked in the cellar for two weeks? We do it this way because we don't want you to be miserable while you have to stay with us. You've done nothing wrong – you shouldn't suffer. But we can't let you run away. This – ' he tapped the cuff again ' – it's not "sporting". It doesn't give you a chance. That's why we use it.'

'You could have picked me up any time, then. Why did you wait so long?'

'That was Conor. He said if you were recaptured right away you would only try again another time. You have to be taught. No matter how far you run, his hand is there to bring you back. He warned you, but you wouldn't listen. This way you learn it for yourself, and you won't forget.'

'What if I'd met up with someone? Not those tame hippies of yours, someone from outside?'

'No one lives out this way now except the kids at Harmony, and they don't encourage visitors. Oh, there are small farms like ours to the west and north, but all those people have known Claire since she was a child. They belong to the dairy cooperative, like us. They are our friends and neighbours. Do you think they'd believe your story?'

'Jesus.' Kate wiped her forehead. 'There must be someone around here who isn't in your pocket.'

'Well, of course. There are all the people in town, but we wouldn't have let you get that far. And Claire's nephew works in the sheriff's office. He's the dispatcher. If any law headed out our way we wouldn't need to rely on the early warning system. We would know about it before they left town.'

'You mean Claire's nephew is in on this too? You've even got the sheriff's office sewn up?'

Chuck grinned and shook his head.

'No, no. Ollie thinks I have a still out in the woods. What a scandalous thing if Claire Bradley's husband were caught making moonshine! Ollie's about as sharp as a pound of wet leather, but he is a boy with strong family feelings. It would embarrass him very much to have his uncle in the lock-up. So you see, we don't take chances. When you leave us and go home, it will be because we have let you go. Right now, Kate, we are the only friends you have.'

This depressing statement was so clearly true that Kate could not argue, and they moved on in silence.

Presently they came to a plank bridge that spanned a small stream – the same stream, Kate guessed, that she had drunk from earlier. On the far side, ending at the bridge, was a road, unmetalled and full of potholes, but still navigable. The Jeep was parked there, with Conor behind the wheel peacefully smoking. He leaned over and opened the passenger door as they clattered across. Chuck helped her down from the saddle, and she stumbled over to the Jeep. Conor gave her a look that would have sheared marble.

'Get in,' he said, biting the words off.

'Brujo's in bad shape again,' Chuck said.

'What's he taken this time, do they know?'

'Acid, Charity thinks.'

'How spiffing. Just what we all needed. How bad is he? Should I have a look at him?'

'He's been crying since yesterday, and he's not making any sense.'

'Nothing out of the way in that. He hardly ever does.'

'No, but worse than usual. He thought Kate was his sister.'

'As I recall, Stephanie Blair has black hair, and she's about eight feet tall. I see what you mean. Dear oh dear, what a tedious fellow he is. I suppose I'd better go and feel his fornicating pulse for him. Good job I brought my bag. Oh, Chuck, call Sam on the radio, would you, and tell him to go on home? He's down at Bryan Fork with the pick-up. I shan't be long, I hope to God.'

Conor was back in half an hour, trotting the pony sedately down to the bridge.

'How is he?' Chuck asked.

'He dreams dreams and sees visions. He'll do for now, I think, but if he keeps this up he'll kill himself. Or somebody else, of course. Bugger the counterculture. How are you going to get home?'

'Very slowly. Barley is a little weary.'

'Put him in the back if you like. He can sit on your knee.'

'Or we could let him drive. Tell Claire I'll be home by supper time.'

112

Chuck floated up effortlessly into the saddle.

'Conor?'

'Yo.'

'I promised Kate you wouldn't beat her.'

'Did you indeed, and I was so looking forward to it. You really must curb this tendency to interfere in the simple pleasures of others.'

He gunned the engine and, with a wicked snarl, the Jeep lurched away up the road. Examining her feelings, which she was able to do without interruption since he did not address one word to her the whole way, Kate was taken aback to discover that the dominant one was embarrassment. She had thought she was being daring and resourceful, and all the time they had convoyed her unseen, like support boats keeping pace with a long-distance swimmer, waiting for her to give up and be hauled ignominiously aboard. Her head ached, her calves ached, her feet felt as if they'd been boiled in brine, but it was her pride that had taken the worst beating of all. *This way you learn it for yourself, and you won't forget.* The bastards, all of them, the rotten condescending bastards. It would have been better to be whipped.

At last they drew up in front of the house. Conor got out, dropped the keys into his pocket, and stood there watching while she took three agonizing steps.

'Feet bad?'

She nodded, speechless with pain.

'Serves you bloody well right.'

He dug his shoulder into her midriff and hoisted her inelegantly in a fireman's lift up the porch steps, dumping her down seconds later like a sack of flour in one of the kitchen chairs.

'I never knew such a girl,' he grumbled, fetching a shallow bowl from the cupboard under the dresser. 'Didn't they teach you anything at that school? You can't expect to go traipsing half across the county without any socks, for God's sake, and still be as good as you were.'

He filled the bowl with hot water, brought a bottle from the scullery and added a generous splash of liquid that made the water turn cloudy. He set the bowl down on the floor in front of her, squatted on his heels, and took one of her feet in his hands.

'This will hurt. Yell if you want to.'

Kate clenched her teeth and did not yell, but he was right, she wanted to. The shoes were full of blood, and it had dried and stuck. Getting the first one off was bad enough. Then he set that foot to soak in the water, and she had to endure the rasp of antiseptic on the raw flesh while he tackled the second shoe.

She sat in a trance of pain, eyes shut, nails grinding into her palms, and wondered if she was going to throw up or only faint. She did neither, and after a while the agony dulled down to a level that was, by comparison, almost enjoyable. She wouldn't have minded staying right there until she was a very old lady. Life would ebb and flow around her, babies would be born and grow up and marry and have babies of their own, and she would sit in the kitchen with her feet in a bowl of water and her eyes firmly closed. When she opened them, Conor was standing in front of her holding one of the blue stoneware mugs. Whatever was in it smelled strong and aromatic, and made her think of Christmas.

'Here,' he said irritably, 'get that down you.'

'Not unless you tell me what it is.'

'Cyanide, little suspicious. Do as you're told. It's Housekeeper's Ruin, actually – tea with brandy in it. Very good for sore feet. Drink up.'

'Don't you think she ought to eat something?'

Claire's voice. She was at the stove, stirring the contents of a huge pot. She looked hot and unhappy, and Kate wondered how long she had been in the room.

'Not yet. Later, after she's had some sleep. Anything you fed her now would probably come right back up again, and she's in a sorry enough condition without that.'

He hunkered down again with a towel in his hands. Carefully he patted dry the swollen, blistered feet. Then he threw out the water, came back with bandages and a tube of salve, and set to work.

'Chuck said you knew where I was the whole time.'

'Yes, we did.' He was concentrating on the dressings and did not look up. 'Sam and his miracles of electronic hello-there. Our resident wireman built us a little black box that sees all and knows all. That's how I found you the other time, when you hid in the cave. I had the box in the back of the Jeep. Since I brought you here we've used it to keep tabs on you whenever you weren't in plain sight, and at night it sits by my bed. You never had a hope, you know. Even without the geese we'd have been onto you in minutes, and after that all we had to do was stay within range of your transmitter. Talk about shooting fish in a barrel.' He sounded genuinely disgusted.

'Is it true you let me get all that way just to teach me a lesson?'

114

'Is that what Chuck told you? Put like that, it does sound a bit brutal. But yes, it was partly that. We can't have you pottering off every time the fancy takes you – it plays hell with the farm work. And after all, I did warn you.'

'What was the other reason?'

'Nosy wench, aren't you? This heel's a mess; you'll have to stay off it for a day or two. Oh God, I don't know. Pure cowardice, I suppose. I kept thinking about the first time you ran away and I caught you. You were so scared and you looked so – so beaten. Never felt such a pig in my entire life.'

'I didn't think people like you worried about that kind of thing. Full speed ahead – damn the torpedoes, and damn anybody that gets in the way. Isn't that what the revolution's all about?'

'No it is not, you quarrelsome brat. This may come as a surprise to you, but even kidnappers have feelings. Hunting people down may be a thrill for some, but I've never much cared for it. I kept hoping you'd get tired of walking and just pack it in. Sit down and take your shoes off and wait for the wagon. Naturally, if I'd had any idea what you were doing to your poor little trotters, I'd have put a stop to it hours before. You don't know when you're licked, that's your trouble.'

He put a pin in the bandage and stood up, looking down at her soberly.

'Are you going to keep me locked up now?'

'What the hell for? You aren't going anywhere. For the next twenty-four hours, you'll have your work cut out making it as far as the bathroom. That reminds me. Claire, can you put your hand on the crutches we got for Chuck when he broke his ankle? They'll be too long, but I can cut them down.'

'They're in the attic. I'll look them out for you.'

'Thank God for a house where nobody ever throws anything away. Finished your tea?'

'Yes, thank you.'

'Let's get you into bed, then.'

'Conor?' Claire said. 'If thee takes her up the stairs I'll do the rest.'

He laughed.

'What's the matter? Doesn't thee trust me?'

She turned to look at him, wiping her hands on a towel.

'Oh, I suppose so. Trust thee more when I can see thee, is all. Go on then, take her up. But let thee lay one hand on that child, Friend Conor, and I'll cook thee. Thee'd look

115

right handsome with an apple in thy mouth.'

He bent over Kate's chair and lifted her, swathed feet dangling.

'I know it's a lot to ask,' he said, 'but could you possibly put your arms round my neck? After the sort of day you've had, I don't want to top things off by dropping you down the stairs. That's a girl. Now hang on tight.'

The room spun as he carried her, and going up the stairs was like being in a small boat in a very rough sea. Too much brandy on an empty stomach, she supposed hazily, and had her guess confirmed when the bed started swinging gently to and fro as soon as he set her down. He unbuckled her belt and began to take off her jeans.

'Hey!' She jerked away indignantly.

'Oh, shut up, I'm not going to attack you. Now hold still.'

He slid the jeans neatly and carefully over her bandaged feet without disturbing the dressings, which was more than she could have done herself. Underneath she had on a pair of plain cotton briefs, so that wasn't too bad; she had worn swimsuits that were more revealing. But under the denim shirt she was not wearing anything. He took the shirt off anyhow and hung it over the back of the chair.

'Why, Miss Jones, you're beautiful without your glasses,' he murmured politely, as he pulled the quilt up to cover her. 'I've done some incredibly silly things in my time,' he added, 'but promising not to seduce you may well have been the silliest.'

'You planning to go back on that?'

'No. Just kicking myself.'

'What *are* you planning to do?'

'Go out and run twenty laps, I expect, and then put my head under the pump. Standard treatment for lubricious fantasies.'

He was almost at the door when she called him.

'Conor?'

'Yes, ma'am.'

'What would you do if I said – *if* I said – that I didn't mind?'

'Didn't mind what?'

'Didn't mind if you did – go back on your promise.'

He came back and sat on the edge of the bed.

'You're drunk,' he said. 'Either that, or you've got a fever.'

He felt her forehead. It was damp, but quite cool.

'Okay, Miss Harper. Just what do you think you're up to?'

'I want to *know*. I just want to know what you'd *do*, that's all.

116

It wouldn't hurt you to tell me. You owe me that much. I've taken a hell of a lot from you. You kidnap me and keep me here, and you won't let me go home. I've had a horrible day and those *awful* hippies, and my feet hurt and my head hurts, and I only asked a simple question, and it's not fair!'

'You are drunk. Never mind. Let's see, what would I do? It's a little hard to say, really. You're much too old to be spanked, and I can't stop your allowance because I haven't been giving you one.'

'I'm not a child!'

'That's a matter of opinion.' He sighed. 'Well now. I suppose first of all I'd deliver my world-famous lecture on the perils of conditioned response to classic erotic situations.'

'You mean this is a classic – whatever?'

'Helpless female in the clutches of brutal male? You must be joking. People in Hollywood have been making a fancy living for years out of that simple, shopworn theme, and don't you fall for it.'

'Why not? You have.'

'No, darling. Nothing so simple. Unfortunately, it's not the scenario I've fallen for, it's you – and I'd have done that if I'd found you peddling lugworms on a live-bait barge. It's inappropriate, it's uncalled-for, and all in all it's a pestilential bloody nuisance.'

'Oh. Well, after you'd lectured me, what would you do next?'

'I should deliver my second world-famous lecture, the one we call Your Mother Didn't Raise You to Fuck Around with Felons. Or dirty old men either, come to that. You don't seem to realize that I am precisely twice your age.'

'I prefer older men,' she said loftily. 'There's something – something different about them.'

'Arteriosclerosis, probably.'

'That's another thing. You know too many long words, and you use all of them. It's a defence mechanism. Bet you didn't know that.'

'You'd lose.'

'Be that as it may. So far you've offered me two lectures, and they don't sound at all interesting. Talk, talk, talk. If you ever got through talking, what would you *do*?'

He looked down at her with such a serious face that the delicious alcoholic buzz enveloping her briefly receded.

'You're very lovely,' he said, 'and very special. You're also very, very young. If you knew how badly I want you, I think it would frighten you. It even frightens me. But Kate, darling Kate, it just isn't on. I cannot look after you, you see. Don't, for God's sake, let this charming pastoral interlude go to your head. An interlude is all it is – it can't be more than that – and once it's over you'll never see any of us again. And that's if everything works out, mind you. If it doesn't, I'll either be dead or I'll be in the slammer for the next five hundred years, and either way I'll be no damn use to you.'

He stood up to leave, and then leaned over and ran a fingertip down her cheek. His hand was not quite steady.

'Don't love me, pretty, whatever you do. There's no future in it.'

It was evening when Claire woke her. She brought a tray with a bowl of the corpse-reviving red soup and a chicken sandwich prepared, touchingly, invalid-style, with the crusts cut off. Kate felt dreadful – dry mouthed and scratchy – and her feet throbbed unmercifully. But she drank the soup, ate the sandwich, swallowed the tablets Conor had sent up for her, and presently began to feel better.

Claire sat in a chair by the window while she ate, talking gently on about anything and everything except the unsuccessful attempt at escape. It seemed this was to be treated as a nonhappening, like some piece of misbehaviour by a child for which there were, nevertheless, mitigating circumstances. Claire had looked out what she called a wrapper for her, an amorphous garment of beige silk with remarkable golden dragons. It looked like something Chuck might have brought back from Vietnam. Kate could have fitted into it with a couple of friends, but she drew it around her with gratitude. It saved the bother of getting dressed, and she couldn't very well sit there eating her supper naked from the waist up.

What Claire thought about her unclothed condition was hard to say, and she didn't seem inclined, in any case, to share her views with Kate. Probably Conor would come in for searching questions later. Though after all, nothing had happened. The odd thing was, she couldn't free herself of the feeling that something *had* happened, something extremely important, if only she could be sure what it was. She had gulped down an overdose of Housekeeper's Ruin, she knew that, and had become silly and coy as a result. Worse than that, she had been vulgar, making flirtatious gestures with no obligation to deliver, like a Hollywood sexpot entertaining the troops. She didn't like herself very much, and the prospect of seeing Conor again made her blush all over. With the most delicate consideration, he had kept her from making an even bigger fool of herself, and she knew she ought to feel grateful to him. Instead, she resented him furiously for having been there to witness her undignified behaviour.

She couldn't think what had got into her. A good deal of brandy, certainly, and she wasn't used to it. But if it were true that all alcohol did was relax your inhibitions, it must mean that, in some part of her that ordinarily was decently repressed, she had actually wanted Conor to stop being noble and scrupulous and – and do what? Throw her on a bed and ravish her? Surely not. However depraved her subconscious, she could hardly have wanted anything that drastic. But she had wanted him to kiss her.

> Whoever loves, if he do not propose
> The right true end of love, he's one that goes
> To sea for nothing but to make him sick.

Which meant, a waspish Beresford professor had informed the class with relish, that foreplay was all very well and most enjoyable, but sooner or later people should screw or shut up. (He was the same professor who had taken issue with Shelley on the grounds that it wasn't 'the desire of the moth for the star' that mattered, but the desire of the moth for another moth. This viewpoint, repeated at home, had caused Charlotte Harper to wonder audibly whether English Lit ought to be retitled Sex and the Single Poet.)

At this stage in Kate's uneasy brooding, Chuck walked in with a pair of crutches under one arm and a pile of books in the crook of the other. The books he set down on the bureau.

'Conor thought you might like something to read. We've cut these things down five inches, so they should be about right for you. Have you ever been on crutches before?'

'No.'

'It's not hard, but there's a knack to it. You have to get the rhythm right. Watch me.' He had to bend his knees absurdly with the short crutches. 'Cheeta the Chimp,' he said cheerfully. 'Feet together, weight evenly on both crutches; that's your starting position. Then you take most of your weight on the left crutch, the rest on the feet – just enough to let you balance. You swing the right crutch forward, like this – not too far, until you've had some practice. Shift your weight. Now you bring the other crutch up level with the first, and then swing your body forward and bring your feet into line with the crutches. Rest. Then you do it all over again. Okay, you try it now, Kate. No, don't poke your chin that way. Back straight, head up, chin tucked in. Better for balance.'

He coached her patiently until they agreed that she could be trusted to go to the bathroom and back. Then he brought her a lamp, 'So you can read in bed. Candles are lousy for reading – you'll hurt your eyes,' and he and Claire went downstairs, leaving her alone and crushed by guilt. They were so thoughtful and caring, so unobtrusively good. They worked harder than anyone she'd ever known, and did not whine about it. In fact they seemed to find it both normal and satisfactory. By comparison she felt trivial and spoiled, and now that she had disabled herself she couldn't even take care of the few marginal chores she had learned how to do. She was a *bouche inutile*, a parasite on the living body of the farm, and the fact that she'd never wanted to be there in the first place no longer seemed relevant.

Casting about for something to distract her thoughts, she remembered the books, and wobbled over to see what Conor had chosen for her. *Pride and Prejudice* and *Jane Eyre*, the stringent Miss Austen and the passionate Miss Brontë. 'Huh!' said Kate, miffed at having her tastes so effortlessly gauged. The other volumes were an odd mixture: *That Hideous Strength*, by C. S. Lewis; Hesketh Pearson's biography of Sydney Smith; a disintegrating copy of Oliver St John Gogarty's *As I Was Going Down Sackville Street*; and one book she'd never heard of, *Wake Up Stupid*, by Mark Harris. This last had a sheet of paper tucked between the leaves. She drew it out and read it. *Darling Occupant*, he had written, *you'll have to manage without me for a few days. I am joining an expedition to Bridgeport, to Forget. Be a good girl and I'll bring you home a commuter. They are loyal and affectionate and make wonderful pets. Conor.* Under the signature was a neat outline of two hearts pierced by an arrow, and below that a PS: *Lay off the booze until I get back. Then we'll see what champagne does for you.*

It wasn't a love letter, of course it wasn't, so why was she feeling so peculiar, like a bottle of soda pop after a good shaking? She wouldn't think about that for the moment. Conor was going away, and until he came back she didn't have to deal with anything more complicated than poking around on these damn crutches. Then, for the first time, it occurred to her that he might not get back. He might be arrested. He might, quite probably, be killed. It was possible that she had already seen him for the last time.

Kate swung herself awkwardly back to the bed, sat down, and remained perfectly still for some minutes, looking at the sheet of paper in her hand. Eventually she put the note in the drawer of the night table, laboured across the room again, and picked up the Mark Harris book. She tossed it onto the bed – one of the problems about being on crutches, she was learning, was that you couldn't carry anything, except perhaps in your teeth – and followed it. Her feet were painful, and in a way she was glad of it.

What was it her mother had told her that the nuns at her convent boarding-school were always saying? 'Offer it up, dear,' that was it. From a bruised shin on the hockey field to the piece of gristle you weren't allowed to leave on your plate at dinner, you were supposed to offer your sufferings to God. In return He docked a few centuries of suffering off the souls in Purgatory, and you got a bit of an edge the next time you put in a request yourself. The similarities between organized religion and standard accounting procedures had always put Kate off, and besides, how appallingly dreary it must be for God, snowed under with the small discomforts of pious little girls.

Still, on the off chance that there might be something in it, she made a formal offering of her raw and blistered feet. *Here's my pain, God – it's all Yours, and please don't let anything happen to Conor.*

THURSDAY, 3 MAY 1973. 9.30 P.M.

Pendleton Harper sat alone in the driver's seat of the Cadillac. Rock Creek Park was not the safest place in the world after dark, but the escort car full of Secret Service personnel was only fifty yards behind, and its motor was running. He had obeyed instructions to the letter because he was afraid to do otherwise, and they had not been unreasonable. In a way it was a relief to be dealing with people who were informed enough to know that a secretary of state could not dispense altogether with his personal protection without attracting the very notice they wished to avoid. If some random marauder were to make an attempt on him while he waited, he would sound the horn and the mugger would be the most astonished man in the District of Columbia. But he didn't think the situation would arise. The sight of the second car should be enough to discourage any prowling opportunist.

As agreed, the two cars were without lights, and the police had placed barriers across the road a quarter mile behind them and a quarter mile ahead. Since this particular stretch of road was only a loop, little more than half a mile long in all, traffic through the park would not be affected. The police had not been told the reason for the barriers. It was none of their business. Their business was to do what Pendleton Harper's aide said do, and they knew better than to question any directive that concerned the most formidable secretary since John Foster Dulles.

Harper looked at the dashboard clock. It was nine-thirty. The man was late. Oh Christ, perhaps he wasn't coming, perhaps they were only playing with him. The evening was warm, and his window was half open. Through it he heard a rhythmic sound gradually asserting itself over the soft night noises of the park. Footsteps. The rear driver's-side door quietly opened, the car jounced briefly under the extra weight, and the door was as quietly shut.

'Good evening,' said a voice immediately behind the secretary's head. 'I'm taking it for granted you've sense enough not to turn around. I'm also taking it for granted those muscle-bound wet nurses back there have been properly briefed. Your daughter's a nice little girl, and we don't want anything to happen to her. Do we?'

122

The voice was liltingly, extravagantly Irish, and Harper's head spun. What the hell was this, the IRA? Come with a modest request for a nuclear warhead to drop on Buckingham Palace? He was not at all sure what he had been expecting – aggrieved Israelis, perhaps, or vengeful Chileans – but it hadn't been this. What in God's name could the Irish have against him?

'Cat got your tongue, then?' the voice enquired.

'I'm sorry. I – yes of course, the guards will stay in the car. That was the arrangement.'

'Indeed it was. I just wanted to be certain there wouldn't be any little mistakes. The consequences would be most unfortunate.'

'Could we please get to the point? First, how do I know you really have my daughter?'

A gloved hand came over his shoulder, and an envelope and a small flashlight were put into his hand. He opened the envelope, took out a thin oblong of card, and switched on the flashlight to examine it. What he found himself looking at was a photograph of Kate, arms outstretched as though crucified, chains on her wrists and about her throat. Her eyes were open so wide that white showed all the way around the iris, and her mouth formed an ugly, anguished O. She looked as if she were screaming. Harper felt suddenly very cold, and at the same time began to sweat profusely. For a moment he was afraid he was going to vomit, but he took a couple of deep breaths and the faintness and nausea passed off.

'Yes, I see,' he said painfully, and turned off the flashlight. He could not bear to see his Kate so humiliatingly exposed. He realized that he wanted to kill the man in the back seat. Not have him killed: he wanted to do it himself – smash the face he must not see, smell the blood and hear the dying groans. Pen Harper had never killed anyone himself. He'd never even hit anyone since his first year in prep school. In the Second World War he had been a paper-pusher, comfortably in the rear, and by the time Korea came up he was already too valuable, one of State's brightest young men. The departmental shake-up in 1961, however, left him without a patron, and he retreated to his old university. There he had stayed, amusing himself in exile by sharpening his manipulative skills on his colleagues, until Hank's plane went down and the calls from the White House began. He had returned to Washington, with charming humility, to pursue his simple and unchanging goal, which was to make himself indispensable. He supposed his policies had helped to bring about the deaths of thousands – hundreds of thousands. The liberal press had certainly told him so often enough. The thought did not disturb him; sentimentality about burned babies had no place in his brand of *realpolitik*. But he had never slaughtered anyone personally, nor wanted to. He wanted to now. The desire rose in his throat like bile, sour and choking, almost sexual in its urgency.

'I see,' he said again. 'But the photograph – it only proves she was alive when it was taken. What guarantee can you give me that you didn't murder her afterwards?'

'You have only my word for it. She was safe and well when I saw her last. Naturally, she's very frightened, and the circumstances of her captivity are a little uncomfortable,' Conor went on, lying shamelessly, and wondering how long he could sustain the bog-Irish brogue dredged up from his early childhood. 'But she's not been harmed at all, and will not be harmed providing you do as you're told.'

'What do I have to do?'

'Not a great deal. Only resign.'

'*Resign?* Resign the secretaryship? For Christ's sake, man, *why?* I've never done anything to hurt Ireland. How could it possibly benefit your cause to get rid of me?'

'That does not concern you. Listen to me, now. These are your instructions. Tomorrow morning you will complain of chest pains. You will check into Walter Reed for extensive tests. The doctors will find nothing the matter, of course, but you will spin a story for them. Tell them it's a matter of national security. Tell them what you like, but make it clear they'll lose their jobs if one syllable ever gets out. That, they'll understand. After four days, your doctors will inform the president that you are a very sick man. Gross cardiac impairment, too weak to withstand surgery, complete rest over an extended period is your only hope for survival.'

'Nobody's going to believe that,' Harper said. 'Look at all the crocks that undergo coronary bypasses and open-heart surgery nowadays.'

'Then make it thrombophlebitis and a pulmonary embolism. I don't care what you and the quacks cook up between you as long as it's laid on thick. And there must be no loopholes, no possibility that some future triumph of medical skill could make you as good as new. You've worn yourself out, my poor fellow, in the service of your country. All those years of unstinting devotion have taken their toll, and you're as near dead as makes no difference. Don't interrupt! Later – in about six months, say – you might recover enough to take a gentle, undemanding chair in something or other at the university of your choice. They'll all be falling over themselves to get you, God forgive them. And you can write your memoirs, that ought to be good for a couple of million. You won't starve. But I warn you, and I warn you now: If ever you try sneaking back into this or any other administration, if ever you even contemplate it, we will take your daughter Kate and kill her, and after that we will kill you. And neither one of you will die kindly.'

Conor, listening critically to his own performance, was pleased to discover that he sounded as acidly convincing as the Angel of Death. He was even scaring himself, pierced by involuntary visions of Kate's body, bloodied and dead, so God alone knew what he was doing to the wretched object huddled in the driver's seat. Maliciously, he decided to increase the pressure.

'As I said, your daughter's a nice little girl. We all think so – particularly our black brothers who have joined us in our struggle for liberty.' The struggle for liberty was usually a safe bet, people seldom asked you liberty for whom, or from what. 'It may be her colouring that appeals to them so. That beautiful golden hair and the skin like the breast feathers on the white swans of Coole.' Watch it, boyo, you're getting a touch carried away. 'As a proud father, I'm sure you're not surprised that she has many admirers. So far, I've been able to restrain their natural ardour. I shall continue to do so, while you follow instructions. If you do not, I shan't feel justified in protecting her further.'

'Jesus Christ.' It came out a moan, and if he had been anyone but Pendleton Harper, Conor would have felt sorry for him. 'I'll do as you say. I haven't any choice. When will you let her go?'

'One week after the news of your resignation is made public. And don't try to speed it up. Four days in the hospital before the statement. It has to look right.'

'Very well. Now get out of here, you son of a bitch. Oh, I'll do as you say, don't worry. I will do precisely as you say. My daughter means more to me than a creature like you could begin to imagine. But I'd rather kiss the sores of a leper than breathe the same air as you one second longer than I have to, so will you please *go*.'

'The saints used to kiss the sores of lepers – they were notorious for it. And no saint, as far as I know, ever died of leprosy.

Good night, Mr Secretary.'

The door opened, the car dipped and lifted, but the door did not close when Harper expected it.

'I am not to be followed,' said the hateful Irish voice. 'If I am followed by so much as a little old lady in a wheelchair, Kate Harper will die. She will die slowly, and she will die cursing the day she had you for a father. Bear it in mind.'

The door closed; the footsteps faded and died. Harper looked at the clock again. It was nine-thirty-seven. The whole thing had taken six minutes. Six minutes to nullify the years of grinding hard work, the manoeuvring, the small humiliations and grievous loss of privacy gladly suffered as the price of power. But he knew something that mick bastard didn't know. He would have to be careful – his heart bounced unpleasantly as he thought how incredibly careful he would have to be. But although he didn't yet know where Kate was, since this morning he had known of at least one place she had been since her disappearance. It was little enough to go on, but it was a start.

'Get a load of that dumb fuck,' one of the Secret Service men remarked, as they drove out of the park. 'Around here they'll knife you for a skateboard, never mind an Italian ten-speed racer. No wonder we got a crime problem, with guys like that going around begging for it.'

The car accelerated, and the demurely pedalling Conor, nylon raincoat rolled up inside the jacket of his jogging suit, stocking mask left behind under a bush, swiftly diminished in the rearview mirror.

The intercom was working, for once, so when the front door bell rang Sean did not have to throw the keys out of the kitchen window. He made soothing sounds at young Julia Anne Devlin who detested door bells, as he went over to the box on the wall and pressed down the lever.

'Yes?'

'Good morning. Can I interest you in a copy of the *Pilot*? I also have the *Watchtower, Muhammad Speaks*, a complete line of incense with the Hare Krishna seal of approval, and forty pounds of Hebrew National salami. Think ecumenical – take a druid to lunch.'

'Jesus, Conor, you're out of your mind.'

'Not at all. Aren't you going to let me in? Marietta's not home.'

'No she's not, thank God, and lucky for you.'

'Luck be damned, I called her office not ten minutes ago. It may comfort you to know that she refused to subscribe to *Time* magazine. Now push the bloody buzzer, will you? I haven't got all week.'

'It's all right,' Conor said as he came through the door of the apartment. 'I'm not asking you to commit any more felonies – you've done your share and more. I just want to get my head down for a bit.'

'You raving lunatic, have you no conception what it's been like up here? There's not a building in New Lymington that hasn't had its meters read and its phone lines inspected every hour on the hour for the last five days. There's more FBI men to the square foot than roaches.'

'Oh really? That's interesting. Put the goons in, has he? Just as well I'm not the villain he thinks I am, or he'd have signed that girl's death warrant. He's a bad man, Sean. Not fit to be anyone's father.'

'You're not fit to be running around loose, and that's a fact. What possessed you to come back here, anyway?'

'Have to keep an eye on the customers. I had a chat with his nibs last night, and put the fear of God up him if I'm any judge. This afternoon I'm planning to look in on mum, but I do need a few hours' sleep first. I can go to a motel, though, if you'd rather.'

'You'll do no such thing. But you're mad if you go near that woman's house. Do you think it won't be under surveillance and bugged and God knows what else? They'll have you, man – you won't get as far as the door.'

'I will if I go as Father Brown's invisible man.'

'You're going to dress up as a *mail*man? That's against the law.'

'Bit late to worry about that. Anyway, I shan't be a mailman. We do not slavishly imitate the classics, we adapt them to the exigencies of today's complex society. Can I use your phone?'

'You'll not be calling her from here, for pity's sake – there'll be a tap on her line. They'll trace the call.'

'Gently, cocker, trust the old man.'

He dialled a local number.

'Gaetano? This is Tony's friend.'

There was a clacking torrent of response.

'Alas, no, I can't make it for dinner – wish I could, but I'm only going to be here for a few hours. I was wondering if I might come around to the shop later and say hello. Will you be there at three? Terrific, I'll see you then.'

'Who the hell's Gaetano?' Sean asked.

'A nice old man. Lost one son in Nam, and when they drafted the second one Tom's friends whisked the kid off to Canada. Gaetano thinks we're very hot stuff.' He leaned over the crib and picked up the baby. 'Hello, *mo chridh*, how's my pretty girl? Been taking good care of your parents, have you?' He bounced her, made her laugh, put her against his shoulder and burped her with the infuriating casualness of the expert, and set her back in the crib.

'Gorgeous,' he said. 'Isn't God clever? Making babies so attractive, so people will love them and look after them. Most people, anyway. Let me have a glass of milk, Sean, if you've got it to spare, and then I'll take myself out of your way.'

While Conor slept with the serenity wrongly supposed to indicate a clear conscience, things were happening some hundreds of miles to the southwest that ought, if there were anything in telepathy, to have brought him bolt upright, screaming. The trouble began with a telephone call. Kate, dozing on the old chesterfield in the kitchen, with her bandaged feet on a pillow, heard it ring, and awoke just enough to remember that she couldn't answer it anyhow. Then Claire came in from the scullery, hastily punched the buttons that released the lock, and lifted the receiver.

'Well, Ollie dear, how are you? It's good to – oh! Oh my gracious goodness. All right, dear, and thank you. I'll tell him right away.'

She slammed the cupboard shut and ran out into the yard, calling for Chuck and Sam. She sounded almost as if she were frightened, which was ridiculous. Claire, surely, would never be afraid of anything. Kate picked up the Mark Harris book from its resting place on her stomach, and had just found her place when Chuck burst in and passed her without a glance, heading for the scullery at a dead run. Almost at once he was back, carrying a small white-enamel tray with a brown bottle labelled Abs. Alc., a smaller bottle with a rubber cap, a wad of cotton, and a hypodermic syringe. He set down the tray and turned to Kate.

'I have to put you out for a while. There's no time to explain – will you trust me?'

She stared at him in frozen disbelief. It was what she had feared before, right at the start – the unforeseen emergency, the captors panicking, the quick needle of death, and the body shovelled under. She had feared it and then forgotten the fear, as she came to know her keepers better. Now it was happening and she wasn't ready, she'd stopped thinking about dying.

'Katie! Do you think I'd hurt you? But there's no *time*.'

Either she would wake up again or she wouldn't. In either event, crippled as she was, there was little she could do. Cooperate, or put up a struggle and filch a few extra seconds of consciousness, those were the barren choices. Her eyes on Chuck's face, which as usual told her nothing, she rolled up her left sleeve.

'Good girl!'

He stabbed the needle through the rubber seal, drew up liquid into the syringe, dabbed at her arm with alcohol-soaked cotton, and deftly administered the shot.

'Two hours, give or take fifteen minutes. Let go, Kate – just let go.'

She started to wilt almost as soon as he withdrew the needle. With an arm under her shoulders he eased her back down onto the couch as Sam strode in from the yard. The two men picked her up between them and carried her out to the barn. Sam had spread a tarpaulin on the cobbled floor, with a couple of fence rails down the centre; they laid the small, limp body down and pulled the tarpaulin over to cover it, arranging the stiff folds to leave an airspace over Kate's face and a channel through which more air could flow. Loops of rope, running through pulleys high in the shadows of the roof, dangled down to the ground. Working fast, they slid the ropes under the canvas bundle and slowly, with infinite care to keep their burden level, they hauled it up until it hung among the rafters, and then secured the ropes.

Meanwhile, in the scullery, Claire was washing out the telltale syringe before putting it back with the bottles in the cabinet where Chuck kept his veterinary supplies. Upstairs, Afeni was stripping off Kate's sheets, flinging the linens in a heap on the floor, neatening the bed, blankets folded under the smooth spread. Then she gathered up the few traces of Kate's occupation – the ribbed sweater, the comb, the loafers with the dark stains inside, the cigarettes and matches – and thrust them hastily in among her own things in the room she shared with Sam. The saucer Kate used for an ashtray she rinsed and dried in the bathroom, and transferred it, and Kate's toothbrush as well, to her own room. Emerging, she checked stride to unlock Conor's bedroom door, slide the panel into place to hide the row of buttons, and leave the door disarmingly ajar. Then she flew up the attic stairs to do the same for the door of the radio room.

When Sheriff Gibbs and his deputy, Will Paton, drove up to the house ten minutes later, followed by a state police car with its lights flashing foolishly in the sun, followed in turn by an unmarked sedan containing two men in dark suits, white shirts, and plain rep ties, they found the Lainez farm – better known locally as the old Bradley place – looking as busy as it did innocent. Claire and Afeni were tending a fire under the huge old iron washpot out in the yard, Sam was lugging a last pail of water for them from the stove reservoir, and Chuck was flat on his back under the pick-up, visible only from mid-thigh downward.

'Doin' your wash on a Friday, Claire?' the sheriff quizzed her, as he manoeuvred his considerable bulk from behind the wheel. 'Your mother like to come back from the grave and haunt you. Hahdy, Miss Tulliver. Hahdy, Sam.'

Claire straightened up and wiped her forehead with the back of her wrist, streaking a smut several inches across it.

'That prize guernsey of Chuck's is about to drop a calf,' she said. 'She's due Monday, and if there's anything like the fuss we had last time I don't see myself getting the wash done in the middle of it, so I'm trying to move ahead of myself. Tomorrow I'll be baking, and wash on First Day I will not, and what business my

130

laundry is of yours, Hailey Gibbs, is more than I can imagine. Morning, Will, glad to see your back's going on better. You keep that board under your mattress and you won't have any more trouble. You fellers are looking right purposeful today – somebody lose something? Brought your friends along too, I see.'

Sheriff Gibbs, however, was not yet through with the subject of washday. He was not a man to be hurried, as his neighbours knew if the Feds did not; nor was he any kind of a fool. Claire Lainez washing clothes on a Friday was odd, and what was odd was interesting.

'Just 'cause your daddy was set against the electric,' he pursued, 'don't mean you got to be as stubborn as he was. If your husband ever crawls out from under that heap of junk he's foolin' with, I'll tell him again what I told him before. High time he got a generator set up for you, instead of messin' with propane tanks and kerosene lamps and all that stuff out of the Dark Ages. Get yourselves one of them little dinguses from Sears and Roebuck – they don't use that much gas – and you could have an electric washer and grow petunias in that old iron pot. It's too much work at your age.'

'I'm fifteen years younger than you are, Hailey, and in better shape than you've ever been, with your cigars and your sippin' whisky. And didn't your mother ever tell you a lady's age is none of your business?'

'Might have. Expect she did, come to think of it. I know she told me not to go around askin' a lot of fool questions and pokin' my nose in where I wasn't wanted. Could be that's what made me run for sheriff. That poor woman always did say I was the orneriest child she ever encountered.'

Deputy Paton and the state troopers were standing around trying not to grin. They were used to Gibbs, but the spectacle of the two dark-suited gentlemen slowly beginning to steam under the strain as they waited for the sheriff to come to the point was so extravagantly entertaining that the observers could barely stand still. They were too polite to make overt fun of their visitors, and too conscientious to withhold cooperation, but to take all this seriously was beyond them. Of course it wasn't fair to expect too much of city people, come all the way from the field office in Haynesville, and both of this pair easterners from the way they talked. No way they would be able to understand how things were in Aurora County.

The notion of Claire Bradley, Eli Bradley's daughter and the sheriff's own kin by marriage, harbouring some female fugitive from the Weather Underground was so richly comic that it seemed a shame you couldn't just quietly take these bull-headed enthusiasts to one side and share the joke. Not that they looked to have much sense of humour, and their excitement on learning that Claire had been raised a Quaker had been quite unseemly. Quakers, they had explained to their rustic audience, were disrespectful of duly constituted authority. Furthermore, they were deeply involved in the antiwar movement, even going so far as to send medical supplies to Communist hospitals in North Vietnam, which was giving aid and comfort to the enemy no matter which way you looked at it.

The rustics had listened solemnly. They had lived alongside Quakers all their lives, and were well aware that these mild-spoken, diligent neighbours were flatly opposed to all forms of violence, and therefore probably the last people on earth to ally themselves with the bomb-happy Weathermen. However, they nodded politely and permitted the experts to enlighten them.

'Let 'em have their fun, boys,' the sheriff had privately advised. 'No sense arguin' with folks that know all the answers before they start. We'll just be sure and cooperate 'em till they're godalmighty tired of it – tag along bein' helpful, and see to it they don't go gettin' the neighbours all upset. More help we give 'em, sooner they'll go home.'

The sheriff stood there now, a hulking figure in his sixties, his small, bright blue eyes slitted in amusement, his weathered face beaming at Chuck, who had at last emerged from under the pick-up.

'This here's Mr Lainez, gentlemen,' he announced. 'Chuck, these fellers are from the Federal Bureau of Investigation. They've come down here from Haynesville to ask us all some questions, and I know you're goin' to do ever'thing you can to help 'em out. Mr Maybush, Mr Grose – you just go right ahead now and ask whatever you want.'

The agents were a little weary of having Sheriff Gibbs oversee all their activities, but his regional knowledge was too useful for them to risk offending him, and this particular assignment presented enough difficulties without the additional handicap of strained relations with the local law.

'Perhaps we could go inside, Mr Lainez,' Grose suggested, 'and Mrs Lainez, if you can spare us a moment, maybe you'd be kind enough to come along as well.'

Shepherded by Gibbs, who had no intention of letting his friends be interrogated without being present to protect their interests, the little party went into the house. The youngest state trooper, who couldn't take his eyes off Afeni, made himself handy helping her dump the contents of the laundry basket, including Kate's bed linen, into the washpot, while Will Paton, who owned the Cold Crossing service station, wandered off to the barn with Sam to inspect the feedline on the tractor, which had given trouble off and on for months. Fifteen feet below Kate's unconscious body they wrangled knowledgeably about airlocks and the ever-present hazard of grit in the fuel tanks of farm machinery, while at the far end of the barn the calves crowded against the railing in hopes of milk.

Indoors at the kitchen table, Claire sat in a daze of gratitude to the Lord, who had considerately arranged matters so that she did not have to lie. Had she been asked, right out, whether she was helping to conceal the person of Catherine Danbury Harper, abducted daughter of the secretary of state, she would have been hard pressed for an answer. But she could in good conscience deny ever having set eyes on the fugitive accomplice of a cell of radical demolition experts. (Afeni, had she known it, came perilously close to filling the job description; but fortunately for her peace of mind Claire knew very little about Sam's activities between his departure from Vietnam and his arrival, sickly and uncommunicative, at the farm six months before.)

In any case, the agents purported to be looking for an armed and dangerous Caucasian female, height five-hour and three-quarters, weight one hundred ten, eyes grey, hair light blonde, name Catherine Hale; uses a variety of aliases; has been known to pose as the relative of a high government official. With all the lying Mr Grose and Mr Maybush were getting through, Claire was even pricked by a twinge of moral superiority, a slip from grace she was heartily ashamed of as soon as she detected it.

The revelation that the FBI was using essentially the same cover story as the one he himself had concocted to mislead the people at Harmony rocked Chuck so badly that for the first few minutes of the interview he was totally off balance, as appalled as the writer of fiction who finds the invention he committed to manuscript on Monday spread all over the front pages of Tuesday's newspaper. The only visible effect of his dismay was to make him appear extremely stupid, and since the agents held conventional views on Chicanos, especially Chicanos with as much Indian blood as this one, a certain dimwittedness in Mr Carlos Lainez seemed to them only to be expected. They were patient with him, framing their enquiries in the simplest terms and taking care to speak slowly and distinctly.

Sheriff Gibbs, who had lost to Chuck at chess more times than he cared to count, was puzzled; but finally he decided that this simple-child-of-nature routine must be a sophisticated joke at the agents' expense. He knew Chuck for a tolerant and kindly man, and it didn't seem like him to make fun of strangers. But then a lot of people were upset with the Bureau these days and no wonder. Probably he considered them fair game. The sheriff himself had been tempted more than once to try a countryman's deadpan tug at one of those conservatively trousered legs, so he could sympathize with the impulse. Nevertheless, Chuck's odd behaviour niggled its way to the back of his mind and dug itself in, for later retrieval if the occasion arose. Hailey Gibbs was no forensic genius, but he did have one trait indispensable in a good lawman: he never forgot anything, ever.

Grose and Maybush had begun to feel like helpless dinner guests forced to sit through a display of photographic slides showing people they didn't know in places they had no wish to visit. It was not that the Lainez couple wouldn't talk – the woman in particular talked like a millrace; there seemed no way to stop her – but it was all irrelevant and, above all, boring. Each question, studiously phrased to elicit a simple yes or no, called forth instead tidal waves of numbingly inconsequential comment and reminiscence, with frequent appeals to Sheriff Gibbs, who appeared to be some kind of relative, for confirmation, arbitration, and additional detail.

Moreover, these people somehow gave the impression that either their interviewers didn't speak the language, or some Pinteresque playwright was supplying the dialogue. In the finest traditions of the FBI, Maybush and Grose were alert to all signals of sexual irregularity, and when their enquiries into the nature and functioning of the household turned up the item that Sam and Afeni shared a bedroom they cheered up at once. But when Grose solicitously wondered aloud why two such nice young people didn't get married, Claire took him up quite sharply.

'Why that would never do at all, Mr Grose,' she said, looking distressed. 'Afeni's family is just dead set against mixed marriages, and I certainly couldn't allow such a thing under my roof when I know it's against their wishes. With young folks the way they are these days, most of 'em, it's a pleasure to see a young girl minding her parents for once.'

Grose fought the urge to shake his head like a swimmer with water in his ear. Either this woman was out of her tree or he was – only he couldn't be, because the Bureau didn't hire crazy people. Pulling himself together, and cutting desperately through an anecdote about the sheriff's sister-in-law, Claire's second cousin Rachel Bradley Owens, whose daughter had run off with an Armenian saucepan salesman, Grose dragged the situation back under control by main force. They would need to search the house, the farm buildings, the entire area. They hoped, he said insincerely, that this would not inconvenience Mr and Mrs Lainez.

'Why, no, happy to help out any way we can. Chuck and Sam can show you around right now, you go anyplace you want and get into anything you've a mind to, just watch yourselves when you come to the goose pen. One of my geese is sitting on eggs, and she gets all fired up at the least little thing. Right nasty nip a goose can give you, if she's in the mood to. And another thing, I wouldn't get too near that cow that's in the barn. She's the one due to calve in a couple of days and a mean-souled creature at the best of times, which this is not. Now if you gentlemen will excuse me, I got a piglet to feed. Hailey, while you're up, just set that pan of milk on the back of the stove to warm. That's the one; thank you, dear. You all come back here now, when you're through, and I'll have coffee for you, and maybe some hot rolls and a piece of ham to put with them.'

While Claire gave the piglet his bottle Sam went off with one search party, made up of Agent Maybush, Deputy Paton, Lieutenant Swenson and Trooper Clay of the state police. Together they inspected the barn, the sheds, the hog pen, the goose pen (circumspectly), the henhouse, and the springhouse, before moving out to run a cursory and useless eye over the fields themselves.

'Where's Conor?' Deputy Paton wanted to know. 'Not gone back to Nam, is he?'

'Hell no. He had enough the last time. Me too. He just ran over to Richmond in the Jeep to see an old friend was passing through. He'll be home tomorrow.'

'You figure he got a little old blonde bomber stashed out here in the bushes some place?'

'Do what? Ain't seen Conor look at a woman all year, 'less she had something real uncommon the matter with her.'

Sam and the deputy shook with imperfectly suppressed laughter, and the back of Agent Maybush's neck turned slowly puce. It was bad enough being stuck with a job like this at all – murky, equivocal, no proper files, no real background information, and what little there was doled out in driblets strictly on a need-to-know basis by the resident agent; quite bad enough, without being snickered at by a bunch of hicks into the bargain. Maybush was never very happy working with regular law enforcement people, especially in rural areas. They were a coarse crowd, from what he'd seen of them, and not as objective as they should be, too quick to think in terms of known troublemakers or good neighbours, instead of viewing everyone with impartial suspicion. Moreover, in his experience, the backwoods were largely inhabited by dangerous lunatics. Remembering his old friend Agent Eisentraub, who had quit the Bureau after a nightmare assignment in the wilds of Vermont involving, among other things, a writer of pornographic books, a weimaraner named Bastard and a chief of police who was never sober except by accident, Maybush could not repress a shudder.

His partner Grose was no happier. With a blank-faced Chuck for guide and Sheriff Gibbs humming and beaming alongside, making him feel he was being escorted by an unusually merry performing bear, he supervised the other two state troopers in their search of the house. They were nicely brought up young men, making the best of a job they disliked. Ferreting around in the personal effects of decent citizens was not at all their idea of what they'd been hired for, and their one desire was to get it over as quickly as possible.

Dutifully they rummaged among the contents of the attic, toppling an old dressmaker's form and as apologetic over it as if it had been a pregnant woman. They admired Daniel's models and looked under his bunk bed, unearthing a stack of well-worn comic books and a gadget for seeing behind you that didn't work. They enthused covetously over the equipment in the radio room, and clearly longed to stay and play with it, but Agent Grose was glowering and they moved down to the second floor to check out Rebeccah's doll house, her closet, and the carved wooden box that held her hair ribbons.

Next they pawed, horribly embarrassed, through drawers full of Claire's ample and uncompromising underwear. In the room across the hall, lace-ruffled bikini panties bothered them even more, and the plastic container of birth-control pills in the dresser

136

was the last straw. They were both married men; they knew what the damn stuff was for, but it was private and it didn't seem right to pick over such things.

They polished off the rest of the room rapidly; not so rapidly, however, that Sheriff Gibbs did not notice something peculiar about the jumble of shoes on the floor of the closet. Men's sneakers and workboots – those would be Sam's and the women's shoes presumably belonged to Afeni Tulliver, but there were two pairs of loafers, one around a size eight or nine and the other no bigger than a six. Nobody in the house had feet that small except the children, and they didn't wear Italian glove-leather shoes. Grose, rattled and irritable, missed the discrepancy, and the sheriff did not point it out. Despite his good-ole-boy facade, Hailey Gibbs belonged to a rarer and far more complex species, the gentleman redneck. His ethics were as sound, and as arbitrary, as those of an aristocratic eighteenth-century whig. The people of Aurora County were, by God, his people. If any of them misbehaved he would attend to it himself, and the rest of the world was welcome to perform unnatural acts upon a rolling doughnut. Let the FBI do its own dirty work.

The ground floor yielded nothing, although Grose perked up at the sight of the veterinary supplies and carefully checked every item on the shelves, yearning for illicit drugs. A drug haul would compensate somewhat for all the trouble they were being put to, and no household could possibly be as clean as this one seemed to be – especially since it included a Vietnam veteran (everybody knew about them and drugs – no wonder we lost the war), a doctor involved in some pacifist outfit and not even an American citizen, an immoral black woman with an insolent hairdo, and a half-witted half-breed married to a member of a subversive religious sect.

With fading hope, Agent Grose peered into the entrails of the piano, and pulled out papery handfuls of dried honesty from the vases on the parlour mantel. In the kitchen, he even ordered the piglet removed from its box by the hearth to make sure nothing was hidden under the straw. Pigs in the house, good Christ – the sooner this job was over the happier he'd be. There was nothing here. Maybe they'd have better luck at the next stop. From what he'd been told it was a nest of hippies, and there were three young white women living there. Please God one of them would turn out to be this Catherine Hale, whoever the hell she really was, and then he could go home. He disliked these rural assignments almost as much as Maybush.

The two agents further alienated the local men by spurning Claire's proffered rolls and coffee, which meant nobody else could have any either, and within five minutes of the return of Maybush's party the whole gaggle had taken off for Harmony. As they drove away Chuck glanced anxiously at his watch.

'*Dios*, I thought they would never leave. Claire, what possessed you? If they had stayed to drink coffee Kate might have woken before we could get her down.'

'I know, I know, but I had to offer. Hailey would have guessed right away something was wrong if I didn't. I just prayed the Lord to put it in those two men's hearts to be in an awful hurry, and He did. Now thee go quick and save that child before she wakes.'

'In New Lymington, Connecticut, today, Mrs Charlotte Harper, former wife of the secretary of state, told reporters she had been notified of the secretary's admission to Walter Reed Army Medical Center quote as a matter of courtesy unquote, but said she had no information to add to the news release already issued by the State Department spokesman. Dr Harper's daughter Catherine, a first-year student at Beresford College, is currently confined to bed at her mother's home, suffering from a virus infection, and was not available for comment. Informed sources in Washington have indicated that, while there is grief and dismay in the nation's capital over the secretary's sudden collapse, it was not altogether unexpected. "He's been running himself ragged for months now," one observer stated, "and no man can keep up that pace indefinitely." The precise nature of Dr Harper's illness has not yet been disclosed, but it is known that he was suffering from severe chest pains when he was admitted to the hospital shortly after ten o'clock this morning. Here now is our correspondent in Washington, Scott Westlake. . . .'

Kate, restored to the kitchen chesterfield with a cold cloth on her forehead and Claire sitting on a straight chair beside her, worriedly stroking her hand, heard the news bulletin as if from an immense distance. She was preoccupied with one essential, ecstatic discovery: she was alive. Sleepily gazing around the room, she felt she was seeing everything in it for the first time. The old wall clock with its fat, painted bird precariously balanced on a spray of apple blossom was the most perfect work of art she had ever seen. The shelf of seedlings in the window was rimmed with golden light that jewelled each tiny leaf like a Russian enamel. Bagel, slouched at the far end of the couch with his nose wedged wetly against her ankle, was without question the world's most intelligent and beautiful dog. She was alive among friends.

The green panel truck with the sign on the side that read PERAZZO AIR CONDITIONING – *Sales & Service – We keep Your Cool*, pulled into the short drive outside Charlotte Harper's house and stopped at the front door. A man wearing green overalls, with *Perazzo* in white script over the breast pocket, stepped out of the truck and rang the door bell. A young black woman in a starched pink shirtwaist opened the door.

'I'd like to see Mrs Harper. It's about the air conditioner in her bedroom. She called last week, but we've had a man out sick and this is the first chance I've had to stop by.'

'Nothing the matter with it that I know of, and Mrs Harper's not feeling well. She's resting right now.'

'Well, I don't like to disturb her, but when she called Mr Perazzo she said particularly that she wanted to see the service man herself. Maybe you could show her this? It's the job ticket they made out at the shop.'

Charlotte Harper was on the sofa, reading the same paragraph of the *Atlantic Monthly* for the third time without taking in a word of it, when her maid brought in the cardboard slip.

'The air conditioner? I don't believe . . . Oh! Oh yes, of course, I remember now. Ask him to come in, would you, Doris?'

Written neatly across the printed slip were the words *Sa bonne s'appellait Nanny Bristow. Taisez-vous, méfiez-vous, l'ennemi vous écoute.*

The second sentence, the old French wartime caution against careless talk, warned Charlotte to be on her guard, but it was the first part of the message that made her heart fly into her throat. Only someone who knew Kate would use Nanny Bristow's name for a password – and Pen's people would never have bothered with such secretive theatrics. There had been half a dozen of them already, and they simply marched in as if they owned the place. This was someone from the other side. When Doris showed the man in, Charlotte was standing, straight and steady and as white as a shroud.

'How good of you to come,' she said formally. 'I knocked over some perfume in my room a few days ago, and when I turned the

140

air conditioner on to Exhaust to try and get rid of the smell, it didn't seem to be operating properly. I know I don't really need it yet, but May can be very hot even up here, and I didn't want to leave it to the last minute.'

'Much better not; as soon as it hits eighty-five we get more calls than we can handle. Maybe you could show me the machine?'

'Yes, of course.'

She led the way into her bedroom. She was still holding the job ticket. Conor took it out of her hand and folded it into a tight spill. He removed the air conditioner's front panel, stuck in the folded card at an angle where it would foul the blades of the fan, and switched on the motor.

'Uh-huh,' he said over the resulting clatter, which sounded like a squad of maniac children running sticks along the railing. 'I think I see the problem. Looks as if I can fix it right here; no need to take it in to the shop.'

He opened his toolbox and took out a Magic Slate, one of those toys that can be written on by pressing down on a sheet of talc, and the writing afterwards erased by lifting the sheet away from the wax tablet below. Snow White and the Seven Dwarfs rioted dropsically around the frame.

'House undoubtedly bugged,' Conor wrote, just to the right of Dopey's nightcap. 'Noise + vibration shd. spoil reception, but safer write, not talk.' He showed her the words, erased them, and passed her the slate.

'Is she all right?' The bold, graceful writing was hurried but firm.

'Yes. Scared at first. All right now.'

'What do you want me to do?'

'Nothing.'

'Why are you here?'

'Wanted you to know K safe.'

A kidnapper with a conscience? 'Kind, but v. dangerous,' Charlotte wrote. 'House watched, phone tapped.'

'I know. After I leave, pl. call Perazzo, thank for sending man to fix a/c. Keep bloodhounds happy.'

Charlotte stared at him, trying to read his face. She saw a tall, thin, serious-looking man with kind blue eyes and a melancholy mouth. He had Kate, precious and beloved Kate. There were no lengths she would not go, nothing she would not do to placate him. But who was he, *what* was he? Nanny Bristow had had a flat, north-country phrase for encouraging the faint-hearted to speak up: 'There's nothing for the dumb.' Charlotte decided to ask.

'Who are you?' she wrote. 'Why Kate?'

'Vietnam,' the scribbled answer came. 'Too many still dying. Get PRH out – no more money for war, *guerre finie*. We hope.'

'PRH in hosp.,' she wrote back. 'News on radio at noon.'

'Part of deal. Resignation next, then K released.'

'Otherwise???'

He hesitated, concentrating on Charlotte's face so long and so hard that she felt he must see right through her skull. At last he began to write again. 'Won't harm K no matter what. Only danger, H's trigger-happy goons.'

She took back the slate. 'Be careful. K's bag handed in Wed., Carrstown, W. Va. Police here called me Thurs. I called PRH. He knew already, through tap on phone.'

He swore, silently but viciously, and then saw the fear in her face and contrived a smile.

'Thanks for warning,' he wrote. 'V. helpful. Any message for K?'

'Tell her to be a good girl. Tell her I love her.'

Conor almost wrote down, 'So do I,' but caught himself in time and merely nodded. He bent over the air conditioner, pulled the spill away from the fan, and let the motor run sweetly for the few moments it took him to tear the job ticket into little pieces and burn them in the nearest ashtray. Then he turned the machine off and replaced the grille.

'There you go, ma'am,' he said in the sudden quiet. 'You shouldn't have any more trouble now. Mr Perazzo will send you the bill.'

'Thank you,' she said, and could not quite keep the tremor out of her voice. 'Thank you *very* much.'

'You're quite welcome. Call us any time.'

She could not bear him to go – he was the only link. Enemy or friend, she was not sure which, still he was the only link. She held out a hand to him beseechingly. He took it and, to her confusion, held it for a moment against his cheek, smiling at her. She was really very like Kate to look at, and like Kate she blushed easily. Her face turned crimson, but he was already out of the room and gone.

In the kitchen, Doris, moodily polishing a copper pan, heard him leave, and drew her mouth tight. Seven years she'd worked for Mrs Harper, and this was the first time she'd ever been made to feel like a nigger. Well maybe not that, quite; but a servant –

someone things had to be kept from, someone who couldn't be trusted with a secret. Just who did Mrs Harper think she was fooling, anyhow? 'Stay out of Kate's room, Doris. She's in bed with a very bad virus and I don't want you exposed to it.' Uh-hunh. That girl hadn't been home in two weeks, and wasn't now – she'd looked.

And there hadn't been no perfume spilled in Mrs Harper's bedroom, either. She, Doris, was in there five days a week and she'd have smelled it. Something real funny was going on, yes *sir*. Mrs Harper telling lies to that bunch of reporters this morning, and Mr Harper sick in the hospital, and those men in dark suits in and out of the house at all hours and calling her 'the help' among themselves, the way you might say 'the washing machine' or 'the vacuum cleaner'. Couldn't blame them too much, they were just ignorant. But Mrs Harper should have known Doris could be trusted. She knew what trouble was; she wouldn't have told anyone, not if they tortured her she wouldn't. But it wasn't fair to shut a person out this way. It wasn't right.

Conor drove back to Perazzo's to return the truck and the uniform.

'You get your story? You get what you want?' the old man asked, his voice loud for the benefit of the long-haired apprentice working at the bench.

'Couldn't have done it without you. My editor's going to kiss me when he sees this. I'll send you a clipping.'

'You got time for a glass of wine? You make time, eh? Just five minutes. Frank!'

He beckoned his balding eldest son over, and the three men crowded into the tiny cluttered lair at the back of the workshop. They sat there sipping the smooth Ruffino and grinning at each other. As usual, they were in agreement: people like Charlie Finley were ruining baseball; the big firms were driving the little man out of business; those fellows in Washington weren't fit to be in charge of a pushcart; and where was the new Garibaldi to set us all to rights? There was news of young Pete Perazzo, now in Vancouver and doing well in the electrical repair business. Angela, Tony's widow, had a boyfriend, but it was all right, he was a local man; if she married him they would still be able to see little Tony every Sunday. Little Tony, so beautiful, so like his papa – there must be no more wars to swallow up the little Tonys when they were old enough to go.

143

Conor finished his wine and stood up. The old man rose too, and embraced him.

'You take care, *paisan*. I don' wanna lose another one of my boys. Antonio, Pietro, is already too much, *capisc*'? You take care.'

'You bet. And thanks for everything. Oh, while I think of it – don't forget to send her a bill. They'll have a mail cover going, and we may as well keep their files straight.'

'*Bene, bene*. That's a smart lady. She did good on the phone; she'll know why I send. If she pay, I tear up the cheque.'

Conor picked up his rented car from a nearby parking lot and drove north to Boston. At Logan airport he turned in the car and caught the shuttle to La Guardia, went into the city by bus, walked across town from the East Side Terminal to Penn Station, and dawdled over an inedible sandwich until it was time for his train. He slept most of the way to Richmond, stopped off at a diner for a huge, greasy plateful of ham and eggs, picked up the Jeep from the garage where he'd left it, and started the long drive home. It would take him most of the day if he didn't hurry, and he wasn't going to hurry. All this bobbing and weaving around the country was a necessary precaution, but it was bad for the reflexes. You got tired, and then you got careless.

Presently he unclipped the hand mike from under the dashboard and tried to raise the farm, but he couldn't get them. Oh well, time enough for that later. He was a long way away still, and there were hills in between. If there were goons about down here, and there would be if Charlotte Harper had told him the truth, Sam would know about it by now – unless their communications system had let them down completely, which wasn't likely. He was almost two hours out of Richmond when he rounded a curve and found himself fifty feet from a state police roadblock.

At two o'clock on Saturday afternoon the farmhouse was quiet. Lunch was long over, the dishes washed and dried and put away. Sam was up in the attic babysitting the radio. After yesterday's crisis had been successfully dealt with none of them believed there would be any more visitations for a while, but as Chuck said, somebody just might have spotted something, and there was no such thing as being too careful. Afeni was setting out tomato seedlings in the vegetable garden, and Chuck was grimly physicking a most uncooperative pig. Claire, who found it hard

144

to believe that any civilized female could have reached the age of eighteen with such glaring gaps in her knowledge, was in the kitchen with Kate, teaching her to knit.

'And over and under and around and through,' Claire said, for the umpteenth time. 'Mercy, child, how'd you ever do *that*? Oh, give it to me.'

The bell of the early warning system pealed loudly through the still air.

'Drat,' Claire said. 'You'd better go upstairs, dear. You can peek from the window, if you like, but don't let anyone see you. It won't be Conor this early, that I do know. Here, I'll come with you and help you up the stairs. Then we can both see who it is.'

Kate, free of her crutches but still tender about the heels, negotiated the stairs slowly, and took up her station behind Claire's shoulder as the older woman peered out. Soon there was the faint groan of an engine, and then an ancient Rambler, with GARVEY'S LIVERY SERVICE painted with more verve than precision on the door, drew up before the house. Out of it scrambled a little girl with long, dark braids. Next came a boy, older, also dark. He held the car door open while an old woman with a face like a walnut emerged, glaring straight ahead, the picture of monarchic disdain.

'Oh, no,' Claire whispered. 'No. I do not believe it. That wicked, *wicked* old thing!'

She ran down the stairs and Kate, watching through a crack between curtain and window frame, saw her reappear at the foot of the porch steps. The little girl came pelting across the yard, ran into her full tilt, and was all over her like a poultice.

'Beccah! Dear heart, what is thee doing here?' Claire was hugging the younger child and stretching out an arm for the boy, who came to her as gladly as a bird to its nest. 'Daniel, thee's old enough to have good sense. What was thee thinking of? I've missed thee both so, thee doesn't know how I've missed thee, but whatever is thee about, running home this way?'

The old lady had arrived in front of the exuberant family group. She jerked her head towards the car.

'Nine dollars,' she said calmly. 'Pay the man.'

'Martha Two Ponies, I could strangle thee!'

'Pay the man,' Claire's mother-in-law repeated, and stumped up the stairs into the house. By the time Claire, with the children still adhering to her skirts, hurried in to ransack the blue delft jar for enough money to pay the driver, Mrs Two Ponies was seated" firmly in the kitchen rocker, getting her pipe going.

'Beccah, take this and give it to Mr Garvey, and thank him for me for bringing thee. Then go find thy father and tell him I need him. Now, Martha, why has thee brought these children home? Thee promised to keep them till the end of the month.'

The old woman rocked and puffed and stared at the wall with eyes as bright and black as chips of mica.

'Daniel?'

'Grandmother had one of her dreams, ma – you know, the special ones? She went and talked to Uncle Peter Sees Far about it, and when she came back she saw Father Montaldo. And Father Montaldo went to Mrs Steinhagen at the trading post and borrowed the money for our fares. Father Montaldo drove us to the airport, and then we took a plane and then another plane, a littler one, and after that we took the bus to the Crossing, and I went and found Mr Garvey and he brought us home. I'm sorry, ma, but you know how it is. You just can't argue with grandmother.'

'Maybe thee can't, but I can. *Dreams!* Heathen nonsense. What thy father will say I hate to think.'

Claire was beginning to cool down a little, but she looked deeply worried, and when Chuck came in with Rebeccah riding on his hip she rounded on him.

'I declare, I do not know what has got into thy mother, but if I was a violent woman I'd hit her!'

'Now is that any way for a good Quaker to talk? Make some coffee, while I find out what this is about.'

He fetched a stool, placed it directly in front of the rocker, and sat down. At once Mrs Two Ponies began talking in an unfamiliar, oddly accented language. Claire, who had made no move to get coffee or anything else, stood there seething, shut out by a tongue of which she understood not one word. She kept her eyes on Chuck's face, but it was no more revealing than the back of the old woman's head. Presently he sighed and got up.

'Well?' Planted foursquare in front of the stove, hands on hips, Claire was a formidable sight. Chuck shrugged helplessly.

'She had a dream,' he said.

'I got that much out of Daniel. What else?'

'It was a teaching dream, one of the ones that are – are sent, you know? It scared her, and she told the dream to Peter Sees Far, and he explained what it meant. It appears that it is necessary for the children to be at home, to – to avert a very great danger.' He was picking his words with care, translating in his head as he went.

146

'Danger to the children?'

'No, to someone else. He was very clear about that, she says. The children have to be here, with us, or the wrong person is going to die. Whatever *that* means,' he added glumly.

'Die? Who's going to die?'

'She doesn't know. Peter either didn't know himself or didn't tell her. But he said the children were needed to be – oh *Dios*, what's the word in English? Guardians, I think. Protectors. Peter said it would be a great honour for them, so naturally she brought them home as fast as she could.'

'*Naturally?* Carlos Lainez, thee is a Christian, or so I've been led to believe. Is thee going to stand there and tell me thee sets any store by this superstitious rubbish?'

'Hush, Claire. Anyone would think there were no dreams in the Bible. Anyhow, she is here, and the children are here, and we must do the best we can. Make the coffee, my angel, and Daniel and Rebeccah will wash their hands and faces because they look so beautiful when they're clean, and then they can have bread and cheese and milk, which they will attend to for themselves with their clean hands.'

He put his arm around Claire's hefty waist and squeezed in a comforting and husbandly manner.

'My mother says she'll go back home tomorrow, if someone can take her to the bus station and buy her ticket. She has her return air ticket, and Father Montaldo is meeting her at the other end, good man that he is. I'll give her a cheque for him, so he can pay back Mrs Steinhagen.'

'Will she be able to manage on her own?'

'She says yes. After all, she got here. You have to give her credit. She was never in a plane in her life before today and she was terrified, but she did it for the good of the children. It may not be your idea of good or mine either, but it was what she thought she had to do, and it wasn't easy for her.'

Claire set her teeth and came as close as she could to scowling. For perhaps two minutes she stood in silence. Then her brow cleared, and she went to the rocker and kissed Mrs Two Ponies on the cheek.

'Thank you, Martha,' she said, without reservation. 'Thank you for taking care of the children.'

The old woman patted her graciously and leaned down to knock out her pipe on the hearth.

*

147

The fourth and last roadblock was only fifteen miles from the farm, right outside Cold Crossing, and the trooper in charge was an old acquaintance. Conor was waved through without hindrance. It was odd, he reflected, how people, even policemen, always assumed that any crimes, except for family murders, were committed either by strangers or by known delinquents. Because you knew a man's name, had once had a beer with him at a church picnic, or sat next to him at an auction, or sold a cow to his brother-in-law, he was automatically excluded from suspicion.

That was what they had counted on when they decided to hold Kate here, where they were an accepted part of the landscape, instead of relying on the patchy anonymity of a big city. He was having doubts about that decision now. Sheriff Gibbs and the state police shouldn't present any great problem. There was no special reason for the state police to take an interest in them, and as for Gibbs, he had known Claire's father forty years. He was an astute old man and very inquisitive, but his bias was in their favour.

Federal agents were another matter altogether, and the discovery of Kate's bag near Carrstown would have brought droves of them into the area. Carrstown itself, almost two hundred miles to the northeast, would be the centre of the search, but even this far out they would be making enquiries, and he didn't like it.

The people at Harmony would inevitably be investigated. They were not popular locally, 'commune' being in many minds synonymous with 'communist', and besides the women wore odd clothes and the men had spurned the dairy cooperative, preferring instead to harbour what their critics called 'them unnatural goats'. Given any suggestion of radical goings-on, they were a perfect target. Fortunately Brujo, the least predictable member of the group, had been out of his head during Kate's brief bid for asylum, and the three women were as likely to babble to the FBI as they were to enlist in the Marines. But an official visit to Harmony was all too likely and entirely too close to home.

On the surface, the operation appeared to be going well. The announcement of Harper's admission to the hospital had come right on schedule, and there was no real reason to suppose the rest would not follow as smoothly. The man was genuinely afraid for his daughter; there could be no argument about that. Although he had disobeyed orders by bringing in the Feds, that had probably been pure reflex, as involuntary as a sneeze. At least there had been no whisper of publicity, which was the really important thing.

Nevertheless, Conor was worried. Moreover, he suspected that he ought to be much more worried than he was, but small bubbles of unwarranted optimism kept breaking up the steady stream of his thoughts and making it hard to concentrate. He faced the possibility that this untimely cheerfulness afflicted him only because he was about to see Kate again. Not being given to self-deception, he acknowledged that it probably did. It was a nuisance and might well be a danger, but since apparently he could not view anything with appropriate alarm, he would simply have to adjust for the distortion, as for a defective gunsight, reminding himself constantly that the situation (tra-la) was really a lot less promising than it seemed.

Though there was still some time to go before sunset, it was almost dark beneath the heavy overcast by the time the Jeep drew up in front of the house. Daniel and Rebeccah came racing into the yard as he switched off the engine, and he realized once again, with a cold slap of dismay, how easy it was for things to go wrong.

'Hello, brats. What on earth are you doing here? Is your grandmother sick?'

'No, no, she brought us –'

'She had a dream and she brought us –'

'In a plane!'

'*Two* planes, stupid!'

'Oh, terrific.' Conor tucked a child under each arm and hugged them. 'Much as I love you both, I could have done without you just now. What does your father say?'

Daniel wriggled free. 'He says the damage is done, and we may as well stay now. Conor, what damage? Why isn't anyone pleased to see us? And who's that girl?'

'Good question. Three good questions. Look, Dan, I can't go into it now. I'll talk to you later. You and Beccah stay close to the house. And don't talk to any outsiders, not even people you know, okay?'

'Okay. But you will tell me later?'

'As much as I can, cocker. You two are a – a considerable complication. For the moment, do whatever the grown-ups tell you and don't argue. Assume that we know what we're about, even if it doesn't make sense to you. Because we do, you know. Push off now, I'm going into conference.'

The atmosphere in the kitchen was soggy with futility, like peace negotiations rudely overtaken by a fresh outbreak of war. Sam's freckles stood out in a spatter of dark brown against the pallor of his skin, and his mouth was as tight as a sprung trap. Afeni had a curiously dusty look, the sweet insouciant roundness of her flesh gone lean and dry. Chuck seemed tired and old and very Indian – one of George Catlin's melancholy chiefs contemplating the decline of the red man. Even Claire's vitality was a little dimmed – the kitchen was warm, but she hugged a shawl about her as if she felt a draught. It was one thing to risk your own life, quite another when children were involved. Only Mrs Two Ponies, the cause of all the trouble, looked entirely comfortable, tipping back and forth in the rocker and sucking on her smelly little pipe. Conor greeted the old lady ceremoniously before enquiring about the person who was uppermost in his mind and unaccountably missing from the room.

'Where's Kate?'

'Oh, Conor,' Claire said, 'thank the Lord you're home. We have had *such* trouble. Federal agents all over the farm yesterday, and now here's Martha brought the children back as if things weren't difficult enough already, and you so late and not a word to tell us when you were coming –'

'The whole area's crawling with troopers. I hit four roadblocks between here and Richmond, and it didn't seem like a very bright idea to use the radio. My God, I need a drink. Claire, where *is* Kate?'

'She's gone to collect the eggs before the rain begins,' Chuck said, pouring whisky. 'She'll be back any time now. Here.' He slid the glass across the table.

'She's alone? You let her out alone, with nobody on the monitor even? Are you demented?'

'Easy, Conor. You've been away. Things are different now. She won't run off again.'

'When all she has to do is stroll down the road into the arms of the Feds? Look, I believe in the Tooth Fairy too, but surely you don't –'

'Hello, Conor.'

He wheeled and then stood perfectly still, the untasted drink halfway to his mouth. She was standing just inside the kitchen door, carrying a brown earthenware bowl full of eggs. She had on a skirt of Afeni's made of dark red printed cotton, very full and graceful, falling almost to her ankles. A black T-shirt clung to her small, high breasts, and her freshly washed hair was tied with a dark red ribbon. She was smiling, but the smile began to fade when he did not speak. Not taking his eyes off her, he felt for and found the edge of the kitchen table and carefully set down the glass before walking towards her. Three feet away, he stopped.

'Well?' he said.

'Well what?'

'Did you miss me?'

The smile revived, glowing.

'You're conceited,' she said.

'Yes, I know. My character is a mass of flaws, but let's not get into that or we shall be here all night. Put those bloody eggs down, can't you? Here, give them to me.'

She held out the bowl, and he put it down on the dresser, again without looking.

'Now then. *Did you miss me?*'

'Yes, I did, very much.'

To Claire, looking on horrified from her place by the hearth, it was as if a hasty-tempered angel had put one large, golden hand squarely in the middle of each back and shoved. One moment Conor and Kate were a yard apart, 'grinning at each other like a pair of fools' as Claire indignantly phrased it to Chuck. The next, they had flown together like two magnets suddenly released.

Kate was not conscious of having moved. She had arrived in his arms, it appeared, by some freak of teleportation, without actually having to go there. She was not aware of the other people in the room or indeed of anything at all except the warm comfort of Conor's throat next to her cheek, the scrape of his chin against her temple, and his arms holding her painfully tight and his fingers moving gently, incredibly gently, stroking the nape of her neck. For those few seconds the boundaries melted, and there was nothing to separate their bodies, not clothes, not even skin; they shared the same pulse and breathed the same breath. Then Conor let out a long, harshly audible sigh, moved his hands to her shoulders, and stepped back, away from her.

'It's no good,' he said. 'I tried, I really did, but it's just no good. I'm sorry, Kate.'

'I'm not.'

'Yes, well, you're a baggage,' he said, drawing her over to the table and picking up his glass. 'And your poor mother saying you're to be a good girl, fat chance.'

'My mother? Did you –'

'I went and saw her. She sends her love. You're very much alike, you two, but I expect you knew that.'

'You *saw* her? In New Lymington? Conor, you lunatic, you could have been caught.'

'I suppose so, but it seemed like a good idea at the time. I knew she must be frantic about you and, not having met the lady, I was afraid if I didn't take the pressure off a bit she might lose her head and do something dumb. A needless anxiety, as things turned out, but I wasn't to know. Anyway, I'm glad I went. I think she's easier in her mind about you now. She's pretty impressive, isn't she? How she ever came to get mixed up with your dreary father I can't think. I saw him too, by the way. Can't say I took to him, precisely, but at least he seems to be fond of you, which is in his favour. Did you hear the bulletin yesterday?'

'That he was in the hospital? Chuck says he's not really sick, though, it's just part of the plan.'

'That's right. What is not part of the plan is that the whole sodding countryside's in an uproar. Somebody found your bag, you wretched child, and the Feds are hopping around getting in one another's way like a plague of frogs. And while I don't want to seem captious or difficult in any way, it would be nice if someone could tell me just what in hell has been going on here.'

With Conor safely home the garrison was inclined to relax, and even to treat the previous day's alarms as something of a joke. Grose and Maybush dwindled from a menace to an unsuccessful vaudeville act, and Chuck recreated the saga of Rachel Bradley Owens and her flighty daughter with such gusto Claire laughed till she cried. Conor was unamused.

'They'll be back,' he predicted.

'But why? They went over the place with a fine-tooth comb; they didn't find a thing. Why should they bother us any more?'

'Oh, use the equipment. *Think*. They're looking for Catherine Hale. They won't find her, because she doesn't exist, but they're not about to go back to the field office and say well, gee, we blew it. They'll go on digging, and after they've tried every place they can think of they'll start again at the beginning. That's how they operate.' He leaned back from the table and looked around at the faces turned to his. 'Lecture,' he said. 'People poke fun at the FBI because they're an easy target. There's a rich vein of silliness running through the whole outfit, and those incompetent hoods they hire as informers don't do much for the image. Also, a quite disproportionate amount of time and effort goes into the sort of weak-minded mischief that's managed far more efficiently by spiteful old ladies.'

'Anonymous letters,' Sam agreed. 'Some sorry li'l scoutmaster gets fired from his job because his wife's a socialist.'

'That sort of thing. But just because they can be fatuous, it doesn't make them negligible. Remember the Berrigans? They thought they were up against a bunch of clowns, and in some ways they were right, but the clowns got them in the end. What the Feds have that the rest of us don't is time. They hang about and hang about, like cats watching a bird cage, and when finally somebody gets careless they are *there*.' He clapped his open hand into a fist and slowly opened it again, palm up. 'With a mouthful of feathers. I'm not trying to frighten you, but they will be back, and we'd better be ready for them.'

He smiled at Kate.

'It's all right, we shan't string you up in the rafters again. Once is more than enough. But we do have to work out some sort of emergency procedure. There's a possibility that's occurred to me, but it calls for such quantities of sheer brassfaced gall that I'm not sure I ought even to mention it.'

'Ve haff vays of makink you talk,' Chuck said. 'Come on, cough it up in mother's hand.'

'The basic difficulty is that Kate would have to help. In effect, she'd become an accomplice in her own kidnapping. Which is where it gets dodgy, because even if she agreed – and there's no sane reason why she should – I don't see how we can ask it of her. If anything went wrong and they found out what she'd been up to, she'd be in bad trouble. Legally I'm not sure what, if anything, they'd actually be able to do to her, but the fallout would be nasty. For one thing, the prosecution would treat her as a hostile witness, and they'd wipe the courtroom floor with her. If the rest of us go down that's our affair – we knew the risks from the beginning. I will not have Kate hurt by this.'

'But if any of you are caught,' Kate said slowly, 'I'll be in bad trouble anyhow. I won't testify against you, and they can send me to jail for refusing. Or I think they can.'

'You'd refuse to testify? For God's sake, why?'

'Oh, don't embarrass me. If you don't know by now, I'm not going to draw you a picture. Look, if you're worrying about what's best for me, obviously the safest thing would be for all of this to go through exactly as you planned it. My father resigns, I go home, and none of the story comes out, ever. That way, nothing can happen to me at all, right?'

'I suppose so.'

'Then it's in my own interest to help in any way I can.'

'There's a hole in that big enough to drive a bus through, but thanks anyway.' He stretched out his hand across the table, and after a moment, she put hers into it. 'Done and done,' he said. 'If it weren't for the social gulf between us, Lady Agatha, I swear I'd marry you. Claire, I'm starving. What's for supper?'

'Chicken pie, and it won't be ready for another hour. I didn't know when you'd be home. Want some cheese and biscuits?'

'No, I'll wait and make a beast of myself when the time comes. One thing I ought to do, I think, is have a word with the children. They ought to be clued in to the point where they don't go and blow the gaff out of sheer inadvertence, but beyond that the less said the better. Or have you spoken to them already?'

'Only to warn them not to talk about Kate. We weren't sure

how much you'd want them told.'

'Okay. Chuck, you'd better sit in on this so they know it's official. And we'll see them in the parlour, that'll be more impressive. Lord, Lord, Martha, I see why you felt you had to bring them back, but I wish you'd learn to keep your dreams under control.'

After the children had been briefed and dismissed, solemn with secrets and privately amazed that their parents would shelter anyone who had run away from home, however dreadful home might be, Conor scribbled a note and sent Sam off with it to Harmony.

'Do I have to go all the way around and leave the Jeep at the bridge? It's going to rain before much longer – you can hear it blowing up already. And I'll be late for supper if I have to walk that last piece.'

'We'll keep yours hot. We're asking them a considerable favour, Sam, no point in putting their backs up before we start. I wish to God they'd go mad and get a telephone. Oh, take a dozen eggs with you. Paul decided it was cruel to keep the fowls penned up, and of course, a hawk got one and the rest are having nervous breakdowns and won't lay. Charity's fit to be tied – after all she's responsible for the commissariat and without eggs the whole system falls apart – but you can't tell Paul anything. In fact make it two dozen, if Claire can spare them, that little girl of Charity's looks like something out of Bangladesh.'

'I got more eggs than I know what to do with,' Claire said. 'And you might take a couple of wholewheat loaves from this morning's baking. Wish I had the feeding of that child, I'd put pounds on her. I'll give you some of those oatmeal cookies, too, children like sweet stuff, and they're wholesome enough. Just tell Paul I made 'em with honey, though, instead of brown sugar, or he'll give 'em to the goats.'

'Did you?'

'If thee doesn't know, thee won't be lying. It's no sin to feed a hungry child.'

They were halfway through supper when Sam returned.

'What's the form?' Conor asked him.

'Paul says it's all right with him, if Alice Mary wants to do it.' He opened the door of the warming oven and took out the fragrant wreckage of the pie. 'Well look at that, now. What a bunch of hogs.'

'Daniel had thirds. Anyway I don't know what you're

grumbling about, there's enough left for two starving navvies. What did Alice Mary say?'

'Said fine, glad to help out. She don't like the FBI much more'n we do. Likes you, though, on account of what you did for Brujo. He's all over it, by the way – till next time, anyhow. No, I believe Alice Mary'd do just about anything you asked her.'

'Which one is Alice Mary?' Kate enquired.

'L'il yellow-haired thing, calls herself Consolation. You probably seen her that day you were over there. Looks a whole lot like you. She's Brujo's girl, if she don't pick up and leave him for Conor here.'

'That'll be the day,' Conor said, and helped himself to more coffee.

It was Sam and Claire's turn to clean up, and when supper was over Conor rose yawning from the table and sat down on one of the settles. He looked up at Kate, who was standing by the hearth, gently prodding Bagel's belly with her toe, an attention that reduced him to drooling ecstasy.

'Leave that scruffy animal alone and come sit by me.'

She hesitated and then came over and perched stiffly at the far end of the settle. Chuck cleared his throat.

'I'm going out to the barn and take a look at Lady Godiva,' he announced to no one in particular and left the kitchen.

'Come on, Mrs Two Ponies,' Afeni said briskly, 'let's you and me get these kids washed up and off to bed.'

'Oh, not *yet* –'

'It's too *early* –'

'Not one more word do I want to hear out of either one of you. Up the stairs, now, and if you're real good I might even tell you a story.'

'A story about Anansi?'

'With lions in it? And crocodiles?'

'You bet, but you got to be good now. Let's go.'

Left alone with Conor, Kate was immobilized by panic. Spinning romantic daydreams about him while he was gone had been a sweet self-indulgence, and his return had given her an unexpectedly violent jolt of pleasure and relief. But faced with reality, the close proximity of a man – not some nice, nervous college boy, but a grown man who wanted her and was not at all shy about saying so – she was, quite simply, terrified. She stared fixedly at the opposite wall, but her peripheral vision was excellent. She knew he was looking at her.

'Sit here, Katie.'

He took her hand and drew her along the smooth wooden boards until their bodies touched.

'That's better.'

'Conor –'

'No. Don't talk. Just stay with me. Somebody's bound to come crashing in before long, I only want a couple of minutes' peace. Christ, I'm tired.' He let his head tilt sideways until his cheek rested against her hair. 'You smell of lavender, like the sheets at home. Dear, oh dear, I wish I'd never set eyes on you. No I don't. "Lavender's blue, dilly dilly, rosemary's green . . ."'

Chuck slammed in through the yard door, dark splotches on his shoulders from the first huge drops of rain.

'She's starting. Conor, I'll need you.'

They went through to the scullery to get what they needed from the veterinary cupboard.

'Can I help?' Sam asked, dish cloth poised.

'You?' Chuck frowned. 'You're good with machines, not animals – but okay, come on. Maybe you'll learn something.'

The three men hurried out into the hissing night. Claire picked up the coffee pot.

'I better make more; they'll be wanting it I dare say. Katie child, make sure there's plenty of hot water for washing. They'll need that too. This'll be a long haul, if the last time's anything to go by. Some of those doctors that go around saying how women make too much fuss over childbearing, and how they ought to treat it like any other animal function, I'd like to lock 'em in with Lady Godiva the next few hours. If cows could write books, reckon we'd find out they're just about as crazy about labour pains as anyone else that's got good sense,' she said, banging the enamel pot crossly down on the stove. 'Oh, it's not so bad really,' she added hastily as she caught sight of Kate's expression. 'Not so bad at all, considering what you get to show for it, which is children, and a greater joy and comfort there never was. Just don't need a bunch of ignorant men telling me it's nothing, is all. Now you, you're a skinny little thing but you got good hips, you'll do just fine. Only don't wait too long. I was close to forty when Daniel was born, and that's awful late for a first child. You have your babies while you're young.'

'I haven't even got a husband yet,' Kate said. Claire glanced at her sharply.

'As to that, if things weren't the way they are, 'pears to me you

157

wouldn't have far to look. My, it's a pity, but it can't be helped. No chance you two can marry, and the other way's not for you.'

'Why not? Oh, I know you'd think it was immoral and – and wrong, but you don't care about Sam and Afeni. You let them stay here, and they–'

'Child, I do care. But they have to live some place, and I'd as soon have them here where I can keep an eye on 'em. Besides that, Afeni's a woman grown. Sam'd marry her in a minute, too, but she won't have him. Don't know why not, but she won't. Anyhow, it's thee we're talking about. Dear heart, I'm not blind. I ache for thee, I truly do. But pet, thee must not. Thee has thy whole life ahead, and there's no way Conor can be a part of it. Thee has to forget all about him. Why, he'd tell thee the same thing himself.'

'He already did.'

'Well, then. And if thee goes and does something that'll make the forgetting harder to do, it'll only be worse in the end.' She patted Kate's arm. 'Some things in life thee can have, and some thee can't, my mother used to say. Conor's a fine man – don't believe I ever knew a better – and thee as young as thee is and away from thy friends, no wonder he took thy fancy. But there's other good men, and thee'll find one and be happy.'

'He said that too, but it isn't true. Oh, you make me so mad, all of you! Acting as if Conor were a – an X-rated movie I'm not old enough to go see. I'm not saying things could ever work out for us in the long run. They probably couldn't. But stop telling me to forget him, because I can't.'

Claire sighed. 'No, I don't suppose thee can. Don't suppose thee'd want to, either. But after a while it won't hurt any more, and that's something. Now I better go up and get those children settled, or Afeni'll be telling them stories all night.'

When Claire came back downstairs she was arguing patiently with her mother-in-law.

'No, Martha, you cannot stay in the barn. It'll be a circus in there till all hours, and you'll not get a wink of sleep. Break your rule this one time and sleep in the house. Take the parlour couch. Or we'll bring Daniel down to the parlour, and you can go up in his room with Beccah. There's two good bunk beds and she can have the top one and leave the lower for you. Come on now.'

'Not in the house.' Mrs Two Ponies had been through all this on a previous visit, and she was adamant. 'A house with rooms on top of rooms, I do not sleep in. Eat, drink, sit, wash, okay.

Sleep, no. And beds on top of beds – you should not let the children sleep so. I will speak to my son. Now I go to the barn.'

'Dear, I keep telling you. You won't close an eye in there, and since you're bound and determined to make that long trip home tomorrow, you need your rest tonight.'

In the end they compromised, Mrs Two Ponies accepting a cot on the porch, which had only earth beneath its floor and the pouring sky above its wooden roof. Once that was settled, the women sat subdued in the kitchen, with little conversation. Rain thrashed at the windows, and the lamps roared like far-off trains. Claire had put a match to the fire, more for cheerfulness than warmth. Above the noise of the storm they could hear Lady Godiva's distressful lowing, and were drawn together in a bond of instinctive female sympathy that did not need to be put into words.

Sam came in, damp, dishevelled, and looking green, to fetch towels and hot water.

'How is the poor thing?' Claire asked, filling his pail from the stove reservoir.

'Not so good. Conor's going to wait a little longer, but he reckons it's a malpresentation, whatever that is.'

'Means he'll have to get his arm in there and try and turn the calf.'

'If you say so.' Sam sloshed two inches of coffee into a mug and gulped it down before picking up the pail. 'One thing I learned tonight: I am not ever going to be a dairy farmer.'

When Chuck eventually appeared, blood-spattered and beaming, to announce that mother and daughter were doing well, Claire rose with a vast sigh of relief.

'One more cup of coffee before you go up?'

'No, but pour me a drink while I wash up. I can use it. She's a beautiful little heifer calf – prettiest thing I every saw. Hoo-*wheee*. If Conor hadn't come back today we might have lost them both. That Lady Godiva is a bitch. We ought to have named her Wrong-Way Corrigan. If she can do things ass-backward she will.' He had stripped off his bloodied shirt and was scrubbing himself energetically at the sink.

'Where are the rest?'

'Conor is cooing at his patient, and Sam's taking a walk.'

'In this rain?'

'He's upset. He never watched a birth before, and he's mad at

159

God for making it so messy. I told him he came into the world the same way, and I thought he was going to hit me. Acted like I'd said something bad about his mother.' He took a grateful swig of whisky and looked around the kitchen.

'Don't tell me — let me guess. You murdered my mother and buried the body under the potato patch.'

'Your mother and I are getting along just fine,' Claire said firmly. 'She's on the porch, fast asleep. You know she was up at four this morning, and nine hours of travelling after. I hope I'm that good at seventy-two, but she's tired out, poor woman.'

'Me too. Go see the baby, and then we can all get to bed.'

But Kate could not sleep. If only it hadn't happened, if only Conor hadn't held her in his arms, if only she hadn't run to him, she might have been all right. She could have gone on pretending that she only liked him. Oh, admired him too, was charmed by him, concerned for his safety; but she would have been spared this humiliating hunger. Claire was right, of course. Once they made love she would never be free of him. If a simple embrace could affect her so deeply, then the Real Thing (she thought of it like that, capitalized, with mingled dread and longing), the Real Thing would unmake her altogether. Like a chemical touched by the catalyst, she would be changed, utterly changed.

She could not stay in bed. She sat in an upright chair with the quilt hugged around her, and did not know whether what she felt was love or misery. Whatever it was, it had taken her over, as though her veins had been emptied and refilled with some foreign substance that might as easily kill her as save her life.

There was a tap at the door and she jumped, but it was only Afeni, stately in a long blue robe and carrying a candle.

'You still up?'

'I couldn't sleep.'

'Then maybe there's hope for you yet,' Afeni said grimly, and sat down on the bed as Kate gaped at her.

'Girl, do you know anything about men?' Afeni continued. 'Anything at all?'

'Well of course I do, I — oh, hell. Not really, no.'

'You ain't kidding. Let me tell you something. Conor's in the kitchen sitting by the fire, and you know why he's down there instead of up where he belongs? 'Cause he's scared to death. He don't dare come near you, 'cause if he did he just might touch you and love you and take you. And he got it into his head you're so delicate and fine you couldn't stand it. He's afraid of doing you

160

harm. I don't mean in your body – in your mind.'

'How do you know?'

'Asked him.' The black woman smiled briefly, in pure amusement. 'It's generally the best way. I been down there with him; we been talking. You two think you're invisible or something? I was right there tonight when you brought the eggs in. I saw his face. Saw yours, too. You're in love with him – you got it real bad – only you're so damn dumb you don't have the first idea what to do about it. And he's so shook up wanting you and telling himself it ain't right 'cause he'd be taking advantage of your youth and inexperience and crap like that, he don't know what to do either. It's a miracle I didn't puke all over my shoes.'

'Did he really say that? About youth and inexperience and stuff?'

'You think I'd make that up? He got mad at me, too, for speaking my mind. Called me an interfering bitch. Said I was trying to persuade him into the very same thing he'd just gotten through persuading himself out of. Said he never ought to of laid a hand on you, and he's going to be good and goddamn sure it don't happen again. That man tearing himself in pieces over you, little snippety thing like you that ain't hardly out of diapers.'

'Afeni! I believe you're jealous.'

'Did I say I wasn't? Sure I am. I had my eye on that beautiful man ever since I first seen him. But he didn't care for women before, like he was turned right off. Chuck told me once he been that way ever since his wife got herself killed. And now *you* show up, and he got lights blinking all over him like a Christmas tree.'

'But look – what about Sam?'

'What about him? Conor don't need me and Sam does, that's what about Sam. I'm his mama and his daddy and his piece of black ass, and he loves me as much as he can love anybody, which ain't saying much. Them little white Southern boys, they all the same – laying in a black woman's lap when they babies, and the rest of they lives they trying to creep back in. I love him 'cause somebody has to – like if you have a baby and it don't turn out right, you still got to love it. Sam, he's my mean old Southern baby, and I'm stuck with him. Conor ain't nobody's baby. He's a man – too good a man to fool with the way you're doing. You think you got a right to sit here playing eenie-meenie, minie-moe – heads I'll have him and tails I won't? God almighty, girl, what do you think a woman is for?'

'You can't say that! It's not right – you know better!' Kate was close to tears. 'I'm more than a woman, I'm a person. I don't need some damn man to give me an identity – I'm a person on my own!'

'Well, good evenin', father.' Afeni was caught between amusement and scorn. 'That the way you want to be all your life, on – your – own? Sure you're a person – everybody's a person. Feller shot Martin Luther King was a person; nothing special about that. But did you listen to what you just said? "I'm more than a woman." Well honey, I'll tell you, there ain't *nothing* that's more than a woman. We are the strong ones, baby. You going to keep all that strength and goodness to yourself, like an old miser? Or you going to give it where it'll do the most good?'

'Claire said I shouldn't. She said I had to forget him. Conor did too. I *offered*, Afeni, I offered before he went away, and he turned me down cold.' The tears were overflowing now, making shiny tracks down her face.

'Wasn't 'cause he didn't want you, though. You know that.'

'He said it was because I'll have to go home soon and never see him again, and he won't be able to take care of me.'

'I knew it. Scared of hurting you, just like he is now.' Afeni stood up and stretched luxuriously. 'Baby, I can't tell you what to do. But if it was me, even if it was just the one night, I'd grab it. I wouldn't worry about what it was going to cost me after, and I wouldn't let him worry either. I would just go on down there and take his hand and lead him up the stairs and into the bed. You grown up enough to do that? Or you gonna sit there crying like a little bitty girl that lost her roller skate key?'

She stalked over to the door, and then paused and came a few steps back.

'You never have a man before? That what's bothering you?' she asked, in a kinder tone.

'No. I mean, no, I haven't, but it isn't only that.'

'Well, you got to start some time, and you may's well start with the best. My first time, jee-*zus*. I was fourteen, and an old white man caught me in the alley coming home from school. Just shoved me down behind a pile of boxes and did it to me, right there in the dirt. Hurt like shit, too – always does if you don't want it. He beat me up, 'cause he was holding his hand over my mouth and I bit him. Must've scrubbed my teeth for a good half hour after I got home, get rid of the taste of that dirty old hand in my mouth. Never told my mother, but she knew. It was right after that we moved up north. Now you dry your eyes, sweetheart, and quit looking so tragic. Whether you do or whether you don't, either way it's not the end of the world. Don't pay no attention to me or Claire or nobody, not even Conor. Least of all Conor – what does he know? You make your own mind up what you want to do. That's the way us big girls have to be – have to take care of business for our own selves.'

Conor had fallen asleep, cramped awkwardly in a corner of the high-backed settle where she had sat beside him after supper. Kate came to a stop a few feet away from him, brought up short by a disabling attack of shyness. After Afeni's lecture she had been so confident. Resolutely she had gone back to the bathroom and washed herself (an embarrassing, self-conscious process, but she had read that it was the proper thing to do). She had brushed her hair, cleaned her teeth a second time, dabbed on a little more of Claire's lavender water, pulled the grubby Band-Aids off her heels and put on fresh ones. She had felt splendidly adult, a woman getting ready for her lover. But now assurance forsook her. What if Afeni had got it wrong, and he didn't want her after all? And even if he did, how was she to wake him? What in the world ought she to say? None of the arduous training in correct behaviour that Miss Hampshire's School had forced upon its students was the slightest use to her now. She simply stood there, paralysed.

He looked younger asleep and painfully defenceless – gentle, troubled, and worn out. Asleep, he did not frighten her at all. As she stood watching him, a random spurt of flame leapt high at the heart of the dying fire, sending shadows trembling across his face, and she thought he moved. The sudden suspicion that he had been awake all the time, watching her through his lashes, made her recoil involuntarily, and she backed into the edge of the dresser and knocked one pot clanging against another. He moved then, and fast. He was on his feet, and on her, before she had time to stir, hard hands gripping her wrists, the peaceful planes of his face distorted in a cartoon scribble of alarm and menace. Then he saw who it was, and his hold relaxed.

'Christ, lovey, don't you ever come up on me like that,' he said. 'I might have hurt you.' He looked down at his hands, still holding her wrists. 'Did I hurt you?'

'No, it's all right. You scared me, though.'

'Not half as much as you scared me.' He let her go, and scrubbed his knuckles across his face, belatedly waking up after the first reflex response. 'What are you doing down here, anyway?

164

What time is it?'

'Almost two o'clock. I didn't think you ought to spend the whole night in the kitchen – you'd wake up stiff as a board. You ought to be in bed.'

'So should you.'

He was sleepy and preoccupied, functioning on some remote wavelength that had nothing to do with her. He was going to be no help at all.

'Yes, I know,' she said bravely. 'But I'm not going unless you come to bed with me.'

His mouth dropped open in honest astonishment as he registered what she had said. There was a long, loaded pause, and her heart sank at his solemn face.

'My dear girl,' he said. 'Are you quite sure you know what you're doing?'

'Yes. At least, I know I want to do it. Please, Conor.'

The smile he turned on her then had all the radiant innocence of a small boy on his birthday morning, when the new bicycle is wheeled out of the closet.

'Christ in glory rules the skies. Well if you expect me to try and talk you out of it, you're mad. Hold on a minute, though – has Afeni been after you?'

'Afeni? No.'

'Of course not. And the cheque is in the mail, I suppose. Oh, the hell with it. I'll take all the help I can get. Your place or mine? Mine, I think – the bed's bigger. Besides, I'd just as soon not be right next door to Claire. I wouldn't put it past her to come barging in with a flaming sword and a lot of uncalled-for remarks.' He bent over the lamp on the table, already turned down low, and extinguished it. In the gloom he turned back to her and held out his hands.

'Katie, my love, my poppet, come to bed.'

When he came back from brushing his teeth in the bathroom she was in his bed, still wearing Claire's nightgown, with the covers drawn up almost to her chin. She looked, he thought, like a child of about ten contemplating a visit to the dentist. He came over and stood by the side of the bed.

'Come clean,' he said. 'You've never done this before, have you?'

'Well . . . No.' She would not look at him. 'Do you mind very much?'

165

He was silent long enough for her to wonder if she was about to be rejected for lack of experience, and if that would be a crushing disappointment or only rather a relief.

'It's going to hurt, that's the trouble,' he said at last. 'You do realize that? I don't care what it says in all those funny books. The first time does hurt – unless you've gone in for some fairly extensive fooling around in the past, which in your case strikes me as unlikely. It's not agony, and it doesn't last long, but it still isn't what you'd call your pure undiluted bliss. And I simply hate the idea of hurting you.'

She sat up in bed, clasping her knees and narrowly examining the blanket. 'I'm not going into a convent,' she said. 'Sooner or later, somebody's going to do it, and I don't want it to be anyone else. I want it to be you.' She looked up at him. 'That's pretty selfish, I guess, but that's how I feel.'

He smiled at her. 'Tell you what,' he said. 'We'll go very gently. We'll take our own sweet time. And if at any point, up to and including the last possible moment, you want to change your mind, well, that's all right too. Okay?'

'Okay.'

'Good girl.' He turned away. 'And you can take off that circus tent you're wearing, for a start.'

He was unbuttoning his shirt when a thought struck him. 'I suppose you have seen a man with no clothes on? Or haven't you?'

'Only in a movie. *If*, it was called. There were all these schoolboys in cold showers, looking miserable. Oh, and my father once, years ago, when I was little.'

He snorted with laughter. 'Now there is a solemn thought. You'll find this a bit different. My God, I hope so, anyway,' he added, snorting again as he dragged off his boots.

Kate scrambled hastily out of the nightgown while his back was turned, and pulled up the covers again. She felt very unprotected with nothing between her and the sheets. She was a little hurt that he should be able to laugh, and puzzled too. Men really were very different; coarse in their feelings, she supposed, and certainly unpredictable in their reactions.

Then Conor came back to the bed, and the sight of his cock in full and arrogant erection drove everything else out of her mind. She could not bear to look at it and could not look anywhere else. It was enormous, monstrous, as threatening as a cannon aimed at her. *That?* she thought, horrified. He's going to stick *that* inside me? Oh, no – no way. All her muscles tensed, ready to run.

He saw the fright on her face and could have kicked himself for a tactless oaf. He'd never made love to a virgin before, that was the trouble. He would have to go very slowly, very carefully – and he wanted her so much that it wouldn't be easy. She was so damned young, even for eighteen. A Saigon twelve-year-old knew more than she did – those heartbreakingly practical child whores with the baby sisters hungry at home, and the slender fingers made for picking pockets. And riddled with the clap more often than not, poor little beasts. He wouldn't think about them now. Now he had to lead his Kate where she was so determined and so afraid to go, and to do it just precisely right would take every scrap of concentration he could find.

He sat on the edge of the bed and, leaning over, took her face between his hands and began to kiss her, lightly at first and then more deeply, probing her softly with his tongue. His mouth was cool and liquid, and tasted faintly sweet. Covering hers, it was miraculously comforting. It seemed to assuage an old, forgotten wound, the pain of which had been a part of her so long that she was only aware of it now because it had stopped. A tide of warmth swept through her, and there was a strangely pleasant ache between her legs. He was not hurting her, though she had fully expected to be hurt. With desperate courage she had opened her gates to the enemy, and now it looked as if he might not be the enemy after all. In simple gratitude she put her arms around him. She had never caressed a man before and somehow expected his skin to feel rough, like a cat's tongue. She was surprised and moved by the silk of his shoulders under her palms, and continued to stroke him as much for her own pleasure as for his, lost in the unforeseen delight of touching.

After a while he drew away from her and sat up. She opened her eyes and saw a stranger, absorbed and stern, all laughter for the moment burned away.

'Let me look at you,' he said, and drew the covers down to the foot of the bed. She was appalled. She had thought of sex, when she thought of it at all, as something that took place in decent darkness, at night, under blankets. To be naked, exposed, stared at – it was too much, she hadn't bargained for that. He was looking down at her body, scanning every inch of it as if he were checking for some unforgivable flaw. She searched for comfort in his face and found none; it was withdrawn, unreadable. *Oh dear,*

Kate thought, *I don't like this. I thought I would, but I don't like it at all.*

She was so lovely it stopped his breath. Dressed, she was a sweet, skinny kid. But now that she was naked the secret generosity of the flesh was all laid bare, the small, unexpected softnesses that would yield so gently to accommodate his own hard angularity. She must have tiny bones. Yet she wasn't a child – though he'd kept telling himself she was when he was trying to stay away from her. Not a child at all, there was nothing childish about that perfect body. Still, she seemed so little, so easy to hurt. A great surge of protectiveness welled up in him, diluting though not entirely vanquishing the damnable male impulse he recognized in himself, to prove his superior strength on something so definitively vulnerable.

He let out a great sighing breath and shifted his gaze, with an effort, back to her face. She looked scared and embarrassed, and no wonder; he was behaving like a lout again. Of course she was upset, poor baby.

'I know you feel shy, but you mustn't,' he said mildly. 'I never saw anything more beautiful in my life. You shine, d'you know that? Like a lamp.'

He put his hands on her. She shivered and was still, and then shivered again. His touch was light, the fingers cool and dry as they drifted over her skin, and yet they seemed to burn like feathers of fire. They captured her breasts and played with them, with a leisurely, benign authority that filled her whole body with soft, swelling heat. The feeling grew too strong, too rich, the exquisite tension building until she thought her skin would split, unable to contain so much sensation. She closed her eyes in fear and pleasure.

'Look at me.'

When she obeyed, he locked her gaze with his and would not release her. All the while his hands moved purposefully, mapping her body as if he were learning it by heart, his eyes never left her face. The patient hunger in them was so disquieting that she longed for darkness as the torturer's victim longs for sleep.

'Conor. Please. Blow out the candle.'

'No. I want to watch you.'

Helpless under those friendly, knowledgeable eyes, she felt panic rise in her like a drowning flood. He felt it too, rising through her skin into his fingers, and opposed it as stubbornly as in the past he had fought terrors of his own.

'Clear your mind. We're not doing something dark and dirty that has to be hidden. You've a lot to learn, my love, my little love, and the first lesson is that it's no use trying to hide from me, because I won't let you. I'm a mean, rotten person and I always get my own way. Now budge over.'

He lay down beside her and, growling softly in his throat, gathered her against him.

'Conor,' she whispered.

'What is it, my heart?'

'I can't – I don't know what I'm supposed to do.'

This time he managed not to laugh. 'That's all right, pretty. You'll pick it up as we go along.' He stroked her reassuringly, and his lips were soft and very gentle. 'Easy,' he murmured. 'Easy now, *mo chridh*. I have you safe.'

For the next hour or more he devoted himself to Kate's education. Her tremulous responsiveness to his touch was proof, had he needed any, that she was not cold by nature. But still she was wholly inexperienced, and very shy. Patiently he set about dismantling the long-established network of alarms and hesitancies that held her captive. He was relentlessly generous. His fingers and lips and tongue were employed with a controlled and delicate ferocity that drove her to such extremes of pleasure she felt herself dissolving, shaken loose and lost. He seemed to be everywhere at once, all hands and mouths, tumbling weightlessly all over her, as lithe and joyous as an otter in a pool. Finally he did something which shocked her so profoundly that she fought him off, protesting.

'But why not? Doesn't it feel good?'

'That's not the point.'

'It's the only point there is.' He rested his head against her thigh and stroked her belly, moving his palm in slow, calming circles. 'If you really hate it then of course I won't do it any more, but you must tell me why.'

'I just don't see how you can stand to do a thing like that. No normal person . . . Well, it's just sick, that's all.'

'It's nothing of the sort.' He was indignant. 'Infantile, possibly. Babies put things in their mouths because it's a way of finding out whether they're good to eat – and you, my darling, are absolutely scrumptious.'

She sat up and stared at him.

'You mean you actually *like* doing it?'

'Well of course I do, or I wouldn't do it. Look, Katie, I love you very much. There isn't one single part of you, not one, that I don't love and cherish. I love your toes and your kneecaps and the back of your neck. I love your breasts and your elbows and your beautiful little ass. How can you possibly imagine that I wouldn't love your cunt? It's not nasty, for God's sake. It's a lovely, loving, hospitable place. And when I touch you there and kiss you and taste you, I don't do it only to give you pleasure. I do it because it pleases me as well. Now come on, tell me. How did it make you feel, really?'

'As if I'd died and gone to heaven.'

'There you are, then; don't be stuffy. There's more to life than the missionary position, thank God.'

He hitched himself up, pressed his parted lips against her skin just below the navel, and blew a gigantic, reverberant raspberry that broke her up into startled giggles.

'Frivolous creature, how can you laugh at a time like this? Now where was I? No, don't tell me, it'll come to me in a minute . . . Aaaahh.'

Physically she was ready, more than ready; melting and open, ambushed by her own body. But still he delayed, allowing more time for the strangeness to subside a little, for the aching thrill along the nerves to become familiar – not something to bridle away from but something anticipated, craved for. With stroking and gentling, with murmuring and soft bawdy whispers, his affectionate invasions gave her no rest as she moved and moaned under his hands, under his sweetly merciless mouth.

'Look, peach,' he said at last, on a half gasp of rueful, barely articulated laughter, 'the old man can only take so much. If you love me, for pity's sake have me now. Otherwise you must go. Run, do not walk, to the nearest exit.'

It was all very well to talk about running. She could not have walked a yard and he knew it, having gone to a lot of trouble to bring her to precisely this stage of pleasure-drugged exhaustion. Raised on one elbow he looked down at her face in the candlelight. The soft, swollen lips were parted, the eyes enormous and hazy with a kind of calm bewilderment. She looked so trustful it terrified him, and his heart turned over without warning, wrenched with pity and tenderness.

'Oh, my love. I don't mean to bully you. You shan't do anything you don't want to. Are you frightened?'

'No. Well – yes, I guess so. A little.'

'But you do want me?'

'Yes.' Slow as sleepwalking, she lifted a hand and touched his cheek. 'Yes, I do.' Her fingers traced the outline of his mouth. Ducking his chin, he kissed her palm.

'Say it, then.'

'I want you.'

'And do you want me to do this?' His tongue flickered in the hollow at the base of her throat, and browsed upward to the other hollow at the angle of her jaw, behind the earlobe.

'Yes.'

'And this?' Brushing his lips across a small hard nipple, teasing it luxuriously with his tongue.

'Yes. Oh, yes.'

'What about this?' A hair's breadth from hurting, he drew his fingernails down her belly, and then up from her knee along the soft smoothness of her inner thigh. Her skin tightened convulsively.

'Brrr, gooseflesh.'

'But you like it?'

'Love it.'

'And here? Do you want me here, inside you? Here? Talk to me. Tell me.' Exploring the secret folds, warm and heavy and sleek with juice, that opened to him willingly now, welcoming his touch. Tenderly, indulgently, he played with her, sliding his finger deep inside, rolling the firm little love-knob gently under his thumb, until she gasped and closed her thighs hard on his hand.

'Yes, God, yes. Oh, darling, please yes.'

He wanted to take her at once, roughly, and was shaken to find himself quite angry with her, as though the long, deliberate preliminaries had somehow been her fault, something she had demanded of him, instead of a discipline he had deliberately imposed upon himself. Whatever the reason, the impulse to violence was there – and strong – and it scared him. He lifted her legs apart very carefully, as if she were made of glass, and knelt between them.

'There's nothing to be afraid of,' he told her, for the second time that week, and hoped to God that it was true.

He entered her in a harsh, sustained assault that would, he told himself, be less traumatic than a lot of drawn-out, tentative fumbling. The sudden stinging, tearing pain shocked her to the edge of resistance, and she cried out. But he lay still and soothed her, dropping small kisses on her eyes and throat and breasts, murmuring that she was his darling, his treasure, his own brave, lovely girl – he had never meant to hurt her. (Had he meant to? Perhaps he had, but there was nothing to be done about it now.)

While he stayed still it wasn't very bad; and he sounded so anxious, so remorsefully concerned. The defensive rigidity melted out of her and then, of course, he began to move again, and it hurt. The good part was over, the skilled, attentive fondling that had scorched her with delight. All pleasure must be paid for – she'd always known that – and the price was this grotesque and painful thing he was doing to her now. Unhappily she braced herself to bear it, knowing that at least, if her book-learned information was anything to go by, it would soon be over. Only it wasn't. The long, slow strokes went on and on. After a while the pain was less, or else she was too distracted to notice it because, incredibly, there was pleasure again, but pleasure of a different kind: primal and powerful, increasing with every thrust. She was going up, higher up, and the only thought there was room for now was that no one had told her, nothing she had heard or read had at all prepared her for the rightness, the sheer physical logic of the act, like running, like dancing. But now it was fast and driving – she was going up too fast, out of control, and she was scared and wanted it to stop, and could not bear it ever to stop, her body thrashing in astonished obedience to his hard cock and clever, loving hands. The world blew up, then, in one long pulsing flare and she was falling, helplessly falling, a galaxy away from the bodies on the rocking bed. There was more of panic than of joy in the wordless cry that escaped her, and it reached him even through the blind egotism of his own crisis.

'There . . . There, my beauty, my darling love. There, my precious girl. Hush now, my dove, it's all right. Conor's here.' Still inside her, putting off the bleak moment of separation as long as he could, he turned her carefully to lie against him, cradling her, one hand obsessively smoothing the damp hair back from her forehead, over and over, as he rocked her into calm.

'Conor, was that – what *was* that?' she asked presently, in a small, blurred voice. He kissed the corner of her mouth.

'That was what they call an orgasm. It hardly ever happens the first time. Very clever of you, peach. And very nice for me.'

He kissed her again, lingeringly. 'Nice for you too, I hope?'

She did not answer immediately, and dread took hold of him and squeezed. Had he, after all, made a hash of it, damaged and distressed the very person he so much wanted to please?

'I wouldn't call it nice, exactly,' she said at last. 'More like being hit by a truck. A solid gold truck.'

Weak with relief, he cuddled her close to him. 'That's what it's supposed to be like, you cuckoo,' he said happily. 'You'll get used to it. Might even get to like it after a while.'

'Oh but I do. I like it already. Can we do it again tomorrow?'

'Good job the vicar left early. Yes, of course we can. Now shut up and go to sleep.'

Later, she mumbled something against his shoulder.

'What?'

'I said, I love you.'

Almost at once she fell asleep. Conor stayed awake for a long time, his right arm slowly growing numb under her head, not wanting to move for fear of disturbing her. The candle had guttered out, and he lay and stared at the dark, and wondered what on earth he was going to do about this guileless, beloved, and crackingly inconvenient complication now that he'd got her.

Kate was not one of those people who take for ever to surface, clambering out of sleep one laborious level at a time. She was either asleep or awake, the transition as brisk as switching on a light. This morning's awakening was unlike any other in her life. From the cold place full of stones, where the blind soldier stalked her with the butcher knife glinting in his hand, she was suddenly in a warm bed with arms around her, holding her tight, and a soft, friendly mouth nibbling at her naked shoulder.

'Darling heart, what could you have been dreaming about? Not me, I hope.'

'Why, what did I say?'

'"No", mostly, and "Don't", and things of that sort. Very agitated you were.' He rocked her gently. His work shirt was rough against her skin.

'Hey, you're dressed – I didn't hear you get up.'

'You weren't supposed to. I had an urgent appointment with a cow. Animals have no tact. How would you like breakfast in bed?'

'Could I?'

'As you've been so good.' Conor stood up and she saw the tray on the night table, with the blue mug of coffee and the cornbread shining with melted butter, and suddenly realized she was starving. She started to sit up, and then remembered and grabbed for the sheet. He twitched it out of her fingers, laughing at her.

'Don't be stingy,' he said. 'Let the old gentleman have his modest pleasures.' He dropped a light, affectionate kiss on each small breast before setting the tray on her knees. 'There you are. Dig in. I ran a bath for you, so as soon as you've done with that lot, you can go next door and have a swim. I've got to get back downstairs; Claire hasn't finished reading me the riot act yet.'

'What did you tell her?'

'Told her the truth – no point in not. I imagine we were fairly audible last night. Besides, when you weren't in your own bed this morning, she must have had a pretty shrewd idea where you'd got to.'

174

'Is she very mad?'

'Livid – with me, that is. Being Sunday, apparently, makes it even worse. She tore a hell of a strip off me for profaning First Day, and when I said the better the day, the better the deed, she boxed my ears. You're all right, though; you're the innocent victim of my beastly lust. Do you think you can manage to look like a victim?'

'Well, I'll try,' Kate said. He inspected her fondly.

'You'll have to do better than that,' he said. 'At the moment you look more like a kitten that's found the dairy. What a satisfactory woman you are. And beautiful, too.' He sat down beside her, the tray tilting perilously, and put his arm around her shoulders. 'Kate, I do love you. You're not sorry, are you? I couldn't bear it if you were.'

'No, I'm glad. I'm only sorry we wasted all that time – a whole week. I can't stand it. But I was scared to death of you. Why was I?'

'Cultural conditioning and female intuition. On some level or other, you knew exactly what was going to happen – which is more than I did, I may say. I never meant it to, you know.'

'I didn't either, until last night. But then I didn't know it would be like this.'

'What is it like, for you?'

'Oh – like Christmas when you're a little kid and everybody loves you.'

His arm tightened around her. She looked sideways at him over the rim of her mug, and was astonished to see tears in his eyes.

'Conor!'

He sniffed, pulled a face at her, and wiped his eyes without embarrassment. 'I'm a sentimental twit – pay no attention. Like Miss America, I am overwhelmed by my own good fortune. Now finish your breakfast while I go back into the pillory. At least it won't be for long – I'm leaving in fifteen minutes to drive old Martha to the bus.'

'Can't you stay here with me?'

'I have a very weak character. If I stay I'll end up making love to you, and I don't want to do that while you're still sore.'

Kate felt herself blushing again. Surely one didn't talk about such things, or anyhow not in broad daylight over cornbread and coffee.

'I don't mind,' she said, not looking at him.

'Possibly not, but I do. Nothing but the best for our Kate.'

175

'Listen, what am I going to say to Claire?'

'I don't suppose you'll have much chance to say anything. Just withdraw your mind and think about Tom Thumb while the tide washes over you. The great thing about Claire is she doesn't nag. Once she's told you what an unprincipled swine I am and what a hopeless little muggins you are, that'll be the end of it. Anyway, she's really not half as cross as she makes out. Having one's worst suspicions confirmed is always soothing to the ego. She'll probably finish up giving you good advice, God help you – how to be happy and useful as a kidnapper's moll.'

He kissed the tip of her nose and left her.

By the time Kate came downstairs, bathed and shining and extremely apprehensive, only Afeni and Claire were in the kitchen. Conor had gone to Cold Crossing with Mrs Two Ponies, taking the children along for the ride, and Chuck and Sam had wisely found chores to do elsewhere. Kate could not quite stifle the feeling that Conor had ratted on her; it would have been easier to face Claire with her lover at her side. But although he could be tender and supportive, especially in bed, he was clearly not the kind of man to encourage dependence in anyone.

She supposed that was natural. For years now he had moved in a world of highly trained professionals, grown men and women who knew their work, coped with their responsibilities, and presumably didn't need their hands held. His first wife would have been that kind of person: confident, self-sufficient, strong. Kate felt a shameful yearning to be spineless, incompetent, and looked after but she knew it was no use. If what she wanted was a sturdy prop to twine herself around, she'd come to the wrong shop. Conor was more like a rough wind blowing through the tidy rooms of her life, snapping the curtains, scattering the neatly arranged possessions. She reminded herself that she'd asked for it, and lifted her chin to confront her outraged hostess. Playing victim might be sound tactics, but it was a paltry role, and she'd be damned if she was going to creep in looking crushed.

'Well, young woman – ' Claire began, but got no further as Afeni danced across the stone floor, threw her arms around Kate, and gave her a greaty stagey hug.

'Peace and love, sister,' she carolled provocatively, favouring the stunned Kate with a tremendous wink from the eye Claire couldn't see. 'Just drawing the enemy fire,' she whispered, as Claire's exasperation crested and broke over her handsome black head.

'Shame on thee, Afeni Tulliver! How thee dares! Peace and love indeed. I blame thee as much as anyone for what's happened. A fine example for a young girl like Kate, and from a good home too. Pure as a baby she was when she came to this house and don't thee tell me different – I know a virgin when I see one – and *now* look! I surely hope thee's proud of thyself. And I'm no better. I ought to have seen this coming – the minute that man walked in last night I knew there'd be trouble, and not one finger did I lift to stop it. Oh, Kate, how could thee be such a little fool?' She slammed down the coffee pot and glared at Kate. Then her expression softened, and she sighed. 'Thee's a child,' she said. 'He's a worldly, heartless wretch with more honey on his tongue than a hive of bees, and thee's a child. How was thee to stand out against him, and thy mother not here to warn thee? I never should have agreed to any of it in the first place. Let one sin through and the rest will follow, like cows through a gate. I promised myself I'd be careful for thee, and I've not done it.'

Claire was coasting now, modulating from fury to self-reproach. She fussed guiltily around Kate, settling her on the sofa, pouring fresh coffee for her, giving her little pats and making comforting noises. Her loving, wounded heart was already busy at its transformations, changing Kate from a wanton into an abused innocent in need of cherishing. Satisfied, Afeni escaped to her vegetable garden, detouring on the way to let the men know that the worst was over.

Conor and Kate lay side by side on the tree-shaded grass, close by the stream that meandered towards Harmony. After lunch he had announced that the two of them were taking a few hours off, and whisked her away in the Jeep, declining the children's helpful offers to keep them company, and ignoring Claire's stormy looks. He had brought along a bottle of wine. They had talked and kissed and taken turns swigging from the bottle, until the wine and the heat of the day made them drowsy and they slept, chastely holding hands, like an old married couple. When they woke it was late afternoon, but Conor seemed in no hurry to return to the farm. He lay on his back, hands locked behind his head, one knee bent and the opposite foot propped up on it, looking insufferably pleased with himself. When Kate moved closer to him he gently fended her off.

'Keep your distance, woman. Otherwise I shall cast off all restraint and assault you madly – and making love under God's glorious blue sky is a mug's game. For one thing, you're liable to find your bare ass nestling in God's glorious poison ivy. I'm a bed man, myself. Sign of advancing age, I suppose. Do you mind terribly?'

Kate tapped at his lips with a field daisy. He snapped at it, troutlike, and missed.

'As long as I can hang around with you, I don't mind anything,' she said.

'Reconciled, are you? To being kidnapped and ordered about and bullied in general? How unliberated of you.'

'You don't bully me; you're the kindest man I ever met.'

'Good Lord. That doesn't say much for the company you've been keeping.'

'Maybe not,' she said seriously. 'I never thought about it before, but you know I have led a very limited life up to now.'

He snorted. 'Never been in an earthquake or a midnight fire at sea, never had any real fun at all. That's the curse of a sheltered existence. Haven't you any weird kin to add strife and colour to your days? Bigamous cousins? Embezzling uncles? Renegade aunts living in sin with abstract expressionists and making vacuum cleaners out of macramé? All I know about your immediate family is your mum, who's a honey, and your father, who is not. Where's the rest of the clan?'

'There isn't one, really. I liked Grandpa Danbury a lot, but he died when I was ten, and my mother doesn't get along with Lalla – that's my step-grandmother. Lalla lives in San Francisco and she's into religions. She was a Bahai for a while, and then she met some friend of Doris Lessing and converted to Sufism, but it didn't take. I'm not sure what she is now. Last time mother and I went out to visit the house was overrun with people who kept chanting and standing on their heads and wouldn't eat anything except raw broccoli. In the middle of it all there was Lalla, with her hair dyed bright orange, scampering around on her fat little bare feet, waving her arms and absolutely drowning in lilac chiffon.' Kate giggled. 'Like it was just awful. Mother kept saying, "Darling, you're quite wonderful – such energy – but shouldn't you stop now?" and Lalla would strike a pose and announce, "I studied the dance under Isadora Duncan, and I *can* dance!" What with the dance and the broccoli people and mice from cellar to roof because all life is sacred, mother said never again.'

'And who can blame her? What about the Harper contingent?'

Endicott Harper, Kate explained, had died long before she was born. Her only memories of Grandmother Harper were of a tall, pinch-mouthed old lady in black, who was always associated with a subliminal flash of overcooked grey, fibrous roast lamb, with little white buttons of fat congealing around it on a stone-cold Royal Crown Derby plate. The other child of the marriage, Pen Harper's elder brother, had died in World War II, and his widow lived in Seattle, as did two of the three female cousins Kate had never seen. The third, an embarrassment to all, was the scourge of Minneapolis, where she headed an organization dedicated to stamping out sex, liquor, irresponsibility in the media, and anything else that might contribute to the simple pleasures of the citizens.

'How very dispiriting,' Conor said. 'No wonder you steer clear. Isn't there anyone remotely bearable in the whole tribe? We can't count Alice Mary – I believe she's your second or third cousin – but for one thing you don't exactly know her and for another she's none too bearable at the moment anyway.'

'Alice Mary?'

'Alice Mary Danbury de Bruycker, a.k.a. Consolation. She's the girl at Harmony who looks like you. Frazzled though you were, you can't not have noticed.'

'God, yes. Talk about weird kin . . . I didn't know she was a cousin, but I guess it figures.' Kate brightened. 'I do have one absolutely terrific aunt – mother's sister, Louisa – but she's in Scotland. She's married to a sexy laird who wears a kilt, and they have two enormous sons who are totally tough in a very grand kind of a way. They all live in a castle on an island in the middle of a lake, or a loch or whatever it's called. Mother and I went over for the summer two years ago, and it was heaven, but it's not really a place you can just stop by when you're feeling low. I mean, three thousand miles and the last bit by rowboat if you can find anyone sober enough to ferry you across. It would be nice,' she added wistfully, 'to have a real family.'

'We'll adopt you. Claire already has, come to that. I must say you've adapted astonishingly quickly to our little rustic home for the unhinged. What on earth do you really make of us, I wonder?'

'You I love, and you know about that, so don't fish. And I'm crazy about Chuck and Claire. Afeni kind of scares me, but I admire her. She's really together; I can't imagine a situation she couldn't cope with. The only one I can't seem to relate to is Sam. I just don't know him at all.'

'Sam doesn't care to be known. He's effective and resourceful and extraordinarily brave – there's nobody I'd rather have watching my back in a brawl. I know he's not very friendly; in fact his personality has all the candid charm of an ingrown toenail, but he can't help that. Some pretty awful things have happened to Sam. It's remarkable he came through as well as he did.'

'Chuck said he used to be with the CIA.'

'*That* ended in tears. He was in the army to start with. Usual thing; poor country boy, parents dead, couldn't see slogging his whole life away for some dirt farmer in Sweatbox, Georgia, so he took the only available escape route and enlisted. One of his instructors, in a spasm of common sense, realized Sam had a natural gift for electronics. The merry pranksters who were running Operation Phoenix were looking for a wireman at the time, and it happened to be during one of those rare but winsome interludes the army and the CIA were on speaking terms. Which is how he came to get in. How he got out is something else again. You don't want the sordid details, do you?'

'Maybe you could give me an expurgated version. Like the cleaned-up Shakespeares we used at Miss Hampshire's.'

'Did you really?' Conor was entertained. 'How splendid. What did Miss Hampshire do about the Bible? It's much worse than Shakespeare – absolutely seething with naughty bits.'

'Miss Hampshire's been dead thirty years; they kept the name for sentimental reasons. Financial, too, I guess. And the Bible was thought to be rather vulgar, especially the Old Testament. I remember Polly Hunnicutt coming back after Christmas vacation one time – she had three older brothers, she always knew everything – and telling the rest of us what they actually *did* in Sodom and Gomorrah. At least, she wasn't too sure about Gomorrah, but she had Sodom sewn up all right. And then some moron brought it up in Comparative Religion, and we practically had to scrape old Mrs Curry off the ceiling. My God, Polly got in trouble, and so did the rest of us. Anyhow. Are you going to tell me about Sam or not?'

'Provided you keep your trap shut about it, yes.' Conor stuck his legs straight out, crossed them at the ankles, and settled his shoulders more comfortably against the bank. Sam, he told her, had been a great success at first. When Sam installed a tap on a South Vietnamese general or a diplomat's mistress or a *New York Times* correspondent, the tap almost always worked, and his employers were delighted with him. The trouble had started when

180

Sam, prowling the bars in an ecstasy of boredom, had fallen in with bad company, notably a Medevac pilot by the name of Fred Orenstein. Orenstein had been a close friend of Chuck Lainez. That was how Chuck and Conor had first met Sam, shortly after Orenstein had narrowly avoided a court-martial for airlifting a number of children out of a village that was being destroyed. 'In order to save it, of course,' Conor said. 'Never lose sight of that.

'Some of the kids were quite badly hurt, and they wound up at our clinic,' he went on. 'Fred used to look in and see how they were getting on, and sometimes he brought us cartons of bootleg penicillin he'd promoted on the H. J. Orenstein Memorial Hash Exchange. His name was Henry, actually, but we called him Fred because of Fred C. Dobbs.'

'Why?'

'Why what?'

'Why Fred C. Dobbs?'

'I keep forgetting you're only just out of the nursery. Humphrey Bogart in *Treasure of the Sierra Madre*: "Nobody tells Fred C. Dobbs what to do." Five minutes with Orenstein and the connection was inevitable. An order was simply a challenge to that lad.' Conor grinned reminiscently. 'Oh, he was a good man, he really was. Bagel was his dog, you know. K. Bagel Orenstein – K for kosher, naturally. After Fred brought his chopper in close once too often and got turned into a fireball by his own artillery, Chuck took Bagel on. We couldn't quite see shipping him off to the family in Texas, and anyway Fred told me once he'd never had a dog when he was a kid because his mother couldn't stand them. Germs and whatnot. So we thought he might not be welcome. Besides, face it, that animal is not everybody's cup of tea. What was I talking about?'

'Sam, to start with. But you really don't want to get into it, do you? I'm sorry, I didn't mean to push you. Let's forget about it.'

'No, it's all right. It just makes me so hopping mad every time I think about it that usually I try not to. May we have the next slide, please? Now this, ladies and gentlemen, is an infantry colonel – a genuine, all-singing, all-dancing son of a bitch. He had a vendetta going against a poor bloody little infant of a lieutenant, who was also a chum of ours, and the upshot was he got the boy killed.'

'Cat was it? Cator Blair?'

'As a matter of fact it was. How the hell did you find out about that?'

'Chuck told me. He said Sam broke the colonel's jaw.'

'That he did, in two places. Sam was only a sergeant, remember, and sergeants who start whomping colonels are not well thought of. What saved him (if that's the word I want) was that his CIA bosses were not thrilled at the prospect of a disgruntled ex-spook shooting his mouth off to all the other malcontents in Leavenworth, some of whom might even get out one day. In the ordinary way Sam would just have had an accident, very unfortunate, very fatal. But it so happened there was a special project under way at the time, and they reckoned they could use him. They shipped him stateside, to a rather chic little nuthouse they've got set up in Pennsylvania. They put him in a nice clean room all to himself, and they gave him some medicine.'

He paused and wiggled the toes of his boots up and down, gazing at them as if he expected them to comment.

'What kind of medicine?' Kate prompted.

'Oh – this and that. Chemicals of various sorts. Synthetic hallucinogens, mostly. They'd been experimenting with various potions, slipping the stuff into the drinks of unfortunate strangers in bars; then they'd sit there taking notes while the winner started crawling up the walls. It wasn't altogether satisfactory, though. Too many random factors and no follow-up studies. Sergeant Sam looked like the perfect guinea pig. No relatives to make trouble, no awkward questions asked if and when he blew a gasket, and just as long as they didn't go too far and start the brains bubbling out of his ears they could keep him around pretty well indefinitely. They'd have got away with it, too, if one of the doctors – *doctors*, Christ help us, it's enough to make you vomit – if one of the doctors hadn't had the marvellously clever idea of seeing how Sam would function in a normal social situation after being dosed up. There was some new stuff he wanted to try, apparently – a ketamine derivative spiked with just a spritz of methedrine as a livener. At least that's what he told Sam, but it may have been only his fun. He was a bit of a sadist, this particular chap. Enjoyed his work. Liked to see the subject sweat a little. Any of that wine left?'

'A third of a bottle. It's kind of warm, though.'

'*Chambré*, we call that. Shove it over.'

Conor took a couple of long swallows, closed his eyes and rubbed them, and then drank again and propped the bottle between his knees, before going on with his story. The doctor had given orders for Sam to be de-toxed and cleaned up. Then he and Sam and two of the sanitarium guards had all driven to the nearest town and gone to the movies and then moved on to a steakhouse for dinner.

'I mean, can you believe this?' He rubbed his eyes again. 'One mad scientist, one country boy with artificially induced schizophrenia, and two run-of-the-mill nutters with guns, all sitting down for a jolly-up at Bert's Beef & Beer? The mind reels.'

The doctor gave Sam his pill, and after a while Sam had become very nervous and excitable, and had insisted on drinking all the beer on the table, the others' as well as his own. Fearful of a scene, they let him. Then, of course, he wanted to go to the bathroom. One of the guards had gone with him. When they did not return, the second guard had followed to see if anything was wrong.

'At least I assume that's what happened. I've only got Sam's side of all this, and he was fairly fuzzy about it, which is undertandable. Anyhow, the second guard doesn't come back either, and the doctor starts getting lonely all by himself. Clearly, the bathroom is where the action is. He's also getting worried, and presently he does something quite stunningly dumb. Instead of telephoning for reinforcements or bribing a waiter or someone to look in and check, he goes along to investigate for himself. He also fails to return, and when the four giant sizzling sirloins, or whatever, arrive at the table everybody's gone. Frantic ditherings among the staff. Has the blue cheese dressing struck again? Are the patrons even now clutching their vitals and writhing in agony? Will they sue? Finally a deputation arrives among the urinals, to find two unconscious gentlemen tidily arranged in a couple of stalls, and a third one on the floor dead as mutton. The corpse was the doctor, of course. Sam owed him. The window was open and the birdy had flown, taking with him Dr Krankheit's walking-around money, which was quite a lot, and the gun off one of the guards.'

Conor drank another mouthful of wine and passed the bottle back to Kate. 'Thirsty work, this Ancient Mariner lark. "The wedding-guest here beat his breast, For he heard the loud bassoon." Let's pack this in and play awful lines from the great poets instead. You must be bored to tears by now.'

'No I'm not, and if you don't get with it and tell me the rest right away I'll hit you with this bottle.'

'There isn't much more, really. You can see how awkward it must have been, though, for the nuthouse contingent. They wanted to get their hands on Sam in the worst way, but they didn't dare tell the more respectable law enforcement people what they'd been up to. And they were terrified that if somebody else picked him up before they did, Sam would start talking. Imagine that lot coming out in court. Probably nobody would have believed a word of it, but there was always the risk of some bloody-minded newsman who'd start digging. In the event, of course, nobody ever did find him. Except us.'

'How did you do it? Did he get in touch with you?'

'No, it was pure luck. He went underground, and none of us even knew where to start looking. We'd lost track of him after they shipped him out of Nam. But Afeni's brother, Tom, is another Saigon alumnus, and he ran across him with some movement types in New York. Tom told Chuck, and Chuck told me, and I went up and winkled Sam out of the West 19th Street Chowder and Bombing Society. And a truly precious bunch of maniacs *they* were, I can tell you – if they ever get their hands on any plutonium we're all for the high jump. By the time I got there, Afeni'd moved in to keep an eye on Sam and see he didn't blow himself up. I brought them both down here with me and did what I could to straighten his head out. As a matter of fact, it was while we were all bitching about old times in napalm country and how rotten things still were out there, that the great get-rid-of-Harper scheme surfaced for the first time. It was more or less a joke to begin with, and then it got serious. I think it was Sam who actually suggested kidnapping you, but don't hold it against him. I made the decision to go ahead, so it's my fault. And that's all I can tell you about Sam, except that you don't want to take liberties with him. That stuff they pumped into him makes absolutely no contribution to mental health, and he's still a bit frayed around the edges. And no bloody wonder,' he added savagely.

'God, what an awful story. Poor Sam. And it's not even over. What kind of a future can he have now? They'll always be looking for him – he'll be on the run the rest of his life.'

'We're getting him out to Canada as soon as this is over. Afeni knows the drill up there. She was at the University of Toronto until she dropped out last year to help Tom get settled when they let him out of hospital. She wants to go back; when Sam leaves she'll go along. We have friends in Canada who'll help him find a job. He'll be all right – as all right as he'll ever be. Finish that last drop of wine, lovey, and then we must think about getting back. It's nearly milking time.'

'What will you do, Conor, after all this?' she asked, as they strolled hand in hand to the Jeep. 'Go back to Vietnam?'

'Not much point in that. The outfit I was with pulled out last November before the Christmas bombing. With so many American troops being withdrawn the South Vietnamese officials turned really nasty, and we couldn't get any work done. Those bastards never did like us above half, and we hadn't the money to spare for bribes.'

'But those were South Vietnamese kids you were taking care of – their own people. They ought to've been grateful.'

'Human nature being what it is, forget it. They were far too busy stealing to worry their heads about casualties, especially very small, very poor ones, but when we moved in and tried to do something they were livid. Foreign interference, paternalistic colonialism, ambiguous political status, you name it. Touchy as a bunch of Marxists.'

'How did you manage, then? It must have been terribly hard.'

'Old General Tizzard, whom God preserve, kept us pretty much under his wing for a couple of years, or we'd never've been able to function at all. He wangled supplies for us, requisitioned housing, promoted a couple of chewed-up ambulances. He was even crookeder than Orenstein, the old darling. What's more, he kept the local thought police off our backs. They were quite convinced we were Communists, and they kept searching the clinic for subversive literature and pinching our copies of *Playboy*. Once Tizzard went, they tried everything they could think of to close us down. If I went back now I couldn't do anything useful, and I'd probably be arrested. Besides,' he added, 'if things work out as they should, pretty soon I wouldn't have any more customers.'

'Where will you go? Or haven't you thought about it yet?'

'Home to Ireland, I expect. I could work in the North. There's plenty of scope there for my kind of stuff unfortunately, though as far as I know they haven't started using napalm yet. But I dare say they'll get to it in time, the clever little lads.'

'Which side are you on?'

'Neither. I never am, really. Death and pain are the only enemies I've time for. God, how pompous can you get? To hell with them anyway – all the kneecappers and the chaps who put bombs in pubs and shops, and set fire to buses with people in them. All the righteous with guns. Give me a kiss, pretty, I need cheering up.'

*

'Stable doors, Claire,' Conor said, and took a bite of bread and cheese. She glowered at him.

'That horse is gone,' Chuck agreed, quartering and coring an apple for Rebeccah, who had a loose front tooth. 'Long gone. They don't have much time. Leave them alone.'

'I will not allow such things to be discussed in front of the children!'

'Then why did you bring it up?'

'Dear heart, I only said —'

'That now Beccah is home she should have her own room back, and I am to go up with Dan, and you will take Katie in with you. I know. I heard you. But Beccah likes to sleep at the top of the house in a little bunk bed, don't you, sweetheart? It's a treat for her. And I like to sleep in my own bed with my own ridiculous wife whom I love very much. There have been enough upheavals around here without turning the sleeping arrangements upside down. Daniel, Rebeccah, ten minutes and then you have to get ready for bed. You have school tomorrow.'

'Oh, Dad, do we have to? I hate that old school, and on Mondays it's always fractions and I can't do them,' Dan complained. 'I like Father Montaldo's school best. He teaches about the Indians and the Mayans and the Incas, and we never did fractions at all, not once.'

'"Without arithmetic, what would life be but a scene of horrors?"' Conor quoted piously. Dan gave him a look.

'Shocking,' Chuck said. 'How are you going to cut up an apple if you can't do fractions? Two halves first, then we cut the halves in half again and there are four quarters. Cut the quarters in half, and you have eighths. Put them back together, like this, and it's one whole apple. Let go of it, it's eight slices, all the same size. Now you eat it, and it's not an apple any more, it's a fraction of Daniel.'

Daniel considered this demented proposition, and reached for the plate.

'How big a fraction?' he asked cooperatively. Parents were decent people on the whole, and it didn't take much to make them happy.

'How much do you weigh now?'

'Ninety-six pounds.'

'These russets go around four to the pound, four times ninety-six. When you've swallowed the last mouthful, the apple will be one three-hundred-and-eighty-fourth of you. More or less. And

186

you can tell Mrs Rouderbridge I said so.'

Much later, in Conor's bed, Kate wriggled like a sleepy puppy, accommodating herself to the body that fitted so comfortingly around her back, knees tucked into the crook of her own, chin filling the hollow where her shoulder flowed into her neck. She could feel his cock, still hard, against her bottom. Wary of hurting her, he had not put it inside her, but had made love to her with his mouth. It still seemed to her a most peculiar skill for him to have acquired, and she tried not to wonder where and with whom he had learned to practise it with such masterful efficiency.

'You know something?' she said, belatedly analytical. 'When you do it that way it's quite different.'

'Different how?'

'It's hard to explain. Sharper and clearer – more exciting in a way – only it's sort of lightweight. Lovely, but not as satisfying.'

'Chinese food?'

'No-o. But caviar instead of roast beef.'

'And I suppose you're still hungry. I don't know what this generation's coming to. *T'es exigeante, tu sais.*'

'*Mais non, ce n'est pas vrai. Simplement, j'ai très envie de toi.*'

'Pretty sexy sort of French you learned at Miss Hampshire's.'

'I picked that up at the movies.'

'I might have known. How about just a touch of roast beef, then? Prime ribs.' He knuckled hers gently.

'You mean we could do that now? As well?'

He shouted with laughter. 'Oh, my blessed, my pearl of price, we could indeed.'

'Would you like to?'

'Very much, only I don't want to hurt you.'

'You won't.'

He did, but not very much, and this time she was not frightened at all but exultant, drifting down afterwards as lightly as a fluff of dandelion seed.

Pendleton Harper sulked in bed in a rotten temper. Wires from the electrodes stuck to his body converged on a wall console, whence the impulses they carried were conveyed to one of a bank of closed-circuit screens facing the nurses' station. The wires were driving Harper crazy. Every time he tried to shift his position they got in his way, catching in the sheets, ripping the electrodes loose if he made an incautious movement. It was like being trapped in a badly designed spider's web.

Nurse Fernandez, whose duty it was this morning to monitor the screens, was an old hand at the job. Usually her attention was divided with impeccable logic between the claims upon it: routine awareness served as an adequate check on patients who were going along nicely, and a sharper vigilance was reserved for the cases where trouble might be expected. Today, however, her eyes kept going back to the EKG reading for Room 401. The pale green peaks and plateaus jiggled along as daintily as they had ever since Room 401 was first wired up. Pretty as a picture – so what was 401 doing here? If Fernandez had been in charge of this madhouse, she'd have had 401 out on the street in a minute. Still and all, the doctors did seem pretty concerned about this Mr Hofstetter, and maybe what ailed him just didn't show up on his EKG. She'd have liked a peek at his folder, but they kept it locked up like it was Liz Taylor's diamonds. 'National Security,' the head nurse had said, casting her eyes up to heaven in pantomimed disgust.

Except for keeping watch on his uninteresting screen, none of them had anything to do for Mr Hofstetter. He had his own private nurses, which was weird in itself. Three of them, working in shifts around the clock, and not one with a word to say beyond Excuse me, Thank you, and Where's the ice machine? Although there was a big red No Visitors sign on the door of 401, and a succession of large, uncommunicative men occupied the hard chair right beside it, that creep in the pin-striped suit trotted in and out of there all day long, sometimes alone and sometimes bringing other people with him, and the guard, or Secret Service man, or whatever he was, made no attempt to stop him.

'Freaky,' Nurse Fernandez said to herself, and forgot the malingering Mr Hofstetter as she spotted a premature ventricular contraction on the screen of that nice old senator in 407. Unlike some people, the senator was really in bad shape. No parade of snooty special nurses there, though; Viola Fernandez was good enough for him – always grateful he was, too, for the least little thing, the old pet. She reported the change in Senator Duncan's heartbeat to the head nurse, who put out a call for the senior cardiologist. Fernandez hoped it wasn't serious, and she also hoped Dr Brodie would get his ass up here in a hurry, just in case. Screw Hofstetter; she had sick people to worry about.

The name of the creep in the pin-striped suit was Arthur Wilberforce, and he wasn't quite as bad as he looked. He was a senior aide on Pendleton Harper's staff, and apart from a handful of indignant doctors, and the three women from Langley dressed up as nurses, he was the only person in Washington who knew that his superior was as healthy as a prize hog. Harper had had to take someone into his confidence, because once in the hospital he realized he would be isolated, cut off from the various agencies which, on different pretexts and under different degrees of misapprehension, were trying to trace his daughter. He would have been lost without a liaison man, and he had picked Art Wilberforce not because he liked or trusted him but, typically, because he had something on him. Wilberforce was a homosexual, which was handicap enough in this scandal-conscious town. But worse yet, the poor man's hapless urges had once entangled him with a predatory young boy. A very young boy. Three years ago, when the confidential report first appeared on his desk, Harper had taken it home, locked it away, and taken no further action. One never knew when it might be useful to have someone around whose fidelity could be guaranteed on the basis of simple blackmail.

His foresight was paying off now, as he'd known it would sooner or later. After returning from Rock Creek Park he had sent for Wilberforce at once and told him everything. He had also told him, in brutal and vulgar terms, what would happen to Wilberforce if he failed to keep his mouth shut. 'And for your sake, my dear Arthur, I sincerely hope you don't talk in your sleep.' Wilberforce had parried this low blow with aplomb. 'My wife and I have separate bedrooms,' he had replied, straight-faced. 'Of course, you don't have that problem, sir. Not being married at the moment yourself. Dear me, I remember Miss

Harper so well from the time she came with us to South America. Such a beautiful young girl – what a tragedy if anything should happen to her.' In other words, you can ruin my life but I can destroy your only child. A delicate equilibrium of shared mistrust had been established, spelled out by neither man but perfectly understood by both.

Harper was waiting for Wilberforce to show up, and the fellow was already fifteen minutes late. Goddamn pederast, keeping him waiting. He snapped his fingers at the woman in the white uniform.

'Bourbon. Two ounces. Use the shot glass. And the same amount of water. No, *no*, not that chlorinated filth out of the tap, the bottled water. That's what it's there for. No ice. Now pass me the brown folder that's in the top drawer next to the closet. The brown folder. *Brown*, not beige. That's right. Now my pen and the yellow legal pad and give me the clipboard. Good. Now crank the bed up, will you. I can't work lying down like this. That's the wrong handle – that's the foot. You're raising the *foot*, for God's sake. Raise the *head*! That's better. Couple more turns ought to do it. Now fold the handle back under the bed, so you don't fall over it and half kill yourself like that fool of a woman yesterday. All right. Now give me my reading glasses.'

Not the least of his present trials was the separation from Albert, his butler, who for three years had anticipated his every want. He had not thought it possible to miss anyone as poignantly as he missed Albert. Kate he was desperately concerned for – and not just because he thought he ought to be, it was genuine enough to wake him sweating in the middle of the night – but Albert was essential to him.

He looked with loathing at the ostentatious arrangement of roses, peonies, and delphiniums on the windowsill. They looked like something out of a very expensive brothel, which he supposed was appropriate since they had been sent by his mistress. The one advantage that might accrue from this idiotic medical charade was that it would give him an excuse to unload Dee Dee. After all, the last thing a cardiac patient needed was an overathletic whore. Certainly he didn't want to see her again. She'd been sucking him off, the dirty bitch, at the very moment when his daughter was being drugged and abducted. He would never forgive her for it.

Propped up in bed with his glasses halfway down his nose and his small mouth turned down at the corners, he looked like an ill-tempered old owl – the only touch lacking was a mouse's tail hanging out one side of his beak. For the fiftieth time he went through the file on Kate, checking and rechecking the scanty facts embedded in a welter of bureaucratic slush.

Fact one: two used disposable syringes, of the sort used by diabetics to inject themselves with insulin, had been picked up at the site of the abduction, and had proved to contain traces of a powerful and fast-acting sedative drug. There were no fingerprints.

Fact two: tests had revealed the presence of that same drug in Charles Belfort Eisinger's urine.

Fact three: a stolen 1964 Plymouth had been found abandoned in Vermont, two hundred miles north of New Lymington. It had disappeared from that town at some time between eight p.m. on Saturday, when its owner had parked it on the street two blocks from his place of work, and three a.m. Sunday, when he had telephoned the police to protest their towing it away from a legal parking spot, and discovered that this time the police were not responsible. (The owner had looked promising to begin with, since apart from a whole sheaf of traffic violations he also turned out to have a record – two convictions for possession of marijuana. But he had been playing the piano, except for brief visits to the bathroom, from nine o'clock that night until half past two the following morning, in plain sight of some fifty assorted layabouts in a bar called P. J. McBurney's. Most of the patrons had known the pianist for years – he always played there on Saturday nights – but that they should all have banded together to perjure themselves in a conspiracy to obstruct justice was stretching paranoia too far.)

There were no identifiable fingerprints on or in the car except for the owner's and those of his three most recent girlfriends. After Kate's bag was found near Carrstown, Harper had become convinced that the pianist's car was nothing but a red herring. Why would anyone drive that miserable jalopy two hundred miles north immediately after committing the crime, if his actual destination lay hundreds of miles to the south? Not, Harper reminded himself, that it had necessarily been a destination at all. It could have been a way-station en route to somewhere entirely different. Or the bag might have been deliberately planted by some accomplice hoping to mislead the pursuit, although in that case you would have expected it to show up in some conspicuous location, not under a bush in the middle of nowhere. However,

Carrstown was the one break they'd had and reports of the investigation were still coming in. So far, they had all been negative.

Fact four: the bag itself. It had been gone over for fingerprints, but so many people had handled it – the child who found it, his father, and what appeared to be the entire staff of the Carrstown and Carr County law enforcement agencies – that little could be hoped for from that. In any case, none of the prints they had fed into the computer matched any that were already on file.

Fact five: no unusual activity had been observed among militant Irish sympathizers. The accent of the man in the park had prompted this line of enquiry, but apart from the normal fund raising, gunrunning, and Paddy-inspired rhetoric, the Little Green Men, as one waggish informer had christened them, seemed to be clean.

Fact six: the electronic and physical surveillance on his wife's house had so far yielded nothing. Except for the night of the crime, the kidnappers had made no attempt to contact her, and it seemed unlikely they would do so at this late stage. Since the initial phone calls telling them of Kate's capture, the only message had been to Harper himself – one brief call making the arrangements that had culminated in that bizarre encounter in the park.

Fact seven: the photograph of Kate in chains had been examined by experts, without result. All the lab boys were able to say was that the background appeared to be some kind of fabric, and that the print had been developed by a reasonably skilled amateur. They also deducted from the quality of the light that the picture had been shot out-of-doors, probably either at mid-morning or mid-afternoon. None of which helped in the least. The only fingerprints on the photograph, and on the cheap dime-store flashlight he had used to examine it, were Harper's own.

Fact eight: fact eight was not so much a fact as a state of affairs, and an exceedingly awkward one. Charlie Eisinger was still being held at the experimental facility in Pennsylvania, and his family had turned difficult, very difficult indeed. Wilberforce was supposed to be bringing down the commandant of that facility to Harper's bedside to discuss the situation. They were now twenty-seven minutes late.

At last there was a knock at the door. Harper's 'nurse' opened it, to admit Wilberforce and a companion introduced as Colonel

Rupert Lund, of the Westwood Sanitarium. Colonel Lund looked like, and had been, a Marine. His appearance was aggressively clean. His skin seemed to have been freshly rubbed down with fine wire wool. His check suit was so little affected by the journey from Westwood to the sodden heat of the capital that he might have put it on (along with the white Sea Island cotton shirt and the crisp navy-red-striped silk tie) ten seconds ago in the hospital corridor. His teeth when he smiled shone with such exemplary whiteness they hardly seemed real, although they were obviously his own. His greying blond hair was cut very short, and his eyes were a pale, freezing blue.

Indeed, the colonel was so obtrusively Nordic, hygienic, and clean-cut – Wilberforce, a tidy and fastidious man, looked like a well-used bathmat beside him – that Harper was deeply disconcerted when he realized that he expected the visitor to smell bad. He didn't, of course. He didn't smell of anything, not even aftershave or soap, and yet there was about him the suggestion of a charnel stench. Wilberforce had been conscious of it for the last three hours and had a fanciful idea that he knew what it was. It was the stale, acrid reek of other people's terror, other people's pain. Lund could shower and scour until he bled, it would never come off.

After Harper had sent the woman down to the hospital coffee shop with orders not to come back for half an hour, they got down to business.

'The Eisinger boy turns out not to have been involved,' the colonel told Harper. 'We've put him through a series of stress interviews, we've held him now for over a week in a monitored stress situation, he's been evaluated repeatedly by our top staff people, and there's no further doubt in their minds or mine that he had no connection whatever with Miss Harper's disappearance. If that were the only consideration, I would recommend his immediate release.'

'But I gather you don't. Why not?'

'It's that family of his. His mother, as I'm sure you know, was a Belfort before her marriage, and I understand her brother, Congressman Belfort, is raising all kinds of cain. Unfortunately, there is sound legal basis for a court action for damages: assault, unlawful detention, violation of civil rights, and God knows what besides. Our legal department is tearing its hair. Young Eisinger has signed a statement, of course, affirming that he cooperated with us of his own free will, but his lawyers would claim he signed

193

it under duress. As indeed he did,' Lund added thoughtfully. 'If we turn him loose in the frame of mind he's in at present, he'll hold a press conference first, and after that he'll sue. He's really very angry, and his mother and uncle will be only too eager to back him up.'

'Colonel, I don't imagine you came all the way down here simply in order to announce that there is nothing to be done. What do you propose?'

Lund sat forward in his chair. 'Insulin shock,' he said. 'Administered under the strictest medical supervision, of course. There'll be nothing to show, you see, whereas for electroshock small areas of the skull are generally shaved to facilitate the attachment of the electrodes, and somebody would be sure to notice. As with electroshock, the insulin treatment ordinarily produces no permanent impairment of day-to-day brain function as a whole, but the patient's memory of the recent past is either erased entirely, or so distorted as to render him useless as a witness.' The colonel's face was alight with honest pleasure as he contemplated this happy solution to their problems. Harper was not a sensitive man, but even he found the colonel's enthusiasm a little disconcerting.

'That seems a rather drastic step to take,' he said. 'Is the procedure safe?'

'In my opinion,' Lund replied, 'entirely too much emphasis can be placed on safety. Risk is the essence of life, sir. In fact you might say that risk *is* life. This nation was not founded by men who were afraid to take a chance.'

Another nut, Harper thought resignedly. Why was it that certain branches of government service attracted people who in other walks of life would be discreetly confined?

'Of course, of course, Colonel. You're absolutely correct. However, in the circumstances – after all, I do know the boy – one feels a certain responsibility –'

'No medical procedure is altogether safe. Given an anaphylactic reaction, a simple shot of penicillin can kill a man stone dead in minutes. But the course I am recommending would be very much healthier for the boy than – ah – various other dispositions of his case that have been considered.'

'I see. Please proceed, Colonel Lund.'

Satisfied with this tacit approval, Lund leaned back again and crossed his ankles, making himself comfortable.

'Mrs Eisinger knows her son was picked up by the police in New

194

Lymington and booked on a charge of using prohibited substances,' he said. 'That's something we can substantiate – the urine test is on file. She also knows that he was handed over within a few hours to representatives of a federal agency – the narcotics bureau will cover for us there if necessary. But that is absolutely all she knows. As far as she or anyone else is concerned, Eisinger dropped Miss Harper off at her mother's house after dinner because the young lady complained of feeling unwell. Let us suppose, now, that young Charles is returned to his anxious relatives in a state of massive incoherence, quite unable to give any sensible account of himself. Let us further suppose his mother is told that on his way to the nearest office of the narcotics bureau, where he was being taken for further questioning, he experienced a psychotic episode during which he attacked and seriously injured the escorting officers, one of whom remains on the critical list. As a result of this vicious assault, which is thought to have been triggered by indulgence in illicit drugs, he managed to get away, and was not recaptured until several days later, when he was apprehended in the act of holding up a liquor store.'

Not only a nut, apparently, but a fantasist on an heroic scale. If only these people would settle for writing pulp novels, which was clearly the métier for which God had intended them, instead of imposing their baroque constructions on the real world. It was time to inject a note of practicality into this insane discussion. It was also time to assert a measure of control.

'Good God almighty, man,' Harper roared, startling Wilberforce from his nonchalant perch on the windowsill next to the despised bouquet. 'You're not dealing with some terrified cleaning woman in Roxbury! Sally Belfort's as smart as a whip. She runs half a dozen committees. That newspaper column of hers is syndicated through half of New England. Colonel, if Sally Belfort Eisinger made her mind up I was going to dance the Charleston stark naked on the White House lawn I tell you I would do it, for the sake of peace and quiet. And that brother of hers is worse. You fool with those people and you'll be up to your ass in congressional investigations before you've turned around twice.'

'With all due respect, sir,' Lund replied with no discernible respect at all but rather with a condescending kindness, 'I don't agree. Most people, even sophisticated people, have a powerful tendency to believe what it's to their advantage to believe. Let me finish, if you will. Mrs Eisinger will also be informed that, because

195

of the high esteem in which her brother, the congressman, is held, some of his influential friends have arranged – strictly unofficially, of course – that provided she agrees to place her boy in a private facility of her own choosing, to undergo a course of rehabilitative treatment, all charges against him will be dropped. Can you imagine a devoted mother passing up an offer like that? She'll jump at it and be thankful. Furthermore, by the time she sees young Charlie, his condition will not be reassuring. He'll be disoriented, amnesiac, and dirty. Ten minutes in his company, and she'll have him safely tucked away in the nearest rubber room so fast he won't have time to change his shorts. Although he could certainly use some clean underwear,' he added, with another flash of that intimidating smile. 'In fact the boy's a disgusting object by any standards, and with a ten-day growth of beard as well he looks as if he's been holding up liquor stores half his life. No, I really don't anticipate any major repercussions, if we stick with the approach I've just outlined.'

'Very resourceful of you, Colonel Lund,' Harper said faintly. 'You're right, of course. Your proposed actions have my full approval, and I'm more than grateful to you and your colleagues for your help and cooperation at this difficult time.' That ought to hold the bastard. Clearly he was a menace to society, but at the moment he had his uses.

'My pleasure, sir,' the colonel said gracefully. 'I only wish we could do more. It must be damnable for you, waiting all this time with no news. You're positive you still want to avoid publicity? We have excellent contacts in the news media. If you decided to go public, there'd be no problem about disseminating whichever version of the facts would serve your purpose best.'

'At this stage, I think it's far too risky. No, Colonel, please don't deliver your sermon again. I understand your point of view, but this is my daughter we're talking about. If Kate has been kidnapped, sooner or later there will be a ransom demand. If and when I receive it – well, quite frankly, I intend to pay it. At the very least, I have to be free to negotiate. The fewer people who know the truth, the greater the hope that my daughter will be allowed to return safely home. I will do nothing – I *dare* do nothing – that might jeopardize her life.'

'I have every sympathy, sir. A father's feelings . . .' Lund wagged his immaculate skull in commiseration. 'This must be hell for you, sheer hell.'

'It's not easy. And unhappily we have to face facts. There is always the possibility, no matter how remote, that she has gone into hiding of her own accord. We none of us know precisely what took place on Winter Hill that night. She may have been so badly frightened that the experience has affected her mind. She may even have left voluntarily with some third party or parties. One hates to think ill of his own child, but there does seem to have been some kind of drug involvement, and I've no means of telling what company she's gotten herself involved with at college. Her mother has been lax, far too lax.' He shifted irritably against the pillows. 'And of course there are other possibilities.'

Colonel Lund had his own excellent reasons for not wishing to dwell on those other possibilities. He deftly turned the conversation.

'And your own health, sir? You're looking better than I had dared to hope, but what do the doctors say?'

'The doctors come around and prod at me and pull long faces. They keep muttering about stress and prescribing tranquillizers. I wait until the nurse is looking the other way, and then I toss the damn things into the wastebasket.'

'Well at least you're in the best place; the care here is the finest in the country.' The colonel glanced at his watch. 'If it's all right with you, Mr Secretary, I think I ought to be starting back. Eisinger's treatment should be initiated as soon as practicable, and I want to be there to supervise. That really is one area of anxiety you can cross off your list. Just leave everything to us; we'll take care of it. And I hope there'll soon be good news of your daughter – and of yourself too.'

'Thank you. You're very kind. Wilberforce here will escort you to your transportation. Oh Arthur, on your way down, stop by the coffee shop and send that cretin of a nurse back up here, will you? I'm not supposed to be left alone, of all things,' he explained to Lund with a grimace. 'Lot of damn foolishness, but we have to follow orders, eh? Like the good soldiers we are. Goodbye, Colonel, and thanks again.'

Harper lay back among his wires and pillows, and brooded. It was all very fine, defusing a tricky situation here, manipulating a potential source of awkwardness there; all very fine, with the telexes coming in, the carefully coded messages conveying damn-all, the sense that right across the nation diligent underlings were running themselves ragged on his behalf. It gave a grand, steadying illusion of progress, but most of it was pure waste motion. What, really, had been accomplished? Zilch. A big, fat, obdurate zero. He was no closer now to recovering Kate than he had been the night he first learned she had been stolen. That was a fact, all right – the real Fact One, the only fact that counted.

It was odd, but Harper had absolute faith that the kidnappers would play fair with him. Otherwise their whole operation was insane, the lethal fantasizing of people who had long ago abandoned reality – people with all too vivid a resemblance to the disastrous Colonel Lund. Lund squared, you might say; Lund carried to the logical, loony outer limits.

On the showing so far, his opponents were in a different class altogether from that chilling visitor. Not only were they intelligent, but they were thoroughly practical as well. They would know as well as he did that with Kate dead, their hold over him would evaporate. His breakdown in health would be briskly disavowed, his resignation – scheduled for today – rescinded. He would continue as secretary of state.

He thought about that, actually thought about it for the first time in years. Helicopters, Air Force jets, red carpets (apt to be made, nowadays, from tacky outdoor carpeting), Secret Service bodyguards, champagne (which gave him heartburn), press conferences, power, Beluga caviar (which he'd never much liked), international acclaim, soaring blood pressure, an ever-open door to the Oval Office, a cowed and awestruck staff, and blissful immunity from the struggle for a cab on a rainy night. And Kate dead. Probably raped first; perhaps tortured to death. Knowing, as she died, that her father could have saved her (easily, so easily), and had chosen not to do so.

She was such a beautiful child. He had watched her with great pleasure when she was little. Not that he ever romped with her – he wouldn't have known how to start. Besides she had her mother and that sour apple of an English nanny, and he'd always been so busy. But sometimes, on days when he was working at home, he used to walk over to the study window and watch her outside on the lawn, making snow angels in the winter, holding solemn tea parties for her dolls in the summer and, when she was older, tirelessly pitching underhand to that brat Charlie Eisinger from up the hill.

Remembering Charlie as a gangly little boy, he was hit with enormous force by the realization that he had just now, quite casually, condemned one of his daughter's oldest friends to a dangerous and terrifying ordeal, simply for the sake of convenience. And he'd known that lad since he was in kinder-garten. Kate's captors had no such ties of long acquaintance to soften their hearts, if indeed theirs were capable of softness, as his own apparently was not. He had done nothing to earn their mercy; in fact he'd broken his side of the agreement within minutes of swearing to keep it. Suppose they were already aware of the hunt he had launched? Suppose they hurt Kate to punish him? Even with the vast resources at his command, he couldn't find the child. All he had done so far was endanger her further.

It would all have to be called off – the risk was too great. When that horse's ass Wilberforce came back, he'd put him to work right away. Cancel the search, every aspect of it, and pray they weren't already too late. He supposed cancellation would still be feasible at this point – they'd told so many different lies, and often it was easier to start the machinery rolling than to stop it. At least they could try.

He recalled with a start that at two o'clock Little Pruneface was being sent over from the White House to see him and to be given the grim verdict by his carefully primed doctors. Not that Harper supposed that the president was pacing the floor in anguish over the health of his secretary of state. The consequences of a certain third-rate burglary were now demonstrably out of hand, and what with Mutt and Jeff, those egregious bunglers, having had to resign, and the Senate hearings scheduled to begin in less than a week, it was doubtful if at the moment the White House much cared whether the State Department was headed by Pendleton Harper or Fred Flintstone.

Without being altogether sure how he had got there, Harper found he had reached a firm decision. He was going to do exactly what that Irishman had told him. It seemed incredible now that he had ever considered any other course. He thought of Colonel Lund and his praise of risk, and winced. As soon as the official announcement was issued, Kate should be safe, and before long, provided the people holding her were not interfered with or driven to panic, she would be set free. He was quite certain about this. That Irishman was a bastard, but an impressive bastard. Credible. Harper had never met anyone who so obviously meant what he said. As for the secretaryship, the fuck with it, he thought, suddenly mutinous. It was no fun any more – hadn't been, really, for quite a while. He didn't snap back from the jetlag the way he used to, his insomnia was getting worse, and his digestion was in ruins. As for his temper, it had never been sunny, but lately he had found increasing difficulty in being even halfway civil to the dolts he dealt with. Last week he had even snapped at the president.

And another thing. How much longer would he have kept the damned job anyhow? Certainly not beyond the next election. He'd become too controversial, had bawled out a few too many fellow cabinet members, and his run-ins with reporters had become so bitter that the whole snarling pack was out for his blood. Moreover, it was by no means certain that the president himself would serve out his term. Defying frantic efforts to stuff it back in, the genie was halfway out of the bottle. This obstruction-of-justice caper – and thank God he, Harper, had absolutely no involvement with *that* piece of lunacy – might yet devour the floundering occupant of the Oval Office with the impersonal efficiency of a column of army ants, and where would that leave Harper? He sure as hell didn't intend to lower himself and start taking orders from El Chumpo. Besides, El Chumpo probably wouldn't want him around. Vice presidents who lucked into the big one seldom cared to be overshadowed, especially by flamboyant superstars identified with the previous regime. El Chumpo (and come to think of it, there had been some pretty disquieting rumours building about him, too) would be happier with somebody like Ted Faraday, who wouldn't make him feel insecure.

That was the choice, then, when you got down to the nittygritty: a possible three and a half years – probably much less, the way things were going – of flashbulbs and dyspepsia weighed against Kate's life. He hadn't thought of the situation in those terms before; he'd been preoccupied with not yielding to pressure, not giving in to demands, standing firm. The habits of power diplomacy had gained such a hold over him that he could no longer recognize an untenable position, even though two minutes' reflection would have told him that, in this private crisis, the armed might of the nation he represented was as much use to him as a leaky bucket.

It showed how stale he was getting, how old and tired. A nice long rest was what he needed. A few months in Jamaica, perhaps, in a borrowed house – a lot of people owed him favours, and most of them were rich. Albert would come too, and take care of him. Whatever else he might have to give up, he would keep Albert. Albert, however, would have to be paid, and so, before long, would the bills for a great many amenities he had become accustomed to getting for nothing. No more perks, and what was he going to do about that?

Into his head floated a fragment of ironic advice, spoken in a soft brogue. 'Write your memoirs,' the Irishman had said. Not kindly meant, perhaps, but all the same it wasn't a bad idea. He'd need an agent, of course. Lazar, that was the fellow's name – he'd be the one. Speedy Lazar, wasn't it? Something like that. Harper reached for the legal pad and made a note: *Contact Lazar re memoirs*. He felt better already.

TUESDAY, 8 MAY 1973. 4.30 P.M.

The Cold Crossing elementary school let out at three o'clock. At three-thirty Daniel called from Billy Paton's house to say he was spending the afternoon in town. Some of the boys had set up a football game, and Billy's father had promised to drive him home after it was over. Rebeccah, Dan said, would be on the bus as usual. But an hour later there was still no sign of her, and Claire had begun to fret.

'That bus ride is forty minutes at the very outside, and even the way she dawdles it doesn't take her more than twenty to walk up from the fork. Where in the world is she at?'

'Maybe she had to stay after school,' Chuck suggested.

'Dan would have told me. Anyhow, Mrs Rouderbridge would have called; she always calls the parents if there's any change. And if she wasn't on the bus, how is she going to get home?'

'Give her another half hour. You know Beccah – she's a dreamer. Probably she found a cricket, or she's teaching a worm to answer to its name.'

'She knows I don't like her to be late. It's not as if she doesn't know the time – she's wearing her watch; I made her put it on this morning.'

'What good is a watch when she never looks at it? Half an hour, and if she's not home by then I will go find her.'

Before the half hour was up, Rebeccah came running through the pasture, braids flying, face scarlet with exertion. Chuck scooped her up as she reached the gate. 'Bad girl,' he said. 'Terrible little girl, you're late and it frightens your mother. Where were you?'

'There were these two men, scary men. I told them my daddy would shoot them dead if they didn't go away.'

Chuck set her back down on the ground and squatted until his face was on a level with hers.

'Two men, huh? And what were they doing, these two scary men?'

'They were up on the ridge, on Berry Hill, hiding all scrunched down in the bushes. They had glasses, buy-noculars like yours

202

that you brought back from the war, and they were looking down at our house.'

'Were they, now. What sort of men – how did they look?'

'They looked funny. They looked – they looked like bankers.'

'*Bankers?*'

'You know. Like Mr Brackage at the Farmers Loan. Dark blue pants and jackets and white First Day shirts. And they had thin shoes on, daddy, like city people.'

'Very suspicious. What did they say to you?'

'Didn't say nothing, to start off. They were hiding, like I said, watching the house, and I was hiding too, watching them. I wanted to see them bury the dead body.'

'Rebeccah, if you're making this up I shall be very angry. What is this about a dead body? Did you see someone hurt?'

'Not ezackly, so I guess they must have buried it before I got there. Bad men always have dead bodies. They kill people – pow, pow, zap – and then they have to bury them so nobody will know.'

'You've been reading Daniel's comic books again. I think I know who your scary men are. They sound to me like Mr Grose and Mr Maybush, and while they are not very suitable company for nice little girls, they do *not* kill people pow, pow, zap. They work for a friend of Katie's father – ' that, at least, was more or less true, though Chuck was less sure about the pow part ' – and they are looking for her to take her home, but she doesn't want to go. That's why she is staying here with us, and that's why we must all be very careful to keep it a secret, and not talk about her to anyone. Did the men see you watching them?'

'What happened was, I coughed. I was sort of forgetting to breathe through my nose, and I had my mouth open like ma says I shouldn't. A little fly popped in and flew right down my throat, and I coughed and coughed. I made a terrible noise, and they came over and caught me.'

'Did you try to run away?'

'Cernly not. I live here. Let *them* run away if they want to.'

'Quite right. So you made a noise and they caught you, and then what happened?'

'They said – they said, Little girl what's your name? And I said, Puddentane, ask me again and I'll tell you the same. And then they asked did I live at the farm. And I said, You mean the farm you were spying on with your buy-noculars? And one of the men got all red in the face and said that word Billy Paton says all the time, the one I am most particuly never to say. And the other man

203

said hush, and he said – he said they were bird-watching. So I asked him, What birds? And he said they were very rare and I wouldn't know about them. He wanted to give me a Hershey bar, but it looked all warm and scroochy, so I said, No. My daddy doesn't let me take candy from strangers. And then the man said – he said, What's your daddy's name? And I said, His name is Daddy, stupid. And then I said about you shooting them, and then I came away. I shouldn't have said stupid, but he was. Big old man in First Day clothes, crawling around in the bushes. Stupid, stupid, he's a droopid.'

'Hush. Run along inside and ma will give you some milk and cookies. No need to tell her about calling that man stupid. She has had too many shocks already the last few days.'

Kate was dumping skim milk into the trough for the calves when Chuck came into the barn.

'They're back,' he said.

'Who are?' She leaned down to shove a hefty bull calf out of the way, making room for the timid one that always got left out.

'Tom and Jerry. Maybush and Grose, the FBI men. Rebeccah saw them and spoke with them. They're about a half-mile away, surveilling the area with binoculars. They told Beccah they were bird-watching. Not very original, but then they don't have to be. You have been running in and out of the house all afternoon – there's no way they can have missed you.'

'God. I really blew it, didn't I? Now what?'

'Now you stay under cover until Conor gets back. He left in the Jeep as soon as we heard so he shouldn't be too long. At some point they'll move in, but I think they will wait until we're all in the house together. That's what I would do, in their place. There's no rush, after all – they know you are here. As long as you are not seen to leave, they can take their time.'

'Chuck?'

'Yes, Katie?'

'What do I do if they come in here and start poking around looking for me, before Conor gets back?'

'That depends. If they're only taking a look around, stay under the straw at the back of Barley's stall until they leave. But if it's a real search and you think they are getting too close, don't wait for them to find you. Call to them, tell them where you are, and come out slowly with your hands in the air. Be very, very careful. I think they really believe this dumb cover story of theirs, so they may expect you to be dangerous – and that will make them dangerous. That man Grose is a bad apple. They're not high up in the Bureau, those two. I don't think they have been told very much, but the field agent in Haynesville will know who you are. Once you get there you will be safe. Say as little as you can until then, and don't talk to the rest of us. Act as if you were afraid of us; it could help you later. Okay?'

'Okay. Hey, you know what? I'm scared.'

'Yes, I know. But it will be all right. As soon as Conor comes we have it made.' He squeezed her shoulder comfortingly. 'Remember how scared you were when he brought you here the first night? You sat in the kitchen like a pet rabbit in a den of foxes. You were so terrified I thought you were going to faint. And now you don't want to be rescued from the terrible villains who were going to eat you up. Some people are never satisfied. Be still now and wait for Conor.'

Out on Berry Hill Agent Maybush slapped at the fly that had just bitten his neck. He missed and bumped the bridge of his nose against the binoculars. 'Ah, Jesus,' said Agent Maybush. He had known he was going to hate this assignment, and he had been absolutely right. And just because Webster Grose had four months' seniority on him, Grose was the one who got to go back and sit in the car with the windows rolled up and the air conditioning on, maintaining radio contact with the sheriff and the state police and setting up the forthcoming raid, while he, Harold Maybush, was stuck in the briers and keeping the Lainez gang under surveillance and being chewed on by every bug in the country. All because of some damn little whore, born with a silver spoon in her mouth he didn't doubt, who couldn't find anything better to do with her time than blow up National Guard armouries. Another Bomber for Peace. Spoiled rotten, this generation was; Dr Spock had a lot to answer for. Look at that hippie outfit they'd checked out over at Harmony, trust funds and dirty feet, playing at hardship like rich kids at a wilderness camp. Poverty was just another high to them, and as soon as they were tired of it they could go back to Fifth Avenue.

'*Kids*,' Maybush said aloud, rancorously. No respect for anything, giving authority the finger every chance they got. Even the youngest of them, like that snooty little girl who'd called them stupid, could use a good spanking along with the rest. Pretty little thing, though – cute, really, with those long braids and the big red bows on the ends. Her father would shoot them dead, would he?

Well, hell, that was the way little girls were supposed to feel about their fathers. He wondered uneasily what would become of her when her precious daddy was in the slammer.

Grose, the crazy son of a bitch, had wanted to go in shooting. Waste them, he'd said; once the woman's in there we won't take any chances, we'll waste the whole fucking bunch. Maybush had been obliged to bring up the public relations aspect of wasting children – particularly American children – to cool that one. He could see the graffiti now, black spray paint fuzzy on ten thousand walls: MY LAI, KENT STATE, ATTICA, COLD CROSSING. Through the glasses he watched the little girl out in the yard with that mangy old dog. Maybush was a sentimental soul at heart. He thought of Webster Grose and felt ill.

Presently a station wagon drove along the road to the farm and pulled up in front of the house. Two young boys bounced out of it, followed more slowly by a tall, stoop-shouldered man who looked familiar. Maybush trained the binoculars on him and swore. It was Paton, the sheriff's deputy. What in hell was he doing out here now, the moron? Surely he didn't imagine he could wrap up the whole operation single-handed? Anyhow, why the kids? If they were his, he must be crazy to drag them into danger this way. And if they weren't his, whose were they?

A rational, consoling thought slipped through the static. Obviously Paton hadn't been on duty when Grose contacted the sheriff's office. He must have missed the alert and had come out here on private business of his own. Now that he thought about it, wasn't Paton, too, related to Mrs Lainez? Kind of a brother-in-law once removed, that was it. His elder brother, Gilbert Paton, who ran the dairy cooperative, had been married to the late Martha Bradley, Claire Lainez's sister. And Ollie Paton, Gil and Martha's boy, worked in the sheriff's office. Not a little proud of his grip on the rich confusions of intermarriage that bedevilled any investigation in Aurora County, Maybush relaxed.

Then he had a truly horrible idea. Suppose Will Paton had found family loyalty more powerful than his sense of duty as a law officer? Suppose he did indeed know about the raid, knew all about it, and had come to warn the household – or worse than warn it? The Hale woman was a little scrap of a thing, from what he'd seen. Put a loose-fitting shirt on her and chop off some of that yellow hair, and from a distance she might very well pass for a twelve-year-old boy. Arrive with two boys, leave with (apparently) two boys, and hope to fool the watchers that way.

They knew he was out there – the little girl would have told them right off. One of the boys had yellow hair.

Maybush dug into his pockets for his Pak-A-Page, the miniaturized unit he could use to communicate with Grose, a quarter of a mile away down on the road. It was stuck somehow, tangled up in his handkerchief, and as he jerked the little thing free it popped from his sweaty grasp as slickly as a cherry pit. He dived for it, letting go the binoculars, but he was too slow. It bounced off a rock with an unpleasantly terminal clunk and came to rest among the briers. He pricked himself badly retrieving it, but he might as well not have bothered. He shook it, thumped it, fiddled with the switch; it was quite dead. Suddenly it was as if the insects that aureoled his head had bored through into his brain. He recognized the symptoms all too well. He was going into what his mother had always referred to, resignedly, as one of his swivets. 'Harry, Harry, now don't get in a swivet!' The admonition had echoed throughout his childhood, and never once had he been able to comply. Like the forty-eight-hour grippe, once a Maybush swivet took hold there was nothing to be done but wait for it to run its course.

The current attack was brought on by his inability to be in two places at once. Grose had to be warned about Will Paton and about the possibility that Catherine Hale might be whisked away, with Paton's connivance, from under their noses. But if Maybush ran down the back of the ridge and delivered the news in person, the girl could be long gone while he wasn't watching. Either way, it was going to be his neck on the chopping block. He tried valiantly to calm himself: breathe in through the nose to a count of three, breathe out through the mouth to a count of five, mentally repeating the word Parma. (He had always been too shy to enrol in a meditation course, and probably the Bureau wouldn't have liked it anyhow, but his homemade regimen was better than nothing. At least while he was doing that he wasn't doing something else which would probably turn out to be wrong.)

Breathing conscientiously from the abdomen, he continued his vigil. He was almost sure the subject had not left the barn; both exits were visible to him from his present vantage point. Although he had dropped the glasses he didn't think he had been distracted for more than a few seconds – not long enough for her to have come out and gone into hiding anywhere else. Besides, the two boys were still in plain sight. They were turning handsprings in the grass, engaged in one of those mindless, pointless, totally satisfying competitive displays he remembered from his own childhood. For the moment, then, there was nothing much to worry about. But what if, what if, what if? Maybush pulled out the traitorous handkerchief and mopped his face. In to a count of three, out to a count of five.

In the sheriff's office in Cold Crossing, Ollie Paton squirmed in his swivel chair. His placid nature was ill suited to this kind of strain. On the one hand, Uncle Chuck's moonshining was in imminent danger of exposure (Ollie knew better than to believe all that bullshit about female terrorists. It was the still they were after, it had to be). On the other hand, the state trooper leaning negligently against the office wall was a powerful deterrent to the phone call Ollie was dying to make. He made up his mind, rose casually to his feet, and pottered over to the window. He gazed out, nonchalant as all hell, and then suddenly stiffened.

'Hey!' he said excitedly. 'There's a guy down the street chasin' a old lady! Got a club in his hand, and carryin' on something terrible. I better – oh, shoot, I can't leave the radio phone, be worth my job if Sheriff Gibbs called in and I wad'n here . . . Pete, maybe you could just get on out there and . . .' He was speaking to the air. Pete was already out of the door in pursuit of the nonexistent molester of old ladies. Ollie lunged for the phone. After all, some old ladies could run awful fast.

On Berry Hill the flies buzzed and bit, and the minutes crawled. The boys in the pasture grew bored or overheated or both and went indoors. For a cold drink, probably, Maybush thought and wished he could join them. Next the black woman, Tulliver, came out carrying a basket, walked up to the vegetable garden, and returned soon after with the basket full of some pale green stuff. Lettuce, he supposed. Some time later the Jeep turned in at the gates and drove straight in through the wide double doors that stood open at the end of the barn. There were several bulging sacks on board, and presumably these would be off-loaded inside.

Grose and Maybush had watched the doctor leave earlier that afternoon. They knew who he was. Although he had not been present for their official visit to the farm the previous Friday, Sheriff Gibbs had given them his description, as well as the licence number of the vehicle. Maybush's mother had always wanted him to be a doctor; the Bureau was a disappointment to her, loyally though she tried to conceal it. Reverence for the medical profession had been drilled into young Harold from an early age, and even now he found it hard to believe that one of the sacred healers, however misguided, could be mixed up in something illegal. But maybe the poor guy was really innocent, maybe the others had concealed the truth from him, told him some yarn or other and he'd fallen for it. Maybush only hoped the doctor could prove he wasn't involved – in this kind of case the mud flew every which way and some of it always stuck.

Feeling hungry, or rather anxious, which for him was the same thing, Maybush pulled out the chocolate bar the little girl had spurned. Unwrapping it one-handed was an awkward, messy job – he was afraid to put down the binoculars in case he missed something – and the chocolate, when at last he had it unveiled, proved to have passed its prime. It made him think of a sliver of mud after a heavy rain, but he ate it anyhow, and quickly. The bugs apparently liked the look of the stuff better than he did and were prepared to fight him for it.

The doctor came out of the barn. The subject walked beside him, swinging an empty pail, and at the sight of her the FBI man was able to acknowledge to himself just how worried he had been in case they had somehow managed to spirit her away. They crossed the yard together and disappeared inside, and a couple of minutes later the doctor emerged once more, followed by Lainez.

Maybush watched rather wistfully as the two men brought the cows in for milking. He knew little about farming, except that it was a hard life: work, work, at all hours and in all weathers, and then half the time you were wiped out by a drought or a blight or a surplus. But the glossy, coffee-ice-cream cows looked beautiful to him, and even from this distance the men had such a noticeable air of being comfortable, at ease with their work and themselves, that he almost envied them. As soon as Grose and his back-up team moved in it would all be over, half a dozen lives shot to hell, and for what? He scratched one of the burgeoning lumps on his neck and wished to God he had listened to his mother and gone to medical school.

Nothing, absolutely nothing, was going right about this case. Agent Grose had been nursing a delicious fantasy all afternoon, involving that classic directive, 'Open this door or we'll blast it open!' But how were you going to blast open a door that stood wide open already, blocked only by a flimsy screen? After a brief, enraging tussle with the screen door, which he tried to kick in only to find that it opened, easily, outward, he settled for striking a dramatic pose in the kitchen doorway, weapon in hand, and yelling, 'Don't anybody move, the place is surrounded!' The moment he'd yelled it, he realized 'Don't anybody move!' was hopelessly outdated. He should have just shouted, 'Freeze!' like Pacino and Hackman and those guys did in the movies. But they were actors, they had scriptwriters doing the words for them, and if they didn't get it right the first time they could go over it and over it until it was perfect. He'd like to see them try it in real life.

The kitchen seemed to be full of people, a frieze of astonished faces all turned towards him. Startled cats scattered like mice disturbed in a pantry, and the basset hound, panicking, tried to crawl under the chesterfield and stuck halfway. Into the stunned and unbelieving silence rose a child's high, excited voice. 'That's him, daddy!' Rebeccah called out. 'That's the man who said fuck!'

'Rebeccah Lainez! Thee mind thy mouth, girl.' Claire was scandalized. Will Paton didn't help matters by letting out a great guffaw.

'Hailey?' he shouted. 'What in blazes are these – these gentlemen up to now?'

Sheriff Gibbs, who had been standing right behind Grose and peering benevolently over his shoulder, moved the agent gently to one side and came into the room.

'Hahdy, Will. Seems like Mr Grose, here, and his friend, they been keepin' an eye on what they call the outlyin' farms, last two-three days, and this afternoon when they were peekin' at this one they spotted a young woman they couldn't quite recall seein' here before. They got to thinkin' it might be this fugitive they been lookin' for, so they figured we better all come along and find out. Reckon you may's well put that handgun of yours away now, Mr Grose; don't appear to me like you're goin' to need it.'

Grose was staring, appalled, at the blonde girl who sat at the kitchen table, where she had been overseeing Dan's homework until they were interrupted. The FBI man looks as if he had just dropped a winning lottery ticket into the incinerator.

'I've seen you before,' he said at last.

'Certainly you have, last Friday.'

'But you had long hair then, right the way down your back. You

210

cut your hair!' It came out a strangled bellow. The blonde girl looked at him with distaste.

'Most people do, from time to time,' she said quellingly. 'It's not a federal offence.'

'And you had a long dress on, like the other women. How come you're wearing jeans all of a sudden?'

'I think it's really sweet that you care enough to notice. But if you'd ever tried feeding hogs in a skirt that trailed on the ground, you wouldn't ask.'

'Let me see your identification.'

'Oh, really, Mr – Mr Grose, isn't it? We went all through that the last time. I am still Alice Mary Danbury de Bruycker, and I have been ever since I was christened. St James's Church, Madison Avenue, February 1950. You could look it up.' At the end of the table Conor choked, and hastily turned the noise into a cough. 'Besides,' she went on, 'Sheriff Gibbs knows me. Don't you, Sheriff?'

'Sure do.'

'You're supposed to be at Harmony,' Grose ploughed on. 'What are you doing here?'

'Visiting. I had a fight with Paul, if it's any of your business, which I very much doubt, and Mrs Lainez offered to let me stay here for a day or two. Harmony is a small house, and when two people out of seven aren't on speaking terms, it makes life uncomfortable for the others. We're just having what the labour negotiators call a cooling-off period. Of course, if I'd had any idea it was going to lead to all this commotion, I'd have let you know. But nobody told me I wasn't allowed to visit friends without filing a flight plan first with the FBI.'

She gave Grose a small, vinegary smile. He had heard of the de Bruyckers, just about everybody had. The name stood for old money and powerful connections, and he had no desire to spend the rest of his working life in Butte, Montana. This sour-faced little bitch had come out on top, her sort always did, and there wasn't one thing he could do about it except scramble through a string of apologies that burned his mouth as he uttered them, and get himself out of the house before he made things worse for himself. He had forgotten all about the state police. They were still in place, naturally, their faces carefully blank. He told them to stand down, loathing them, and rounded on the only available target for his wrath.

'What the fuck are you so fucking cheerful about?'

'Me? I'm not cheerful.' Maybush had been grinning like a dog without knowing it. He rapidly rearranged his face into an expression of suitable chagrin, but Grose was not to be put off.

'Then why were you smirking that way?'

'Indigestion?' Maybush offered incautiously. He had a miserable ride back to town.

Will Paton, still simmering with amusement, collected his boy Billy and headed home, but Sheriff Gibbs paused on his way out.

'Little girl of yours ain't lookin' so pert today,' he said to Chuck, laying an immense, calloused palm against Rebeccah's forehead. 'Thought so. She's burnin' up, like to scorch my hand. You better keep her home from school tomorrow. My granddaughter Cissy, Elizabeth's girl, she told her mother Beccah was talkin' kind of wild at recess today, makin' up a lot of crazy stuff, and now I believe I know why. Got a real fever on her. Miz Rouderbridge was tellin' me one of the Swenson kids is in the hospital with meningitis. You better have Conor check this one out – and I sure would keep her home, was I you. The boy too, 'case he might be comin' down with it. So long Claire, Chuck. Conor, I'll see you around. 'Bye, Miss de Bruycker – ah, Consolation, that is.'

'Alice Mary to you, Sheriff. I don't feel particularly consoling just now.'

'Can't say I blame you. I'm right sorry about that nonsense. That feller Grose is entirely too excitable for his own good; he's been chasin' around like a half-trained hound dog ever since he got here. He'll learn, I guess, one of these days, long as somebody don't blow his fool head off first.'

Chuck went out to walk the sheriff to his car, and Conor swooped on Alice Mary and hugged her.

'Was there ever such a performance? I haven't heard anything like it since my Aunt Rose told the Provos where to put it. Rolled 'em up, you did, horse, foot, and guns. I can't begin to thank you.'

'My dear, it was a pleasure. Mother always said I'd come into my own as a dowager, and at last I can see what she meant. What would you like me to do now?'

'Stay here overnight, if you can bear to. I don't think they'll come back, but I'd rather not risk it.'

'What do you mean, if I can bear to? For one of Claire's dinners I'd stop over in – in Camden, New Jersey, and I can't say fairer than that. I love Charity like a sister, but she's the second worst cook in the world.'

'Who's the first worst?'

'Me, of course – otherwise I'd do it myself.'

Chuck walked back through the kitchen door, headed straight for Rebeccah, and felt her brow. 'I know, I know,' Claire said. 'She's as cool as I am, cooler; I just checked. Now what do you suppose Hailey would do a thing like that for?'

'One thing for sure, he doesn't want Beccah to go to school. Or Daniel either.'

'That old bugger knows something,' Conor said. 'I've no idea how much, or how he got on to it, and I can't conceive why he should cover up for us. But that was a warning all right, and a nod's as good as a wink to a blind horse. Beccah my love, I think you are about to have a short vacation. Come here a minute. As you're looking so ravishing you can sit on my knee. That's a girl. "This is the way the ladies ride, tippety, tippety, tip." Now I want to hear all about school today. What did you do first?'

'First we had assembly, and Mrs Rouderbridge said how glad she was to see Dan and me back at school. And by the way, I don't think she's going to like it one bit if I have a vacation just now. She said I missed a lot going away to grandmother's, and I was way behind in substraction.'

'Never mind about substraction, you'll soon catch up. Then what did you do, after assembly?'

'We had the Pledge of Allegiance. You want me to say it for you? I know it all the way through.'

'Not now, lovey, thank you all the same. You say it for me some other time. What happened next?'

'The big kids went off to their part of school to do all that stuff they do, and the sixes and sevens – that's me, I'm a seven – we sat down very quiet and nice in our places and did reading. "Run, run, as fast you can, you can't catch me I'm the Gingerbread Man!" I like that story – it's exciting – but I don't like it when the fox gobbles him up. I think he should have gotten away. And then we did singing. We sang "This Land is Your Land" and we sang "The Erie Canal" and we sang "*Jump* down turnaroun pickabaleacotton, *Jump* down turnaroun pickabaleaday," and Elnora threw up, and then we had break.'

'Tell me about break.'

'Well, I got my skipping rope, and Cissy Barrett got hers, and we did Lincoln Lincoln I been thinkin', until we was plum-tuckered out. And then we sat on the fence, and I told Cissy about grandmother's house and Uncle Peter Sees Far and what it was like going to Father Montaldo's school. And I told about coming back in an airplane – two airplanes – because Cissy's never been in an airplane, not once. And I told about the lady with the blue stuff on her eyes that gave me a yucky colouring book with elves and flower fairies, yuck, and Dan got Scenes from American History, and it wasn't fair. But the crayons were okay so I kept those, and Dan let me colour in Pocahontas and Captain John Smith and he said I did a great job.'

'I bet old Cissy Barrett was green with envy. Did you tell her anything else?'

'I told her about the princess, that's all.'

'Ah. Now which princess would that be?'

'The one that's staying here, of course, the secret princess. The one that looks like *her*.' She pointed to Alice Mary. Claire was so taken aback by Rebeccah's account she quite forgot to tell her again how rude it was to point. 'I told old Cissy how she'd run away from the wicked witch's castle,' Rebeccah went on, making the most of her unusually attentive audience. 'And they chased her and chased her with flying monkeys and – and heticoppeler gunships and everything, but my daddy rescued her and brought her here to live with us. And I told her it was a big, big secret and she mustn't tell anyone ever or she'd get big green warts all over her tongue.'

'So it is a big, big secret. And you know, Beccah, you promised you wouldn't tell it to anyone either.'

'But I didn't. I only told Cissy, and she's just a kid, like me. She doesn't count. I didn't tell any grown-ups. You want to know what we did next, after break?'

'Tell me another day, lovey. You run along now and play until suppertime. I have to take care of something in the barn.'

'Can I come?'

'Not this time, it's private.'

'Hey, Beccah,' Dan said nobly, 'I finished my homework, you want to play Snap?'

'Sure.'

'Get the cards out then. And you better not cheat.'

Except for the children, who had been sent upstairs to work on their reading books, all the members of the household were grouped around the kitchen table listening to Chuck's little transistor radio. The president was paying tribute, in the ringing clichés of both his principal speech writers, to that diplomatic genius and selfless public servant Pendleton Harper, whose exertions in the cause of international peace had tragically undermined his health to the point where he could no longer bear the burden. The torch would pass to worthy hands. The policies so brilliantly initiated by Dr Harper would be faithfully carried on by one whom he himself had imbued with his own shining faith and high ideals. Edward Faraday, as they were all aware, could be counted upon – blah blah blah and so forth. The questions that followed the president's statement were muted and respectful, as if the reporters felt themselves to be taking part, even though at second hand, in a deathbed scene. Right after 'Thank you, Mr President', Conor leaned over, switched the radio off, and looked around the circle of intent faces with a kind of awe.

'Well get a load of that,' he said softly. '*We* did that. Us. With a little help from our friends. Good Lord, we could have done it years ago! Who shall we get rid of next?'

'There's a cardinal in New York I've had my eye on,' Claire began, and was drowned out by Conor as he threw his arms around her, whooping. Suddenly everyone was hugging everyone else, and Claire was crying and laughing and mopping her eyes with a kitchen towel. Bagel started to bark, and the piglet woke up, contrived to fall out of its box onto its head, and set up a counterpoint of piercing squeals, while Chuck went for the whisky bottle and sloshed out huge celebratory portions.

'Mafeking is relieved!' Conor crowed, waving his glass above his head. 'But nothing like as relieved as I am.' He kissed Alice Mary. 'You must think we're nuts,' he said. 'And I can't explain. But be happy for us.'

Alice Mary smiled at him, a very different smile from the brackish grimace she had bestowed on Agent Grose. 'I am happy for you,' she said. 'And you don't need to explain. If you did it, then it's all right.'

Conor turned to the others. 'Did you ever believe we'd bring it off, did you really? Claire, I know you did – you're the Faith Lady – but did anybody else?'

'Of course,' Chuck said. 'You think this Indian stick out neck just for kicks? Me plenty coward, cover ass at all times, same like the generals. It was a good plan, it deserved to work, and it did. But without my Katie we would all be in the lock-up.'

'*Your* Katie? I'll have you know that is my Katie, you thieving savage. And you can take your Apache paws off her this instant!'

'Sioux paws. You want to be a bigot, you get your facts right.

215

Afeni, pick up that little pig before somebody steps on him.'

By the end of the evening everyone but Claire was mildly drunk, as much on euphoria as on whisky. Even Kate's new-found cousin, the alarming Alice Mary, lost some of her icy poise and became almost friendly. In fact, the way she smiled at Conor was positively warm, but Kate was too happy to be jealous. She felt enfolded by this dear adopted family who made her feel so safe, so loved. She'd never felt like part of a family before. Her father's departure from Walden Avenue, and the subsequent divorce, had merely made official what had long been his absence in all but physical fact. Once Nanny Bristow had gone home to England to put the fear of God into a large, noisy household in Wiltshire, Kate and her mother had been very much on their own. Kate had always vaguely felt she was missing something, without being at all sure what it was. Now she seemed to have found it. She was full of love, crammed with it, spilling out sweetness like a honeycomb. When at last Conor took her up to bed, she began to tremble as soon as he reached for the buttons on her shirt.

'My dove, you're shaking. What is it? Are you cold?'

'No, it's just – I just want you.'

'Well, you've got me.' He finished undoing her buttons and bent down to press his face for a moment in the warm hollow between her breasts. 'Bad bargain that I am, I'm all yours – God help you.' He unfastened her jeans and slid them down over her hips until they fell around her ankles. She stepped out of them, and he took hold of the top elastic of her underpants and very carefully, very slowly rolled them down, inch by inch, dropping onto one knee at the end as she lifted one bare foot free and then the other. Still kneeling, he slipped his fingers between her thighs, delicately probing. Then he stood up and smiled at her.

'You really do want me, don't you?' he said. 'You weren't just being polite.' He pulled off his own clothes and joined her on the bed.

'Conor?'

'Mmmmm.'

'You do such beautiful things for me. I want to do them for you, too, but I don't know how. Will you teach me?'

'You are the most astonishing girl.' He stroked her hair. 'I must have been a saint in my last life, for I've done nothing in this one to deserve a bonus like you.'

'Sweet talk, I love it. Now show me.'

He showed her. But after a while he took her head between his hands and lifted her up, away from him.

'What's the matter, am I doing it wrong?'

'You're doing it quite sensationally right. Another thirty seconds of that and I'd come, and I don't want to yet, because then I'd probably go to sleep. And when I'm asleep I don't know you're there, and that's a terrible waste.' He sighed. 'Oh, God, I wish I were your age, then I could stay up all night – so to speak – and love you every hour on the hour. Which is what I'd like to do and what you deserve.'

She wriggled up beside him and kissed his shoulder. 'You're too thin,' she said disapprovingly. 'I can feel your bones.'

'You prefer the stockbroker type, no doubt.'

'I prefer you, always and always. Conor?'

'Yes, peach.'

'Can't there be anything for us? Afterwards, I mean?'

'Afterwards? I don't see how. Look, lovey, I'm trained for a certain kind of work, and that's what I have to do. I can't see myself spending my days rolling up to some state-of-the-art fancy hospital in my Mercedes, raking in thousands of bucks for operating on witless adolescents who've smashed themselves up diving into empty swimming pools while stoned out of their embryonic minds. I know somebody has to do it, but it isn't going to be me. I'm the blood-and-muck type and there it is. Once this caper's over I'll be moving on to somewhere that's messy and dangerous, just the way I like it, and wherever it is there's one thing certain: it'll be no fit place for you. Darling girl, you can't tie yourself to a nutcase like me – there's no future in it. I told you that before. Get on with your life and be happy – and safe, please God.'

'I don't think I can bear it.'

'Ah, but there's now,' he said, turning her onto her back, kissing her breasts. 'There's this, now. And now is as much as anybody ever has, really. Make the most. Anything to come, be glad of it. And always take your coat off the minute you come indoors, or you won't –'

'Won't Get the Benefit when you go out again.'

'Right! Where on earth did you get that from?'

'Nanny Bristow, of course.'

'Of course indeed. Bet she'd be shocked right out of her stays if she could see you now.'

'Don't! Don't even think of it, you'll summon her up like a, a –'

'Spirit from the vasty deep?'

'Right. And she'll come stumping in, in that awful grey felt hat like a mixing bowl, and send me straight to my room.'

'The hell she will. I'll sprinkle the old girl with a few drops of cod liver oil and she'll simply dissolve. Whimpering faintly.' His hands moved over her. 'Now what have we here? Interesting little arrangement, I wonder what it's for.'

'Shall we see if we can find out?'

'What a good idea. Of course it may take us a while. There are so many possibilities. But as my dear old professor used to say, time spent on research is never wasted.'

You can't stop time, Kate knew, but sometimes you can stretch it. Last night the minutes, magically accommodating, had made up what seemed a whole exquisite lifetime: gentle and rough, funny and solemn, greedy and achingly tender. But now that it was over, all she could think of was that only five nights were left. After that, the beautiful lean body she had come to know better than her own would be off limits, no longer to be touched and stroked, submitted to, enjoyed, and satisfied. The sad mouth that smiled for her, the mouth she had once traced with such tentative fingers, would no more fold softly over her own in the slow kisses that first soothed her need for him and then inflamed it. She would have to manage without him, and she didn't at all see how this was to be done.

Kate picked up another carrot, sliced off the fluffy green top as if she disliked it personally, and scraped the root clean of earth and outer skin before chopping it into lengths to add to the growing pile Claire would put in with the brisket for tonight's supper. I've learned to cook, I've learned to knit, I've learned to milk a cow, and I've learned to fuck, she thought resentfully. And six days from now I'll have to be a student again and pretend to have significant opinions about the Romantic Movement, whether Wranglers fit as well as Levis, and if the vegetables at Mammy Nature's Nosheteria are really organically grown or just recycled rejects from the A&P. 'And who the hell cares?' Kate muttered, sniffing, and reached for another carrot.

Sam came in and stopped beside her. He snatched a chunk of carrot as it fell from the flashing knife blade and popped it into his mouth, crunching down hard with his small white teeth.

'Katie,' he said very quietly, 'I have to talk to you. Real private. Be in the barn in five minutes. Something you got to know.' He helped himself to another piece of carrot and was gone without once looking at her.

'I can't believe it,' Kate said. 'You've got it wrong, you must have.'

'How do you suppose I feel? But it's possible. You think about

219

it a minute, you got to admit it's possible. How much do we know about her? I mean really know? We just took her on trust, 'cause she's Tom Tulliver's sister and Tom's okay – at least I hope to God he is. This thing has me so shook up I don't feel too sure of anybody right now.'

'But she came down here with you, you must have thought she could be trusted. You must have known *some*thing about her.'

'I met her in New York with Tom, when I was hiding out. He was weak still, after the hospital, and she was living with him and looking after him. Week or so after we met up, she moved in with me and the rest of the outfit, just showed up one morning with a backpack and a sleeping bag. When Conor come to get me she rode right along. Why, she could've been using Tom all that time, just to get close to his friends.'

'Oh, it's all crazy. I mean, why would she do that? Somebody like Afeni, why would she want to work for the CIA?'

'Might not've wanted to, might not've had the choice. Tom was pretty deep into the movement, they could've pressured her that way. They're good at pressuring. Fact is, that is one of the things they're best at.'

'God, Sam, I don't know. It sounds so contrived, so – so silly, like something on television. Are you sure you heard it right?'

'Yeah. Dead sure. Now if somebody had come up and told me, I never would have believed it. But I got this by accident, it was random. See, I check out the Company frequencies ever' once in a while, just to see what's happening. It's habit more than anything, habit and curiosity. Like driving down a street you used to live on?'

'I thought it all went out in code, though, that kind of message.'

'Scrambled. What man hath scrambled, man can unscramble; that's what they used to tell us, and it's the truth, long as you got the right l'il deelybob for doing it with. I took care of all that kind of stuff, in Nam. And this morning I was just diddling around, not looking for anything special – feeling pretty good, you know, after last night, and not paying much attention? Took me a while to figure out what I was getting, and at that I only picked up a part of it. I don't even know when they're planning to move in. But they're using that Green Berets unit, I got that much, and I have seen those boys operate. They don't leave *nothing* – not a blade of grass. You got to get out of here right now.'

'What does Conor say?'

'He don't know about it yet.'

'You didn't tell him? Why ever not? If you're trying to make out Conor's in on this too –'

'Hell, no. He's a lousy actor, is all. He'd give it away in five minutes, and I ain't ready for that yet, not till I've got you clear away from here. Don't forget, Afeni knows how to work the radio. I taught her myself so she could run it when I wasn't around, and I taught her good. I can't take a chance on her getting word out to her control and blowing this thing wide open when we ain't set up for it. You let me get you stashed while I can still do it, before them motherfuckers – excuse me. Before they hit us. Soon as I get back, I'll tell Conor the whole thing, and he can decide what-all we're going to do about Afeni.'

The implications of Sam's bombshell had only begun to get through to Kate. She wasn't afraid for herself yet – she hadn't thought that far – but she was terrified for Afeni. She had done her homework, she'd read Greene, Deighton, le Carré. She knew what happened to double agents.

'What do you think he'll do? What would you do?'

'Feeling the way I do right now, I'd be liable to put a bullet through her head. Don't know what Conor'll do, but it won't be nothing like that. He's a forgiving kind of feller, which I am not. Besides, he ain't the one she's been whoring around with the last six months. Man hates to be made a fool out of by his own woman.' He let out a grim, ashamed-sounding laugh. 'She'll get a helluva better deal out of Conor than she would out of me, I'll tell you. Now quit fretting yourself over her – she sure as hell ain't paying no mind to you. But I am.'

'I suppose you'll take me over to Harmony.'

'No, I don't believe I will. Those FBI men looked like they fell for that switcheroo we pulled on 'em, but you never can tell. Fine thing if I was to take you down there and they was still hanging around, like Conor said, waiting for something to break. We could walk right into 'em.'

'Where, then?'

'There's an old falling-down cabin between here and Harmony; been standing there empty ever since old man Sonnenfeld died last year. You could hole up there while we get things straightened out some, get the kids out of the way, all that. Then one of us'd come by and pick you up.'

'You're going to leave me there by myself?' Kate was ashamed of herself for sounding such a baby, but she couldn't help it. She could have faced any danger with her friends beside her, but to be alone, not knowing . . . Not knowing what was happening to them, to Conor. Sam gave her a reassuring smile.

'Don't reckon you'd be there more'n a few hours. It ain't fancy, but there's a roof on it, and it's all I can come up with right now. And right now is when we got to go.'

'It'll be pretty tough getting out of here without somebody seeing us. They'll want to know where we're going.'

'Take you out same way Conor brought Alice Mary in, inside a feed sack. Lucky you girls ain't no bigger. I can say I'm picking up a couple of propane tanks in town. There's an empty one in the barn been waiting for the next trip. That big freezer of Claire's is such an old guzzler, nobody going to think twice about it.'

'Yes, but hey – what about the black box?'

'The what?'

'That gadget that picks up the signals of this damn thing on my arm.'

All the colour drained from Sam's face, leaving his freckles standing out like specks of mould. Then it came flooding back in a dark tide. 'Jesus Christ in the morning.' He shook his head, as if to clear it. 'I forgot. How could I forget a thing like that?'

For the first time Kate realized how rattled he was.

'The transmitter,' she said. 'Can't you deactivate it or something?'

'Not without taking it off of you first, and Conor has the key. I could file through the cuff, but we don't have that kind of time. You wait here a couple minutes, I'll be right back.'

When he reappeared he was moving fast, light on his feet, whistling softly under his breath. He looked keyed up and curiously happy.

'Did you wreck the monitor?' she asked.

'No ma'am. I pulled out what you call your capacitor. L'il bitty thing made out of paper and foil. Costs about a half a cent, and without it there's five hundred bucks' worth of circuits laying there deader'n Old Man Mose.' He patted his shirt pocket. 'Got it right here, too. No way anybody is going to fix that baby. Going to have to wait for poppa.'

He took her by the shoulders. He had never put a hand on her before, and his grasp was surprisingly loose and easy for such a large, powerful man. He's like a quarterback taking care not to bruise his mother, she thought and was touched. They were kind people, all of them. Sam was harder to know because he kept people off, at arm's length. But after what Conor had told her, she was eager to make allowances. (And Afeni, the traitor, the double agent calling down death on them all, how kind was she? Afeni, who had guided her into Conor's arms and Conor's bed, even though she loved him. Perhaps because she loved him. None of it made sense.)

'I'll back the pick-up in here,' Sam said. 'We can load the tank, and then I'll load you. Be pretty bumpy, I guess, going out there, but it's just a few miles, and I won't do no cowboying around. It's worth it, anyhow, for you to be safe. That's the only thing that matters. I got myself to think about, too.' He grinned at her. 'Old Conor like to kill me if I let anything happen to you.'

The great war chief Bad Heart Bull, known to those with prosaic, dull perceptions as Daniel Bradley Lainez, was out on his pony scouting for white-eyes. The pony's name was Barley, short for Barley Sugar – a terrible sissy name for a war chief's mount, but he wouldn't answer to any other. Bad Heart Bull made the best of a sorry job and simply addressed him as Horse, unless he really needed to get his attention. Then, damn it, he had to call him Barley.

Bad Heart Bull was enjoying his second day out of school. Yesterday morning – Tuesday, that was – his father had called up Mrs Rouderbridge at the Cold Crossing school and told her he was afraid Beccah might be coming down with something bad, which was crazy on the face of it because any fool could see the kid was perfectly fine. Nobody who put away three helpings of pancakes and about a pint of apple sauce at seven in the morning was coming down with anything worse than plain old greed, and what had gotten into dad was more than he could figure. Anyhow, it appeared Mrs Rouderbridge had been very much concerned, and had said that neither one of the children ought to come to school until the doctor was quite certain what the trouble was. This was all right with Bad Heart Bull, because Tuesdays there was always a spelling test, and Wednesdays they had to study sentences, a piss-poor occupation for a warrior.

He had left the family tepee soon after breakfast with a canteen of lemonade and a bag of oatmeal cookies. Pemmican would have been more fitting, but he'd never had any and wasn't sure how he'd like it. Besides, his mother had confessed as how she was fresh out of pemmican and it would have to be cookies or nothing. Trouble with cookies was they always broke up and went to crumbs. He reached down into his saddlebag, fished up a couple of substantial fragments, and crammed them into his mouth. Horse could have the crumbs later. Horse was a sucker for oatmeal cookies no matter how broke up they got.

There seemed to be a shortage of white-eyes today. Earlier, he had watched from cover as Will Paton rattled by in his old wagon heading for town, but there was no way a pony could stalk a Chevrolet even when the Chevrolet was falling apart. Bad Heart Bull brooded over his chances of saving up for a motorcycle, but those things cost an arm and a leg and anyhow his mother wouldn't let him. And anyhow who ever heard of a war chief leading his braves into battle on a motorcycle? 'Honda Harley Davidson, Kawasaki Yamaha,' he crooned to himself, more or less to the tune of *Gaudeamus Igitur*, and headed the pony east. Last spring there had been a pair of orioles nesting near the old Sonnenfeld place, and the queer little bag of a nest had still been hanging from its branch last time he'd checked. Wouldn't hurt to take a look and see if they'd come back.

He found no orioles, but there was a red flash that might have been the crest on a pileated woodpecker, and he put up a whole flock of goldfinches – flittery little creatures as giddy as butterflies. He cranked up a pailful of ice-cold earth-smelling water from Joe Sonnenfeld's well and gave it to Horse, then sat down in the sun at a safe distance from the spookily abandoned cabin. He and Horse shared the rest of the cookies, and they had started home again when he heard a car coming. Dan Lainez would have pulled up beside the track to be neighbourly with whoever came by, but Bad Heart Bull was not about to risk it. He whisked the pony into cover and slid down from the saddle to duck behind the bushes.

It was only the pick-up from the farm with Sam driving. There was a sack of something in the back and one of those big old tanks of propane gas for ma's freezer. The track didn't lead any place except up to Sonnenfeld's, and the boy wondered idly what Sam was doing out this way, but he didn't wonder much. Grown-ups were always doing the damn-foolishest things, and if you asked them why, not only did they not seem able to give a sensible account of themselves, but they were liable to think of something you ought to be doing. Next thing you knew, you were sent off to wash your hands again or finish your homework or feed those miserable chickens. Unless you really needed them for something, it was generally best to leave grown-ups alone.

The pony, ambling along at his normal unheroic pace, had

covered little more than a mile when the boy heard the pick-up returning. Once again he left the trail and hid, watching through the young leaves. The tank was still in the back, he noticed, but the sack had gone.

'White-eyes!' Bad Heart Bull snarled as the pick-up vanished around a bend. 'Treaty breakers! Squaw killers! You wait till Little Big Horn, that's all. You just wait.'

'Why, there you are, Sam,' Claire said. 'I was looking all over for you.'

'Went into town, picked up a couple of gas cylinders. One on the freezer's running low.'

'That it's not. I looked at the gauge just yesterday and it was more than half full. Any excuse to get to that old town. You've been drinking beer with Will Paton down at the gas station, I know you. Not that I mind having a reserve – all that good food in there, be a sin and a shame if anything happened to let it spoil. Didn't take Katie with you, I suppose?'

'Hell no. What kind of a crazy thing would that be? With the FBI poking around like they was doing a survey on crop rotation in Aurora County . . . We greased through it once, but right now the closer she stays to home the happier I'll be.' His face clouded as he thought about her question. 'What do you mean, was she with me? Ain't she *here*?'

'Well she must be. Oh, don't look at me that way. Of course she must be. It was only I tried to find her to beat some dough for me and she wasn't in the house. And she left a whole heap of carrots not done, just sitting there in the sink, which is not like her one bit. Maybe Conor took her off some place with him, like he did the other day.'

'Maybe Conor took who off some place?' Conor enquired, knocking the dirt off his boots outside the kitchen door.

'Katie,' Claire said. 'You know where she's at?'

'Haven't seen her since breakfast. I thought she was with you.'

'So she was, to begin with. Let's see now. I went upstairs to make the beds, and after that I had Beccah try on that new dress I'm making for her so I could get the hem pinned even. And when I came down again she'd vanished. And left a mess of scraped carrots on the draining-board and the rest of them not touched. I finished 'em myself.'

'Who's minding the box?' asked Conor. They looked at one another, bewildered.

'Why, nobody, I guess,' Claire said slowly. 'These last two-three days, and things being as they are between you two, there didn't seem the need –'

'Oh, for God's sake, I'm not worried about her running away. Somebody may have gone off with her, don't you see? Caught her away from the house and just grabbed her. If we could do it then so could the FBI – or anybody!' The last words were an angry shout as he raced up the stairs two at a time. In a moment he was back, carrying the box.

'The alarm isn't going,' he said, setting it on the kitchen table, 'so she can't be far away. Check the house, Sam, while I look outside.'

When Conor came back Afeni and Chuck were with him, but there was no word of Kate. Afeni had been watering the vegetable garden, and Chuck had been replacing a couple of broken rails in the hog pen fence. Neither of them had seen the girl since they had left the house after breakfast.

'I simply do not understand it,' Conor said crossly. 'If she's not here, and obviously she's not, why isn't the monitor sounding off?'

''Cause it's dead,' said Afeni, looking up from an inspection of the silent box. 'That little red warning light that starts to flash off and on when the batteries get low, and otherwise it's on all the time – that's out, see here? Thing ain't working.'

'It was all right this morning,' Conor said. 'I checked it when I first got up. I always do. It's a habit. And I put new batteries in on Saturday, right after I got back here. Jesus God. Here, Sam, you'd better take a crack at it, after all you built the fucker. See if you can get it to go. Claire, you call up Ollie at the sheriff's office, tell him you've got a message for his Aunt Dorry –'

'But I don't. And if I did, I'd call her direct.'

'You tried and her phone doesn't answer. And you found that recipe she was asking for, or something. Anyway *call* him, chat him up, see if you can pick up any gossip. Ollie loves to talk, and he doesn't have a thing to do all day but mind the switchboard and the radio, and type reports. If there's anything going on he'll be longing to tell somebody all about it.'

'Recipe, recipe,' Claire mumbled, unlocking the cupboard. 'Peach marmalade, she did want that one. Oh shoot, but I gave it to her before. Getting old, that's my trouble. Brains are withering away. Can't remember my own name hardly. Just clean forgot I told her already. Hello? Hello, Ollie? This is Claire. Listen, dear . . .'

'So I asked him – well, you heard me – how things were going,' Claire said after she put down the phone. 'And he said quiet as the grave, and he was so bored he was thinking of sending away for a set of those language records, so he could improve himself and get a better job. Asked me did I think Arab would be a good one to pick, what with them taking over the world and everything. Ollie's bored, and he don't know beans. And if it was anyone around here that picked Kate up he'd have heard. Even if those FBI fellers got her, they'd surely let Hailey's office know about it, wouldn't they?'

'Those two lunatics? Who knows what they'd do, but yes, you'd think they'd at least pass the word to the sheriff. Although with that pair nothing would surprise me.' Conor scrubbed his cheeks with his fists. 'Sam, we don't have anyone in the Haynesville field office, do we? No, I asked you that before.'

'All I got is the name of a guy in the radio station there. He's a newsman, he might have a contact. Never tried him before, but he's on that list old Tom gave me, he ought to be okay. Want me to check?'

'A reporter, is he? No, better not. His professional instincts might run away with him. Look, this is ridiculous. Kate's just gone rambling off somewhere, in that idiot-child-of-privilege way she's got, and we're working ourselves into a lather about nothing. But all the same she'd better be found. I'll take the Jeep. Sam, you stay here with the radio, and –'

'Let me have the pick-up, Conor,' Sam said. 'Then when young Dan gets back, Chuck can take the pony. You know I can't ride worth a damn, and she may be in the woods where the pick-up won't go. Afeni can go on radio watch – she knows that contraption as well as I do. I'm getting no place with this baby,' and he tapped the monitor. 'Whatever's wrong, it don't hit you in the eye right off. Could find it in the next two minutes, or could take all day, depending on luck – and I don't feel lucky. C'mon, let's go find her. Either one of us sees Dan, we'll send him on home with the pony. And Afeni, you stick to that radio like a burr. Something comes up and we have to raise you in a hurry, you *be* there!'

Once the two men had gone, the kitchen filled up with a sluggish silence, barely ruffled when Afeni, leaving to stand by at the radio, murmured that she might as well take the monitor with her and work on it upstairs. Chuck didn't even hear her. He sat at the table holding his elbows, a hunched-over, pre-Columbian statue.

'And what ails thee?' Claire demanded tartly.

'I don't know. Something is very wrong. I don't know what.'

'Well of course something's wrong: we can't find Katie.'

'Yes, I know, but something more, only I can't get a hard grip on it. Like a dream you almost remember, but it keeps sliding away.'

'Dreams! I declare there are times thee's as aggravating as thy mother.' She turned, out of tidy habit, to relock the telephone cupboard and gave a sudden exclamation.

'What is it?'

'That old pistol of Sam's – the one Conor was using the day I got so mad at him. When they frightened that poor child for those foolish pictures.'

'What about it?'

'It's not here.'

'Maybe they forgot to put it back afterwards.'

'It was right there yesterday morning early, lying on the shelf under the rifle rack.'

'So it was,' Chuck said. 'I remember. I noticed it when I was speaking to Mrs Rouderbridge at the school, and I was going to get rid of it, only something came up and I forgot. Even locked up, I don't like handguns around the house, especially with the children home. It was there yesterday, and now it's gone.'

They were staring at each other in mounting dismay when Chuck cocked his head and stood up.

'That's Daniel,' he said. 'I can hear the pony. Claire, get the shotgun down and some shells – and tell Dan to let down the stirrups for me.'

He ran upstairs to the radio room.

'Afeni, can you get through to the Jeep with this thing?'

'Sure.'

'Then do it, I have to speak to Conor . . .'

'Conor? Where are you?'

'About – oh, five miles out or so on the Harmony road. I met Dan and sent him back. Is he there yet?'

'Just got here. Listen, come back to the fork right away. I'll meet you there on the pony as soon as I can.'

228

'What's the trouble?'

'I'll tell you when I see you. Now move it!'

He was already out of the room when Afeni called after him.

'Chuck? Chuck, I found out what's wrong with the monitor.'

'Can you fix it?'

'No, it's –'

'Then don't bother me.' He started down the stairs.

'*Listen* to me, fool! There is a part missing – that's why it don't work. I can't fix it because I don't have a spare. But don't you see? That capacitor didn't get up by itself and run off and join the army. Somebody took it. Somebody don't want Kate found. Somebody in this house.'

He stared up at her from halfway down the flight.

'Who would know enough to do that, to disable it just that way?'

'I'd know, and Sam would. And, Chuck? It wasn't me.'

'Oh, Christ.'

He clattered down to the kitchen, boots skidding on the polished treads, and paused to drop a handful of shells into his pocket and take the shotgun from Claire's reluctant hands. She caught his arm as he headed for the door.

'Carlos! Dear heart, thee wouldn't – oh, thee wouldn't –'

'No.'

'Then why is thee taking the gun?'

'For Conor.'

Daniel was out in the yard, standing patiently at the pony's head. He gaped when he saw the shotgun, but handed up the reins without a word as his father settled himself in the saddle.

'Take care of the women,' his father said, as he dug his heels into the rough barrel belly. Dan looked to see if it was a joke, but it didn't seem to be. And if it wasn't a joke, if it was for real . . . Oh, brother.

Kate was bewildered, furious, and very badly frightened. She would have been even more frightened, except that she was in such extreme physical discomfort, it tended to block out everything else. The jouncing ride on the bed of the truck had left her shaken and bruised, and the sack was stifling. When the pick-up finally lurched to a stop she had waited impatiently for Sam to free her from the smelly, scratchy wrapping. Instead, she was heaved up without warning, sack and all, over a broad shoulder, carried a short distance, and dumped face down, with painful carelessness, onto what felt like an unyielding hammock. She was scared, disoriented, unable to see. It was like a distorted replay of the day she was kidnapped, and she reacted as she had then, with stillness and silence. Maybe something had gone wrong, maybe they had somehow been intercepted, and Sam was trying to pass her off as a sack of meal.

Be silent, be still, play dead – at least that way she could hardly make things worse. She waited, shrinking, for someone to untie the top of the sack, which was drawn tight above her head. Instead, hands began fumbling at the other end, where her feet were. There was a ripping, sawing noise, and all at once her legs were free, but only for a moment. Then, to her astonished fury, an enormously heavy, living weight sank down onto her thighs, pinning her helpless. Outraged, she found her voice.

'Sam!' she yelled, struggling with all her strength. 'Sam, damn you, get *off*!'

But he didn't get off, he didn't speak, and now rough hands were dragging at her ankles. First one was grabbed, circled with something far too tight – rope? tape? a strap? – and secured as brutally as if she were a dead animal. Then the second ankle was treated the same way. This couldn't be Sam, that much was clear, unless he'd flipped. Some drugs, she'd read once, could produce psychotic episodes long after people had stopped taking them. Suppose that was what had happened to Sam. Suppose this whole thing – the accusations against Afeni, the flight into hiding – was the result of some unforeseen chemical flashback. If it was, he might do anything. He had killed a man before.

230

The crippling weight heaved and shifted, reversing itself. The ripping noise came again, and then her arms were out of the sack, but not free, not for a second. The wrists ground together in a bone-cracking hold as more of the too-tight stuff was whipped around them. A moment or so of hurried manipulation, more shifting of weight, and her bound hands were jerked together into the small of her back and strapped there, secured to some additional restraint that held her whole body down. It was then she began to scream, and to this there was, finally, a reaction: a numbing, neck-wrenching blow to the side of her head. The heavy folds of sacking cushioned the impact enough so that she was not quite knocked unconscious but only knocked silly, shocked and sick, wavering in and out of consciousness like a patient coming out of anaesthesia.

At some point later on, her head cleared altogether for a while and she was able to think coherently, if not very usefully. It was hard to breathe with the dusty, sour-smelling burlap still muffling her head and shoulders, and the battle for air, or perhaps the crack on the head, was causing a dull and distant roaring in her ears, but she could hear nothing else except for a bird singing somewhere nearby. Although her body was no longer cramped under that vicious weight, she was in a great deal of pain. Her head pounded, her neck was very sore, her arms and shoulders ached and throbbed in revolt against the unnatural position in which she was held. She still had some feeling in her hands – enough for them to burn as if a thousand electric needles had been driven into them – but her feet had gone quite numb. Both ankles hurt, though, so fiercely that in her more confused moments she half believed they were gripped in the jaws of some wild animal.

From time to time her diaphragm heaved in a brief, retching reflex, and bile flooded her mouth, but she fought to keep from actually throwing up. She had read of people who choked to death on their own vomit when they were unable to move, and it seemed a particularly disgusting way to die. She would not – *would not* – let that happen to her. Apparently whoever had treated her like this didn't especially care if she lived or died, but Kate cared. The curious, limp fatalism that had periodically weakened her over the last ten days seemed at last to have been burned out of her nature. That petrified creature in the cave, dully awaiting the release of death, had been some other person altogether, and one she had no time for. *This Business Under New Management*, she thought a little hysterically and forced down the silly giggle because if she laughed she might cry, and if she cried she might suffocate. She wouldn't give them the satisfaction.

Only who were they? Was it a demented Sam she had to deal with, and if so would he snap out of it in time, before she was seriously hurt? Or had Sam been silently immobilized, even killed, leaving her in the hands of the unknown enemy? And where was she, anyhow? Inside a building of some sort – she was reasonably certain of that, because the air was so still. There was less light, too, even allowing for the sack, than there would have been outdoors. Unless it was already night; but then surely it would have been cooler, and the bird wouldn't be singing.

Kate hoped she was now alone, but it was extraordinarily unpleasant not to be quite sure. The fear that her mysterious attacker might still be within a few feet of her, silent, motionless, watching – that was in some ways the least tolerable aspect of the fix she was in. It was almost worse than not knowing who had tied her up like this or why. In books, Kate reflected, people managed to wriggle free by Houdiniesque contortions or they did resourceful things with sharp-edged stones or cigarette lighters. Or else they were rescued. Well, there was no question of escaping out of this coil unaided; she was trussed as tight as a Thanksgiving turkey, and with about as much consideration for her comfort. What she was tied to seemed to be a primitive kind of bed, the rustic, homemade variety, with a web of knotted ropes in place of bedsprings. The knots dug into her at intervals, and the whole thing sagged under her weight so that her spine was forced into an unnatural arc, with her feet, lashed to the end of the wooden frame, higher than her shoulders. She could move her upper body a little, and it was just possible, with enormous effort, to turn her head, so that for a while it was her left cheek that was punished by the rough sacking and the criss-crossing ropes, instead of her right. Like shifting a heavy suitcase from one hand to the other, the relief was purely temporary, and lasted for a shorter time with each alternation.

The cuff containing the useless transmitter bit into her wrist as she squirmed, testing the intractable bonds. If only Sam hadn't disabled the monitor, the others would have been able to find her. Probably that was why he'd done it, intending from the start to separate her from any hope of help. Then again, he could have been telling the truth, protecting her from Afeni's deadly masters, who had caught her now in spite of his precautions. If Sam was on the level, he was presumably a captive too – or dead.

If he'd somehow got clear, surely he would have come to her aid by now. Or maybe the enemy was really still there, maybe her crawling fear was well founded and he sat beside her now, while Sam waited nearby for a chance to set her free. She had better not struggle any more. If the man saw her move he might hit her again – harder, this time. Presently the bird outside, defying the sleepy noonday heat, let loose another string of liquid trills. Kate did not hear them. Between pain and fear and insufficient air, she had fainted again.

The most frightening thing for Dan was the sight of his mother sitting in her rocker, totally idle, in the middle of the day. Not just taking a break with a mug of coffee between chores, but sitting there as if she might never get up, never move again at all except to rock slowly, distractedly forward and back. It was long past dinnertime, but she had done nothing about preparing a meal, which in itself was shocking. Dan was beginning to be very hungry, but he did not like to ask for anything. In the end she made him so nervous, rocking away, not speaking to him (although her lips moved sometimes, forming words that never went beyond their own sketched shapes), that he went quietly to the pantry, helped himself to bread and cheese, poured milk from the jug in the refrigerator, and retreated upstairs to his attic bedroom. There, however, he found Beccah already in possession, with all her dolls, and an extravagant supply of pound cake and strawberry jam which she never would have got away with if their mother had been even halfway on the ball.

Beccah was all right, he supposed, at least for a girl, but she was disposed to be sociable – wanted to play that game Conor had taught them, the Clergyman's Cat – and he wasn't in the mood. He finished his bread and cheese, swiped a good-sized slab of cake, and slouched gloomily in to join Afeni in the radio room next door. He sat on the floor in a corner, munching silently, and since she didn't seem to mind having him there he got his nerve up after a while and asked her what all the upset was about.

'Katie's gone off some place and we can't find her,' Afeni said unhelpfully.

'Well, sheesh, I know *that*. Conor told me when I met him on the road. But how come everybody's having conniptions over it? Ma's acting so peculiar I never have seen nothing like it, and dad taking off that way with the shotgun and telling me to look after you girls, like there was a war party fixing to burn us out. And all 'cause that fool girl's gotten herself lost in the woods or some such. Don't make no sense.'

'Honey, there is more to it than you kids know about.'

'Oh, come *on* – you wanna bet? I know Katie's run away from home, and I know the cops and the FBI were looking for her when they came by here day before yesterday, and I know Alice Mary was pretending to be her when all the time Katie was hid out in the barn. But the way I figure, you all got something more on your minds than fussing over some runaway. If dad's in bad trouble, you ought to tell me. I ain't an old blabbermouth like Beccah – you can trust me.'

'Think you're real smart, don't you,' Afeni said absently, adjusting her earpiece. 'You know this and you know that. If you know so damn much maybe you can tell me where Katie's at, so I can radio Conor to go bring her in.'

'What about Sam? Ain't he out looking too? I saw him two-three hours back, heading in from old Sonnenfeld's cabin. He should've gotten home long ago.'

'You saw him where?'

'I just told you. On the track leading down from Mr Sonnenfeld's. Least, he went up there first, and then after a while I saw him come back down.'

'Daniel.' Afeni was looking at him in a very hard, scary way. 'Now you think back, and you think good. When you saw him going up there, was anybody with him?'

'No. No, he was on his own. Had one of them old propane tanks in the back of the pick-up and a sack of something, that's all. Wasn't nobody else along.'

'A sack in the truck? A full sack?'

'Yes'm, it looked like it was full.'

'Now when you saw him the second time, when he was coming away from the cabin, was the sack still there? Did you see it? Think, Dan. Don't say if you ain't certain.'

'No, ma'am,' Dan said, after a moment. He could see the pick-up in his head, see it jouncing by below him, framed in a pale green fretwork of new growth. 'No, that sack was gone. Tank was still in back, but that's all.'

'You're a good boy, Daniel, a good sharp boy. Now get out of here. I got work to do.'

Afeni didn't praise people often, so when she did you could figure you'd earned it. But if he was so terrific, how come Afeni was crying? As he went back to his own room he could hear her, in a high, wobbly voice, calling Conor in the Jeep.

'Aurora to Retriever. Mayday, Mayday. Aurora to Retriever. Mayday.'

Kate was more or less conscious again and wishing she weren't. It was quite astonishing how much pain could be caused just by tying a person up tight. And now, on top of everything else, she wanted – wanted hell, desperately needed – to go to the bathroom. Her bladder ached, and her sphincter muscles quivered with the strain. That would be the final humiliation: to wet herself like a baby. She squeezed her thighs together and heard herself moan in misery.

Then all at once she heard something else, not sure at first if it was only the pulsing of her blood, and then sure. It was something outside the sounds of her own body. It was an engine, and it was getting louder. Tyres on a rough track, spitting and crunching; then a long, sour squeal, and the engine died. A metal door slammed, shockingly loud, and then came footsteps, a heavy booted tread coming closer, coming right up to the bed.

Was it the man returning to hurt her again, or could this be help? She was going to make no movement, no sound, do nothing at all, until she knew which. The footsteps stopped. The sacking was dragged away from her head and shoulders and, blessedly, she could breathe and see. Stiffly she turned her head once more, seeing first the scuffed, familiar boots, then the work pants, then – straining her neck as far as it would go – the blue check shirt, the red hair, and the white, freckled face. And he didn't look crazy, not a bit. He was as calm as an archdeacon. It was all right.

'Sam,' she croaked joyfully. 'Oh thank God!'

'No,' he said, and then she saw the gun in his gloved right hand. 'I have to,' he said, sounding dull and tired, like a decent, worried man explaining to a child that the old dog has to be shot. 'I got nothing against you. If it wa'n't for them I'd as soon turn you loose. But I have to do it. I was just going to do it right off, through the sack, but then it didn't seem right – not giving you time to say your prayers or nothing. I have to do it, though. And if I don't, they'll find somebody else who will. Wouldn't save you, and it'd be the finish of me.'

'But why, Sam, why?' If she could start him talking, even if it only bought her a few extra breaths . . . Talkling, people in trouble usually wanted to talk, and he was in trouble, that was plain. So was she . . . into Thy hands oh Lord – but she wasn't going to give up, not this time. '*Why?*' she asked again.

'They want you dead. And if I don't do it for 'em, they'll lock me up in that place again and give me that stuff in the needle that makes it like you're in hell. Stinking and burning and devils eating on you.' Grotesquely reasonable, he allowed her the briefest glimpse of his landscape of madness. 'Only this time they'll go on; they won't ever stop. They'll go on till I die. I'll be in hellfire then for sure, where their worm dieth not and the fire is not quenched, just the way my granny told me, God rot her soul.'

'We won't let them touch you,' Kate said determinedly. It wasn't exactly easy to sound confident and reassuring when you were tied to a bed, your bladder was bursting, and someone was about to kill you, but she made a brave try. 'Conor and Chuck, they'll see to it you're safe, they'll get you away to Canada and you can start over.'

'Conor and Chuck don't know shit from a shovel.' A trace of contempt had crept into the flat voice. 'I been using them all along, same way the colonel been using me. This whole kidnap thing, it was the colonel's idea from the start, and I sold it to 'em so good they ended up believing they thought of it themselves.'

'That was smart of you, Sam. You really had them fooled. You're a whole lot smarter than they are. And I bet they never suspected you, not once. Did the colonel ever tell you why he wanted me to be kidnapped?'

'Sure he did. What's the matter – you think he don't talk to me or something? He got a lot of respect for me, the colonel has. See, him and his friends, they just don't like your daddy worth a damn. They figure he's too buddy-buddy with the Russians and the Chinks. Specially the Chinks. Colonel was in Korea and he purely hates Chinks. When your daddy went to China that just about blew it. They figured he got to go, and now he's gone.'

'That's right, he's *gone*. Don't you see? They've got what they wanted. You don't have to kill me; there's no sense in it now. You can let me go. I won't tell the others, I promise. You just untie me, and we'll go back to the farm, and we won't say a word to anyone.'

It was not going to work. His face was turned away from her now, and she could no longer see his expression, but it wasn't going to work. She hadn't got through to him at all. He was bored with talking, running out of patience – she could feel it. Only some pathetic, vestigial remnant of courtesy had prodded him into answering her questions at all. In two minutes, one minute,

236

less . . . The hand with the gun twitched slightly, lifting. Think of something else to ask, quickly.

'What good will it do you to kill me, Sam? When I don't go home, my father will go to the police, and it'll all come out. And you'll be arrested too, along with the others. You'll be tried for murder.'

'Not me. I'll be long gone. They promised me. Going to California or any place else I want. New name, new ID, and a whole lot of money. Two hundred thousand dollars, they going to give me – two *hundred thousand*. And never have to go back to that place again. Conor's the one headed for Death Row, not me. This gun got his fingerprints all over it. Anyhow, colonel wants it done this way. This way, your daddy can't ever make no comeback. Putting his own family concerns ahead of his country, making deals with terrorists, telling all them lies . . . Colonel says won't nobody ever trust him again. Going to make ever'thing he ever did look bad, too. No more getting in bed with the Commies, that's what the colonel said. Time they're through, won't nobody dare take his shirts to a Chinese laundry, even.'

'Well okay, that's what the colonel wants. You don't owe him a thing, though, do you? All he's ever done for you is drive you crazy –'

'Not crazy. I ain't crazy!'

Wrong. Tilt.

'Well of course you're not, I know that, and it's a miracle you aren't after everything they did to you. But why do you have to care what some old colonel wants? What do you want for yourself, Sam?'

'Out. I want *out*. Want to be a rich man in California, and sit in the sun and look at the women, and never see the colonel or the doctors or any of 'em long as I live. Don't ever want to see a face I ever seen before. Peace and quiet, that's what I want, and being let alone. I ain't never been let alone. My whole life somebody been on my back – move your ass, do this and do that and do it right, and get beat up if you do it wrong. Now I am going to be peaceful.'

He turned back to face her squarely and lifted the gun.

'It won't hurt,' he said with dreadful solicitude. 'Be over so quick, you won't even feel it. Just one hell of a loud noise, and then nothing. Be all over.'

Kate squeezed her eyes tight shut. Her last thought was a shaft of pure rage: this sorry maniac is going to murder me and get clear away with it, get paid for it, and Conor will get the blame. Oh, Conor, oh, Jesus –

There was a noise so loud, so appalling, it was like being inside a clap of thunder. But there was no pain; Sam had told the truth about that. Even her bladder didn't ache any more. But if I'm dead, she wondered suddenly, how come my hands and my ankles still hurt? And the side of my face feels all wet and the back of my shirt. And my jeans.

'Kate! Oh my poor love! It's all right. You're all right now. Keep still, my treasure, I don't want to cut you.'

Conor was slicing through the tape with his knife, freeing her hands first, then shearing through the rope that held her body down. His face was frightening, it looked so different – so old.

'Chuck, throw something over it for God's sake. There's a sack on the floor here, that'll do. I don't want – okay, that's better. Thanks.'

He had been kneeling at her head, blocking her view with his body. Now he moved down to cut her ankles loose.

'This is awfully tight. I'm afraid your feet are going to hurt like hell when the blood gets moving again. The bastard, the miserable, fat-headed, murdering bastard. Here, let's give them a rub for you. Easy now. I know it hurts, poor baby.'

'Conor,' Kate said in a whimper, 'I'm sorry, I'm so sorry – Conor, I wet my pants.' She burst into tears, and he put his arms around her.

'Darling heart, it doesn't matter. Please don't cry. What *does* it matter? We'll get them off, shall we? Just let me wipe your face first.'

'What is that? What's on me? There's stuff all over me, all over my back too. What is it?'

'It's all right – don't worry about it. Get me some water, could you, Chuck? From the well out back? And a cloth or something. We've got to get her cleaned up. Can you sit up, if I help you? That's a girl. Easy does it. That's the way.'

On the floor close to the bed was a long, sprawled shape. From the waist down it was Sam; the rest was covered with the sack. There were dark splotches at the upper end, soaking through the burlap, and on the wall were bright, glossy red stains – one enormous one and a mass of splatters, with here and there clots and flecks of something yellowish-grey and soft. One of the clots slid gently down the planks as she looked, and plopped onto the floor. Chuck came in then with a pail of water and a rag, and

Conor stripped her shirt off, threw it on top of the sack, and began to clean her shoulders and back.

'Oh, shit, it's in her hair as well.' He was talking past her, as people are apt to do in front of someone gravely ill. Then he caught sight of her face and managed a not very convincing smile. 'Never mind, lovey,' he said. 'You're a bit of a mess, but you're alive. That's in your favour.'

He dipped the cloth in water and very gently and carefully went over her face again, murmuring as soothingly as an old nurse. Chuck, who had tactfully turned his back and was poking into the one musty closet, came over with an army blanket.

'Here,' he said, 'put this around her – she can't wear those clothes again. I'll get fresh water to wash off her head.'

He picked up the pail of tainted, pinkish water and went out again, while Conor pulled off her jeans and panties and wrapped her in the blanket. Grabbing handfuls of the harsh wool, he briskly rubbed her shivering body.

'I f-f-feel like a wet d-dog being t-t-towelled off,' she gasped, through chattering teeth.

'D'you think you can stand, or are your feet too numb still? Hang onto me and we'll give it a try.'

'My hands – I can't –'

'Of course you can't – I wasn't thinking. Come on, I'll carry you. I just want you away from this shambles.'

Outside the cabin the sun blazed through the leaves in a shifting dazzle of light. Conor put her down on the ground.

'Right. Let's have that bucket over here, could we? Now I'm going to put my arm under your shoulders, and you tip your head back as far as it'll go. *Right* back, that's it. Good girl.'

'Ow!' The water was icy.

'Cold is it? Never mind, it won't take a minute. Every penny makes the water warmer.' He was ladling water over her forehead with one cupped hand, and the back of her head was in the pail, lapped by the chill wetness.

'All done. Sit up now. There you go.' He peeled off his shirt and used it to rub her head. Drops showered from the rat's-tail ends of her sopping hair, making rainbows as they flew.

'Conor?'

'Yo.'

'Sam's dead, isn't he?'

'Good Lord, yes.'

'That's his blood you've been washing off me.'

'I'm afraid so.'

'Which one of you . . .'

'I did. I blew the poor bugger's head in half with a shotgun. He was going to kill you.'

'Yes, I know. Does that make it all right? Killing him?'

'Nothing ever makes it all right. I just couldn't think of anything else to do. If I'd jumped him you'd have been badly hurt, probably killed. I *could* have rushed in and flung myself on top of you, which would have been spectacular but not very useful. He'd just have shot me first and finished you off afterwards.' He rubbed his knuckles across his mouth. 'God, I feel a fool,' he said. 'I've known that man the best part of three years, lived in the same house with him for the last five months, and I never saw it. Not a bloody inkling, not a glimmer. Kate, I hate to fuss you, but did anything emerge at all about what the hell he thought he was up to? I mean, was he just off his trolley?'

'Oh, no. At least, he was a little weird, but he knew what he was doing, all right. But he said they made him do it, they were going to take him back if he didn't. He – he said he just wanted to be – to be let alone.'

Kate began to cry again, clutching the blanket around her, crouched over in a damp, distressed huddle. Conor stroked her wet head.

'My poor girl, what a thing, what a godawful time of it you've had. You tell us all about it on the way home, okay? Come along. Upsydaisy. Chuck, I'll drop you off where we left the Jeep, and you can bring the pony home. We'll have to make a separate trip and pick the Jeep up later. God, logistics . . . In you get, lovey, that's the way. Budge over a bit and make room for Chuck, and we'll have you home in no time. Nice hot bath and a spot of Housekeeper's Ruin, you'll be as good as new.'

'You can't just leave him there, like that,' she protested as he got in beside her.

'Not going to. I want to get you organized, and then we'll come back and – tidy things up. But darling, it's not Sam. What's there, I mean. It's got no more to do with him now than his coat or his boots. Sam's gone.'

'He was going to be a – a rich man. In California. And sit in the sun and look – and look at –' A fresh welling of tears brimmed over and slipped down her cheeks.

If she had walked in a couple of yards ahead of Conor she might have been able to warn him in time, but he was right on her heels. In any case, her reactions had been disastrously blunted by the events of the last few hours. When she stumbled into the kitchen, holding the blanket around her, and saw Afeni, Claire, and the two children stiffly lined up in a row on the chesterfield, the sight was surprising – it was odd – but it did not set her inner alarm bell jangling as it should have. Then she caught the reek of cigar smoke. But by the time she had turned her head and found Sheriff Hailey Gibbs sitting in a straight pine chair, with a blue-black revolver negligently tilted against his knee, it was already too late. Conor was in the room and the gun was coming up, held casually in the sheriff's relaxed grip, but aimed right at him all the same. He was so close behind her that she heard the tiny sound of the breath catching in his throat, but when he spoke his voice was steady and only mildly reproving.

'Now really, Sheriff. "Never never let your gun pointed be at anyone." Be with you in a minute.'

He led Kate over to the rocker, settled her into it, and went to the dresser for the whisky bottle. Only after he made her a drink and lit a cigarette for her did he turn back to the sheriff. Gibbs spoke first.

'That ain't Alice Mary,' he pointed out.

'How right you are. That is not Alice Mary.'

'Sure does look like her, though. Piece of luck for you, the way things turned out. If it was luck.'

'Simple opportunism. We certainly didn't plan it in advance. If you care to go along with a stately old gullible named Jung, you could call it synchronicity – the inexorable whatsit of events. Or as Jack the Ripper more succinctly put it: it seemed like a good idea at the time.' He was talking entirely at random, giving himself a few seconds' breathing space to assimilate the shock of the sheriff's presence. 'And don't blame Alice Mary,' he added. 'She hadn't a clue what that tatty little masquerade was really about. She just thought it was a lark.'

'They related?'

241

'Distantly. Very dominant genes in that family, apparently.'

'Don't suppose you feel like puttin' a name to this young lady for me?'

'That rather depends.'

'On what?'

'On your immediate plans. Have you got Will Paton lurking in the parlour with a platoon of state cops, or is this a solo?'

'I come out on my own.'

'Wasn't that a bit rash?'

'You got to remember I know these people,' Gibbs said. 'Claire, now, her sister Martha was married to my cousin Gil; I've known Claire since she was no bigger than Rebeccah. I ain't forgot you, either. When you was a kid in your teens and your daddy sent you down here summers, back when old Eli was alive. You and Will Paton forkin' hay, brown as a pair of Indians and near as naked.' He looked over at Claire and ducked his head apologetically. 'Excuse me. Didn't mean to offend nobody. Now I don't say you all couldn't jump me, if you'd a mind to,' he went on, 'and cut my throat and bury me under the hog pen. I don't say it couldn't be done. But it sure would surprise the hell out of me if you tried.'

He looked down at the Smith & Wesson .38 in his lap with a faintly embarrassed air, as though wondering how in the world it had got there. He eased it back into the holster, grunting as he shifted in his chair.

'Tell you what I wouldn't mind one bit,' he went on. 'I wouldn't mind you pourin' me some of that fine sippin' whisky I see on that table there, and then I wouldn't mind havin' a rundown on what's been goin' on in this house, and how come I got the FBI buzzin' around my poor old head like wasps at a church picnic. I'm a lazy man,' he continued plaintively. 'Some fellers'd give their eye teeth for a big case like this – get their picture in the papers, maybe go on TV, even. But it's just more work to me, and I hate workin'. I am paid by the county to uphold the law around here, and when folks go breakin' it I got to take steps, but as to *what* steps – why, that's between me and my conscience. So you give me my whisky, young Conor, or whatever you're callin' yourself these days, and then you tell me about these terrible bad things you all been doin', and we'll see if we can't work something out.'

Conor brought the sheriff his drink. 'What if I don't tell you?' he asked. Gibbs beamed at him.

'Why, that don't hardly arise, son.' He took a sip of whisky, savouring it, and smiled more widely than ever. 'Now that is good liquor. Goes down just as pretty as a day in spring. No, that don't arise. 'Cause if you don't talk to me, you are goin' to wind up talkin' to a bunch of real mean fellers that work for the You Ess government, and if you are in so much as one-tenth part of the trouble I think you're in, you are all going to jail.'

Claire had been sitting staring at them as if they had both gone mad. Now she burst into speech. 'Conor! Before thee says one more word, *where's my husband*?'

Conor looked stricken. 'He's perfectly all right, I promise you. God, I'm sorry. I should have told you right away. He'll be along later; he's riding the pony back.'

She closed her eyes in thankfulness and, stretching her arms around the bewildered children, hugged them tight. Conor turned his attention back to the sheriff.

'All right, it's a deal,' he said. 'But you don't need all this mob here, do you? Let the children leave – they've heard too much for their own good already. And Kate –'

'Who?'

'The one that's not Alice Mary. She's been through a very bad time indeed. I'd be grateful if you'd let Afeni take her upstairs and look after her.'

'Well, I don't know. Seems like I ought to have a talk with the young lady.'

'Yes, of course – but later? Couldn't you do it later?'

'You guarantee she'll still be here? Later?'

'Yes. I'm not trying to pull a fast one, Sheriff. We're in your hands, and we know it. But she's had about all she can take.'

'Is that right? Okay. You girls can go. Just don't leave the house.'

Conor helped Kate up out of the rocker. 'Have a bath and pop into bed,' he told her. 'I'll bring the sheriff up afterwards, if he still wants to talk to you.'

Hailey Gibbs watched as Kate, draped insecurely in her army blanket, toiled up the stairs with Afeni's supporting arm around her. When they had gone he looked at Conor under his eyelashes.

'She have anything on under that blanket?'

'Not a stitch.'

The sheriff shook his head in disapproval. 'My mother,' he said, 'she used to wear *corsets*. Big old pink things from Sears and Roebuck. Whalebones and laces and hook and eyes and I don't know what-all. Keep out a twelve-inch shell, those things could

243

have. Kids nowadays, all they got is a little bitty wisp of something, and you could see right through it anyhow. When they ain't runnin' around bare naked under a blanket. Probably end up with pneumonia. You remember corset covers, Claire? And camisoles? Come to think of it, I bet you're still wearin' em.'

'After all the time you and those nice boys from the state police spent picking over my underwear drawer,' Claire said acidly, 'you certainly ought to know. You're getting to be a dirty old man, Hailey.'

'Very likely. Little more of that fine whisky wouldn't be refused, Conor. Now let me see. Miss Tulliver and your friend with the blanket, they're upstairs. They better be. Claire's right here, soundin' off as usual. Chuck's ridin' in, I believe you said. You sure about that?'

'Positive.'

'Leaves Sam Aitken. Where's he at?'

'Sam's dead.'

Claire's hand flew to her mouth, and she cried out in protest.

'I had to, Claire. He was going to shoot Katie. Chuck was there – he'll tell you.' Conor put his head in his hands. 'It's all gone wrong,' he mourned. 'Everything's gone wrong. We never meant to hurt anybody, that was the whole *point*. But there was all this stuff going on that we didn't know about.'

'Well, imagine that,' said Gibbs. 'Now maybe you can sympathize with me, 'cause just about ever'thing that's gone on is something I don't know about, and I am good and godalmighty tired of it. You just killed Sam Aitken, is that right? Maybe you better start there.'

'It won't make sense unless I start at the beginning. Probably it doesn't make sense no matter how you tell it,' he added, looking suddenly exhausted, and sat down at the kitchen table.

'It's your story – tell it whatever way you want,' the sheriff said with commendable patience. 'You look like you could use a drink; maybe that'll help get you started.'

Haltingly at first, with much use of 'I forgot to mention' and 'Of course we had no idea at the time', but gaining in fluency with judicious doses of sour mash, Conor laid out the whole wretched tale, fitting the pieces together in the light of the appalling new information Kate had acquired from Sam. Meanwhile, Claire, relieved of her most immediate anxieties over Chuck and Kate, and filled with distress for Sam, took out her feelings as she always had – by working. It had occurred to her, with a rush of guilt like a wave of scalding steam, that no one in the house had been fed since breakfast. Furiously she sifted, measured, stirred, kneaded, and banged baking sheets around, interrupting occasionally to amend Conor's narrative each time he tried to take all the blame on himself. When he reached the part about Kate in the cabin, Claire stopped working and leaned against the wall, her eyes lowered, her broad shoulders bowed.

'We could hear voices,' Conor said, 'so we took our shoes off and crawled up under the window. It was pretty well blocked with morning glory, so there was a good chance he wouldn't spot us if we looked over the sill. Kate was tied down to the bed frame, and he had the gun in his hand. We could have gone round to the door, I suppose, and jumped him – the window wasn't big enough. Or we could have tried to talk to him, but it was such a hell of a risk. I think he'd have killed her before we got anywhere near him. While I was still trying to decide what to do, he lifted the gun and pointed it at the back of her head, and I stopped thinking and shot him. Both barrels. Kate got blood all over her, that's why we had to take her clothes off. And then we come back here and find you in charge, grinning like a bloody Cheshire cat,' he finished bitterly. 'Christ, what a fuck-up. Sorry, Claire.'

The sheriff got up from his chair, groaning gently, and padded on small, springy feet to the kitchen table. 'Claire, them rolls goin' to burn if you don't pull 'em out the oven,' he said, 'and hungry as I am, I never did like a burned roll. You got any ham? I had my hopes up last week, when them FBI fellers was here, but they was in such a powerful hurry to go on and bother the next bunch of folks that I never did get the chance. My daughter Elizabeth, Cissy's mother, she sees to it I got food in the icebox,' he told Conor, 'but she could no more cure a ham than grow feathers. Buys that flabby garbage from the supermarket they call Virginia ham. Pink as a peony and got a kind of shimmer to it, like fish been dead a long time.'

He helped himself to a modest tot of whisky and sat down across the table from Conor.

'Hailey,' Claire said, flicking rolls off the tin with a spatula and folding them in a linen napkin, 'I've been thinking who I'd ask to take the children. Does thee suppose Will and Dorry Paton might do it? Will's not the closest kin we have, but he and Ollie live the nearest, and Ollie's no use, being a bachelor. I can't ask Gil, with Martha gone. Children that age, they still need a woman to take care of them. If Will took 'em, Dan and Beccah could stay in the school, where their friends are. Dorry's a good mother, even if that Billy of hers does have a mouth like a midden. We *could* send them back out to Martha Two Ponies, but she's an old woman, and who knows how long it might be for? Years, maybe, and if anything happened to Martha . . . I guess I'll ask Will and Dorry first.'

'What in the name of good sense you talkin' about, girl?'

'While we're in jail – Chuck and me. The children will have to go some place; they can't stay here alone like Robinson Crusoe. Then there's the stock; I guess that'll have to be sold off. Oh my, there's so much to think of.'

'You got your heart set on goin' to jail?' the sheriff enquired. 'Or would you care to discuss it?'

'Discuss what? Kidnapping and now killing as well. Was I a lawyer I wouldn't even take the case, there's just nothing to argue about.'

'Only way you'll need a lawyer is if you're arrested, and I ain't arrested nobody yet. Now from what I can make out, if that poor bastard Sam was tellin' the truth, you people been workin' for the government. Makes no never-mind whether you knew it or not, that's what you been doin'. If you turn it around a little, that is, and look at it just right.' He tilted his head to one side and screwed up his bright little eyes by way of illustration. 'Course, there's some folks wouldn't see it that way, but I don't know what good it'd do, bringin' a bunch of strangers into this. Seems to me we'd do better to keep it in the family.'

He tipped his chair back (Claire stifled an automatic admonition) and stared down his nose at Conor.

'I ever tell you about my boy, Bobby Lee? He's my youngest – you wouldn't remember him I don't suppose. He was just a little feller, those summers you came down. My wife died when he was five, and I raised him myself, pretty near. The two girls helped out, best they could, but they was only younguns themselves, so I had the raisin' of him. He was goin' on nineteen when they shipped him out to Vietnam, and he was twenty and two weeks when he caught a couple of shell fragments high up in his spine. Year and a half ago, that was. He's in a veterans hospital up north. Special surgical unit, they got him in, but now they're talkin' about movin' him down here to Haynesville. I been to look at that Haynesville place, and I wouldn't leave a yeller dog in there. But the surgeon up north, last time I was up to visit with Bobby Lee, he took me on one side and he said they can't keep

246

him there much longer. Nothing more they can do for him, got to move him out. That's the rule, is what the man told me.'

The sheriff took out his handkerchief and blew his nose with a loud, angry, trumpeting sound.

'The government,' he said scornfully. 'They take your boy and get him all broke up, and they send him home a quadriplegic. Year and a half of cuttin' and sewin', and he's still a quadriplegic. So now they goin' to stick him in some goddamn stinkin' dog pound till he rots, and for what? Can you tell me what he was doin' over there in the first place? Government says he was keepin' the Chinese Communists from takin' over the You-nited States, but they pulled the rest of the boys out a while back and I ain't seen no Chinese Communists runnin' around Aurora County. All I know is, I got a boy can't feed himself or wipe his own nose, got to piss through a tube and shit in a diaper. Can't even read a book 'cause ain't nobody got the time to turn the pages for him. He lays there and watches the TV.' Gibbs blew his nose again, and drank the rest of his whisky. 'That's what the government done for Bobby Lee,' he said. 'Yes, sir. They fixed it so he gets to lay on his back all day and watch "Hollywood Squares", and reruns of "I love Lucy". So one way and another, I ain't that crazy about the government. Never was, even before, but I didn't think too much about it then. I think about it now, though. Early mornings, when I don't sleep too good, I think about it all the time.'

Claire set a platter of ham-stuffed hot rolls on the table between the two men. The sheriff's hand hovered over the dish, selected a roll, and popped it, whole, neatly into his mouth. He chewed with a nice blend of delicacy and appreciative greed.

'Still the best ham in the county,' he pronounced, after swallowing. 'Be a shame to waste a talent like that in the penitentiary. Now I take it you all don't intend to make a habit of this kind of thing?'

'My God no,' Conor said, and Claire shook her head, shuddering. Hailey Gibbs ate another roll.

'Well now,' he said, brushing off crumbs. 'You take me up to see that little girl, and if she tells me you ain't none of you mistreated her, barrin' poor Sam of course, then I believe I'll let her decide what ought to be done. Her bein' the injured party, as you might say. The federal government I ain't worried about. They ain't payin' my salary, and after what they done to Bobby Lee I don't figure I owe 'em no favours. Which one of you goin' to take me up?'

'I am,' said Conor, and led the way upstairs.

The two girls were in Kate's room. Kate, very pale, with a towel wrapped around her freshly washed hair, lay in the little bed, and Afeni sat beside her. They were holding hands, but Afeni stood up and moved away when the sheriff came in. He nodded amiably to both of them and approached the bed.

'You are Miss Catherine Harper, is that right?'

'Yes.'

'And your daddy is Dr Pendleton Harper, that was secretary of state up until yesterday?'

'Yes, sir.'

'And Conor, here, abducted you and brought you down here and kept you prisoner.'

'Yes he did, but it was to stop the killing in Vietnam. It wasn't for money or anything.'

'You must've been pretty scared.'

'I was at first, but then I got to know them.'

'They do anything bad to you while you been here? Tell me the truth now, girl.'

'No, never. They're just the kindest – Conor even went to see my mother and tell her I was safe, so she wouldn't be so worried.'

The sheriff glanced at Conor inquisitively. 'That so? You didn't tell me that.'

'I forgot.'

'I don't want to hurt your feelings, son, but I don't believe you were cut out for this kind of work. Terrorists are supposed to terrify people, not go runnin' around makin' up to pretty girls' mothers.'

He turned back to Kate. 'Way I look at it,' he said, 'it's up to you to say what you want done. You want these folks arrested and charged, I'll do that. You want me to take you down to the FBI office in Haynesville and tell 'em a story, so you get to go home but nobody here don't get in trouble, I'll do that. Or you want to stay here a while longer, and go back next week like they fixed it, then I'll do what I can to keep the feds from catchin' up with you. Just tell me what'd suit you best, and whatever that is, that's what we'll do.'

Kate had risen bolt upright in bed, bundled to the throat in flowered calico; her cheeks were flushed, and her eyes shone.

'You really mean that, Sheriff Gibbs? You're not going to arrest them or – or put them in jail or anything? I can stay?'

Gibbs patted her knee under the blanket. 'Guess I got my

248

answer,' he said, looking pleased. 'Now don't you worry about a thing; we'll take care of it. You lay back and get some rest.' He turned to Afeni. 'I'm right sorry about Sam.' She nodded silently, and the two men left the room.

Back in the kitchen, after reassuring Claire, Gibbs engulfed another roll and dropped two more into his pocket. 'Come on, boy,' he said to Conor. 'Get a pick and a shovel, and let's go. We got a dead man to bury.'

They met Chuck on the way, and paused long enough to bring him up to date. As the pick-up truck jolted away up the narrow track, the sheriff looked sideways at Conor, rubbing his fleshy chin.

'Conor?'

'Yo.'

'That's a real pretty little thing, that Miss Harper.'

'Yes, isn't she?'

'I'm gettin' as nosy as an old maid, and I hate myself for it, but I can't help it. You screwin' her?'

'Every chance I get,' said Conor, unoffended.

'She like it?'

'As far as I can tell, she likes it very much.'

'Mmmm. No wonder she ain't in no particular rush to get home,' the sheriff said and let the subject drop.

THURSDAY, 10 MAY 1973. 2.45 A.M.

Kate woke in the dark with no idea at all where she was. A square of window showed over to her left – a sky cloud-streaked, with wan edges of moonlight. The square was much smaller than her window at her mother's house, the wrong shape for her college dorm. No, she wasn't in New Lymington, she was at the farm but the window was on the wrong side for Conor's room. She must be back in Rebeccah's bedroom, and the narrowness of the bed confirmed it – the child's bed she had slept in until shameless Conor had brought her in to share her nights with him. Her body was sore all over. She shifted in the central hollow of the mattress, trying to get comfortable, and gasped as a sudden stab of agony went through her ankles. Fully awake at last, she remembered everything and wondered how she could have slept at all. Oh, of course: Conor had given her a pill. It had worn off now, though.

Presently she got out of bed and crept down to the kitchen. There was enough light filtering between the trays of seedlings for her to make out the hands of the clock if she stood up close. It was a quarter to three, the dead hour, with too much left of the night to be lived through alone. Bagel thumped his tail at her, and she knelt on the hearthrug to pet him. He rolled over at once, huge paws batting the air as he offered his belly to be tickled. She obliged him and ducked her face against his head for a comforting swipe of warm, floppy, wet tongue. Plainly what she needed was something to hug, and Bagel, while better than nothing, could be improved on. She hauled herself back upstairs by the banister rail and went looking for Conor.

'That you, Kate?' he said, as she slipped into his room and closed the door.

'Yes.'

'Dope not working?'

'It did for a while, but now I don't think I can go back to sleep.'

'D'you want to come in for a cuddle? I'm not equal to much else, I'm afraid.' He moved over against the wall, and she climbed in beside him, turning her back so that he could curl himself around her.

'You've got one of those awful tent things on again. Bloody

250

acres of it. Where are you? I can't find you.' She sat up, hauled the nightgown over her head, dropped it on the floor, and burrowed back under the covers.

'That's much better,' he said, fitting a hand over her breast. 'What a kind girl to come and visit me.'

'I'm not being kind, I'm being selfish. You've just about ruined my sleeping habits, you know? It doesn't feel right any more, being in bed alone.'

'Well shit, if that's all that's bothering you I'll buy you a teddy bear.'

'Creep.'

'Darling, I'm sorry. I don't mean to be nasty. But I feel nasty.'

'Because of Sam?'

'Partly.' He stirred restlessly.

'But what else could you have done? Are you sorry you didn't let him kill me?'

'That is the sort of crack that, as you grow older and wiser, you will learn not to make. Unless you want your husband to beat you black and blue. The situation never should have arisen, that's the point. I ought to have seen what was happening to Sam and done something about it before. If I'd been on the job I'd have realized the state he was in and found out why – after all, I'm supposed to be running this show. And what was I doing instead? Following my cock around like some cuntstruck adolescent.'

'You mean it's all my fault.'

'Oh, shut up. Look, if I'd been concentrating on the operation, as I should have been, I'd have had Sam's confidence. He could have come to me, told me the bind he was in. I'd have helped him; he didn't have to sweat it out like that. But he didn't trust me enough, and that's my fault, not his. *I wasn't paying attention*. I saw him every day and I never saw him at all – I was too busy screwing.'

His hand had tightened on her breast until he was hurting her. She put her own hand over his, and the bitter grip relaxed.

'Darling love, that's nonsense and you know it,' she said. 'He was programmed for this months before you ever laid eyes on me. Let alone laid me. They set him up and he set you up, all of you. Chuck and Claire, Afeni – they didn't see it either, so why pretend you're the only one responsible? You want to find somebody to blame, take a look around. You could say it's my father's fault, for keeping the war going. Or the president's fault, for being too weak to control my father. Or Colonel Whatsisface's fault, for

251

being crazy enough and wicked enough to turn poor Sam into a hit man. Or it was Sam's own fault for punching out that officer in Saigon or Cator Blair's fault for getting killed.'

'Kate, I told you before – shut up.'

'I will not shut up; somebody has to get you off this guilt trip of yours. I could make out a case against poor Charlie Eisinger, for taking me up to Winter Hill and making everything easy for you, just because he wanted to get into my pants. Then there's Sheriff Gibbs – you could blame him, because he didn't tell the FBI as soon as he guessed there was something funny going on. Or maybe it really is your fault after all, but you better stand in line because *boy*, do you have competition!'

After a moment she felt his rigid body settle in small, nuzzling movements against her back, and his chin moved into its accustomed place on her shoulder. He kissed her neck.

'What a shrew,' he said. 'I do love you. What are you studying at that silly college, anyway?'

'Literature and art history, why?'

'You're wasting your time. You ought to be a lawyer – you've a superb natural gift for obscuring the issues. Now think lovely thoughts and go bye-bye; we've got one hell of a lot to do in the morning.'

Conor waited until she was sound asleep before he crawled down to the foot of the bed and hopped over onto the floor. He wrapped a towel around his middle and paused on the landing to work out where Chuck would be. Claire had taken Afeni in with her, for comfort or at least for company, so presumably Chuck was sleeping in the room Sam and Afeni had previously shared. He went in. Chuck was there but not sleeping.

'Conor? Wait, let me light the lamp.'

'No. Let's go downstairs. I don't want to disturb the others, but we've got to talk.'

In the kitchen Chuck reheated leftover coffee, moving around as quietly as the cats. Presently he and Conor sat facing each other with the old enamel pot on the table between them.

'Carlos, old chum,' Conor said, 'I hate to be an alarmist, but has it occurred to you that we're up the well-known creek? That colonel of Sam's must know where we are.'

'Of course.'

'And when Sam doesn't check in with his control, they'll know something's gone wrong. I mean, there must have been an arrangement: a daily radio signal – something. They'd have kept him on a pretty tight rein, wouldn't you say?'

'They would have been fools not to.'

'Precisely. So if you were Sam's colonel, and you didn't hear from him on schedule, and there were no news flashes about kidnapped girls named Harper being found murdered, what would you do?'

'First I'd try to contact him by radio. I'd keep trying for quite a while – at least twelve hours from the time the signal should have come through, maybe as much as twenty-four. But after that I would send a couple or five real mean sumbitches on down here to check out the situation stat.'

'Right. And while I'm as vain as the next man, I know when I'm out of my class. The FBI I can just about cope with, but not these lads. They'll be melon thumpers – holdovers from Operation Phoenix, I shouldn't wonder. What they used to call a Health Alteration Unit. Remember?'

Chuck nodded, looking sick.

'At the moment,' Conor continued, 'I'm about as close to screaming hysterics as I ever want to be, and my judgement's not reliable. I know it isn't, because what I'm tempted to do is rout everyone out of bed this minute and run, and that makes no sense at all. Where the hell would we go? We'd be pretty conspicuous in a motel, and we're far too hot to foist ourselves onto friends and risk getting them killed as well. Besides, who'd see to the stock? We can't just leave them – and we can't ask a neighbour to fill in. What'd we tell him? Anyway, the goons might show up when he was here and take him out just for practice.'

'No.' Chuck was decisive. 'Moving everyone out is no good. Afeni should go, I think. She was too close to Sam; they'll know about her. But if she and Sam have both vanished we may be able to persuade the goons that the two of them left together. It makes a better story that way. And of course we have to find a safe house for Kate. I have an idea about that, but first there is one thing we have to settle.'

'I want to be buried in a pet cemetery. You get a better class of visitors.'

'Jokes I need like a hole in the foot. Us dumb Indians, we ain't got no sacred relics, like now, then we got to make with the brain, which is enough of a drag without you making funnies.' The dark man drank the rest of his coffee and started again.

'Okay, *kemosabe*, here's the pitch. We thought we'd won, right? Harper resigned, Faraday gets the job, and pretty soon

Congress should get around to cutting off the cash flow for those crooked bastards in the South. Everything just the way we figured it, right?'

'Right.'

'But if this colonel person gets his way, all that gets fucked. We'll be the villains – which is not important so long as you like the food in jail – but also public opinion will swing back in favour of more military aid.'

'How d'you make that out?'

'It's obvious.' He rose to his feet and struck an oracular pose. '"And I say to, you my friends, that United States foreign policy is not to be dictated by a handful of extremist criminal elements." And similar crap, six ways from Sunday. The peace movement will be set back ten years, and the South Vietnam government will demand a shipment of nukes to make them feel loved and wanted. They might even get one.'

'I take it you're not just trying to depress me. You do have something in mind other than a suicide pact?'

'I'm getting there. Conor, you're the only one of us who's met this guy Harper. What kind of a man is he?'

'A prick,' Conor said.

'Well sure, but what kind of a prick? Can you trust him to act in his own best interest, or can you not trust him at all?'

'Useful point,' said Conor thoughtfully. 'After Kate, and in some areas well before her, I'd say self-interest was certainly the most powerful factor in his life.'

'And if the colonel person exposes this whole story – except for his own part in it, of course – then Pendleton Harper will be ruined. No honourable retirement, no portrait hanging on the wall with all the other lousy portraits, probably not even a million-dollar book contract, though nowadays anything is possible. But anyhow, Harper will be disgraced. Finished. I don't think he'd like that, do you?'

'So?'

'So you set up another meeting. You go see the bastard, you tell him all about the colonel, and you show him how to cover his ass.'

'The fuck I do. I don't care if they hang him from the yardarm of the *Victory*. Besides, I'll get killed.'

'We still have Kate. Harper doesn't know how we feel about her. She'll be your safe-conduct pass. And to save her, and himself, Harper will stop the colonel – immobilize him and his murder squad as well. He has to, for his own sake and for Kate's. We can't do it, but he can.'

'It's a thought. As a matter of fact,' Conor said, beginning to brighten, 'it's an absolutely bloody brilliant thought. There's only one thing the matter with it. There must be hundreds of loopy colonels around, and we don't know which one we're looking for.'

'Yes we do. He's the man in charge of the Westwood Sanitarium, or he was when Sam was there last year. We don't know his name, but Harper can have the records checked. They'll find him. If the man can be stopped at all, if it's not too late, Harper's the one to do it.'

'Chuck, you're a genius.'

'It may not work –'.

'It's a chance. And it beats sitting around waiting for a lot of rude, unfriendly people to come and start altering our health. Notebook, where's my notebook?'

'What for?'

'Charlotte Harper's phone number; I bet the line's still tapped. It's the safest way to set this up. Then we'll call Tom Tulliver in New York; he'll have to get down here and take charge of Afeni.'

In New Lymington, in the house on Walden Avenue, Charlotte Harper picked up the bedside extension on the second ring. 'Your daughter's fine,' the soft, unmistakable voice said in her ear, 'but she's in some danger. Not from us, from another – interested party. I have to see her father this evening, same time and place as before. It's vitally important.'

'You know he's still in the hospital –'

'He'll have to leave it. We don't want to endanger his health,' Conor lied, remembering the tap, 'he can come in an ambulance surrounded by cardiologists if that's a factor, but he has to be there. This is Kate's *life*. And tell him to bring an aide with him – someone he can trust. I need a witness, and Harper's going to need a runner.'

'Wait! Oh, please wait –' But she was pleading with a dialling tone, and Conor was already looking up another number.

Tom Tulliver reached out his good hand for the phone, which, like his extra-long king-size mattress, rested economically on the floor. 'Uh-huh,' he said. 'Uh-huh. Right. You wanna tell me why?'

'The weather's so beautiful down here. I really think today will be a perfect May day.'

'Well, I wouldn't want to miss that. Guess I'll come on down.'

'That will be delightful,' Conor said primly. 'We're expecting some other visitors as well. Old colleagues of your sister's roommate.'

'Oh really? They work for the same company?'

'Yes, indeed. I'm getting some melons in specially. For thumping, you know.'

'Right. Okay, man, I'll see you. Have to get me some wheels, like it may take a little time, but I'll be there soon as I can.'

The girl beside him had raised herself on one elbow. Tom put the phone down and slapped her lightly on the rump.

'Out, pretty mama,' he said, rolling off the mattress. He collected her scattered clothes and dropped them across her slender bare thighs. 'What you do with your shoes?'

'What you mean, out?'

'I got to leave, and don't nobody stay in my house when I ain't here. Now cover the body, mama, and haul ass.'

'Shee-it! Where you going, then?'

He grinned. 'Gotta make a house call. Have a nice day.'

It was past four in the afternoon when the monster motorcycle with Tom Tulliver astride it roared up in front of the farmhouse. By the time he had kicked the stand down and stood back, stretching, Dan was two feet away. Reverently the boy gazed at the black and chrome dragon.

'Honda Street Machine?'

'You got it.'

'Can I touch it?'

'Sure you can, just leave them saddlebags alone. And don't try riding it or I'll whip your ass.'

'Yes, sir. Sir?'

'Yeah?'

'Excuse me for asking, but how do you manage? With your hand an' all?'

'Listen, boy, this thing's stronger than a regular hand. After your five little fingers'd curl up and quit, it just holds on. Where's Darlene?'

'Who?'

'Darlene. Or she still calling herself Afeni, I guess. My sister.'

Chuck came down the porch steps. 'Tom, you made good time,' he said. 'Afeni's in the house, but before you see her I have to give you a rundown. Here, come in the barn and look at my new calf.'

He took the black man by the elbow, steering him away from the house, but checked his stride to look back over his shoulder at Dan, who was running worshipful fingers over the immense padded saddle.

'Daniel!'

'Yes, sir?'

'Don't try and ride that thing.'

'No, sir, I won't.' They all think he was crazy or something? Not that he wouldn't have liked to, but as his mother had pointed out so often, with disheartening emphasis, there were some things in life you could have and some you couldn't. '*Vrooom*,' Dan growled to himself, very softly. '*Varrrooooom!*'

In the barn, Chuck wound up a bald, brutal synopsis of recent events. 'And Conor left this morning, but the goons may already be on their way. So you see there's no time to fool around; you have to get Afeni out of here right away.'

'How 'bout Miss Ann?'

'Miss – Oh, Kate. She's in the safest place we could think of. If they track her down there, we're blown anyhow.'

'Well don't tell me where – I got no need to know. Just so she's away out of this. Two minutes' interrogation from those babies, she'd crack like an egg. But what's Claire gone do? And the kids? You really think you can get away with this craziness?'

'It's the best chance we have. Maybe the only one.'

Tom nodded. 'I ain't done too much praying lately,' he said, 'but they say the Lord hears the cry of the sinner, so maybe I'll have an edge. Don't count on it, is all. Darlene ready to leave?'

'I think so. She packed a duffle bag –'

'Hide it. Or burn it. I can't take no more baggage this trip. We better split now.'

Afeni was standing with Dan, beside the motorcycle. Tom put his arm around her and kissed her cheek. 'Told you to stay away from that honky,' he said with affectionate callousness. 'Next time your brother gonna find you a *brother*.'

'You have a place to go?' Chuck asked.

'We got kin a few hours' ride from here. I figure to hide out a while. Keep a low profile, like they say. Can't tell you where to reach me, but I'll call you tomorrow, see what's happening. Get aboard now, girl. Watch out for them saddlebags and hold onto me. Stay cool, man.'

They took off, stones flying. Chuck sighed.

'Daniel, I'll need you to help me with the milking. Your mother has to stay with Beccah.'

'She gonna be okay, dad?'

'She'll be fine. It's only an allergic reaction; as soon as she has the antihistamine it will clear up in a few hours.'

'Then why don't you give it to her now? And why did you make her eat that stuff in the first place? You know canned crabmeat makes her sick. I don't see how you could do that to your own kid.'

Chuck looked down at his son's troubled face, and did not need to be reminded that this, too, was his 'own kid', understandably anxious in case such unfatherly behaviour might affect him next.

'Better sick than dead,' he said soberly. 'Your sister is too young, and she talks too much. You're old enough to be sensible, I hope. I wish to God your grandmother had kept the two of you safe with her, but it's too late for that now. We're in bad trouble, Dan. I'm expecting company, and not the kind you put out the lace tablecloth for.'

'Those FBI men again?'

'No. Much worse. These are really bad guys. Killers.'

'Why don't we call Mr Gibbs then? And the state cops?'

'There's not a lot they could do. The men who are coming don't care about the law. They make their own. It shouldn't be possible, but it is.'

'Well, I think it sucks.'

'Daniel!'

'Sorry, dad. It just slipped out.'

'It never should have slipped in. Billy Paton again, I suppose. When I think that boy comes from a good Christian home . . . Now listen, Dan, if these men come – I hope they won't, but if they do – we have to tell some lies. I know, I know – we don't tell lies in this family. But this is one time we do, because people's lives depend on it. We say, if we are asked, that Sam and Afeni left the farm yesterday afternoon in the Jeep. I let them borrow it because Conor is away and won't need it for a few days. They said they were going to Charlottesville to visit friends. Okay?'

'Got it. Dad? Where is Sam?'

'He has gone away.'

'To Charlottesville?'

'No. Further away than Charlottesville.'

'How much further?'

'He told Kate he was going to California,' Chuck said carefully.

'Gee, I wish I could go to California. What else do we have to say?'

'First, about Kate. Kate was never here: you never saw her or heard of her. There *is* no Kate; there is only Alice Mary, who was here for a while and then went back to Harmony.'

'Where's Conor at? I don't mean really, I mean where do we say he's at?'

'We don't know. Yesterday morning a man came in a car – we don't know who he was – and Conor went away with him. Conor told us he would not be back before Monday. He didn't say where he and the man were going. That's all you know. *All*. That is all any of us know.'

'You were right about Beccah, dad. This is just too complicated – she'd have blown it for sure. What did the man look like? The one that came for Conor?'

'He didn't get out of the car, so we couldn't see his face clearly. Dark hair, I think, and a big moustache, the kind that hangs down over the mouth. That was all we saw.'

'What car was he driving?'

'A green car.'

'That won't do it. Boys always notice what make a car is. You might not, but I would.'

'A Dodge, then, a green Dodge, late model.'

'Coronet. Okay. You better tell ma. Not that she'd know a Dodge from a T-bird anyhow. But don't worry, dad. You and me, we'll handle it. And Afeni's brother, that came on the bike, we never saw him, right? Like Kate. He was never here.'

'Oh, Dan. Don't be too good at this. At least, be good at it, this one time for all our sakes, but try not to enjoy it too much, okay? We better milk now and have it done. Later there may not be time.'

As the stuttering clatter of the helicopter grew louder, the five men settled at the kitchen table looked uselessly upward and then at each other. 'Damn thing's about to come down the chimney,' one of them grumbled.

'Is this what you were expecting?' asked the spruce elderly man across from him.

'Hadn't reckoned on a chopper, no, but it figures. Fast in, fast out, and while they're airborne nobody can touch 'em.' He looked at his cards. 'Carl, I'll raise you five.'

The noise of the aircraft abruptly died, replaced not by silence but by a raucous honking as the geese in their pen protested the earsplitting invasion. Then, not so much audible as felt on the air like drumtaps, came a brief ruffling of little soft thumps, all run together, ominous as a suddenly accelerated heartbeat. The geese were cut off mid-clamour, and Chuck Lainez started to his feet.

'Sit down, Chuck, sit down. They'd as soon shoot you as the geese. Sooner.'

The screen door to the kitchen was quietly opened, and three men filed in. Within seconds they were joined by two more through the inner door that led from the main hallway. All five wore olive drab, with no insignia of any kind, and all five carried machine pistols with long tubes extending the barrels. Chuck had seen weapons like that before, though never in the hands of people he wished to know better.

'Which one of you is Lainez?'

Very slowly and carefully, keeping his hands in plain view and well away from his body, Chuck stood up.

'I am,' he said. 'Who are you, and what do you want?'

'Do you know a man named Samuel Aitken?'

'Sure. He was on a visit here with his girlfriend.'

'Was? When did he leave?'

'Yesterday. They both left; they were going to Charlottesville for a few days. I let them borrow the Jeep.'

'Very generous, considering it doesn't belong to you.'

'The owner is away. He left the Jeep for me to use. He wouldn't mind if Sam had it; he's borrowed it before.'

'Okay, Lainez, move away from the table. Slow and easy. Get over there and face the wall. Feet apart, hands behind the neck. Very *good*!' The singsong drawl was insulting, a schoolyard taunt. 'Rest of you do the same, one at a time. You next, Fatso.' He gestured with his weapon at the heavyset grey-haired man to the right of Chuck's empty seat. The man smiled and stayed where he was.

'Now just you hold on there, sonny,' he said pleasantly. 'My daddy always told me, first thing you do, you find out who you're dealin' with. By rights, you all bein' the visitors, you had ought to tell us your names first, but while you're makin' your minds up you may's well have ours. This over here is Mr Carlton Brackage. Mr Brackage is the president of the Farmers Loan, that's our bank down in Cold Crossing. Right the other side of him is Mr Gilbert Paton, the head of our dairy cooperative here in Aurora County, and next to him, lookin' like he never seen a M-10 before, that's Mr Paton's brother Will. Will's my deputy. And I'm Hailey Gibbs, sheriff of this county, and don't nobody hold a gun on me. So you just set that fancy piece of hardware down some place where the cats won't get on it, and let's see if we can get you boys straightened out.'

At the end of the pasture nearest the house, the Huey pilot sat with long legs dangling out of the doorway and listened to the night noises. Moonlight gleamed dully on the weapon balanced across his thighs. In Vietnam a rustling in the dark could mean death coming in black pyjamas to blow your head off, but this was the US of A, the peaceful countryside, and the small sounds here would surely be innocent – a cow recovered from the stampeding panic of the chopper's brash arrival and settling again into the long grass; a bird returning to its perch; a randy hound heading for an in-season bitch in the next parish. The pilot was a farm boy himself. He didn't know for certain what the others were doing up at the house and didn't want to. He could have made a pretty accurate guess, but guessing was not what he was paid for. His job was to fly the aircraft and guard it while it was on the ground. He was also supposed to monitor the radio, but the lure of the sweet night air was too strong. Anyhow, why would anyone want to contact them now? They knew what they had to do. He was just glad he wasn't one of the guys that had to do it. Shame about those geese, though – the pilot had always had a soft spot for geese.

Fifty feet away, Tom Tulliver sat halfway up a tree, perched on a limb with his back against the trunk, in much the same attitude as the pilot of the helicopter. He had been there quite a while, and he was cramped and stiff, but he did not move. The four little eggs hooked to his belt might not take kindly to any further jouncing around. He had climbed up without them and drawn them up after him on a cord, with the same breathless delicacy he had employed as a child in fishing for coins through storm gratings, with a blob of chewing gum at the end of a thread. Those dimes and nickels had, more often than not, been eating money; they had meant life, then. The mean little eggs were death, but not his own if he could help it. Bringing them down from New York had scared him shitless. Each one had been snugly nested in its own polyurethane cocoon, surrounded in turn by further layers of plastic bubble wrap, and the whole lethal clutch suspended on gimbals inside a padded steel box. Nevertheless, the knowledge that they were there, right behind him in one of the Honda's black saddlebags, had made his long ride a haunted one. He had more than half expected to lose his elegant black ass and everything attached to it, with each bump in the highway. Oddly enough, now that he was sitting in this dumb tree with the fuckers cosying up to his gall bladder, he felt a lot safer. If he blew it now it would be because of something he did himself, not because some sleepy truck driver had absentmindedly jumped the centre reservation.

Nobody at the house knew he was here, which was just the way he wanted it. Chuck would have had a coronary on the spot. At five o'clock that morning, while Tom was extracting the grenades, by a nicely calculated mixture of camaraderie and straight blackmail, from the current Grand Master of the West 19th Street Chowder and Bombing Society, he had already decided that this piece of private enterprise would have to be concealed from the Lainez family. They didn't believe in violence. Tom Tulliver was not addicted to it himself, but his principles were elastic enough to allow for doing unto others before they did unto you – or unto your friends. He hadn't told Darlene about the eggs either. When he left her off at the motel forty miles away he had simply said he was coming back to keep an eye on things, so that if Chuck's scenario didn't work out too well he could maybe lend a hand.

'With what?' his sister had enquired. 'You got an army you forgot to tell me about?' Never a woman to waste her breath, however, she hadn't tried to talk him out of it. But then she didn't know about the eggs.

The back of his neck itched, and he lifted his left arm with great care until he could reach around to scratch the place with his metal hand. Something had bitten him. Come to that, in the two hours he had been stuck up here just about everything for miles around had bitten him, but after Nam you didn't pay much attention to stuff like that. He lowered the hand again, adjusted the grip around his branch, and watched the Huey pilot sitting there swinging his legs in the cool, silvery light. Finding himself in such a good spot in relation to the chopper had been pure dumb luck. He had chosen this particular tree because it was well leafed out and because it commanded an excellent view of the farmyard, the barn, and the kitchen entrance to the house. He'd been expecting a motorized approach – bulletproof limos, something unobtrusive along those lines – which was why he'd figured the eggs would give him more of an edge than an automatic weapon. (He'd wheedled one of those out of the West 19th Street stockpile too, but it was still in his saddlebag. After what Chuck had told him he was pretty sure the opposition would be similarly equipped, and he didn't like the odds.)

The chopper had taken him completely off balance, and the surprise had lasted just long enough to keep him from tossing one of his little friends right then and there, before the men could leave the aircraft. Being professionals, they spread out as soon as they hit the ground, and then it was too late. Unless you could be sure to get the whole bunch at one time, there was no sense hitting them at all. Even if there were only one survivor, that man's first priority would be to reach the house and slaughter everyone in it. Standard operating procedure.

Tom, being a professional of sorts himself, had relaxed and made himself as comfortable as he could. The massacre of the geese did not surprise him, it simply confirmed that at least one of the fingers on the trigger of an LISP was undesirably itchy. Prevention was out of the question now. Chuck's plan was the only hope and not a very dazzling one at that. If the rest of this crowd was as jumpy as the goose killer, the outlook fell somewhere in between lousy and forget it. What would be left was vengeance. He could, and would, take the mothers out as they took off. There were four eggs; only one of them needed to connect with the chopper, and Tom had always been a right-handed pitcher – not flashy, but accurate. He could do it. No sweat.

*

At the precise moment when the Huey pilot lowered his legs out of the doorway and settled down to enjoy the familiar softness of a country night in May, Pendleton Reville Harper, three hundred miles away, thumped a heavy first into the smarting open palm of the hand he had already, repeatedly, hit. He was flushed with shock and anger.

'But I *know* the man!' he exploded. 'I mean literally: I've met him, I've talked with him. His name's Lund, Colonel Rupert Lund. He was sitting by my bed in Walter Reed just two days ago, oozing sympathy, wanting me to tell him what he could do to help. Young man, are you absolutely sure of your facts?'

'Yes. But you can check. Have Wilberforce call the Sanitarium. If Lund's there, tell him Kate's been released – she's safe with friends. Don't tell him she's at her mother's house; we don't want a goon squad showing up there for God's sake. If he presses hard for Kate's exact location – and he will – then you'll know. Because he'll have to eliminate her, and to do that he's got to find her.'

'You were prepared to kill her yourselves. Why should I trust you?'

'Why should we trust you? You gave us your word you'd keep all this to yourself, and as far as I can see you never had the slightest intention of sticking to it. Anyway, we weren't going to kill her. All that was for your benefit; you had to be convinced the danger was real. But we'd never have hurt her.'

'And now you're trying to convince me again. More lies?'

'Christ no, you've cornered the market; there aren't enough to go round. Look, you can check,' Conor repeated. 'It can do no harm. Have your man call. What have you got to lose?'

'What if Lund isn't there?'

'Find out where to reach him. If they say he can't be reached they're lying. Don't accept it. Keep pushing till you find him. Men in his position don't drop out of sight; even when they go to the men's room they've got their beepers with them. You *must* check this out. Kate wasn't in danger before, or not from us, but she is now. And if that doesn't bother you, think of yourself. How are you going to like being the Benedict Arnold of the twentieth century?'

'It's my word against his,' Harper said.

'It is for about five minutes. After that you'll have to produce Kate – and you can't.'

The truck, outwardly disguised as a telephone repair vehicle, was lavishly fitted with the most sophisticated communications equipment. It had been rushed to Rock Creek Park at Conor's insistence. Now the three men sat together in a cramped rear compartment, separated by soundproof glass from the operational section, which was manned by two stone-faced technicians whose every move was scrutinized by a pair of equally glum Secret Service men. In fact everyone in the van appeared monumentally cheesed off except for Conor, who merely looked anxious and tired, and Arthur Wilberforce, who was as alert as a terrier with a nice aromatic rat hole. Pendleton Harper stared at his aide with dislike, and sighed gustily.

'*I* don't know,' he groused. 'A man sacrifices everything, even his health, in the service of his country, and right away everybody's out to bring him down.' Conor was amused, in spite of his grinding anxiety, to find that Harper, like many a superstar before him, had started to believe his own publicity. Harper sighed again in ostentatious martyrdom.

'Arthur,' he said, 'you'd better move up front and start calling.'

Left alone together, Kate's father and Kate's lover sat watching Wilberforce's back through the glass, as if the seams of his Cardin blazer might suddenly fly open to reveal the solution to all problems. Forced into physical proximity by the van's close quarters, in every other way the two were light-years apart. But while Conor in his time had dealt with a number of people who resembled the former secretary of state – the US Embassy in Saigon had been full of them – Harper had never been exposed before to a man like this self-contained conspirator sprawled bonelessly in the swivel chair two feet away. The fellow seemed content to sit in silence, but Harper was never comfortable for long without the sound of voices, especially his own.

'What happened to your Irish brogue?' he asked idly.

'Oh, that. I couldn't be bothered.'

'But you are Irish?'

'More or less. I'm as much Irish as I am anything, I suppose.'

'And yet you say this – this act of terrorism, this abduction, blackmail, God knows what – has nothing to do with Ireland?'

'No.' Conor was too tired for anything but the truth. 'It was to stop the war. In Vietnam.'

Harper's eyes bulged, and his jowls seemed to inflate like a bullfrog's throat. 'Good God almighty, man, are you mad?' he bellowed. 'Where have you been? In a cave? The war is *over*. The last American troops were pulled out six weeks ago. You must know that.'

'Your ground war's over, that's all. You think dead people don't count, just as long as they're not Americans? You've gone on bombing the shit out of Cambodia, and in case you hadn't noticed, plenty of people in Vietnam are still dying. The ARVN is quite the most incompetent army I've ever seen, but as long as the generals go on getting money and materiel on a non-stop bloody conveyor belt they'll find a use for it. After all, how many things can you do with high explosives and aircraft parts? You can't eat them or wear them. You can't even swap them for a brand-new secondhand bicycle, so you chuck 'em at the enemy and the enemy chucks stuff back at you, and more and more civilians on both sides go on getting killed. It won't be easy, but try to look at this from our point of view. First there were the Paris peace talks. Good. Then there was the Christmas bombing. Bad. A truly monumental bummer. Then there was the cease-fire. That looked good, except pretty soon it turned out nobody was taking any notice of it. Bad. All American troops out by the end of March. Good. Saturation bombing of Cambodia from US bases in Thailand. Bad. And just a few days ago the Congress voted to approve more money for increased weapons and supplies to South Vietnam. Bad, bad, bad. The yo-yo theory of foreign policy, and you, Dr Harper, are wholly responsible. Oh, I know all about old Westy and his creative accounting, the New Math we used to call that, but even a general can read signals as clear as the ones he was getting. He told you what you wanted to hear, so you had an excuse for what you wanted to do. This has turned into your personal war, your very own shambles, and you've prolonged it virtually single-handed. Nobody else could have got away with it, and nobody else will.'

Characteristically, Harper's ego plucked from this indictment what appeared to him the ultimate compliment, the tribute to his unique power over events. But even as he glowed with satisfaction, his internal computer dutifully activated the module for righteous wrath. 'You are a traitor, sir,' he intoned. 'A traitor to the generous land that has nurtured you, sheltered you in its bounteous—'

'Balls. According to you, the war's over. Besides, I'm not an American. I can't possibly be a traitor.'

'An enemy agent, then, striking at the very foundations of democracy.'

'Have it your own way.' Conor shrugged. 'But don't forget I came here of my own free will to try and save your daughter's life – at some risk to my own, if you don't mind me mentioning it.'

'That is true,' Harper conceded, not pleased at being thrown out of his oratorical stride. 'And of course there is that contemporary problem, the so-called generation gap. I realize patriotism is out of favour with young people today, but for a man with my background that emotion is a sacred one. When my country's freedom is threatened, I feel it deeply. I feel it here.' He pressed his hand to his liver.

'That's not patriotism,' Conor said, absentmindedly professional, 'that's martinis. Or bourbon, or whatever you've been killing the pain with lately. Listen, you ought to get those boys at Walter Reed to run a liver function series while they have you. And when you get out, lay off the butter and the hollandaise sauce and all those goodies. Grilled fish, poached chicken, and a glass of white wine, that's what you ought to be having. Go on stuffing yourself with booze and cholesterol and you'll do yourself in. Not that I care,' he added, returning to reality, 'but don't say you weren't warned.'

Harper relinquished his hold on his gut, contemplated a future of grilled fish, and changed the subject.

'Tell me one thing, if you will,' he said. 'Why did you do it? Are you a Communist agent? A Marxist intellectual? Why is it so important to you that the North Vietnamese should win this war?'

'I couldn't care less who wins,' said Conor patiently. 'I just want it to stop. Militarily, the South are so abysmal that even with all that free hardware there's no way they can actually win. They couldn't hack it with American troops doing most of the fighting, so they're hardly likely to get there on their own. In which case, the North had better be allowed to take over and be done with it. It's the only way to stop the killing.'

'That is a shockingly dangerous argument, but it doesn't answer my question. Why did you – you personally – feel justified in taking such extreme measures, such extraordinary risks? What's in it for you?'

Conor looked at the man sitting across from him, at the great pink slab of barbered face that revealed only the mild interest of a man confronted by an oddity: a dancing chicken, say, or a bifurcated banana. It was a face lightly etched with the wrinkles of age, sagging here and there under the pull of gravity, the cheeks permanently flushed with damaged capillaries that had succumbed to decades of good living. There were no traces here of reflection or self-knowledge, no scars left by the decent distress that haunts good men with great responsibilities. Telling that face about napalmed children would be as productive as reciting the Sermon on the Mount to a rhinoceros. Wincing inwardly, Conor realized he would have to present the face with the only explanation that might penetrate the wall of well-kept flesh and strike some kind of response from the man inside. If, indeed, there was a man inside.

'My wife was Vietnamese,' he said, disgusted with himself for making such sleazy use of the dear and lovely dead. 'She was working in a South Vietnam orphanage when it was bombed. By South Vietnamese airmen flying American planes and dropping American bombs. She was killed. Now do you see?'

It became clear that Harper did see, or thought he did. His politician's eyes misted over with the easy emotionalism of a man who will depopulate whole provinces without a tremor, and then weep all night when his dog dies. Sickeningly, he reached across and patted Conor's shoulder. 'You poor boy,' he said. 'You poor, poor boy. You've done wrong, of course: we both know that. But I do understand.'

Much to Conor's relief, for he was beginning to be quite dangerously angry, the unctuous sympathy vanished as quickly as it had come, and the expression on the big bland face reverted to curiosity.

'You took a hell of a chance, coming here like this. You could have dumped Kate, left her to take her chances, and you and your accomplices could simply have disappeared. Presumably the prospect of my own downfall wouldn't have kept you awake at night. Why did you come back to warn me?'

'First, because of Kate. Second, because now you owe me,' Conor said gently. 'We're in this together now, and too many people know it for you to wriggle out. People have seen me and heard me. Wilberforce, the Secret Service detail, the whiz kids up front. You can't kill them all.' Harper bridled, but Conor swept on. 'You can't disown me, you can't doublecross me, and if you try it I'll blow the whistle on you and everything will come out. Everything. I've got tapes and copies of tapes, half a dozen sets, all held by people you've never heard of, and if anything happens to me one set goes to the *Times* and another to the *Washington Post*,' he announced, inventing freely. 'The original bargain stands, and don't forget it.'

'The bargain?'

'The one you made with me. The one you broke and I kept. If you ever want to see Kate again, this time you'll keep it. No, I won't hurt her. I couldn't. But I guarantee you she won't come home. Behave yourself and she'll be returned to her mother on schedule – or she will if we can stop this bastard Lund – and you retire gracefully from public life with your reputation unsullied. God knows it's not a reputation I'd be specially attached to myself, but that's what makes a horse race. Obviously it matters to you, and I daresay you'll find it a financial asset.'

Harper slapped his knee. 'That reminds me,' he said, cheering up. 'Do you remember suggesting I should write my memoirs? Well, I've been in touch with that Lazar fellow, the agent, and he thinks we should have no difficulty getting two million. That's for the whole package, of course, paperback deal, subsidiary rights and so on, but even so . . . Not an inconsiderable piece of change, don't you agree? I've already had an approach from my alma mater – not much money in that, but it makes a useful base, and one would have a secretary and all that. And Lazar tells me that CBS has expressed interest in –'

Wilberforce came back into the rear compartment. 'I've reached him. You were right,' he said to Conor, 'they tried to stonewall it, so I called Doug Sims at the White House – he never leaves his office before ten o'clock, no wonder his wife walked out on him. I always had a feeling we might need him sooner or later. That's why I've let him win every time we've played tennis for the last year and a half, and God knows it wasn't easy – he serves like Daffy Duck. Anyhow,' Wilberforce went on, dragged back onto the track by a wordless snarl from Harper, 'I had Doug talk to them, and after that everything opened up. Lund's at Lurie Field. It's a small installation near Roanoke – Army officially, but it's used by the Agency as well. Lear jets, light aircraft, helicopters – that kind of thing. Anyhow, I got Lund, and he's desperately anxious to find out where Miss Harper is. I told him I had no information on that, and his voice went up half an octave. He's on the line now,' he told Harper. 'Wants to speak with you personally.'

'And so he shall.' Harper levered himself out of the chair. 'So he shall.' He looked down at Conor. 'You don't trust me an inch, do you?' he said unexpectedly. 'That's all right. If I were in your shoes I wouldn't trust me either. Come along and hear this for yourself.'

He marched into the forward area, Conor and Wilberforce at

his heels, and took the receiver from one of the technicians.

'Lund? Pendleton Harper. Before you say anything at all, I think it only fair to tell you that you have been under surveillance for some time. Very close surveillance. We know precisely what you've been doing, and we have full documentation. Photocopies, tapes, and witnesses. Lesson one, Colonel. Never assume everyone else is dumber than you are.'

You have to hand it to the son of a bitch, Conor thought, he's a quick learner. There was a rattle of protest from the other end of the wire, audible only as a series of percussive squawks to the others in the van. Harper cut the babble short with regal indifference.

'Colonel Lund, I am not currently interested in a summary of your legal defence, although at a later date I'm sure I shall find it fascinating. Right now I am only concerned to ensure that the unauthorized and totally irregular unit you have recently dispatched be recalled without delay.' This frontal assault had, for Conor, a certain reassuring familiarity, since it appeared to be a straight steal from his Aunt Rose, who based all her dealings with children on a firm assumption of guilt. Asking you if you'd done something, in her view, was simply an invitation to untruth. The approach had always worked for Aunt Rose, and it worked for Harper now. The colonel did not deny sending out a strike force. Instead he made a brief, ill-advised attempt to challenge Harper's authority, on the grounds of his recent resignation. This was scraping at an already raw spot and did him no good. Harper first referred darkly to Doug Sims at the White House, and then threatened to take the matter up directly with Doug's employer. The president stood a good deal in awe of the Duchy of Langley, but even he could be counted upon to veto a rogue operation of this sort, and the colonel knew it.

'Very well, sir,' he said at last. 'I'll radio the officer in command and instruct him to return at once.'

'You do that, Colonel. I will stay on this line, which you will keep open, and you will inform me as soon as contact has been established. I suggest you move your ass on this one with all possible speed. You will also consider yourself restricted to Lurie Field until further notice. Now get on the phone!'

'Is it possible,' Conor asked into the sudden quiet, 'to link this line to a speaker so that we can hear both ends of the next conversation?' He was trembling like a whippet with fatigue and stress, but his voice was low and level.

'Couldn't be easier,' the senior technician replied. 'Only have to press the button. That is, if – ?' He looked enquiringly at Harper.

'Oh go ahead. Why not? Short of giving the entire story to AP and UPI, we could hardly spread this thing around much further.'

The button was pressed, and the van was loud with background noises: voices in the distance, footsteps, the dry flutter of papers, and an indecipherable hodgepodge of electronic doodling. Then a voice, shockingly loud, came through the speaker.

'Dr Harper?'

'Is that you, Lund?'

'No sir, this is Major McMichaels, Colonel Lund's aide. I'm to inform you that, most unfortunately, we don't seem able to reach the unit in question.'

'What the hell do you mean, you can't reach them? Don't they have a radio?'

'Of course, sir.' The voice was affronted. 'But it doesn't appear to be manned. Either the operator's been reassigned, or there's a faulty equipment problem. They radioed us on arrival, but we've heard nothing since, and we're getting no acknowledgement of our signals. The colonel wishes me to inform you that we'll keep trying, and we'll let you know as soon as we make contact.'

'Wait a minute. What's-your-name – McMurray, is it?'

'McMichaels, sir.'

'Doesn't the unit commander carry a beeper?'

'We can't reach him on that from here, sir – he's way out of range. Once we contact the aircraft, the operator there can buzz him, but we can't get him direct. I understand there's a transceiver installation in the house itself, and the colonel's having that tried now, but so far there's been no response.'

'That's hardly surprising,' Conor muttered to himself. He scrubbed his face with his knuckles and spoke up. 'I hate to spoil the party when we're having so much fun with all that expensive gadgetry, but has anyone considered the telephone? I know it's a comedown, but there is a phone at the house, and unless those silly sods have cut the wires out of sheer habit, surely Lund could simply call up and speak to the chap himself?'

'McMichaels!' Harper snapped. 'I am about to give you a telephone number. Write this down.'

Slowly and distinctly Conor spelled out the number of the

271

Lainez farm, with Harper relaying it digit by digit to the man at Lurie Field.

'Now read it back to me. Very good. Have your colonel call that number immediately. As soon as he's spoken with the unit commander and ordered his recall, I want him to get back to me here. Keep this line open. And Major!'

'Sir?'

'I shall require an immediate sitrep on the current status of all civilians in that house.'

'I'm afraid I don't quite –'

'Yes you do. I want to know they're alive and well. And by God, Major, if you and your boss are interested in your own survival, they'd damn well better be.'

Kate sat in the dark, with her backside on the hard vinyl seat of a chair that had been designed in a spirit of revenge, and her forearms leaning on one of those 'linen-look' tablecloths with artful plastic irregularities that furrow the skin. She had not wanted to leave the farm and had argued fiercely, but her presence there would have endangered them all. Chuck had been very definite about it, and Chuck was in charge. Conor had driven away as soon as the morning milking was done, despite Claire's forceful lecture on the need for a good breakfast, the kind that would keep people going. He had stopped her mid-harangue with an emphatic kiss, full on the mouth, which left her for once quite speechless. Kate walked out to the Jeep with him. He turned and hugged her very hard, his cheek pressed against the top of her head.

'It'll work,' he said. 'I promise you. First thing I met when I walked out of the house this morning was a cross-eyed black cat going from left to right, which is practically tops on the Good Omen Chart. Only thing that beats it is a one-legged bishop and those are hard to come by in Aurora County. Be a good girl and do as Chuck says while I'm gone.'

He kissed her lightly, and traced with a fingernail the barely visible curved line at the corner of her mouth. 'Smile for me, lovey,' he said. 'That's better. No, don't watch me out of sight; it's bad luck. See you later,' and he was gone.

Soon after breakfast Will Paton's old Chevy arrived at the farm to collect her, and she was driven, half-stifled under a tarpaulin, to the house where she would stay until, one way or another, the emergency was resolved. A door under the sagging carport gave unobtrusive access to the house, and she was quickly bundled inside and abandoned. Most of the day she had spent alone, and the hours since morning had crawled as if the clock were paralysed. She could no longer see its smug, vindictive face. She had been warned to turn on no lights, stay away from windows, ignore the telephone if it rang. There was a big television set in the living-room, but she must not turn it on. 'And don't draw the curtains,' she had been instructed. 'Around here, you draw the

273

curtains and right away the neighbours know damn well you got something to hide – and they ain't about to give up till they find out what it is. Every old woman for miles be bakin' a pie so she can come knockin' at the door with a dish in her hand. "I'll just set it right down on the kitchen table here"' in a sprightly falsetto '– and before you know it she's goin' through the closets.'

So Kate sat in the kitchen with the moonlight streaming through the window painting the linoleum with a checkered parallelogram of brightness that made the rest of the room seem even murkier. The clock ticked, and periodically the old refrigerator startled her by wheezing into action with a rattle and a harsh, metallic snarl. She was hungry, but afraid to open the refrigerator door. The light would go on, and someone might be passing; someone might wonder who was scrounging for food in a dark kitchen in an empty house. There was a cookie jar on the counter, but it was empty except for a few sour-smelling crumbs. The bread bin yielded half a sliced loaf, plastic wrapped. Kate drank water from the tap, chewed tasteless, rubbery bread, and brooded over the irony of being reduced, in the name of freedom, to the punishment diet of an eighteenth-century convict. Feeling cranky about the menu might be immature, but it was better than fretting herself to rags over what could be happening at the farmhouse. Her faith in Conor was very strong, but she doubted whether even he was totally immune to the workings of Murphy's law: 'Whatever can go wrong, will go wrong.' There was an awful lot that could go wrong.

'Oh, Jesus,' she said aloud, 'why doesn't somebody come?'

The room smelled of stale smoke. She wondered if she might risk another cigarette; there was a half pack in her shirt pocket, but what if someone saw the flare of the match in a supposedly unoccupied house? Oh really, she admonished herself, people had better things to do than keep up a ceaseless watch on a perfectly ordinary house where there was obviously nobody home. Paranoia, however alluring, must be controlled. Nevertheless, she groped her way out into the hall and ducked behind the door at the head of the cellar stairs before she lit the match. Once again she was out of the action, parked maddeningly on a siding with nothing to do, but she could at least try to avoid doing anything wrong. Had she known how closely her thoughts echoed those of Agent Maybush a few days earlier, among the briers on Berry Hill, she would have been astonished and annoyed.

For the record, Agent Maybush was at this moment drinking beer at Will Paton's service station in Cold Crossing. Paton was off some place, but his nephew Ollie, after putting in a soporific eight hours at the sheriff's office, was minding Uncle Will's petrol pumps with the indolent good humour that made him such peaceful company. The beer was poor, thin stuff – almost as bad, Maybush considered, as that Colorado Kool-Aid some people went crazy over – but at least it was cold, and hanging out behind the pumps with Ollie was a lot less wearing than sitting in a dank tourist cabin with Webster Grose. Grose's disposition had been further soured by frequent gastrointestinal crises, the result of eating all his meals at the Dixie Diner where they hadn't changed the frying oil since Easter, and his diatribes against what he mistakenly imagined to be Southern cooking were varied only by outbursts of profane complaint from the bathroom itself. Agent Maybush couldn't figure out why the two of them were still here. He'd asked Grose and had been snubbed so soundly that he would have been prepared to bet Grose had no idea either but wasn't about to admit it. Four months' seniority and he thought he was the new J. Edgar Hoover. Maybush eased the tab off another can of beer and indulged himself with soothing visions of a future in which Grose had been permanently exiled to Montana.

The female child was clearly very sick, the blotched and crimson face so swollen that the eyes were mere watery slits, swallowed up like the rest of the features in a shiny, edematous mass. The major did not stay in the room any longer than it took him to verify her condition. Whatever was wrong with the brat – and no one in the house seemed able to give him a straight answer – the disease was probably as infectious as it was repulsive, and he didn't want to catch it. In any case, she was unlikely to be a source of useful information. The major had interrogated young children in the past and had found them unsatisfactory. The carefully calibrated psychological pressures so effective in dealing with adults were markedly less so when applied to an age-group that had not yet learned the difference between fantasy and reality. As for physical coercion, the operator was handicapped by unpredictable fluctuations in the durability of the subjects, some of whom showed a frustrating tendency to go into irreversible shock, with terminal results.

Normally he would have threatened the child as a means of putting pressure on the mother. However, the unexpected and inconvenient presence in the house of a cross section of locally prominent citizens, two of them law enforcement officers, made it difficult for the major to move ahead on orthodox lines without considering certain extraneous factors.

Crudely viewed, his options had been reduced to two: he and his unit could pursue their investigation with civility and restraint, in which case they would achieve nothing. Or they could employ their customary techniques, extort such information as these people might possess, and then terminate everyone on the premises and burn the place to the ground. The major's bias, by temperament and training, inclined him to the second of these two choices, although it seemed a pity about the house. He had been all over it, and it was just the kind of place he would have liked for himself. In need of modernization, of course – that bathroom was a nightmare – but the building was sound and beautifully maintained, and the proportions of the rooms were satisfying, even noble in their small-scale way. There were several really fine pieces of furniture, too. He'd have liked to spare the house, but standard operating procedure required its destruction.

Getting rid of its occupants posed no such ethical problem; there were far too many people in the world already. However, there were practical considerations. The removal of such a comparatively large and influential group risked causing a scandal that not even his superiors would be able to contain. It was annoying, too, that the doctor was away. They'd get him later, of course, but it would have to look like an accident. Unlike Aitken and his black bitch, who were marginal strays and would not be missed, the doctor was a professional man with some degree of standing among his peers. If he vanished, questions would be asked and if he died accidentally, no matter how discreetly it was managed, somebody might make undesirable connections between his death and the tragic fire at the Lainez farm. People nowadays were so damn suspicious.

The major left a man in the child's bedroom to maintain surveillance and, still undecided, went back downstairs. As he entered the kitchen a telephone began to ring. Chuck started to rise from his chair without thinking, and one of the guards lifted his weapon warningly.

'Get that,' the major snapped to no one in particular.

'I don't see the phone, sir,' said the man nearest to the sound, gazing around helplessly.

'It's in the closet, in the wall there,' Chuck said. The man opened the unlocked door and flinched at the sight of the shotgun in the rack on the back wall. The major would kick ass when he saw that – they ought to have checked the house for concealed weapons right after they moved in. Then he picked up the phone. After a moment he turned to the major.

'It's for you, sir. Code Red.'

While the major stood there, as rigidly at attention as a man can be while holding a telephone receiver in the operative position, the kitchen could almost be thought of as holding its breath. The scattered cards and the little piles of money on the table, along with the beer cans, the whisky glasses, and the ashtray with the sheriff's messily frayed cigar butts, were frozen in a pattern of vivid, unnatural significance, like the paraphernalia of some strange religion. The cats had gone into hiding, and Bagel, wailing like Marley's ghost, had been confined to the root cellar for his own protection before the major and his troops arrived. An eighty-seven-pound lapdog with oncoming habits was apt to be taken the wrong way. Everyone jumped when the piglet, waking famished and aggrieved at being kept waiting so long for its supper, set up a thin, furious squealing. One of the men swung around, machine pistol at the ready.

'It's a piglet, sir,' Daniel said soothingly. 'Just a little pig. In the box there, see? It's hungry, is all.'

'Make it shut up, then,' the man said. 'The major's on the phone. You just get down there, kid, and keep that thing quiet.'

'Affirmative, sir,' the major was saying. 'Understood. Routine retirement procedure, Code Red . . . No, sir, negative on that. No casualties at this time, sir, civilian or other . . . Affirmative. No sweat, sir.'

He replaced the receiver, tidily closed the cupboard door, and turned to the five men who still sat grouped around the table, as they had for the last twenty minutes.

'Gentlemen, excuse me,' he said and took a long breath which seemed to hurt him. 'I have to apologize for this – ah – incursion. It appears an error has been made. My superiors have instructed me to offer Mr Lainez their – ah – their sincere regrets, their very sincere regrets for any inconvenience we may have caused you as a result of this error. This most unfortunate error. Now if you'll forgive me, we'll be on our way.'

'Just a goddamn minute, Major,' said the big man who had first challenged him. Oh, Jesus, Chuck thought, don't blow it now, Hailey, let them go. Then he realized the sheriff was right.

277

Innocent people would not tamely settle for an apology after an incident like this; they would be furious, they would protest, they would demand satisfaction. And if one of them happened to be county sheriff, he'd insist on it. With his heart in his throat and his wife and children at hazard, Chuck offered up brisk simultaneous prayers to both his sets of gods and composed himself for disaster.

Gibbs was on his feet, very large and formidable, and plainly very angry. Even his paunch had a kind of majesty to it, a dignified buttress testifying to years of quiet prosperity. The major eyed him nervously.

'What about them geese?' Gibbs demanded.

'Excuse me?'

'Geese, boy, geese – big white critters with long necks and web feet. Just before you fellers come bustin' in here they was yellin' hell to breakfast, the way geese always do when something upsets 'em, which is what you done with that eggbeater of yours. Then there was some firin', and ain't nobody heard diddly-boo out of them birds since. You killed 'em, didn't you? They was makin' a racket, and one of you trigger-happy nitshits give 'em a burst.'

'I deeply regret –'

'You can regret all you want, sonny, but geese cost money. One gander, five geese, and as I recall one of them geese was on a settin' of eggs that was about due to hatch, so that's an additional financial loss right there. Wilful and *pree*-meditated destruction of private property. So you tell me now, who's goin' to compensate Mr Lainez? You all come marchin' in here, wavin' a whole lot of dangerous hardware and scarin' folks half to death, and that's bad enough. But mistakes will happen, and I don't believe anybody here is goin' to be bothered suin' the government for trespass, wrongful detention, extreme emotional anguish, or any of that stuff – although they *could*, you understand, and if they want to go ahead and do it they got all of us here for witnesses. But right now, what Mr Lainez wants to know is, who pays for the geese?'

'I'm afraid I have no authority –'

'Far's I can see, you didn't have no authority for one single thing you done since you got here, but it don't seem like you allowed that to incommode you none. I'm talkin' dollars and cents, Major, and I intend to have an answer.' The sheriff turned to Chuck. 'What you reckon it'll cost you to replace them birds?'

Chuck shook his head. 'It's not that simple,' he said. 'If I buy

278

mature birds, now that there's no colony already here for them to join, they won't settle down. I would have to keep them in the pen day and night, which means I'd have to feed them instead of letting them forage, and that would raise the cost to the point where it's no longer an economic proposition. No, I'll just have to start over with goslings, and that's a pain as well – raise them by hand, watch over them. It will be two, three years' work before I can replace what these people destroyed in five seconds.'

'So we got to take into account the cost of the goslings, plus feed, plus time and labour, plus fixin' up the pen which probably got shot to hell along with the geese, all added to the market value of the dead birds – Chuck, I believe you wouldn't come out even for less than seventy-five, eighty bucks.'

'Of course,' Chuck offered, getting into the spirit of the thing, 'it's possible one or two of the carcasses could be used for meat. They won't be fit to sell, but we might be able to salvage something for our own table. That would knock a few dollars off the total.'

'Only one way to find out, and that's go look. You better come along, Major.'

From his observation post in the tree, Tom Tulliver watched in wary disbelief as the little procession – Chuck, Gibbs, and one of the men in uniform – left the house and, using flashlights, made a lengthy inspection of the battered goose pen and its pathetic detritus of blood and feathers. Presently they returned, with the sheriff in fine voice.

'Wouldn't get a bowl of broth out of the whole damn lot,' he was proclaiming indignantly. 'And I don't want to hear any more about "puttin' in a claim through the appropriate channels", either. What'll happen, the "appropriate channels" goin' to say they never heard of you, and I don't blame 'em. If I'd never heard of you myself I'd be just as happy. Cash on the barrelhead, Major, or me and Will goin' to have to take you fellers into Cold Crossing and make further enquiries. There's a pair of FBI men hangin' around town wastin' the taxpayers' money. Maybe they'd like to sit in.'

They went back into the kitchen, where the major, scarlet with humiliation, went through his pockets, ordered his men to do the same (even the guard upstairs was sent for to add his contribution), and eventually came up with sixty-seven dollars and fifty-nine cents.

'You willin' to settle for that, Chuck?' asked Gibbs. 'Course, we all know it ought to be more, but this way at least you get *some* compensation. Start writin' letters and fillin' in forms and you'll still be goin' at it twelve months from now. If I's you, I'd take the cash.'

Chuck consented gracefully, wrote out a receipt for the money, and even went so far as to offer the deflated, and now penniless, commander of the murder squad some of Conor's good sour mash. This, however, was declined. Sheriff Gibbs accompanied the discomfited force to its transportation and stood there, grey hair fluttering wildly in the down draught, as the helicopter took off. He even waved goodbye – a formal, satirical side-to-side motion that semaphored 'good riddance' as clearly as if he had bellowed the words at the top of his lungs. Then he came slowly back, closing the pasture gate behind him as the sorely tried guernseys raced away once more in witless panic. Moving like a tired old man, he plodded along until he stood under the tree where Tom Tulliver sat hidden.

'You can come down now,' he said. Tom was so startled he nearly fell off his branch, which would have been the finish of them both.

'How d'you know I was here?' he enquired, recovering his balance and stroking his little eggs gently with his fingertips, as if they were children to be cajoled back to sleep.

'Your sister called me, soon's you left. That young woman got brains, unlike some folks I could put a name to. I spotted you right after I got here. But then I was kind of lookin' out for you,' he added consolingly. 'You figure to stay put up there enjoyin' the view all night?'

'No way. I got to lower something down first, though, before I can move, and – Sheriff?'

'Yeah?'

'What I got here is kind of – well – volatile, I guess you could call it. I'd feel better if you was to back off a piece. Like about fifty yards? And lay down flat with your arms over your head?'

'How you goin' to get the stuff down?'

'Got a piece of cord here; that's how I pulled 'em up. Gone let 'em down the same way, real slow and easy. Just it's kind of hard to see, with the ground in shadow, and if they land a little too quick that's all she wrote. So if you could back off, like I said . . .'

'Bullshit,' said Hailey Gibbs. 'You let 'em down slow, the way you said, and soon's I can reach 'em I'll take and steady 'em down

280

the rest of the way. Now you do like I say and don't talk so damn much. I'm in charge here.'

Ten sweaty minutes later the eggs were safely back inside their steel housing.

'Where's your car?' the sheriff asked.

'I come on a bike. Left it back at the fork. I didn't want to set the alarm off.'

'Come on in the house and get your breath back, have a drink, and then I'll give you a ride to the fork.'

'I don't need a drink.'

'I do. You ought to call your sister, too, tell her you're okay. Not that you deserve to be, foolin' with stuff like that. Leave them buggers right here, we'll pick 'em up when we leave. And I never seen 'em, understand? Where d'you ever get hold of 'em anyhow?'

'Off a friend of Sam's. In New York.'

'New York? Oh well, that's all right, then. Don't believe I'm obligated to do nothing about that. They can take care of their own crazy people up there. I'm just a dumb old country lawman; I can't get the whole world shaped up all by myself. Got enough crazies here in Aurora County to keep me occupied.'

In the kitchen, Chuck, Carl Brackage, and the Paton brothers were already into the whisky. The poker game had been abandoned by common consent. Their hearts had not been in it in the first place, and certainly nobody felt like going back to it now. Gibbs leaned over the table to glance idly at Chuck's cards.

'Lord God,' he said. 'You know what you got here?'

Chuck looked up. 'I wasn't paying much attention,' he said. 'Why, what's wrong?'

'Aces and eights, boy, that's what's wrong. Aces and eights. Same cards Bill Hickok had, day he got careless and sat with his back to the door. That's the Dead Man's Hand.' He walked over and lightly, reverently, laid his palm on the top of Chuck's sleek black head.

'Always touch a lucky man,' he said. 'Sometimes a little bit rubs off.'

Later, the sheriff dropped Tom off at the fork, helped stow the metal box, and waited to watch its imperturbable guardian start on his way. Then he drove to his own home in Cold Crossing. It was a big old house, much too big and empty now with his wife dead, the girls off and married, and Bobby Lee away in the hospital up north. It wasn't as comfortable, either, as it had been when Jane was alive. She'd had a knack of spreading comfort, and the worn, old-fashioned furniture had fitted him like an old jacket. After her death the girls had cleared out a lot of things – nothing but dust catchers, they'd called them – and made him buy new stuff that they said was more up-to-date. Sectionals, and Danish modern, and a rocker-recliner in dog-vomit vinyl that was cold and clammy in winter and hot and clammy in summer. Looking back, the sheriff was amazed that he'd let them do it, but he'd been so miserable at the time, he hadn't really cared. Nowadays he lived mostly in the kitchen – not that they hadn't gotten their well-meaning paws on that too, but at least in the kitchen he didn't have to sit and look at sculptured wall-to-wall carpeting cunningly made to resemble cowpats in an ill-kept barnyard. Leaving his car under the carport, he went first to the kitchen. The whole house was in darkness, but he did not turn on the lights.

'Kate?' he said softly. 'It's me. You all right, girl?'

There was a sudden rush of movement, and a wild projectile, all arms and legs and rounded chest, thumped into him headlong.

'Oh, Sheriff, I've been going crazy! I didn't know what was happening, and you were gone so long!'

She was shivering, and he wrapped his long arms around her and patted her back. 'Hush now,' he said, 'take it easy. Everything's fine.'

'Did they come?'

'Sure did. It was a little hairy there, for a while. But Conor must've done what he set out to, 'cause they was still tryin' to make their minds up whether to give us a real hard time when the feller that sent 'em called up, and after that they went off just as nice as pie. Only thing got hurt was the geese, and we made 'em pay for those. Now you slip out and get in the back of the car and lay down, and I'll take you home.'

'But I want to know what *happened*.'

'Chuck'll tell you all about it when you get there. Just let's you and me move on out. I'm an old man and I need my rest.'

Colonel Rupert Lund sat straight-backed in a black swivel chair in the small private office adjoining the control room at Lurie Field. He had not moved for some time. Fidgeting was a sign of weakness and one that no real man would permit himself. He very much wanted to let his right hand slide into his pocket, but consciously resisted the impulse. He was not some neurotic housewife who creeps downstairs at three in the morning because she can't remember whether she turned the oven off. He was a colonel of Marines, a responsible and disciplined officer, and once he had taken care of something it was taken care of. He knew what he had in his pocket; he didn't need to fondle it just to reassure himself it was still there. But he wanted to, and the desire in itself was a weakness. His thin mouth drew down at the corners in self-disgust. With his spotlessly clean hands clasped on the desk in front of him, clasped tightly to keep that right hand from sneaking towards the pocket, he waited for word of the returning helicopter.

A baby-faced boy in uniform tapped on the half-open door and entered, looking nervous.

'Colonel, sir. Major McMichaels says you asked to be notified when we heard from Alpha Foxtrot.'

'I'm aware of that, soldier.'

'Yes, sir. Sorry, sir. They just called in. They expect to touch down in twelve minutes.'

'Very well. Radio back and tell them on no account to leave the aircraft before I come aboard. I'll be waiting for them on the runway. No one is to leave the aircraft until he has been personally debriefed by me.'

'Yes, sir.'

The six-foot child saluted, wheeled smartly, and marched out. Normally things weren't too formal at Lurie, but this Colonel Lund had a very tightening effect. The young corporal had never met him before, and would not mind in the least if he never did again.

The men in the control tower could not hear the chopper's engine through their soundproof windows, but they could talk with the pilot and watch the ungainly craft creep through the air, hover briefly, wobbling a little like an overloaded bumblebee, and then drop gently down by inches to settle on the asphalt. One of the watchers took off his headphones and walked over to stand by a window.

'That guy Lund certainly is on the prod,' he said over his shoulder. 'He's right out there, stiffer'n my granddaddy's hat rack, waiting for 'em to get the door open. Man, he's looking mad. Ground crew got the steps in place, but it looks like he don't want 'em around – he's waving 'em off and they're heading back inside. Don't blame the guy; he just don't want to be contaminated. You can pick up a social disease from a ground crew at a range of one hundred feet if you're fool enough to get downwind of 'em. That's a scientific fact. There goes Colonel God now, stomping up the steps.' He switched to the nasal bellow of a track announcer. '*And* he's almost up at the top, *and* he's through the starting gate, *and* now he's out of sight on the backstretch. We don't know who has the lead; it's anybody's race but the smart money's on the colonel, *and* – Oh Jesus! Jesus *Christ*!'

There was no need to tell the others what was happening, even if he had been capable of it. Through the floor-to-ceiling glass of the tower, they had a grandstand view. The Huey had blossomed into a glorious orange flower, streaked with scarlet and white. For one second, five seconds, it shone like some incredible Fourth of July extravaganza, before billowing black smoke poured out to smear the terrible brightness that had swallowed Alpha Foxtrot and every soul on board.

It was their last night, and at first Kate had been morose and unloving, lying curled in a sulky ball with her back to him, angry tears slipping sideways across her face to wet the linen pillowcase. Half of him was consumed with sympathy and remorse, and the other half wanted to smack her. It was their last night, and she was wasting it. But presently she stopped crying and allowed him to kiss her wet cheeks and stroke her hair as, little by little, he persuaded her hostile body to uncurl. Now, much later, she lay collapsed against him, throat arched, lips parted, slack in the aftermath of tension repeatedly, explosively released. The harsh, runner's gasps muted and slowed as her breathing steadied. In the candlelight a faint shimmer of sweat gleamed on her skin, outlining the curve of a breast, the nipple small and soft after love. He bent his head and kissed her eyelids, oily-damp against his mouth.

'You look so beautiful like that,' he said. 'Innocent satisfaction of innocent greed. "What is it men in women do require? The lineaments of gratified desire."'

'William Blake,' she murmured, conscientious but drowsy. 'I never quite knew what it meant.'

'You do now, I hope.' His hand rested between her thighs, cupping, cosseting. 'I love playing with you and making you come; in a way it's almost better than fucking. One's not distracted by one's own sensations.'

'That's a little kinky, isn't it?'

'Certainly not.' He pinched, evilly, and she let out an indignant yip. 'Now that's kinky,' he continued. 'Deliberately inflicting pain. I like to inflict pleasure, which is a power trip too, I suppose, but comparatively harmless.' His voice dropped to a lecherous growl. 'I'm a kind master; I'm good to my slaves. Every night I go to the slave quarters, pick out a girl, take off all her clothes. The others look on enviously as I lead her away, naked and trembling, to my sumptuous private apartments.'

'Are you naked and trembling too?'

'Of course not, I'm the prince. I have these absolutely smashing robes, gold tissue and embroidered crimson silk and whatnot.

And a bloody great emerald collar round my neck, I think, don't you?'

'Sounds faggy.'

'A lot you know about it. Anyway, I arrange her on the bed, legs nicely parted, and secure her wrists and ankles with massive chains.'

'Oh, not chains, Conor. How cruel.'

'*Padded* chains,' he explained loftily. 'The parts that actually touch the skin are lined with lots of lovely foam rubber.'

'Well that's okay, I guess. What's the bed like?'

'An immense four-poster, covered with white fur rugs.'

'Hey, fantastic. Not very practical though – think of the cleaning bills.'

'I refuse to think of anything so boring, and do stop interrupting. Whose fantasy is this, anyway?'

'Ours,' said Kate firmly, and he laughed.

'How very improper. Where had I got to?'

'She's chained to the bed, naked and trembling.'

'Oh, goody. I cast off my robes and loom over her helpless form, murmuring lascivious details of all the marvellous depraved things I'm going to do to her, while I fondle her with excruciating delicacy. Then, when the poor thing's practically beside herself, I take pity on her. No, keep still; you're chained, remember? You can writhe a bit, but you can't go hurling yourself about. I open the lips of her creamy little cunt, and I lick it and suck it and tease it with my fingers and make her come and come and come until she's exhausted. Does this turn you on at all?'

'If you'd take these damn chains off I'd show you. What happens next?'

'She's lying there in a sexual stupor, satisfied beyond her wildest dreams, thinking it's all over now and she can go to sleep. Suddenly she gives a start. Her eyes fly open and she whimpers in alarm, because my hand has begun to move again between her legs, and I do this, and then I do this . . .'

Conor's hand, from being quiescent as a warm cushion, suddenly reacquired fingers – intrusive, experimental fingers, eliciting soft mews of protest and pleasure.

'Conor I can't – mmmmm – I can't possibly, it's too much.'

'Nonsense. The Chinese, now,' he informed her (fingers independently, deliciously busy), 'the Chinese , before they came over all Calvinist and lost interest in sex, had some very interesting theories. One of which was that a woman ought to have seven orgasms to a man's one. And since I'm old and tired and generally not the devil with the women that I used to be in the dear dead days when the reg'ment was stationed at 'Pindi ... Oh, God.'

'What?'

'You have simply no idea at all what you do to me. Feeling you all slippery and melting and excited, and knowing I did that. It makes me positively weak with lust. How about if I unfasten this little chain, and then I take your hand like this and put it just here ...'

'You call that weak? It feels pretty powerful to me,' she said, as he surged and thickened under her fingers. 'You and your old lust. Lie a little, why don't you? Tell me you love me.'

'Of course I do, you ninny. What's more I'll respect you in the morning, too, I swear I will.' He slid over on top of her, gliding inside her welcoming body with a grateful sigh. 'O my America, my new found land. Oh, Kate, my blessed girl, I love you so.'

'It's an unusual situation,' the chief of surgery said. 'Irregular, really, I guess. But I like the boy, and I'd like to help him. So if a big shot like Walter Brehn is prepared to come up here and try that microsplice technique of his on Bobby Lee, you're not going to hear any argument from me. I'll give Brehn the whole mothering hospital if it'll do any good. You have to remember, though, there's no guarantee this'll work.'

He got up from behind his desk, walked over to a corner closet, reached up to the top shelf and took down a pack of cigarettes. He lit one, replaced the pack, closed the door, came back, and sat down again.

'Trying to cut down,' he explained. 'The idea is that every time you smoke you have to stop what you're doing and go through this damn fool rigmarole. You're deliberately choosing to have a cigarette, instead of just lighting up automatically, and it helps you cut down. Or that's the theory.'

'Does it work?'

'I'm still getting through two packs a day, but I guess the exercise is good for me. Now where were we? Oh yes: this is no certified cure-all, this operation. It's new, it's experimental, and while Dr Brehn's had some successes with it, I can't say to you that after surgery Bobby Lee's going to be okay, because we don't know that. Also, all surgical intervention carries its own risks. This is a lengthy and complex procedure, and the insult to the body is massive. What I'm saying is, the body may die. On the other hand, what kind of a life does he have now?'

The doctor ruffled his hair until it stood on end, and glared across the desk. 'If you ever tell anyone I said what I just said,' he rumbled, 'I'll deny it. But some of the cases we see here, you wonder what the fuck the triage nurses thought they were doing. What Bobby Lee has now, maybe, is a chance; and it's the only chance left, because I'll level with you, we're not up to that kind of stuff around here. We do a good job, but miracles are beyond us. Down in New York, at Special Surgery, Brehn's been doing two, three miracles a month. Maybe he can pull one off for your boy. Don't get your hopes up, now, but this guy's the top man in his field, and even if it doesn't work out for the kid, at least you'll know he had the best.'

Sheriff Gibbs nodded slowly. 'That's all I want,' he said. 'I just want to be sure we tried ever'thing.'

The surgeon looked curiously at the bulky old man in front of him. His clothes weren't shabby, you couldn't quite call them that, but they'd clearly seen a lot of wear, and so had their owner. And in all the time his son had been a patient at Brackley, the old man had never once given a hint that he might have important connections. He'd been concerned, he'd been stubborn and argumentative when the situation had seemed to him to warrant it, but never once had he thrown his weight around, or even implied that he could do so if it suited him. He'd just been the worried, ageing father of a quadriplegic son. Now all of a sudden, when they were about to ship Bobby Lee Gibbs out because there was nothing more they could do for him, had come this letter from a world-famous neurosurgeon, politely requesting permission to use the facilities at Brackley for a revolutionary surgical procedure, to be performed upon one Pfc. Gibbs, R.E.L. The chief of surgery was genuinely attached to young Gibbs, and delighted at his good fortune, but he was also inquisitive.

'You have some kind of an edge with Dr Brehn, is that it? Knew him way back when? Saved his life in the war or something?' The doctor was making a joke of it, but he really wanted to know.

'No, sir.' Gibbs shook his big head. 'I never met Dr Brehn. Friend of mine, though, he knows him. Reckon he put in a word for Bobby Lee.'

'It must have been a very forceful word.'

The sheriff's face creased in a startlingly attractive smile – amused, reminiscent, and very fond. 'I believe it probably was,' he said. 'This friend, he's kind of a forceful feller.'

Kate was in the visitors' lounge, looking a frump in the oversized gingham housedress they'd bought her on the way north. Pink-lensed aviator glasses hid a third of her face, and her telltale hair was stuffed out of sight under a polyester scarf in a sickly shade of lavender. Gibbs had started to walk right by her before he remembered. He took her by the arm and walked her to the parking lot. There, leaning on the door of his old Ford, he told her about Bobby Lee's last chance.

Kate wiped her eyes, blew her nose, and achieved a huge, watery grin.

'Oh that's so great,' she said. 'That's just so great. I'm so happy for you. And Conor did that?' The painful pleasure of saying his name made her eyes fill up again, but the sheriff tactfully pretended not to notice.

'He gets around, old Conor does,' he said. 'Pushin' out a secretary of state, puttin' the blocks to the CIA, stoppin' a war – well it ain't over yet, but it will be. Little thing like fixin' things up for my boy, that's just a five-minute chore. Kind of thing you fit in between feedin' the hogs and hosin' down the barn.'

He looked at his watch. 'We got a while,' he said. 'Don't want to show up too early. On th' other hand, there's too many folks altogether that knows a little bit about all this, and half of 'em I wouldn't trust around a glass corner. Including your daddy. No offence. So I figure what we'll do, we'll get ourselves into that town right away, while there's still a mess of traffic and plenty of folks on the street. Once we're in, we can take a little time out some place. Go see a movie, maybe. I ain't been to a movie since *True Grit*. Course they show 'em on the TV, but they chop 'em up into such little bitty pieces you can't follow 'em. Just when you think you got a hold of what's goin' on, some faggot with a lot of teeth starts trying to sell you a lawn mower or something, and you got to start all over.'

'A movie would be fine,' Kate said.

'That's what we'll do, then. And when it's time, I'll just drop you off and light out for home. Anybody want to ask me questions, I can prove where I been, and why.'

They stopped at a McDonald's for cheeseburgers and french fries. Kate thought nostalgically of the feasts at the farm, and then thought of Conor again and had to leave most of her cheeseburger under the paper napkin, because her throat seemed to have swollen up inside. Hailey Gibbs stood treat, as he did later at the movies, and Kate couldn't argue since she had no money. They sat through a scratchy print of *High Noon* at a dilapidated rerun theatre, partly because it was close to the rendezvous point and partly because the sheriff had a great respect for Gary Cooper; as he pointed out, they were in the same line of business. The audience seemed to be almost entirely made up of students from Beresford, and at first Kate was terrified of being seen by someone she knew. But after a while the movie took over, and she was too busy being more and more enraged with that little prig Grace Kelly to worry about anything else.

It was quite dark when they came out. They left the sheriff's car parked where it was, and walked until they reached the entrance to the tiny public garden. There was a fountain in the centre, and around the basin, set back far enough to avoid the splash, were eight curved wooden benches. Two young people were mildly necking on one, and a number of children who ought to have been in bed hours before were romping on another. The rest were empty, except for a woman in a dark skirt and a white shirt sitting quite alone and motionless, with her hands folded in her lap.

'That your mother, Kate?'

'Yes.'

'You go on, then.' He gave her a little push. 'And come back down and see us real soon, you hear?'

She took a step forward, then turned back quickly and gave the sheriff a hug and a kiss on his wrinkled cheek. 'Bobby Lee will be all right, you'll see,' she whispered. 'I know he will. And Sheriff? Thank you. Thank you for everything. And I love you.'

She walked slowly, hesitantly along the gravel path, through the darkness under the trees, and came out again into the lighted area around the fountain.

'Mama?' Kate said – Kate, who had addressed Charlotte firmly as 'mother' since the fifth grade. 'Mama? I'm back.'

Sheriff Gibbs was stopped three times before he drove clear of New Lymington, and each time the pattern repeated itself: aggressive excitement at the sight of his licence plates, followed by disappointment when he showed his official ID. When the officers asked him, most politely, what he was doing so far from home, he was able to answer them with the amiability of a man telling, if not the whole truth, at least nothing but the truth. They didn't even bother to write down the name of the surgeon at

Brackley VA Hospital. They had picked up a number of indignant smalltime sinners in the trawl, which was some compensation for not so far having found the man they'd been ordered to look for; but this old country sheriff with the big smile and the slow, southern voice was so obviously genuine there was no need to waste time checking him out.

Once he'd put the first hundred miles between himself and Kate Harper the sheriff pulled off the highway and found a motel. No sense pushing too hard. If Bobby Lee was going to be coming home one of these days, he'd need his daddy around to take care of him. Before he went to bed, Gibbs charmed a handful of change out of the motel manager and used the pay phone to call his daughter Elizabeth in Cold Crossing. After giving her the good news about Bobby Lee, he asked her to call the Lainez farm and relay it to Conor.

'Tell him ever'thing went off just fine. Ever'thing. Tell him I'm about to have a good night's sleep, and there ain't no reason in the world why he can't do the same. You just be sure and tell him that.'

'What about these maternity clothes?' said Kate's Aunt Louisa. 'Do you want to pack them, or shall I pass them on to the rector's wife for the jumble sale?'

'Let's have a bonfire in the courtyard and incinerate the lot.'

'Darling, how rude. Inverness is hardly the fashion hub of Europe but I did my best. As a matter of fact they may come in handy. I think Kirstie's been at it again – she's got that look, half sheepish and half pleased with herself. I give her another week before she corners me in the breakfast room, says "Och, Madam!" and bursts into tears. What a prospect. I might as well be running a day nursery.'

Louisa Fleming subsided onto Kate's bed, kicked her shoes off, and lit a cigarette. 'Stop pootering and sit down a minute,' she directed. 'There won't be time to talk in the morning – getting off is always such a muddle – and while I don't want to be a nag I *am* concerned about you.'

Kate perched on the broad stone windowsill. Louisa tossed a pillow at her. 'Put that under you, fathead; you'll get piles.'

'You sound like Nanny Bristow.'

'Lucky for you I'm not. I can just imagine Nanny Bristow's views on unwed mothers. Be serious, will you, Kate. What are your plans? It's all very well waltzing calmly back to Walden Avenue with a little stranger and no explanation, but what *will* people say? I know your dismal pa's not secretary of state any more, but he's still a national figure. Make no mistake, an ever-so-slightly illegit grandchild is going to raise one hell of a lot of eyebrows. You'll be besieged by reporters.'

'I don't care.'

'You will when you can't wheel Lottie Claire's carriage outdoors without forty flashbulbs popping in her face. Anyhow, think of Charlotte. Horrid for her.'

'I suppose it will be, poor mother, but she's determined to have me come home. Besides, what else can I do? I can't batten on you and Alastair for ever. And if you do so much as whisper the word adoption, I shall scream,' she added quickly.

'So I should hope; it's far too late for that. I admit I pushed the idea slightly before she was born, but once you've fed them that's *it*, even I know that. What about this young man who keeps writing you letters?'

'Charlie? Oh, come on, Louisa, I can't marry Charlie.'

'Why not? He doesn't have two heads, does he? Your mother says you've known him for ever and he's a very nice boy. And he's prepared to take the baby as well, which is really a very generous offer.'

Kate made a vulgar noise. 'He can stick it in his ear,' she said ungratefully. 'Look, I don't in the least want to be married to Charlie, and after the first chivalrous glow wore off I bet you anything he wouldn't like being married to me either.'

'So you get a divorce; at least you'll have *been* married. You've led a sheltered life, you don't know what people can be like.'

'I told you, I don't care.'

'I heard you, and I think you're being terribly selfish. Think what it'll be like for poor Lottie Claire in a few years' time. Other children are so cruel, you can't want to expose her to that.'

Kate slid down from the windowsill and came over to sit on the end of the bed, nipping at Louisa's toes through her sensible wool tights.

'This little piggy went to market –'

Louisa screeched and retracted her feet under her quarter-inch-thick Harris tweed skirt, accepted defence against the rigours of a Scottish spring. 'You little horror,' she said. 'It's a good thing you're going home. How I've put up with you all these months I can't imagine.'

'You're an angel of patience, and so's Alastair. Even the boys have been darling, although I do think Lachlan was a little out of line, drawing that big red A in Magic Marker on the front of my best smock.'

'Kate, he didn't! Why didn't you tell me? I'd have skinned him alive.'

'That's why I didn't tell you. After all it was pretty funny, and I didn't have too much to laugh at right around then.'

'I'll say this for you, you do have guts,' Louisa told her with affection. 'And believe me, you'll need them.' She prodded Kate's midriff with her toes. 'Lovely and flat again, aren't you? What it is to be young. Listen, Katie-lamb, if it gets too awful you can always come back here, you know. The flower of Highland manhood would be hammering at the gates in a minute. We've

ever had a wedding at the castle, or not in my time. We could
put on a super bash.'

Louisa's fine-boned, mischievous face wore the expression of
one suddenly preoccupied with such concerns as heavily
decorated, leaden fruitcakes, tiny sandwiches containing fish
paste, and cases of Krug champagne. Kate, however, was not to
be enticed by catering.

'The trouble with your generation is you think a husband is the
answer to everything, and it's not. Look at mother.'

'On the other hand, look at me. And God knows, sweetie, I
am not a prude. I'm all in favour of people shacking up, or
whatever it's called, if that's their thing, but a baby's another
matter. You do have to think of the future. Babies aren't like the
mumps or something; once you've had them you *have* them.
They're *there*, and before you know it they'll be fourteen years
old with spots. It's no use just waffling along as if everything
would solve itself, because it won't. I suppose the father –'

'Shut up, Lou,' Kate said. 'You're a honey and I love you, but
shut up. I'm not going to discuss it. I don't know where he is,
there's no way I can contact him, and I wouldn't if I could, so
forget it, okay?'

'Does Lottie look like him at all?' Louisa pursued, unsnubbable.

'Yes she does. Now cut it out, will you?' Kate got off the bed
and went back to emptying dresser drawers. 'Do you think the
rector's wife might like one argyle kneesock, low mileage, driven
by a little old pregnant lady on Sundays only? I can't find the mate
anywhere; one of the dogs must have eaten it.'

'Any luck?' Alastair Fleming asked his wife later, as she sat
brushing her hair before coming to bed.

'Not a sausage. She refused to talk about the man, but she
won't even consider anyone else,' Louisa complained, sending
the bristles hissing through her red-gold mane. '*I* think she's still
besotted with him. She's being noble, that's what it is. Doesn't
want him to know about the baby because he might feel in duty
bound to marry her, and she'd rather not have him at all than have
him on those terms. Heaven protect us from children with
principles. I know I bitch about Lachie and Dand but at least
neither one of them would recognize an ethical dilemma if it was
gnawing on his ankle.'

'A reprehensible viewpoint. You're a bad mother,' said the laird.

'Yes, isn't it restful? Seventy-two, seventy-three . . .'

'Wish I could lay my hands on the bugger, I'd sort him out,' Alastair said balefully. 'But we don't even know who he is.'

'Speak for yourself.'

'What? Lou you *devil*, what have you been up to?'

Louisa gave him her wicked, triangular cat smile. 'Interfering,' she said. 'Well damn it, somebody had to. Not only do I know all about Kate's demon lover but I've had a delicious lunch with her unofficial father-in-law. At the Ritz, I might add. Sole meunière, crepes suzette, and a very respectable port with the Stilton. Eighty-six, eighty-seven, eighty-eight . . .'

Alastair erupted out of bed in his striped pyjamas and snatched the hairbrush away from her. 'Come across or I'll skelp you,' he snarled, coming over all Scots in the heat of the moment. 'And I want it straight, mind – forget the bloody menu.'

'You're not to breathe a word to Kate, then, but I've been sitting on this one so long I'll burst if I don't tell someone. A couple of months ago I heard from Charlotte. She'd had a letter from a Mrs Lainez, who lives on this farm place where Kate was. The woman was worried about Kate. She didn't know about the baby, she was just in a fuss because she'd written Kate several times and had no answer, so she took the logical next step and wrote to her mother. Charlotte didn't send me the letter, but she said it was very touching and sweet, and the upshot was she went down there to see Mrs Lainez for herself. They took to each other, I guess, because Mrs L. told Charlotte everything.'

'Was the chap there too?'

'No, no. He's in Ireland, at one of the big hospitals in Belfast. He's a surgeon, specializes in children, Charlotte says.'

'Is he married?'

'He was, but his wife's dead so there's no problem.'

'What a thing to say.'

'Well I know it sounds callous, but I'm only being practical. His name's Kilmoyes, by the way. He went to Eton, and his father's a general, no less. Retired, of course. They're Anglo-Irish, which is a bit of luck because that means they're Protestant. The last thing we need is a lot of old priests mumbling around being difficult. He lives near Cork – the father that is – and Charlotte sent me his address.'

'So being the world's prime busybody, naturally you sat down and wrote to him.'

'Naturally. For one thing I love Kate dearly and I want her to be happy. For another, I don't believe in marriage between first cousins, and in case you haven't noticed, Lachie's falling head over heels. I never saw a worse case of sheep's eyes in my life. shan't have a moment's peace of mind till that girl is safely hitched. I don't know what it is about her lately but no man is safe. Even the postie falls apart when she says good morning, and he's the sort that wouldn't bat an eye if it was Raquel Welch in a see-through nightie. Anyhow, General Kilmoyes wrote me a very nice letter back, and we made a plan. And then when I went down to London last week he popped over to Heathrow and took me to lunch.'

'New drawing-room curtains from Harrods forsooth. I might have known there was more to it than that.'

'Well, I do think you might. After all, one can get quite adequate curtains made in Edinburgh, but you're so trusting.'

'I never will be again. And I hardly like to ask, but did you really order new curtains?'

'Certainly I did, I may be devious at times but I *never* tell lies. Dove grey watered silk with a narrow stripe of charcoal and cinnamon. You'll faint when the bill comes but they're going to look sensational. Put that hairbrush down, Alastair, if you hit me you'll be sorry. The general is an absolute dear, with the most gorgeous silver hair just like Lloyd George – all right, all *right*! He married rather late, sort of fortyish, and his wife died young. This is his only child, and spoiled rotten I shouldn't wonder, but that's Kate's problem not mine, thank heaven.'

'Did you tell the general about Lottie Claire?'

'Yes of course, and he was thrilled, bless him, only he thinks it would be better if they got married. I said I thought so too, and we cooked up an extremely shaky plot which I am *not* going to tell you about in case it doesn't work out, but keep your fingers crossed. Oh, and General Kilmoyes knows your mother. He used to run across her at deb dances when she was a girl, although I can't picture your mother ever being a girl – still, we are as God made us and I'm not saying a word against her, not one word. But that makes him almost one of the family, doesn't it?'

'God forbid,' Alastair said with feeling. 'Although it could be worse, I suppose. At least the wretched girl didn't fall for a ticket-of-leave man with a wife and six starving children.'

'I should think not indeed. I always knew it would turn out to be someone perfectly acceptable, Kate has excellent taste. After all she *is* my niece.'

*

It was nearly one o'clock in the morning, with a cold spring rain falling, and the hospital parking lot was deserted except for one man, a distracted figure striding back and forth, his green smock flapping dankly about him. Archibald Conor Kilmoyes, MD, FRCS, was as close to despair as he had ever been.

It wasn't just the work. The injuries were obscene, but no worse than he was used to, and at least there were none of the napalm burns that had haunted his nightmares for years. Also, these children were stronger to begin with, relatively well cared for and well fed. They could survive wounds that would have finished a Vietnamese child within hours. What he had not been prepared for, and could find no way of handling, was the hate. Seven-year-olds bragging of what they'd do to the dirty Prods when they got out, and bright-eyed little boys of nine and ten heatedly arguing the merits of various forms of homemade petrol bomb, as they surreptitiously poked lollipop sticks under casts to scratch the itches.

An hour ago one child – a new patient, whose left thigh was so badly shattered that months of surgery, years even, lay ahead of him – had confided to Conor in his hoarse, street arab voice that he'd killed a soldier last winter. Well, not all by himself – it was him and his big brother Ned. Got the bastard with a brick, Neddy had, knocked him cold, and then they'd done him with his own bayonet. Almost certainly the story wasn't true. What had driven Conor out, bareheaded and coatless, into the wet, was how much the child wanted it to be true. He yearned to have done it, he was on fire with the great slaughterous image of it, and if the doctors could rebuild his bones and muscles skilfully enough so that eventually he could walk on two legs again, then probably one day he really would do it. The boy was twelve now; he'd be fourteen at least before he was off crutches, and they took them young in the Provos.

Conor's crepe-soled shoes made only a faint, sucking slap on the ground, and the rain was one of those deadly, soundless Irish downpours, so the crisp footfalls coming up behind him were clearly audible. *Well if it's a bloody gunman that'll solve all my problems*, he thought, wheeling to confront the danger and finding himself looking down at a tiny woman in a dark cloak, her grey hair drawn back smoothly under a stiff white cap of antique and frivolous design.

'Matron! What on earth are you doing out here at this hour?'

'I saw you from the window. The Fallon girl died. We couldn't have saved her but the parents were hoping still – you know how people do. I've been with them just now. The mother's out of her mind with grief, poor soul. I said the same things I always say, and for all the good it did I might as well have read them the Act of Establishment in Chinese. One of these days I shall lose my head entirely and tell the bereaved the truth – that if God's not dead then He's retired, and we're on our own with neither rhyme nor reason to any of it.' She cocked her head sideways at him and gave him a little rueful smile. Then she looked more closely. 'Dear man, you're drenched,' she said. 'Do you not have a mackintosh?'

'I suppose so, somewhere. I wasn't thinking.' He told her about the new patient, and she shook her head.

'Jesus, Mary, and Joseph, what's to be done with these children? But fretting yourself to flinders won't help. You look dreadful, Mr Kilmoyes. Have you not been sleeping?'

'Not very well, no.'

He did not tell Matron that even when he did fall asleep it was worse than lying awake, because with sleep came the dream. The details varied, but in essence it was always the same dream. He was an intern again, on ER duty, and an ambulance came sirening out of the night with a cargo of casualties. 'This one first,' the triage nurse urged him, and he worked like a galley slave on the boy with the crushed chest. Miraculously, he got him stabilized, and turned at last to the next victim. It was Kate, and she had bled to death not three feet away from him. He grabbed the triage nurse by the arm, shouting, and she was not the nurse at all but Sam Aitken, with half of his head blown away.

Matron was looking at him with concern, and he wondered what had been happening to his face.

'You could ask one of the house doctors to prescribe something for you,' she said doubtfully. He shook his head.

'Downers to get to sleep, uppers to get going in the morning. No thanks. I'll stay off that merry-go-round as long as I can.'

'You should get away for a while, you know. Otherwise it's yourself will go to pieces and be no use to anyone. I know what I'm talking about, my dear, I've seen too much of it. The only ones who can keep on without a break are the ones that don't care.'

'Matron darling, you're a fraud. I happen to know you haven't had a holiday in eight years. Can you stand there and tell me you, of all people, don't care?'

'It's not the same thing at all. I'm an administrator. If my

298

temper's gone or my judgement's faulty I may drive my staff to drink, but I won't be killing patients.'

Conor winced, and she put out a rope-veined hand and rested it for a moment on his sopping green sleeve.

'It hasn't come to that yet, Mr Kilmoyes, and it won't if you're sensible. Now get out of those wet things and run away home. And think about what I've said. I must go. Good night.'

Her small navy-blue shape vanished in the drizzling dark. He watched the white, disembodied half circle of her cap bob briskly along until it disappeared through a distant doorway, and thought that she was a harsh woman, possibly a saint, and almost certainly right. He didn't like her any the better for it.

When Conor walked through the gate at Cork airport two days later, he was still in a vile mood, and finding Zorba the Mick waiting for him instead of the general did nothing to improve matters. Zorba the Mick, whose real name was Dennis Cafferty, was married to Bridget, who had been the general's housekeeper for thirty years. His presence at the airport meant that Conor would have to drive the old Daimler himself, since no one not prompted by an uncontrollable death wish would voluntarily submit to Dennis's driving.

Conor just didn't feel up to it. He had looked forward to slouching in the passenger seat with his eyes closed, breathing the cool damp air, lulled by his father's gently plaintive comments on the world, the weather, the Irish postal system, and the vagaries of his new Labrador retriever, a beautiful moron suitably named Widgeon. What he absolutely did not want was to take the wheel, negotiate twenty miles of lovely countryside and shameful roads, dodge three trucks and one tractor blundering around corners on the wrong side, and be subjected yet again to Dennis's highly coloured recollections of the Easter Rising, an heroic fiasco he had in fact been too young, and much too frightened, to take part in.

At last Conor drove through the lodge gates, avoided the worst of the driveway's potholes by some form of reflex radar, managed not to flatten the idiot Widgeon, who loved the Daimler and wanted to play with it, and coasted to a stop outside the front door. He left Dennis to put the car away and stumbled into the house, tipsy with weariness but vaguely comforted, as always, to be home. Bridget met him in the hall and took the overnight bag from his hand.

'Mr Archy, my dear, you'll be wanting your tea. The general says you're to go straight in. I'll bring a fresh pot directly.'

Started without him, had they? That meant company. What a time to choose. Here's hoping it's not the vicar, Conor thought uncharitably. One more crack about Christian witness out of that old bat and I'll strangle him with his own collar. Oh well, better get it over. Conor opened the drawing-room door.

The Queen Anne wing chairs flanking the fireplace were occupied by two elderly gnomes, both wearing disgraceful tweeds that looked almost as ancient as their owners. The older of the two had very blue eyes, a cloud of shining white hair, and, at the moment, an uncharacteristically shifty expression.

'My dear chap, how splendid. You couldn't have come at a better time,' the general said, avoiding Conor's eye. 'There's Billy Fitz, the decent man, come to give me a going-over and stayed for a little something.'

'So I see. How are you, Billy?' Dr William Fitzgerald, the Kinsale GP, was several cuts above the vicar.

'Better than you, if appearances are anything to go by,' said the fierce little man. 'My God, Archy, don't those heathen Ulstermen feed you at all? You've lost half a stone.'

'He lives on cold sausage rolls and whisky,' the general said gloomily. 'If he didn't come down here at weekends for a bit of Bridget's cooking he'd starve to death. Sit down, old boy, sit down. Have a scone.'

After Bridget had cleared away the remnants of a substantial tea, Conor headed for the drinks tray, but Dr Fitzgerald stopped him.

'Before we get our noses into a jar, come with me to the study a minute and I'll run a stethoscope over you.'

'Like hell you will. There's nothing the matter with me.'

'You've got the shakes, you're underweight, and you're the colour of the main attraction at a three-day wake, otherwise you're fine. Come along now.'

It occurred to Conor, frighteningly, that there must be something gravely wrong with his father, and that Dr Fitzgerald wanted a word in private. He led the way to the study and closed the door behind them.

'What's he got?' he demanded.

'The general? Ach, he'll see us all under the ground. Liver like a breadboard and his blood pressure's up a touch, but the heart and lungs are sound, and a billygoat would envy his digestion. For seventy-eight the old fellow's a holy miracle, so he is now. There's only one thing really wrong with him and that's yourself, Archy dear. He's worried to death about you, and now that I've seen you I'm not surprised. Isn't there a medical man in Belfast with eyes in his head? A child of three could tell you you're pushing the limit. Take off your shirt, like a good chap, and let's have a listen at you.'

Conor argued, lost, and submitted with very poor grace.

'I ought to have you in for an ECG,' the doctor said finally, as he fitted his instruments back into their scuffed leather case. 'You've a resting heartbeat of one hundred and six, and there's a perceptible arrhythmia; you must have noticed it yourself. Gets worse when you lie down, does it?'

Conor nodded.

'How much are you smoking?'

'Too much.'

'That's part of it, then. But what we're up against here, basically, is stress and exhaustion, and you know as well as I do there's only one remedy for that.' He was scribbling on a pad as he spoke. 'Here's a chit for some iron and another for B-12. I'll get back to you with the full results of the blood tests, but I can tell you this minute you're anaemic. Now *take* the bloody things; they'll do nothing for you sitting in the bottle. You've a couple of nasty varicosities in your right calf, too; it's the surgeon's occupational hazard, of course, along with bunions and fallen arches, but at your age you shouldn't be in as bad a way as this. Keep up at the rate you're going and you'll be flat on your back with phlebitis before you're forty. You have to take a rest.'

'I suppose I could manage a bit of time in the autumn.'

'Have you heard a word I've been saying?' The little doctor was exasperated. 'Not in the autumn, nor yet in the summer. *Now.*'

'Billy, if you could see those kids–'

'I don't need to. I was with the Eighth Army in North Africa when you were in short trousers, and I've seen enough injuries from high explosives to last me a lifetime. But, Archy, you cannot save the world single-handed. Let somebody else have a turn. You're rapidly approaching the point of MHTG.'

'What the hell's that?'

'More harm than good. Once upon a time, if you can remember that far back, you learned the first rule of medical care: *primum non nocere*, don't leave the poor bastards worse off than you found them.'

'It's a fucking conspiracy,' Conor said crossly. 'I had the self-same rocket from Matron a couple of days ago.'

'Do you tell me, now? Clearly a woman of sense. Get right away from it, boyo. Six or eight weeks off the wards and you'll come back like a giant refreshed.'

'What a brilliantly original simile.'

'Ach, get stuffed,' said Dr Fitzgerald. 'You always did have a nasty tongue on you.'

'No, but honestly. Loafing around here for weeks on end with nothing to do but shoot pigeons, and watch that half-wit dog of the old man's failing to find them. I'll go off my head.'

'Don't stay here, then; you've the whole world to choose from. Your father was telling me about that farm of yours, over in America. Why not go there for a bit? Fresh air, lashings of good plain food, and a little mindless manual labour to give you an appetite.' Fitzgerald was smiling persuasively, but his eyes were anxious. 'I'm right, Archy,' he went on. 'Trust old Billy Fitz, I've never steered you wrong yet. Will you do it?'

It was true, Conor admitted to himself, he did feel rotten; he'd felt rotten for so long he had forgotten what anything else was like.

'Oh Christ. Oh, all right.'

'Grand! And you're not to be putting it off, mind you. Spend this next week turning over your cases, and then I want to see you out of the place.'

'Don't be an ass, Billy. I can't possibly do it in a week.'

'If you were to walk under a bus or drop dead of a myocardial infarction, which is a great deal more likely, other people would see to your patients. Nobody's indispensable, not even the great Kilmoyes. Now let's go and tell the general you've seen the light of reason, and then we can all have a drink.'

Julia Anne Devlin got off the floor and looked up hopefully.

'Wow-wow?' she asked.

'That's right, pet,' Claire said, 'go play with the nice wow-wow.'

Julia set off with the forward-tilting sailor's roll that was, at seventeen months, her normal gait. She flailed across the kitchen and collapsed on top of Bagel, who groaned theatrically. Claire was folding laundry at the kitchen table. When Chuck first bought the generator she had kicked like a steer, and for weeks she had pointedly ignored the electric clothes washer that followed. But with Julia still in diapers, and Lottie in the house as well, they'd never have managed without it.

There was a sudden commotion out in the hall, and an alert-looking yearling pig came sliding and skittering over the stone floor, pursued by Marietta Devlin with a broom.

'Mother of God, get on out of it!' Marietta scolded, catching the lean rump a whack as the animal fled into the yard. She propped the broom against the wall and pushed a strand of curly brown hair out of her eyes. 'The creature's possessed,' she said. 'Put him out one door and he runs around the house and comes in at the other.'

'He was hand raised,' Claire offered in mitigation. 'Got it fixed in his head he belongs in here with the rest of the family.'

'My great-granny in Connemara used to let the pig in the kitchen to lie by the fire, but we've come on a bit since then I hope.' Marietta was disapproving, but her frown gave way to a reluctant grin. 'At that, if it's a choice between him and the New Lymington roaches, I'll take the pig. At least I know where he's been. Julia, get off that poor dog. You'll smother him.'

'Wow-wow,' said Julia intelligently, thrusting a small brown hand between Bagel's slobbery jaws.

'She can't hurt him, he's solid rubber.' For the twentieth time Claire swivelled to peer at the clock. 'Sean ought to be back soon.'

'You still haven't told Katie about Conor?'

Claire shook her head. 'I'm scared to. What she'd do is, she'd run.'

303

'That's what Chuck said, but I don't see why.'

'For one thing, the child's shy. She'd likely be afraid he wouldn't be glad to see her. And then there's Lottie. Chuck was as happy as I was when Dan and Beccah were born, but some men are queer about babies. He'll get used to the idea quick enough, but it'll come as a shock to start off. He'll have put all this behind him, you see. And he's got an awful temper.' She gave Marietta's hand a swift, desperate squeeze. 'I'm nervous myself, and that's the truth.'

Five miles the other side of Cold Crossing, Conor woke out of a light doze, yawned, and looked around. He was jittery enough at present to dislike being driven, but after the first fifty miles his eyelids had begun to droop and he had been grateful to relinquish the wheel of the Jeep to Sean Devlin. He wondered again what it was that Sean wasn't telling him. Whatever the opposite of a poker face might be, Sean had it, and from the moment they met at the airport Conor had been positive that something was up. He didn't suppose it was anything very terrible. The dear man couldn't look him in the eye, but he seemed embarrassed rather than distraught. It was good that he and Marietta had come to live at the farm. PhD's seemed to be moving rather sluggishly on the labour market just now, so the arrangement provided at least a temporary solution to the Devlin family's problems. But for Conor it also meant that the absence of Sam and Afeni would be less painfully obtrusive.

He still wasn't sure if this trip was a disastrous error or not. In the past the farm had always been a haven for him, a small enclave of sanity in a world growing madder by the minute, but that was before Kate. Without her there, would the old healing process still work, or would he be ghost-ridden, galvanized by irrational hope each time someone came through the door? How frightful if Sean's evasive manner meant that Claire had imported some offensively suitable young woman to take his mind off Kate. With the best intentions, she was quite capable of such a clanger, and his skin crawled with foreboding. They'd just have to get rid of the girl as tactfully as possible. He didn't want to be unkind, but he was tired and ill – Billy Fitz had been right as usual, damn the man – and there were definite limits to how much he could take.

Riding through the outskirts of the Crossing, they went past the sheriff's house, and all at once Conor jerked up straight and stared back over his shoulder.

'Sean, who's that getting out of Ollie Paton's car? The big tall chap on crutches, with the brace on his leg?'

Sean glanced in the rearview mirror. 'That's Bobby Lee Gibbs,' he said. 'He still uses a wheelchair a good part of the time, but Ollie takes him over to Haynesville three times a week for therapy at the VA hospital, and he's coming along fine. The sheriff's getting him one of those cars with the special controls, and once that comes he'll be able to drive himself.'

'Three cheers for Walter Brehn,' Conor said contentedly. 'God he's clever. I wish I could do that stuff. Talk about engraving the Lord's Prayer on the head of a pin.' He turned to look at Sean and was met by a wide-open gaze of such transparent guilt that he was goaded into candour. 'Look, cocker,' he said, 'I'm the old maestro, remember? You can tell me. What's this hideous piece of news you're sitting on? You look like the Third Murderer having doubts.'

'Jesus, Conor, I don't know what you're talking about.'

'The good Lord never meant you for a liar. Now come clean.'

'I can't. Claire would kill me. I *promised*.'

'Oh, well.' Dread gave way to a long-starved sense of the ridiculous and Conor began, weakly, to laugh. 'Tell you what. I'll guess, and if I get it right you can wiggle your ears. Chuck left home with the fat waitress from the Dixie Diner. No? Let me think. Claire's been born again and turned the barn into a permanent floating revival meeting. Carl Brackage had a sex-change operation. Lady Godiva gave birth to an aardvark last week and you're afraid to tell me.'

'Not yet, she hasn't,' Sean said, hoping to change the subject. 'She's not due for another four days.'

'You mean I'm just in time? Oh, splendid. What a treat. Poor Sean, it's not fair to tease you. Keep your black secret, just put up a quick petition to St Dymphna and mention my name.'

'Who's St Dymphna?'

'The patron saint of nervous breakdowns, you ignorant mick. I understand she's very booked up, but tell her it's an emergency.'

As soon as they drove through the gates, all Conor's doubts coalesced into a single, soggy conviction: this was going to be a monumental mistake. The place was saturated with Kate. Kate coming out of the barn with an empty milk pail; Kate sitting on the porch steps, legs drawn up under her, braiding Rebeccah's hair; Kate leaning from an upstairs window, laughing. In Ireland, overwork and worry had driven the thought of her out of his

305

mind, at least while he was awake. Now it was as if every moment he had ever spent with her, all the trivial memories safely locked away for the past year, had settled on him in a punishing cloud, stinging like bees. He had total recall, and it was unendurable. He would have to go home, as soon as he decently could. A month spent trudging through the bogs with Widgeon would be paradise compared to this useless, exquisite pain.

Chuck ran down the steps, and although it was still daylight Conor caught himself looking for the lantern that should have been in his old friend's hand, as it had been the night he first came here with Kate. Stiffly he climbed down from the Jeep, with the shrivelling certainty of loss alive and vicious under his ribs.

'*Tahi, kemosabe*,' Chuck said, grinning. 'You look terrible.'

'Always the soul of tact.'

'What can I tell you? I haven't seen a face that colour since Billy Paton came on as Typhoid in the school pageant of health last winter. You should have been there,' he went on, lifting Conor's two small bags out of the back. 'Beccah was a lady-in-waiting to Queen Hygiene, and Dan was Air Pollution. Claire thought it was boffo, but in my opinion Mrs Rouderbridge's porch light is definitely out. Come on in. There's a house full of women waiting to kill you with kindness.'

The kitchen was dark after the bright evening outdoors. Claire's face, vivid with welcome, came swimming out of the murk as she swooped to hug him, and then Marietta was greeting him, shyly putting up her cheek to be kissed. Over her shoulder he saw another familiar figure at the end of the room, a small woman with straight brows and a soft, gleaming fall of butter-pale hair. Dear God, it was Alice Mary. Claire's good intentions had brought off a right disaster this time. The girl was staring at him with what appeared to be horror, and he couldn't imagine why. No matter what Chuck might say, he didn't look all that bad. It was Alice Mary, it had to be, yet the face was Kate's, and he knew then that his mind had gone, tipped over the edge at last into delusion.

'Conor!' a voice cried out, and it was Kate's voice, but then it would be. *Where visual and auditory hallucinations are present, schizophrenia must be our provisional diagnosis,* a dry stranger noted in some still-functioning corner of his brain, as he put his hands over his eyes and blundered off to one side until he hit the wall and stayed there, shaking. A small, raw, keening sound forced itself from his throat.

Alone of the people in the kitchen, it was Claire who realized something of what was happening to him, and Claire who put strong arms around him and held him tight.

'That's enough,' she said loudly. 'Thee quit that this minute, thee's frightening Katie. Not to speak of the children.'

The awful little sound trailed into silence. His face still hidden, he asked cautiously, 'Katie? It is Katie?'

'Well, of course it's Katie. Who did thee think it was, Mae West? Thee'll have to start wearing glasses if that's the best thee can do.'

'You ought to have told me,' he said, like a reproachful small boy.

'I can see that,' Claire said. 'And from the looks of her, we ought to have told Katie too.'

'You mean she didn't know I was coming?' Conor freed himself gently. 'Lord God of Israel, what a crew.' He went over to where Kate stood and put his hands on either side of her face. 'It *is* you,' he said. 'Hello, pretty. Sorry I made such a spectacle of myself – I was afraid I'd slipped a cog for a while there. Claire and her surprise parties.' He moved her head a little from side to side, studying her. 'Well?' he said.

'Well what?'

'Did you miss me?'

'I never gave you a thought.'

'If Rebeccah is to be believed,' he said, as he took her in his arms, 'you're about to get big green warts all over your tongue.'

When, satisfied that she was real, he was finally able to let go of her, he found that Chuck had poured him a drink, and was taking rolls out of the oven. 'It's only a snack,' she said, 'I kept supper back in case thee was held up, but these'll do to be going on with.'

Conor took a swallow of whisky, steadied himself, and turned to inspect the gathering. 'I apologize for that exhibition,' he said. 'Very poor form. Good Lord, that's never Julia Anne Devlin. Last time I saw you, my girl, you hadn't a tooth to your name. And Daniel's grown at least a foot, and Rebeccah's more beautiful than ever. Hey, brats, good to see you. Now who's this?'

'Daniel, Beccah, run along outside and play,' Claire ordered quickly, in a tone that put argument out of the question, as Conor stared at the chesterfield. Plumped down among pillows and waving a tiny starfish hand in what appeared to be the friendliest greeting, was a baby about three months old. Conor looked at the baby speculatively. Presumably it was another little Devlin, but in that case why hadn't Sean mentioned it? Besides, its colouring was all wrong. Even allowing for future modifications, there was no way the dark Devlins could have been responsible for the deep blue of those enormous eyes, let alone the pale, warm gold of the fuzz that aureoled the shapely little skull. The baby beamed at Conor, kicked one fat leg, and hiccupped. A trickle of milk appeared at one corner of the upcurved mouth. Kate leaned over and dabbed at it with her handkerchief. She picked the baby up.

'Whose is it?' Conor asked again, puzzled. Kate took a very deep breath.

'Yours,' she said. 'Half of it, anyhow. And it's not an it, it's a her – she – whatever.' She glared at him defiantly over the baby's head. 'Lottie Claire,' she said bravely, 'this is your papa. Conor, Lottie Claire.'

'Jesus fucking Christ,' Conor said. Claire brought her hand down on the table with a ringing slap that sent three cats hurtling out from underneath it.

'Language like that I will not have, now or any other time, and well thee knows it,' she snapped.

'I'm sorry, Claire. Look, forgive me, I know it's bad manners, but I really am awfully tired. If nobody minds, I think I'll go and lie down for a bit.'

He went very slowly up the stairs, and they heard this door close. Kate sank onto the chesterfield, still holding Lottie Claire, and started to cry.

'Oh, hush,' Claire said, 'thee'll set the baby off next. Can't have the pair of thee bellowing like bulls. We were wrong, Chuck and me. We thought this'd be the way to do it, so's not to give either one of thee time to get in a fret, but we were dead wrong.' She sat down abruptly in the rocker and wiped her forehead. '*Now* what'll we do?'

Kate stood up again and dumped the baby in Claire's lap. 'Hold that,' she said briskly and blew her nose.

'Where's thee going?'

'Where do you think?' She headed for the stairs. Outside Conor's door she paused for a moment, wiped the palms of her hands on her jeans, and then knocked. 'Conor?' she said.

'Now what?'

'May I come in?'

There was an interval, which stretched. 'I don't know,' he said at last. 'Have you got an appointment?'

'Well *shit*,' Kate said, walking in and shutting the door behind her with fierce restraint. Conor sat hunched over on the edge of the bed, head down, elbows on knees. Presently he raised his head and looked at her, and her insides turned to water. He looked tired and very ill, the lines that bracketed his mouth gone deep and angry, the crumpled skin around his eyes bruised with weariness. He also looked furious and unmistakably himself: Conor, bloody-minded past belief, and her heart's dear love.

'I thought I told you if anything happened you were to get an abortion,' her heart's dear love said with hostility. 'I did tell you. I even gave you the name of the best man to go to. It's not as if it was illegal any more. This is inexcusable, Kate – what were you thinking of, landing yourself in such a mess?'

Kate put up her chin. 'I am not in any kind of a mess, thank you, and neither is Lottie Claire. You don't have to do anything about us, we're perfectly fine. The reason I came up was to tell you that this – this *humiliating* situation was no idea of mine. I never wanted you to know about the baby at all.'

'I hate to seem critical,' Conor said nastily, 'but lugging the child down here may not have been the most effective way of keeping it a secret.'

'I know that, you dope, but nobody told me you were going to be here. If I'd known, naturally I'd have left her with mother. In fact, if I'd known you were going to be this rotten I wouldn't have come myself.'

He scrubbed his knuckles over his face in a gesture so familiar she could have wept. 'Look,' he said, 'try to pretend I've been cut off from civilization for the past year – which is not far from the truth, as it happens. I don't know anything about anything, right? Just give me the highlights.'

Kate did so. 'And when Lottie Claire was two months old we came back from Scotland,' she concluded, 'but mother's house was impossible, reporters kept calling up and some of them even started hanging around outside the house. People are so damn *nosy* –'

Conor gave one of his reluctant snorts of laughter, and Kate scowled.

'All very well for some,' she said. 'Anyhow, there was a letter waiting for me from Claire, saying why didn't I come to the farm for a while and bring Lottie, and it seemed like the perfect answer until mother and I could decide what to do next. So we came. But none of it has anything to do with you.'

'The fuck it hasn't. For one thing, this is my house – a fact the rest of you seem to have conveniently forgotten. For another, that's my child downstairs. I'm sorry to behave so badly. It was the shock, you see. I'm a bit jangled at the moment. I haven't been all that well.'

'Do tell. The way you look, I'm surprised they even let you into the country. What have you been doing to yourself?'

'I told you I'd probably go to Ireland. Well I did, and it's shitty, and I let it get to me, which is the short answer to that. Now look, peach, what have you got in mind? About the baby, I mean.'

'Mother and I are going to take care of her; it's all arranged. I guess we may have to move some place where people don't know us, but mother never was crazy about New Lymington to start off with. We only went there because of father. Charlie wants to marry me and adopt Lottie, but I think that's a terrible idea.'

'You're damn right it's terrible. Who does this fellow think he is, pinching my family?' Conor demanded with superb illogic.

'It's Charlie Eisinger, for heaven's sake. The boy I was with when you kidnapped me. Your friend Sean punched him out and shot him full of dope, and then that awful man Lund got hold of him. You can't have forgotten.'

'Lund had him, did he? I didn't know. Poor devil.'

'Not so poor as all that. At least, it must have been pretty bad at the time, but now he's written this novel about life in a CIA nuthouse, and Doubleday is bringing it out in September. He says they're really excited about it – they think it'll be a big best seller. Charlie's going to tour the country doing talk shows and be on Johnny Carson and the Today Show and everything. Sally Belfort – that's Charlie's mother – she says he can't make his mind up whether to sue the CIA for a million bucks or send them a case of Scotch.'

'Well thank God he's all right. I never meant to let him in for anything like that. Still, he's not having you and what's-her-name for a consolation prize.'

'Her name's *Lottie Claire*; you might at least try to get it right. Anyhow, I wouldn't dream of marrying Charlie. It's dear of him to offer, but I don't want to marry anybody. Nowadays you don't have to have a husband just because you have a baby – look at Mia Farrow.'

'I haven't the slightest desire to look at Mia Farrow. I'd much rather look at you. Darling Kate, I wish you'd sit down. I'm getting a crick in my neck. Besides, you look much too dangerous standing up. If I say the wrong thing you'll probably brain me with the washstand.'

He patted the bed beside him. Decorously, Kate sat, keeping her back straight and her knees together. He leaned across and very gently bit her neck. She smiled, but did not move.

'Something's happened to you,' he said, playing with the ends of her hair. 'Not that you weren't absolutely gorgeous before, but you seem a lot more *there*, if you know what I mean. More defined.'

'That's what Aunt Louisa said. She said it was having the baby – it brings out the best in women.'

'Not necessarily. What it does bring out is whatever's there already, good or bad. In your case, the results are spectacular. You ought to be careful, you know. If I'd had a couple of drinks, there's no telling what I might do. Even half a can of diet soda . . .'

'Stop it,' Kate said. 'I've been through enough today. This isn't fair to either of us. I don't know just who's been doing what, but we're being manipulated, and I don't like it.'

'Oh, I don't know. It's rather soothing in a way – people pushing one around for one's own good. Like being made to put a sweater on before you go outside. Boring, but at least somebody cares whether you live or die.'

She stared at him. 'You have been through the mill, haven't you? You'd never have said that a year ago.'

'A year ago I thought I was accomplishing something. Muscles Mouse, changing the course of history. Drunk with power, you might say. Nothing like a stint on the Belfast barricades to fix that. More to the point, a year ago I had you.' He looked down at his feet.

Kate felt as if someone had been inflating her heart with a bicycle pump. 'I could live with you, I guess, if you wanted me to,' she said slowly. 'If that would help. And if Lottie'd be too much, I know mother would take her. She offered to before.'

'Oh lovey, *don't*!' There was such pain in his voice and in his face, that she drew back. 'Don't turn me into a charity case, I couldn't bear it. You don't owe me a thing – quite the reverse. When I think of you sweating out that whole baby business on your own, months and months of it . . . Oh Christ, why do I always let people down?'

'You don't. You just think you have to do everything. You're

311

crazy, you know that?' She took his hand in both of hers and held it against her mouth.

'It's no joke, alas.' His hand was tense, resistant, but not quite pulling away. 'When I came in, downstairs, and saw you, I was quite sure I'd gone bananas. I've been so close to the edge lately, it just didn't occur to me you might be real. My dear good girl, you can't get yourself tied to a loony – life's too short.'

'It's my life. I can do what I want with it,' Kate said without thinking and then froze. Of all the stupid, self-betraying things to say ... She'd promised herself to play it totally cool, and yet there she was forcing herself upon him, like those people on street corners thrusting blurry adverts into your hand, touting porn shops or fortune tellers or the end of the world. Using your own politeness against you, to make you accept something you didn't want.

'Scrub that,' she said. 'It was a dumb thing to say. Let's take it from the top.' The trouble was, she couldn't think of anything to say next, except 'But I love you', and that was the one thing that must not be said. They sat and looked at each other in helpless silence. Then Conor took his hand back, used it to rub the nape of her neck, and, moving closer, pulled her against his chest.

'Stop being so bloody tactful,' he said. 'I love you. I want to marry you. Not because of Lottie Claire and not because of anything else except pure selfishness. It's a very poor offer, and if I had your best interests at heart I'd advise you against it. But I'm not letting you go again, not now. I must have been round the bend the first time.'

'I'll run away,' Kate said into his shirt. 'I'm good at that.'

'You're no earthly good at *getting* away,' he pointed out. 'Anyway, I'll hound you. I'll – I'll picket you. Grow a beard and totter up and down outside your front door in sandals and an old sheet till I'm taken up for committing a nuisance. You don't want me to go to prison, do you? Not for committing a nuisance. It's very low class, like peeing in public.'

He was rewarded with a muffled giggle. Then Kate sat up. 'I just thought of something awful,' she said. 'Do you realize I don't even know your name?'

'Conor. C-O-N–'

'I mean the rest of it, dummy.'

'Oh dear,' he said. 'I was hoping to avoid this.'

'Why, what is it? Ludwig C. Hasenpfeffer? Percy von Klutz?'

'Worse. Now look here, you're not to laugh. It's Archibald, Archibald Conor Kilmoyes.'

'What's wrong with that?'

'Archibald?' He pronounced it with fastidious loathing. 'Sounds like an Edwardian chorus boy.'

'It does not either. I think it's sexy.'

'Do you really? No, of course you don't, but what the hell – if I can put up with it, you can.'

He had just begun to kiss her properly when there came a peremptory knocking on the bedroom door.

'I don't know what thee's doing in there, and I don't want to,' said Claire's voice. 'But it's time and past time for Lottie's feed, and supper be on the table in a half hour.'

Conor swore, but he got up and opened the door to Claire, who was carrying a fractious Lottie. He took the baby, bringing her over to the bed, and then stared fascinated as two tiny, growing spots of damp darkened the front of Kate's shirt.

'Well I'll be damned,' he said. 'I've read about that, but I've never seen it. How terrific.' He jiggled his daughter, who was chewing frantically on a couple of spitty fingers. 'You've got it wrong, lovey,' he told her, 'it's the thumb you're supposed to go for. Never mind, grub's coming.'

He put her on the bed and, bending down, started undoing Kate's buttons. Glancing apprehensively past him at Claire, Kate received the full force of a look that was part outraged propriety and part self-congratulation. Inside her head, a piece of the puzzle slid into place with an almost audible click.

'You've been catching up on your correspondence, haven't you?' she said to the older woman, as she settled Lottie at her breast. The little fists stopped beating the air, and the baby began to produce a succession of startlingly loud growly noises as she sucked. 'Greedy little beast,' Conor said approvingly.

Claire looked fussed. 'Well, I wrote *thee*,' she temporized.

'Uh-huh. And a couple of other people, while you were about it?'

'Oh shoot,' said Claire, red faced. 'I did as I thought right, that's all. Conor, thee come on out of here; it's not fitting.'

'That's where you're wrong. If a man can't watch his own wife feed the baby, whose wife can he watch?'

'Thee's not married.'

'An administrative oversight. It'll be attended to as soon as possible. Dearest Claire, do go away, I have to talk to this chit.'

The door closed behind her. Conor sat down again.

'That's very pretty,' he said. 'Don't forget it's my turn next.'

'Smartass.'

'Abuse, that's all I get. Vilification and abuse. And I try so hard.' His face clouded. 'I'm only here on leave, you know. Sooner or later, I'll have to go back. I can't just walk away from it.'

'I didn't suppose you could.'

'What about you, though? It's not exactly Fun City over there. Besides, it's dangerous. If you did come, you'd have to move in with my old man, in the South. It's a big house, and he's a decent old boy. You'd like him.'

'There you go again,' Kate complained. 'Always trying to get rid of me. Watch it, Lottie, you cannibal, that hurt. Whithersoever thou goest, and all that crap,' she told Conor. 'Man, you're stuck.'

'Am I?' he said. 'My God, I hope so. It's about time.'

Contemporary Romances

Once a Lover £1.95   **Diana Anthony**
Set in New York and San Francisco, *Once a Lover* is the
moving love story of Lainie Brown, a young artist, and
Jean-Paul Vallier, a blinded sports superstar. Then he
regains his sight and Lainie fears she will lose his love. But
she learns painfully and joyously why she is so worthy of
Jean-Paul's enduring devotion.

Celebration £1.50   **Rosie Thomas**
Bel Farrer, a wine columnist, was a high-flying career girl.
But beneath her glittering professional appearance was a
vulnerable heart. Both the titled aristocrat bound by an
ancient code of honour, and the reckless, carefree playboy
claimed her heart and she had to make a choice.

Perfect Dreams £1.75   **Carolyn Fireside**
The world of high fashion, Hollywood and the jet set is
the backdrop for this rich love story. Gabrielle Blake, a
photographer's model, is independent, intelligent and lov-
able. Among the rich and famous men who fall in and out
of Gaby's life is Terry Baron, a young journalist who
finally rescues her when her career collapses. But is it too
late for them to rescue their love for each other?

Perhaps I'll Dream of Darkness £1.35   **Mary Sheldon**
In this compelling and beautifully written story of love and
obsession the lives of a teenage girl and a burned-out rock
star entwine fleetingly — with disastrous results. Probing
deeply into her characters' lives, Mary Sheldon creates a
portrait of frustrated passion that leads to tragedy, and
captures both the grace and terror of obsessive, idealistic
love.

FONTANA PAPERBACKS

Helen MacInnes

Born in Scotland, Helen MacInnes has lived in the United States since 1937. Her first book, *Above Suspicion*, was an immediate success and launched her on a spectacular writing career that has made her an international favourite.

'She is the queen of spy-writers.' *Sunday Express*

'She can hang up her cloak and dagger right there with Eric Ambler and Graham Greene.' *Newsweek*

FRIENDS AND LOVERS £1.75
AGENT IN PLACE £1.95
THE SNARE OF THE HUNTER £1.50
HORIZON £1.75
ABOVE SUSPICION £1.50
MESSAGE FROM MALAGA £1.75
REST AND BE THANKFUL £1.75
PRELUDE TO TERROR £1.75
NORTH FROM ROME £1.50
THE HIDDEN TARGET £1.75
I AND MY TRUE LOVE £1.75
THE VENETIAN AFFAIR £1.75
ASSIGNMENT IN BRITTANY £1.75
DECISION AT DELPHI £1.95
NEITHER FIVE NOR THREE £1.95
THE SALZBURG CONNECTION £1.95

FONTANA PAPERBACKS

Belva Plain

– the best-loved bestseller –

Evergreen   £2.50

A rich and tempestuous story of Anna Friedman, the beautiful, penniless Jewish girl who arrives in New York from Poland at the turn of the century and survives to become matriarch of a powerful dynasty.

Random Winds   £2.50

The absorbing and poignant story of a family of doctors – Dr Farrell, the old-fashioned country doctor who dies penniless and exhausted, his son Martin who becomes a brilliant and famous brain surgeon, but is haunted by his forbidden love for a woman, and Martin's daughter Claire, headstrong, modern and idealistic, whose troubled romance with the unknown Englishman provides a bitter-sweet ending.

Eden Burning   £2.50

A romantic saga set against the backdrop of New York, Paris and the Caribbean. The island of St Felice holds many secrets, one of which is the secret of the passionate moment of abandon that threatened to destroy the life of the beautiful fifteen-year-old Teresa Francis. A story of violence, political upheaval and clandestine love.

FONTANA PAPERBACKS

Fontana's Family Sagas

Molly £2·50   Teresa Crane

Molly is a spirited young woman who escapes poverty in
Ireland for a new life in Victorian London. Courageous
and passionate, she fights the prejudice against her sex
and her class — and wins.   A compelling story.

The Cavendish Face £1·95   Jane Barry

A love story to sweep you off your feet. Set in London of
the 1920s and '30s, it tells of a young woman's struggle
against the stifling conventions and corrupt morals around
her and how she seeks a way to love freely the only man
who has ever had a place in her life.   A captivating novel.

Futures £1·95   Freda Bright

Caro Harmsworth is the perfect twentieth-century woman
— young, liberated, independent, and determined to be a
success in the high financial world of Wall Street. A strong
contemporary story of love and success — and of the
woman who has to chose between the two. . .

FONTANA PAPERBACKS